Ordinary Citizen

XANDER STERLING

To Lisa
Hope you enjoy every minute of Vina's adventure!

To: All my fellow Beautiful weirdoes!

And of course, to my family. I love you all

and thank you so much for all your support!

Editors: Xander Sterling, Lynda Harlos and Robynne Lokat

ISBN 978-0-9879631-0-9

Chapter 1 – *The Intruder*

A slightly cooler night than normal, Vince noticed, an unnerving chill crawling up his spine as he stepped out of the tiny silver Porsche that had been a recent perk from his new position at work. He had been promoted a few months earlier but still couldn't wrap his head around the drastic changes that had taken place in those few short months. The house, now in his line of sight, was the most obvious example thus far that he had been moving up in the world. What he did not see or notice, was the car parked just beside his yard that did not belong to any neighbours.

The sleek, modern structure peered out from behind massive palm trees and assorted tropical shrubbery and sat atop a slight hill that was his yard. It had a few concrete balconies with glass railings, a thought that had terrified him at first, but he soon realized just how sturdy they were after his first visit during the showing. The previous owners had only lived there about a year and kept it in excellent condition. Prior to that, the gleaming estate was brand new and considered a 'monument to modern architecture', as hailed by a few Los Angeles area housing and architectural magazines.

As Vince approached the front door, exhausted from a particularly tiring day at the office, and with paperwork to still finish, he ran his fingers through his short dirty blonde hair with a brief sigh before reaching for his keys. It took only a moment for him to remember that he did not indeed *have* keys to his home anymore due to a padlock that required a pin number authorization, something he still wasn't used to and wasn't sure he ever would be. He punched in the number, 713, wearily on the keypad and pushed open the behemoth steel and glass door, stepping inside and pausing at another odd chill that seemed to take over his entire body before closing the door behind him.

Vince looked down at his watch. 11:00 on the dot. Vanessa was sure to be sleeping by now; she never was much of a night owl. Vince carefully removed his shoes and headed past the foyer into a slightly narrower hallway dimly lit by half cup sconces on either side of the wall. Walking straight ahead, he entered the airy living room where one could sit and stare out at the glistening city through the large windows that made up the wall. The house was situated on an excellent piece of property in the "bird streets" of the Hollywood hills area and just so happened to have a spectacular view of L.A. due to some rather remarkable natural landscaping. The buildings along the skyline glistened and sparkled like a layer of diamonds against the horizon under the night sky.

Vince looked around the living room for a moment wondering how he was going to find the time to finish the briefs his boss, Mr. Crane, had given him earlier that day. He placed his leather briefcase on the end table next to one of the large ultra-modern white sofas and headed into the kitchen that was directly to the right of the living room. He walked around the large marble-top island and pulled a tall Baccarat glass from the top shelf of one of the steel cupboards that blended so seamlessly into each other that you didn't know where to open them half of the time. Vince had expressed confusion at the matter when he first viewed the house, to which he received a look of disbelief as the very unfriendly real estate woman pulled one of the doors open during the showing with an almost undetectable scoff.

Grabbing a bottle of Pellegrino out of the steel refrigerator and pouring it into the glass, he felt another unsettling chill run through his veins for no apparent reason. He walked back into the living room and sat quietly, burying his face in his hands, overwhelmed by the task before him that was to be accomplished before he could get some of the much needed sleep his body had been craving. Leaning back in the couch, he could see up through the open concept living room to a small break in the hallway between the master bedroom and the bathroom on the second floor separated by a glass railing. It had taken quite a while for Vince to get used to the utter lack of privacy his new abode provided when he and Vanessa first moved in, but she absolutely loved the open space and freedom it seemed to provide.

Looking back down across the living room and directly into the dining room, which sat on the opposite side of the living room, he noticed that her mug was still sitting on the dining room table where she liked to sit and read while enjoying a cup of chamomile tea before bed. For such a simple mishap, it seemed to make him more uneasy than one would think seeing a mere cup of unfinished tea would. He sat there and stared at it for a while longer in the darkened silence before reaching for the briefcase he had set on the end table moments earlier. He switched on a small glass cylinder lamp to lighten up the room just enough so he could see the paperwork he was supposed to concentrate on when he heard a slight noise from upstairs. On any other night, he would have ignored it and continued working. Tonight however, something seemed wrong, so he headed cautiously out of the living room and back down the dimly lit hallway to the airy foyer. He paused at the bottom of the steps that curved up the far right wall from the front door.

He stood motionless for a second, waiting for another noise. Nothing. He started slowly up the stairs, passing his favourite picture of him and Vanessa kissing and cutting the cake on their wedding day without so much as a glance in its direction let alone the little smirk he made to himself each and every time he had passed it before that night. Placing his foot quietly on the final step to the top level so as not to make any noise and wake Vanessa, he peered down the hallway to the master bedroom. The door was shut, which was also unusual. Being claustrophobic, she never kept any door shut and certainly not while sleeping. This was the primary reason for her immense love of their new home. Open concept and mainly glass architecture was a dream come true as far as she was concerned. As long as there was very little enclosed space, utter lack of privacy was no issue to her.

He stood and waited a moment longer; one eye on the door, before deciding to call to her softly enough that she would hear it if she were awake but still wouldn't rouse her from her slumber if she wasn't.

"Vanessa ...?"

After a moment, there was another slight noise of someone shifting around in the room behind the closed door so he walked carefully down the hall towards the bedroom. He could feel his heart pounding in his chest and all the way down to his toes although he wasn't sure why. Keeping one eye on the door, he paused again briefly at the railing that separated his bedroom from the upstairs bathroom and looked down at the living room. Everything still as he left it. Light dimmed on the end table beside his briefcase and the glass coffee table still in front of the huge white couch ... nothing getting up and walking away on its own yet.

He sighed deeply and pushed open the double doors to his master bedroom and felt the bile rise to the back of his throat when he saw Vanessa there, on the king sized bed, throat slit and lying in a pool of her own blood. Her dark hair stretched across the pillow on which her head lay. He instantly began to panic but ran to the side of the bed to try and help her even though he knew it was too late. Just then, he saw a brief dark shadow in his peripheral line of sight. Instantly, he heard a loud crack and felt a sharp bludgeoning pain in the back of his head.

He fell to the floor with a scream as pieces of broken wood landed around him. Had he been more coherent, he would have grabbed one of the sharp pieces and begun flailing, but all he could focus his now blurred vision on was the dark figure standing over him pointing a knife at his chest. He sat in complete disbelief at what was transpiring for a moment before making a surprisingly quick comeback to complete consciousness and kicked at the assailants knee cap.

He heard a loud cracking noise followed by a blood curdling scream as the unknown murderer fell to the floor. As Vince tried to pull himself up using the stool at the end of the bed, the man slashed at Vince with the large hunting knife but missed, only slightly cutting the back of Vince's calf. Turning around, Vince kicked him right in the face and knocked him flat on his back. He then jumped onto his attacker, putting both hands around his neck and squeezing with all his strength.

"You son of a Bitch!"

Vince's words leaked hatred from his mouth like toxic oil from a broken car as he continued his python grip around the intruder's neck. The man, having dropped the knife after being kicked in the face, picked up a piece of broken wood and stuck it into Vince's arm. No reaction. All Vince could focus on as he felt his hands tighten around the beating red, bulging neck was utter fury and hatred towards the complete stranger. Another hit with a larger piece of wood sent Vince flying out into the hallway.

Both coughing and choking while lying on the floor, momentarily apart, the intruder was the first to get up. He scooped his knife off the floor by the bed before stumbling over to Vince, who by that time, had managed to pull himself upright. He ran clumsily at Vince with the knife as Vince quickly knelt down and the attacker's foot lodged itself hard into Vince's side. Vince looked up in time to see him flying through the small stretch of glass railing and down to the floor below with a scream.

Vince dropped to the floor, exhausted from the fight and shock of seeing his slain wife sprawled out on their bed and peered over the edge. The man lay one level down in a pile of broken glass from the railing, one blank, open eye staring up at him, limbs contorted and sprawled in a huge expanding pool of blood. The white sofa now splattered with red dots sat beside him; the end table on which the dimmed light rested, sat untouched, casting a faint yellow glow that illuminated the gruesome scene.

*

Vince sat in the cold brightly lit hallway, feeling numb. It was as if he had been hit by a lightning bolt and was in shock. He was unable to feel the pain and fury he knew he was supposed to, unable to really see anything around him. Like a veil had been placed over his head, preventing him from thinking, hearing or seeing anything and leaving him alone with his thoughts. An older, very friendly African American gentleman smiled brightly as he offered Vince a cup of coffee.

"No thanks," Vince replied with very little enthusiasm.

It was wonderful that everyone was being so nice, but he couldn't express the little bit of gratitude that he did feel. In fact, he could barely move he was so deep in thought. What happened? Why was that guy there? What did he want? How did he get in? How long had he been there? Why did he have to kill Vanessa like that? Where am I?

The last question must have come out as an audible whisper because the friendly black man that had taken a seat beside him replied, "You're at the Police Station."

No reply from Vince. He had noticed the black short sleeved uniform on the man complete with utility belt and gun and others walking around in the same attire but the visual failed to register in his mind until the words came out of this friendly strangers mouth.

"How you holdin' up son?" the uniformed officer asked.

Vince wanted to respond but couldn't. The words were right there, all the questions, all the thoughts, all the anger, but it wouldn't come out.

"I'm Sergeant Omar Reaps," said the friendly African American policeman after waiting for a response from Vince and not getting one. "Just let me know if you need anything, OK?"

Again, no response from a disconsolate Vince, until the man started to walk away and Vince managed to look at him and mutter quietly "Thank you." Omar nodded his head slightly, turned around and started walking down the hall, leaving Vince alone again with his acid thoughts.

He couldn't figure it out. 'Why? Why did he pick my house?' Vince wondered. 'What would have happened if I hadn't come home right then? Or if I had come home earlier would she still be alive? Why did he have to kill her anyway? Isn't that a last resort even for criminals? What did she do? She must have been just sleeping or she wouldn't have been in bed when I found her. What if he had raped her before slicing her throat?' All these thoughts jumbled around inside Vince's mind. Then in a flash they stopped and only one thought prevailed. There was no way to ever know the answer to any of these questions. From then on, that one mind frame was all Vince could focus on. He will never know, but he did know that his beloved wife, Vanessa, was dead and he would be without her forever now.

It was quite a short questioning session that had taken place between Vince and the investigating officers but it felt like a lifetime of haggling, questioning and debating. This was punctuated only by moments of silence accompanied by sympathetic looks from the officers as they waited for their questions to be answered by a rather unresponsive Vince. Somewhere, he heard a distant ringing but figured it was in his head. Before tonight Vince, in his 27 years of life had never actually seen a dead person, with the exception of a few open casket funerals he had attended as a child and into his teens.

Vince would usually be described by others as friendly, passive and only daring to harm others when his friends and family were under attack. This proved to be true even under the dramatic circumstances in which a threat to one of his loved ones occurred. If someone had attacked him however, he would usually just turn the other cheek. Not always to be the bigger person, but mostly because he wasn't naturally aggressive and didn't want to instigate trouble. He had never so much as been in a fight in high school. A few strongly worded squabbles maybe, but certainly nothing physical. In many ways, he was still the same odd little boy he had always been. Even though he had long since left the days of torment at school and was now much more the type to be envied by others (something he still didn't understand or really place too much credence on), he never really forgot it and so he still never intentionally set out to hurt anyone.

With that truth, in retrospect, none of this made sense to him. Even religiously and philosophically, it didn't add up. Why would God let this happen? If Karma were true, it still didn't seem a fitting punishment for anything he had done in his life. Any way he looked at it, it wasn't fair. Vince hadn't even so much as *wished* something like this on his worst enemies throughout his life. Not even thoughts of destructiveness towards others. He wracked his brain for an answer but couldn't produce one.

The police had informed him that from what it looked like, the hooded man was only there to steal random valuables, not for anything particularly malicious, just petty theft. This made the question of 'why' so much more confusing, but he let the officer continue.

"His name was Jamie Stetson," said the officer slowly as if to make sure that the words registered in Vince's mind. Vince said nothing, still deep in thought. "He's been arrested before for drunk driving and petty theft. Never gone into anyone's house to steal before though, just stores," continued the large guy with a crew cut and the mandatory black uniform.

The officers continued to ramble on about general nothingness that hadn't even come close to producing the answers Vince had been hoping for. The more he thought, the more he couldn't think, the more he tried to answer his own questions, the more questions he had and the more he tried to feel what he knew he was supposed to feel, the more he felt numb to the world. Void of all human reaction, he tried to regain it but couldn't. He knew he would have to, to carry on a normal life but now didn't seem to be the time. He also wondered why exactly he found himself trying to rationalize how he was going to get back to

11

normal and why he couldn't do it right now. A tragedy had just occurred and he felt nothing anymore, except wanting to get back to 'normal'. It was like he had skipped the first four phases of death and was already in 'acceptance'. This couldn't be ordinary behaviour. Was the simplicity in his thoughts an indication of a deeper psychological problem? Who knew these things?

*

The next morning came as nothing less horrible than the day before as Vince found himself waking up to the thought, 'Was it a dream?' He had something similar to this before upon waking up from a deep sleep, but wasn't familiar with it in this context. Previously when it happened to him, he had dreamt about winning the lottery or taking an amazing vacation in the Caribbean somewhere and as he lay in bed for a while longer, eyes still closed, he realized solemnly that it had just been a dream. This on the other hand, was a horrible hoping that reality was actually fantasy, even if subconsciously, he knew it wasn't.

The hope was only fleeting though, and the severe emptiness overcame him once more. Blinking one eye open, it was at this point that Vince also realized the bed he was in was not his own, but that of the Sheraton suite he would be calling home for the next month or so. Aside from letting the ash settle as the police and crime scene investigators combed and cleaned out his actual house, he just couldn't be there right now. Vince pushed back the red check pattern comforter and grabbed one of the white pillows, preventing it from falling over the edge, before finally sitting up and staring blankly around the room. It was a fair size, but still comfortable and well put together.

The Spanish yellow walls and tan line patterned carpet perfectly offset the dark simplistic furniture. Brown floor to ceiling curtains that were presently opened only a crack, allowed the morning light to shine a thin ray onto his tangled clothes that sat on the floor at the foot of his bed. As he looked around momentarily, he couldn't help but feel like this was not the only place he was alone; he was alone in the world ... For a second while remembering how much of life he and Vanessa would never get to experience together, a single tear fell from his left eye. He ignored it and pulled his tired body from the bed. The recent promotion and everything that came with it, in perspective, really meant nothing to him at this moment, for he couldn't put a price on the love he had for her.

As he looked at the clock he realized it wasn't morning after all, it was 6:32 p.m., which when he thought about it a little more, made perfect sense seeing as his suite faced west and the sun was at present, trying to peek in through the crack in the heavy curtains. He had slept over 13 hours and was still tired. Grieving certainly took its toll on the body as well as the mind. He stood by the window for a minute, squinting out through the slit between the material at the downtown Los Angeles buildings. Everything he had worked for, everything he had tried to be and everything he had planned for his life, life itself for that matter, seemed more surreal to him now than ever before. The majestic buildings he gazed out upon were a mere dream now, something that seemed to him like it would vanish forever if he just reached out and flicked it. The people down on the streets were now just ghosts, appearing and disappearing to and from behind buildings where they vanished from any existence at all.

His thoughts danced around the lack of reality in flashes but always returned to Vanessa. Vince had lost his way and all roads in his mind led back to her, only she was not really there. He tried to clear his head of any thoughts at all before taking off his plain white tee shirt and wandering into the bathroom to take a shower. He stood in front of the mirror, placed his palms flat down onto the white granite countertop, and looked at himself in the mirror while finding his thoughts returning to the vacuous essence reality currently had to him.

He peered intently into his own blue eyes and wondered, 'What is blue?' Did he really look like this or was his own reflection merely a continuous figment of his imagination? What exactly made him 'good looking' as most people had called him lately? He had been something of an ugly duckling in his early years and had only recently grown into his body and good looks. Were people serious when they complimented him or were the comments borne of good manners? He looked at himself in the mirror and for this one dreamlike moment in time, genuinely saw a stranger staring back at him.

In truth, he had always felt like he was never good enough for anyone. Until he found Vanessa, that is, but now the only person who had truly loved him was gone. He had been thrown to the ground, hit rock bottom, cast out of his home and he felt nothing now. Everything had been taken from him. He once again tried to shrug off any thoughts that came to his mind and kept a blank and safe mentality. He then pulled off his boxers and got into the steaming hot shower.

As he got out and dried himself off, he noted that being clean did actually improve his mood a bit. Life didn't seem like that constant feeling of just waking up and not wanting to get out of bed anymore. Still empty, still surreal, still painful but not as lazy now.

Coming out of the washroom and glancing around the room again, he thought about going down to one of the restaurants for dinner but decided against it and instead climbed back between the white sheets, pulled the red comforter over himself and quickly fell into another deep sleep.

Chapter 2 – *The Love Lost*

As he lay in bed after waking yet again, Vince began to go over pieces of his life in his mind, replaying them like videos on a mental projector screen. He could clearly remember most of the moments he spent with Vanessa. How they met, what they did, where they went and the moments they shared were all as clear as day, as if they had only happened the week before. Dreamlike and flashing from one joyous moment to the next, he still couldn't wrap his mind around the fact that it had all ended, never to return.

The day he had met her was nothing out of the ordinary. Vince had just taken a job as a lawyer at one of the most prestigious law firms in Los Angeles, J.P. Crane & Associates. A couple of friends who were already working for the firm had helped him secure the job there and the other one that wasn't under their employ, Jake McCraun, an old high school buddy, had strong connections there. Vince was shown to his new office as a tiny smile played around on his lips throughout the orientation process. He knew corporate life just didn't look like this at all, especially straight out of Law School. The dark mahogany, teak and oak furniture, the large black leather chairs and the sheer size of the spaces that made a cubicle look like an empty spot in an ice tray, this place was definitely a step in the right direction. He had dreamed about working somewhere like this all his life and now it was happening.

Vince walked around his new office after being left alone for a brief moment by his escort. He wandered over to the window behind his behemoth desk and stood rooted in the plush carpeting staring out at the Los Angeles skyline. Taking a seat in the equally large chair behind the desk, he fiddled mindlessly with the various stationary and office supplies that were placed there by his secretary before he had even started. It was around 11:00, when his company escort had left for a minute to fetch documents, that Vince saw one of his friends who'd come to greet him.

"Hey I'm heading out for coffee, want to come with?" asked Trey, one of the guys that had helped Vince get the job, peeking his head into Vince's office.

"Yeah, Hold on a sec," Vince replied with a smile as he picked up his briefcase and started towards the door "I've got to let, uh ... that guy that was showing me around, what's his name?" he asked Trey as he came into the hallway. He had always been terrible at remembering names but did his best to be polite.

"Marco?" Trey replied with uncertainty and a faint twisting of his face as a small lock of his longer, dark hair fell out of place and down over his forehead. He flicked it back as Vince spoke.

"Yeah that's it. I've got to let Marco know that I'm heading out. Hold on," Vince stated as he looked down the hallway in search of the man who had been showing him around the building for the entire morning.

"Don't worry about him," replied Trey, "he's just from HR, you don't work for him. Come on." And with that, he headed down the beige coloured hallway. Popping his head into various offices along the way, Trey all but shouted at other members of the firm he had gotten to know and managed to convince Dave and Micah, two of Vince and Trey's mutual friends, to come down with them.

"Come on man its Vince's first day! We gotta show him around a little," Trey demanded of Dave from the doorway.

"I can't. I still have to finish this briefing before I leave early today to catch my flight to New York," Dave shot back in that usual half exhausted, half whining tone Vince had grown accustomed to, his rather ordinary face contorting a bit with aggravation.

"Dude! Get your ass out of that chair and come downstairs with us! You're going to miss the congratulatory party tonight; the least you could do is come have coffee with us before you jet off to see your little Manhattan mistress!" Trey's voice came through clear and authoritative in comparison to Dave's.

"She's NOT my mistress! She's my girlfriend. A mistress would mean someone *on the side* of an established relationship, moron!" Dave stated flatly.

"Whatever dude, get your ass downstairs with us before I punch you in the face," Trey threatened jocularly as he pushed himself off the wooden doorframe and continued down the hall. Vince followed suit and looked back to see Dave emerging from his office packing papers into his briefcase as he followed them towards the elevators. Just like usual, doing exactly what he's told.

Trey, walking two steps ahead of Vince, almost ran right into Micah as he swung around the corner into *his* office.

"Shit dude, don't you ever knock or anything before you come charging into someone else's space?" Micah said, frustrated at almost being knocked over.

"Why? I was coming to invite you to come down for coffee with us. No need to get in a snit about it," Trey snapped back.

"I know," said Micah, unbuttoning his navy pinstripe blazer that complimented his slightly darker skin tone and short, perfectly placed dark hair, "I heard you screaming all the way down the hall. It's a wonder no one has reported you yet."

"That's 'cause everyone loves me. And besides, it's always so goddamn quiet and boring around here, we need some life from time to time before we find someone slumped over their desk, dead from overworking themselves."

"Yeah. Right. Maybe if you actually *did* any work you'd realize that it won't, in fact, kill you," Micah snorted, eyeing Trey from the side.

Trey shrugged off everyone's partly annoyed looks and comments and started strutting towards the elevators again.

The sun shone brightly outside and Vince had to shield his eyes to block out the penetrating rays. They all walked over to the Starbucks across the street and stepped into the over-air conditioned space. Everyone ordered their usual Grande latte's and stepped aside to let Vince order, still bickering amongst themselves in regards to who had the latest one night stand with the hottest girl.

"No dude, I guarantee you this girl *way* outdid that chick you picked up at Status last weekend … I'll get another one, you watch. I'm doing this tonight! It's probably gonna start a fight again. Remember last time when that guy got all up in my face and I had to knock him out 'cause he thought I hit on his girlfriend?" Vince overheard Trey's immature gloating as he decided on a Grande frappuccino.

"What the *devil* are you getting that for? Its freezing in here and back at work," Micah asked.

"I don't know, I just felt like getting one. I'm sick of all the bloody lattes," Vince answered, barely looking away from the menu overhead.

Dave, Micah and Trey all picked up their respective drinks and headed over to the separate island the sugar and cream were placed on and carried on with their previous conversation, seemingly forgetting that Vince was still with them. Vince walked over to the pickup counter and watched his friends publicly making fools of themselves with their constant boasting, bickering and a seemingly unprovoked flick of a stirring stick at Dave's face.

"Grande frappuccino!" the barista stated loudly as she propped the frozen drink up onto the counter beneath two hanging yellow lights.

Vince reached to grab it and instead caught the hand of the woman that had been waiting next to him. He turned to look at her and was momentarily shocked into silence. She was stunning. How had he not seen her when he came in? Her long dark hair fell down her back in soft waves just below her shoulders. She was wearing a dark grey skirt suit with a bright red waist belt and black pointed toe heels that stretched out her already long legs. Her light brown eyes locked on Vince's as she flashed a very white toothy smile in slight embarrassment.

"I'm sorry," she muttered shaking her head slightly then looking back at Vince once more.

"No, No, I'm sorry. I didn't realize I grabbed the wrong -"

"Grande frappuccino!" the girl behind the counter cried again, propping another cold drink up onto the kidney shaped counter.

"I think you have the right one actually," the beautiful woman remarked as she grabbed a straw the girl had forgotten to give her from slightly behind the counter.

"Well I guess we ordered the same thing," Vince responded rather unnecessarily, "but I still grabbed the wrong one - you ordered first. I think in all fairness that means I should buy you another one sometime."

The woman bowed her head slightly and looked up at Vince with a tiny smirk.

"Yeah I guess so," she replied. "Well I work at the marketing firm across the street so maybe we'll run into each other again and you can repay me for this severe inconvenience."

Vince was surprised by the coy sarcasm in her voice, but he still smiled.

"I'm Vince. I actually work across the street too, at J.P. Crane and Associates though, not in marketing," he said extending a hand which she took in her own and shook more firmly than he had expected her to.

"Vanessa," she said as she turned to leave, realizing they were now in the way of others who had been anxiously awaiting their daily caffeine fix, "See you around."

She glanced back, a little smile forming on her perfect red lips as she walked towards the door, pushed it open and headed out into the bright mid day sun that seemed to encompass her in a soft glow like that of an angel.

Vince turned to see his friends sitting, mouths agape and staring at him incredulously. It was as odd an occurrence to him as it was to them as he was generally very shy. For some reason though, he wasn't with her. He walked over to them and sat down without a word and tried to ignore the tentative glares before Trey inevitably broke the silence.

"Unbelievable! Any other man on earth would have been shot down right then and there but this guy gets a date with a gorgeous woman for grabbing the wrong coffee," he said, motioning to Vince just in case Dave and Micah weren't sure who he was talking about. Vince shrugged his shoulders, still not saying a word and everyone's looks of disbelief ceased as they resumed their previous conversation and laughed about how drunk they had gotten last time they went out.

*

It had been another few weeks before Vince ran into Vanessa at the same Starbucks they had met in. He had been working long hours and doing favours for the higher ups in order to stay on their good sides, at least for the first few months. His boss would stop by his office every now and then and demand to know why any given project he could think of at that moment wasn't completed yet. By the time his boss, Cameron, a short and brooding character, had started making personal demands, those that should have been handled by his secretary, Vince began to think things couldn't get any worse. He didn't realize that he clearly lacked a certain perspective at this point, as things *could* get much worse.

Vince headed downstairs and out into the blazing light of day in search of yet another venti Colombian blend with 2 raw sugars. 'This is ridiculous. If he's so caught up on the fact that I don't finish things quick enough, even though I do hand them in on time, why the hell am I the one who has to do his coffee runs?' Vince thought angrily to himself.

Bursting through the cafe doors, he rushed over to the counter where, surprisingly at midday, there was no line up, and ordered Cameron's coffee. As he moved to the pickup counter and picked up the venti coffee, he heard a voice behind him,

"That's not my frappuccino."

He turned around to see Vanessa sitting nearby on a stool at a high table pushed against the window.

"Oh hey!" Vince stammered, "Uh no its not, it's actually not mine either so I guess we're both out of luck today."

"Well, whose is it then?" Vanessa asked pointedly with a slight frown.

"It's actually for, uh, it's for my friend that I work with. I was coming down anyway and he asked me to grab it for him," Vince tried to lie so as not to seem like a mere go-getter working for the biggest law firm in the city.

"Well, where's yours then?" Vanessa returned, sensing the insecurity in Vince's voice.

"Oh I actually came down for something else."

"Oh ok then ..." Vanessa said now slightly snickering to herself. "You don't have to lie to me you know, I don't care if you're the coffee boy, the janitor or the CEO ... I know what it's like, my boss is a bitch too. I swear sometimes she demands stupid things just to piss me off because she knows it's not my job ..."

Vince relaxed a little, bowed his head and chuckled a bit at his own immaturity.

"Hold on," he said before walking over to the counter and ordering 2 Grande frappuccinos. He grabbed them and took a seat on one of the high stools next to Vanessa.

"I believe we are even now," he said, handing her the drink and a straw. Vanessa smiled, took the frozen beverage in her hand and flung back her long dark hair with the other, sending the most amazing smell of Dior pure poison perfume washing over Vince, who almost audibly moaned, as she removed the straw from the paper wrapping.

"Yes, I think we are ... but won't your boss get angry that you're taking so long only to bring back a cold coffee?" Vanessa asked raising both eyebrows and looking at the Venti Colombian blend Vince had ordered moments earlier.

"Yeah, well he can wait. And besides I'm pretty sure he can figure out how to use a microwave," Vince responded coyly with a laugh.

*

Not too much longer, and the wedding day had arrived. The two years they had spent together flashed by with the speed of a lightning bolt and yet, they both felt as if they'd known each other their entire lives. Vince and Vanessa had done a lot of out of the ordinary couple's things together for two people who had actually known each other for such a small amount of time. Among their many endeavours were a Caribbean cruise which both of them would remember as, "The one where it rained *all the time*", and would describe it as such to their friends upon being asked how it was, a cross country tour of Europe and a trip to the Amazonian rainforest.

The trip across Europe was pretty much all they had hoped it would be and more. They decided to stay away from Paris, London, Madrid, Rome and most of the other major tourist areas, opting instead for the lesser known areas in Luxembourg, Switzerland, the Czech Republic, Slovakia, Germany, Belgium and Holland. Both had been to the major areas in Europe before and while they did find them to be amazing vacation spots, rich in culture and experiences, they really wanted to explore more of the 'behind the spotlight' places throughout the continent. This choice proved to be a beneficial one as they met many kind, friendly and funny people along the way, including an older couple in Fehmarn, a town just outside Hamburg, who referred to themselves as "Die besten Bäcker in Deutschland," (the best bakers in Germany) and offered to bake Vince and Vanessa as much cherry strudel and Mandelschnitten as they needed to prove it.

When Vince asked what Mandelschnitten was, the kindly older lady responded, "It ist de, how you say ... almond cookie," with a large smile.

Vince and Vanessa had travelled to Prague and from there ventured out to Karlovy Vary to stay at the renowned Grande Hotel Pupp for a weekend after they had both expressed an intense desire to see it if they ever went back to that area of Europe. From there, they travelled on to remote locations in Slovakia such as Piestany for a small spa retreat, Luxembourg, Holland and Switzerland.

The rolling landscapes, enchanting little villages, historical architecture and the overall romantic charm of being in such a culturally diverse place was the perfect backdrop for Vince and Vanessa's European getaway together.

The trip to the Amazon was definitely different from Europe to say the least. But they had expected this. Instead of luxury hotels, quiet towns and cobblestone streets they resided in a compound of several "huts" that were surrounded by forest and water. The luxurious huts included saunas, fireplaces, private lounge areas and bridges connecting the different parts of the themed resort together over the water. Bountiful meals were served that contained a more impressive display of fruit than Vince had ever seen in his life and balconies on each private hut or cabin sat right over top of water that was suitable for swimming around in all day if one was so inclined.

It wasn't any better or worse than Europe, just very different, each with their own set of strengths and wonders. They spent most of their time right at the resort instead of travelling from country to country. They had gone on a tour of the surrounding Amazonian rainforest and had witnessed and incredible abundance of wildlife and flora. Vince had never seen such enormous trees anywhere before and the moss that hung from them soaked the air in a pungent aroma that felt intoxicatingly natural and almost carnal when mixed with the scent of rain and the forest floor. Vines with large multi-coloured leaves that climbed up and down the trunks and shrubbery into the forest canopy completed the scene.

Vanessa had stopped to admire a brilliant azure dart frog that created a strong, beautiful contrast against the centre of the deep scarlet bromeliad it was currently sitting in and Vince couldn't help but compare her to the spectacle she was observing. She was bright and beautiful and natural standing in the centre of the lush forest. Everything about her seemed perfect. She was peaceful and serene; a glowing angelic force of nature. At that moment, he knew he loved her.

*

The wedding day was one of the best days Vince could remember in his 27 years of life. A few months earlier him and Vanessa had just gotten back to their shared house in Los Angeles after a romantic dinner out and settled in front of the fireplace to enjoy some Dom and chocolate covered strawberries. The flames that flickered and crackled quietly beside them provided the immediate surrounding area with just the right amount of warmth and illumination.

Vince pulled one of the berries from his side of the plate by the stem and reached across to place it in Vanessa's mouth. Before it reached its destination, he turned the large berry around by the stem to reveal a glimmering 1 carat solitaire ring embedded in the decadent dessert.

Vanessa stopped and looked momentarily confused but then screamed with joy upon realizing what it was and shouted "YES!" as she flung her arms around Vince, once again bathing him in the scent of her Dior perfume.

"I haven't even asked you yet ..." Vince said playfully with a broad smile.

"Ok ok, go ahead," Vanessa said as she sat back and eagerly awaited the assumed question.

"Vanessa, love of my life," Vince started, "will you make me the happiest guy in the -"

"Yes! Yes! YES!" Vanessa shouted once again throwing her arms around him with the biggest smile he'd ever seen as she cut him off mid sentence.

Now it was the wedding day. The only thing Vince had regretted was that neither his nor Vanessa's parents could be there due to the fact that they had all passed away several years earlier. This loss of both their parents was another one of the central bonds he had formed with Vanessa. All of their mutual and separate friends had arrived and Vince made Trey, Micah and Dave all his Best Man seeing as he couldn't choose who his 'best' friend was out of the three. The ceremony was held at Crystal Point Hall in Los Angeles and was decorated in all white peonies and roses, Vanessa's two favourite flowers.

She had fallen in love with them as a little girl after seeing them in her grandmother's garden. They were always there, right in the middle of all the other flowers and resonated with a young Vanessa in a way she couldn't explain. She had always felt a connection to them and had willingly taken care of them every year. Her grandmother had later told her of a time when Vanessa said she wanted to grow up to be just like her "pretty white flowers."

When her grandmother inquired as to what exactly she had meant by that and asked how she could grow up to be a flower, Vanessa responded, "Because they stand out from all the other flowers and they look like they were planted there by angels."

Vince had heard this story from Vanessa and kept the flowers his little secret until the wedding day because that was exactly how he felt about her; she stood out among all the others and seemed to him, like an angel. He had placed the white peonies on the side of the altar that he would be standing on and the white roses on the side Vanessa would be entering to with a mixed bouquet of both flowers sitting in between them. The entire room was illuminated by the soft light of white pillar candles placed around the room in various types of white painted antique candle holders.

The guests had all gathered in the large French chateau style banquet hall room that looked as though it had built in the previous century by skilled artisans plying their trades. The large 12 foot mirrors that graced the walls were framed in intricately carved white painted oak and looked like something from the Palace of Versailles. The grand crystal chandeliers dropped from the ceiling that was painted midnight blue with clusters of stars so it appeared as though the chandeliers themselves were floating in the sky.

Vince looked out quietly, reverently over the crowd of friends and other family members that had come to join him and Vanessa on one of the most important days of their lives. Right then, the back doors opened and in came the wedding party, followed by Vanessa. It's safe to say that she had never looked more beautiful or stunning in her entire life. Love is blind as far as the eye can see, but everyone agreed she looked amazing.

The long white fishtail gown draped at the hips in a decadent display of silk and Swarovski embellishment that looked as though it were shot at the centre of the dress and splattered outward, creating a star effect. The white silk was ruched and tucked into the top of the strapless sweetheart bust. As Vanessa walked, the six foot train that flared from the dress dragged and swirled behind her.

She wore a large multi-diamond necklace and chandelier style diamond earrings. Her thick dark hair was done up in waves and held at the back with a diamond encrusted butterfly hair piece that also held in place the small white mesh veil that fell over the side of her face where the hair swept up, leaving the other half exposed. Her brown eyes were locked on Vince as she gracefully made her way to the stage, a crystal swathed, pointed toe shoe peeking out from underneath the luxurious gown with each step.

By the time she reached the platform on which the two would exchange their vows, Vince was utterly speechless. The minister carried on and each said their vows and exchanged their rings but all Vince could focus on was her. Her face, her beauty and her elegance all seemed to meld perfectly with the raw sexiness that she had always had about her.

After the ceremony, most of the guests had left for a few hours while Vince and Vanessa took hundreds of pictures in the serene gardens at the back of the lot the hall was located on. The rest of the night seemed like a dream. People ate and drank and danced under the haze of the crystal chandeliers. Champagne flowed and spilled, all night long, people laughed and chatted amongst themselves at their tables as the music, which included Journey's classic, played in the background.

"While the movie never ends, it goes on and on and on and on. Strangers waitin', up and down the boulevard, their shadows searchin' in the niiight. Street lights, people, livin' just to find emotion; hiding somewhere in the night ... Don't stop believin', hold on to that feelin'!"

Trey, Micah, Dave and Vanessa's Maid of Honour, Teresa, all gave their speeches. Some, like Trey, opted for humour, throwing in the old ball and chain joke one too many times. Others made heartfelt observations of the couple that had most of the guests welled up in joyous tears. Vince smiled to himself when he overheard one of Vanessa's friends eagerly telling her date, "Oh, Just one more dance and then we're good to go."

Vince and Vanessa stayed around to thank everyone they could for coming and for their gifts and support. After everyone had been acknowledged, Vince and Vanessa took to the stage and announced their departure upon which all of the guests erupted into applause as they made their way out into the limo and off to their honeymoon suite for the night until their flight to Tahiti the next morning.

Vince sat in the doorway; his arm propped up against the frame and looked over at Vanessa lovingly. She finished taking off her shoes and lay down on the bed still fully dressed. Vince slowly walked over, placing both hands on the bed on either side of her, leaned down and kissed her ever so gently on her perfect red lips. He sat for a moment longer and stared into her eyes until he again leaned down and kissed her. She tasted so good.

Then, he couldn't control it any longer as passion tore through him like a bolt of lightning. They both started tearing off their wedding clothes and throwing them onto the floor. Vince took Vanessa in his arms and began eagerly caressing her long slender legs, sliding his hands up her whole body until he reached her hands which he pinned down above her head while he leaned down to kiss her neck. He let go and once again, slid his hands down and back up her small frame, gently massaging her smooth skin as he moved. Pressing his body against hers, he slid himself into her as she audibly moaned. It was the perfect end to the perfect day and Vince couldn't remember ever being happier.

*

Things settled down a bit for Vince and Vanessa after they returned from their honeymoon. It had been yet another magical time in both their lives and they relished in it every day, lounging around the Tahitian beach and taking the odd surfing or diving class together. Other than that, they didn't do near as much 'touristy' stuff as they had on previous trips. Mostly, they just enjoyed each other's company and took every opportunity to unwind and relax under the hot sun before returning to the real world.

Vince hadn't taken to the whole work idea easily at first but quickly settled in and became more productive than ever, working relentlessly on advancing his career. He couldn't afford to waste the opportunity to work for J.P. Crane and Associates. This job, he figured, if he worked hard enough, would give him more than everything he needed in life that wasn't already provided by his loving wife.

He met every demand his boss made of him, even seizing opportunities to showcase his accomplishments to the higher ups. He never missed a deadline and even got most of his briefing and other things that would allow for themselves to be completed early, handed in quite a bit ahead of time. This also meant putting in long hours and taking on more responsibility than he knew was needed. He didn't mind though, he knew it would pay off some day.

What he did mind however, was his boss, Cameron's, increasing disdain for him. It was as obvious to everyone else as it was to Vince that this was due only to the fact that Vince far outperformed him and Cameron, as a result, was simply jealous of all the garnered attention Vince received. Of course the jealousy only served to detain Cameron, while helping Vince because in the minds of the partners, everything said or done against Vince by Cameron was passed off as merely personal prejudice. With this growing contempt Cameron was harbouring, the demands became greater and more ludicrous, and usually accompanied by nasty comments and snide remarks, to each of which a thousand barbed responses raced through Vince's head, but he kept his mouth shut.

In the courts, Vince had an astonishing success rate and almost all of his clients had given him raving reviews, calling him professional, astute, meticulous and always willing to provide the clients with the most informed course of action. It wasn't long before Vince had taken over Cameron's job as one of the partners in the firm. Vince was ecstatic upon hearing the news as it normally takes anywhere in the vicinity of three to ten years to even be *considered* for partnership, but Vince had done it in two! He had not expected it because he had thought it impossible, for as far as he knew, he was the youngest attorney to be promoted to partner of a major law firm ever.

"Mr. Torres, Patrick would like to see you in his office," called Vince's secretary from one of the phone lines.

"Thanks Jean, tell him I'll be right there," responded Vince.

Normally, the thought of being called into your boss's superior's office would be an intimidating endeavour. Not for Vince, seeing as he had not once yet been reprimanded for anything but instead had received nothing but praise and acknowledgment from Patrick. Although rumours of Patrick's wrath and cunning ran rampant around the office, Vince had only witnessed evidence to the contrary. This was no doubt due to his reputation as a 'rising star' within the firm, but it didn't really matter to him. As Vince arrived at Patrick's secretary's desk, he could hear him inside.

"Take a seat and he'll be with you in a moment," said Chloe, Patrick's pretty, blonde secretary motioning to one of the couches.

A bit of noise could be heard behind the closed doors then some raised voices shouting. This shocked Vince as he couldn't imagine anyone yelling at Patrick like that, especially seeing as Patrick was supposed to be the one with anger issues. But the noise was too blurred to tell who it was.

Vince sat and waited uncomfortably outside Patrick's office while the voices behind the door continued their tonal fluctuation until everything went quiet. Vince, hearing footsteps coming towards the door, sat upright on the suede couch that was positioned directly across from Chloe's desk.

The door flew open and Cameron came rushing out. It was one of those slow motion moments where their eyes locked on each other as they passed without saying a word, though the tension and hostility was quite tangible. Vince watched as Cameron stormed down the hallway to the elevator lobby and disappeared behind one of the sleek, quiet doors.

Chloe pressed a button on the desk phone and said, "Mr. Crane, Vince is here to see you, as you requested."

She threw in that last part because she knew that Patrick had a tendency to forget such mundane things as who he had called to his office mere moments earlier. With that, Patrick came out of his office, looked around for a minute appearing somewhat frazzled and walked over to Vince who had risen upon seeing the door open and shook his hand with a firm grip.

"Vince … so glad that you're here. Come in and have a seat," Patrick said motioning towards the door.

Vince walked in and followed instructions, planting himself in one of the oversize leather chairs situated in front of Patrick's desk, who came around the other side pouring a glass of scotch from an intricate crystal decanter for himself and offering Vince one, which he politely refused. 'Was it even legal to drink at work?' he wondered to himself before figuring if you're the founding Partner of a major law firm, you can probably get away with it.

Vince noticed Patrick's pinstripe suit was perfectly pressed even at 7 p.m. and that ever-present green pocket square in a strange fold was still sticking out of his left breast pocket. Vince briefly pondered if Patrick actually changed several times throughout the day or if he simply did very little work.

Patrick sat down and swivelled in his own oversized black leather chair for a moment and stared Vince dead in the eye before starting in, "Vince, I called you in here to tell you that you've been doing an incredible job, as you are well aware, and also to tell you that effective Monday, Cameron will no longer be with the firm, as you are *not* yet aware. His behaviour and performance simply do not live up to the expectations we have in place here. You are the person I have put up as a recommendation to the other partners and they've all agreed, after much discussion, that you are the most suitable candidate."

The words coming out of Patrick's mouth in rapid succession threw Vince's nerves into overdrive. He experienced an incredible adrenaline rush upon hearing this, as it was all happening so fast. He knew what the words meant, but the weight they carried refused to register in his mind. The only distinct thought Vince could remember from that moment was 'I did it!', although it wasn't official yet. Patrick rambled on for another solid ten minutes as Vince tried not to visibly smile or laugh.

He was the one who everyone thought would never really amount to anything in high school. He had never been the one to win the 'most likely to succeed' award at prom or even really been considered one of 'the popular kids', whatever that meant. As far as he knew or felt, most of the so called 'popular kids' held nothing more solid behind their title than the jealousy of others for not being like them. Whether it was good looks or talent in sports or the biggest house, the only real reason they were dubbed 'popular' was because most people wanted to *be* them, not because they harboured any amiable feelings towards them. Only a small percentage of them were actually nice people who didn't go out of their way to be cruel to others, and actually earned their title.

Recalling this, and remembering how long the wait seemed to be to earn this new life when he grew up, he now realized how far away it all seemed. He would have never imagined at the time, that in only a few short years he would become the youngest partner ever at one of the biggest law firms in Los Angeles. He would have never guessed that the life he knew then and dreamed of escaping from would become meaningless, completely irrelevant and distant, like smoke dissipating into the air.

After he was done explaining the procedures that would follow their conversation, they negotiated on Vince's new salary which ended up being much higher than he had expected and Patrick even offered to throw in a company leased Porsche. This deal, as far as Vince knew, was far more than any other attorney being promoted to partner was offered, especially with as little seniority as he had and he gladly accepted the offer. As of this moment, it seemed as though Vince's entire life had come together. Like all the various colours on the painter's palate had united to form a masterpiece. All his hard work had finally paid off and he now had everything that he needed out of life. All he had to do was keep it and enjoy it.

Chapter 3 – *The Daravians*

Vince sat alone in his suite and went over all the various moments in his life. Everything that had mattered to him, everything he had loved, and everything he had worked for was now either forever torn from him or had somehow, in the wake of tragedy, lost all meaning entirely. What was he to do now? He would have to sell the house; of that much he was sure, but what about his career? How was he supposed to return to work as if nothing happened and still continue on with the same passion and enthusiasm as before?

He decided he couldn't. He would have to resign only mere months after being promoted to the position he worked so hard to achieve. Better resign, he thought, than the slow inevitable deterioration of his performance and energy which would make way for a newer, much more motivated and ambitious attorney looking to climb higher on the career ladder. Once he became more comfortable with this thought, another question presented itself. If he was to quit, then what exactly would he do for a living?

Vince racked his brain for an answer but couldn't produce one at that moment. 'No, I can't quit,' he recanted to himself. There's no need to be irrational about it. Vanessa was gone now and his career was the only small shred of his life he had left that had meant anything and still did. He couldn't just throw it away. If that was all that was left of his life, he would not simply discard it after all the hard work, all the bullshit, all the politics and all the money it gave him. He knew of course, that all the money in the world couldn't bring Vanessa back or buy the love that they had shared, but a career was at least something to focus his energy on.

Besides, he was extremely lucky to have even attained the junior position he started at the company with right out of law school let alone the position he had been promoted to now at such a young age. He had been aware of this fact since the first day he set foot into their downtown Los Angeles building. He must continue. Yes, he was absolutely devastated over Vanessa's brutal murder but he wasn't about to let fate take *everything* from him. The love he had for his job paled in comparison to the love he had for Vanessa, but this was a separate part of his life that had been the other half of who he was. If one half of your life gets destroyed or becomes void, fill the vacant space with whatever is left.

His boss and some co-workers had already contacted Vince to express their sympathy, but Patrick mostly expressed an interest in when Vince would be returning to his post. If Patrick, as cold as his intentions may have been, simply assumed Vince would take some time off then come back to work, then that seemed like the most sensible thing to do. After all, Patrick wasn't the one who had just experienced a traumatic event in his own personal life, so he must have a clearer frame of mind than Vince did by this point.

Vince wandered over to one of the chairs situated behind a desk from the big soft bed he spent most of his time in lately and began to contemplate just how long he should wait before returning to work. A month? Two? For what, to grieve? Vince wasn't sure his body or mind could handle any more of that anyway. Maybe he could suppress any emotion, guilt or turmoil he felt long enough to get back to work and recover naturally without anyone ever knowing.

That sounded like a good idea. Better to be at work feigning normalcy and level headedness and be busy actually doing something to keep his mind occupied than to sit in a hotel room and wallow in self pity and crippling body and mind numbing depression. On the other hand, what if the stress became too much for him to handle? Everyone would accept at face value his attempts to act as if everything were ok, maybe not at first, but eventually, and they would begin to treat him as if he were in a proper frame of mind even though he wasn't.

A little test, he decided, making his way over to the unpacked suitcase that was lying in front of the closet. He had left it there in hopes that if it were at least near the closet, he would eventually be inspired to put its contents away so as not to ruin the drape or hang of his expensive suits. He unzipped the one side and flipped open his large beige discreetly labelled Prada suitcase and clumsily riffled through the soft wools and cashmeres and eventually produced his favourite white on white stripe Gucci dress shirt and set it on the bed to be ironed while he searched for a pair of suitable pants. After another moment of half consciously digging, he ferreted out a pair of grey glen check Dior homme dress pants.

A quick check through another slightly smaller matching suitcase revealed a pair of black rounded toe Zegna oxford style lace ups and matching black leather belt. Vince took his time ironing the pieces and after draping them over his toned torso and legs he wandered into the bathroom. He stood again, palms flat on the cold countertop and stared at his reflection. This time, he saw something slightly more concrete gazing back at him. He finished applying his facial creams, aftershave and styling paste that gave his hair that natural feathery look he could always be seen sporting and realized he was back to at least *looking* like his old self again. He fished the extra large bottle of Prada's Infusion D'homme out of his toiletries bag, sprayed his neck and wrists then headed downstairs for dinner with himself. He figured if he could comfortably and confidently accomplish this, then he may be ready to head back to work sooner than he had planned and continue on with his life.

Stepping off the elevator onto the marble bank emblazoned with a large decorative, six pointed star, Vince looked around momentarily for something he would recognize as some sort of restaurant. Spotting nothing immediately and remembering nothing from when he had checked in, more focused on getting between warm bed sheets at the time, he walked over to the concierges' desk and asked where he might find some place to get dinner.

"We have the lobby bar and the Brasserie restaurant within the hotel sir, but if you wish to dine outside the Sheraton, there is a wide selection of -" The concierge stated in a friendly but automatic manner.

"The Brasserie," Vince stated cutting him off, not particularly interested in leaving the confines of the building just yet, "Where can I find that?" he asked.

"It's right down this hallway here," he answered pointing a very white finger to a passage behind Vince, "and to the right, you can't miss it."

"Thanks a lot," Vince said turning around and starting for the hallway the kindly but odd man had pointed out, now realizing that he was absolutely starving.

He also took a mental note that he had just conversed with another human being and was, for once in what seemed like a long time, in full command of the English language. He found his way to the restaurant as he passed down the right side of the hallway. Following the hostess, he took a seat at one of the dark tables with light wood trim and was again able to uphold a normal conversation with a complete stranger without breaking down. He sat and ate lazily, watching other couples enjoying some time out together, pushing thoughts of him and Vanessa doing the same out of his mind with relative ease. Was this a good thing or a bad thing? He couldn't tell and when he thought about it some more, he didn't really care. It made life easier.

Upon making it back to the room, and not paying much attention to the bill he was sure to be racking up at the hotel, he landed face first onto the made up bed and let out a sigh as he lifted one half of his face up for air and looked around the empty room with the exposed eye. He was able to behave fairly normally in public but he was also fairly certain that it wasn't supposed to be as taxing a task as it had just been.

Each individual thing, when focused on, he could accomplish with little difficulty but the combined energy it took trying to act normal continually was an overall gruelling feat. Maybe with a couple more weeks practice, he would have it down to an art. 'That's it,' he thought, 'just a couple more weeks to recoup and try and get back to being a functioning part of society.' Vince picked up the phone and called Patrick to let him know he would be back sooner than originally planned.

*

The next few weeks passed much quicker than Vince thought they would. Maybe just knowing when the time off would come to an end helped to speed up the process. He had gone out for dinner and even into public on the odd occasion several more times in those weeks with only minimal problems. One time walking through a park, he found himself staring innocently, although absentmindedly, at a group of children who were playing some sort of game, much to the dismay of their parents and chaperones who were observing from nearby benches. Other than that one little uncomfortable incident and a few times walking into something or someone, Vince had managed to act relatively normal. No mental breakdowns and no hysterics ... definitely progress.

Returning to work however, wasn't quite as easy. Seeing as everyone had heard the news that seemed to spread like wildfire in that place, he was painfully reminded of what he was desperately trying to forget each and every time someone stopped by his office to offer their heartfelt condolences. Once or twice, someone in the firm that he couldn't stand would stop by and in his mind, only offer sympathy because he was one of the partners.

'Sure,' Vince thought to himself when Carl meandered into his office. Vince generally gave Carl a wide berth due to the fact that before Vince had been promoted above him, he had had a penchant for making petty complaints about anything and everything Vince did behind his back while taking credit for work other people had done. Now that he was working under Vince however, he never missed a chance to suck up, but Vince knew Carl hadn't changed at all and was still generally hated by everyone. After Carl had offered his sympathy in person, Vince resigned himself to levelling a dark look in his direction before muttering, "Thanks," but thinking, 'Now that you've said your peace, get out.' Eventually he decided to make a companywide announcement,

I would like to thank all of you who have offered your sympathy and everyone who sent cards and gifts for your support through this difficult period. However, as this is something I'm trying to move past in my life, I would now appreciate all conversations on the matter to cease. I know you will respect my wishes and I thank you again.

-Vince Torres, Partner, J.P. Crane and Associates.

After that, the only people who mentioned it again were Vince's close friends in the firm. Vince had already gotten over the weird feeling of being his friends' new boss, especially seeing as he was newer to the firm than they were and they were probably secretly a little resentful, but he couldn't get over all the fake apologies and sympathy cards from everyone simply because he was their boss.

He sat at his desk in his new office, which wasn't really much nicer than his old one but definitely a lot bigger and started to pick up where he left off on the contract draft from the day before.

"Hey buddy, how's it goin?" Trey asked as he swung around the doorframe into Vince's office.

"Not too bad, just trying to get some work done," Vince answered without looking up, hoping to imply that he wanted to be left alone. Unfortunately, subtleties were almost always lost on Trey.

"Yeah yeah, you're always working. That's why you made partner," Trey said jokingly, but Vince wasn't in the mood for his antics.

"You know Trey, you're not supposed to come bursting into my office calling me buddy and everything at work anymore. You know I don't mind you coming in to chat every once in a while but if Patrick or one of the other partners saw you do that, we'd *both* be in shit," Vince stated flatly and inevitably sounding less friendly than he was trying to come across so Trey wouldn't despise him.

"Right," Trey responded with an undertone of hurt that Vince hadn't heard before seeing as he wasn't overly emotional. "I guess I'll just leave you to your work boss," he finished and promptly left.

Vince stared at the empty doorway for a moment and wondered when Trey had become so sensitive. 'I'm the one who just been through a tragedy, not him,' Vince thought. Maybe he started to change when Vince was promoted above him. Was that when it happened? Had Vince really just been too busy working to notice his friends attitudes towards him were changing? 'No, No,' he reprimanded himself silently, 'It must have been while I was away for so long. Or maybe it was after the wedding. Trey didn't even have a steady girlfriend at the time; he must have been upset that I was already getting married. Well no point in wasting energy I don't have worrying about Trey's newfound feelings,' Vince thought as he continued on with his work.

The hours seemed to drag on even though Vince had tonnes of work to catch up on and knew there wouldn't be anywhere near enough time. He sat and worked on everything he needed to accomplish but it didn't seem the same as before when he … 'never mind,' he thought quietly to himself as he dropped his pen onto the pile of papers in front of him and pressed his face into his hands with a long, tired sigh. It doesn't matter. Of course it's never going to be the same now, or ever. Nothing will ever be the same for that matter. The essence of life itself had shifted its basic meaning so many times in the past few months so that nothing seemed solid to him anymore. Maybe *that's* the basic fact of life - nothing is certain. Nothing is forever. Nothing stays as it is, good or bad, real or surreal, love or hate. It's all as volatile as quicksand under your feet. One minute it's there, and the next, it's gone. When he thought about it this way, it didn't seem so bad, and he was overcome with a sense of calm realizing that even this horrible stage would twist itself around into something new eventually.

It was true as far as he could tell. Up until he started working at J.P. Crane & Associates, his life had been relatively boring. School, odd jobs to pay for school, random dating, Friday and Saturday nights out with the guys ... his life had only started to skyrocket with the start of his new job. All the excitement and prestige, the hard work and seeing it pay off so quickly. Then of course, it wasn't long afterwards that he started dating Vanessa, with whom he'd had more life experiences in the two short years they dated and was worth more than any paycheque he had worked so hard for. Then he got married. 'Holy shit,' he thought, 'I've already been married, made partner at the biggest law firm in L.A., owned my own multi-million dollar home and been widowed all by the ripe old age of 27.' To top all that off he had also already killed someone, and this was somehow the least of his worries and anxieties that kept him up at night. All of this had happened within two and a half years. It had been nothing but an ever-changing and experience rich time in his life.

The problem was what to do now? He felt like he had already gone through all of life's major stages and couldn't help but feel like he was too young to have experienced so much yet. All of the fast paced drama, all the love, all the excitement, the ambition, the rush of it all came to an end at the speed of lightning, ended by a brick blockade of death, misery, grieving, guilt and fury.

And now after all those dramatics, there was nothing. Like a hole, like life was supposed to be over for him. He had already gone through it all, seen it all, lived it all and it was almost as if it were supposed to be his time that was up, only it wasn't. He was trapped here in a meaningless, lacklustre, trance-like reality with nothing more to do or say that hadn't been done or said. With that, the feeling of calm gave way to the feeling of desolation. Vince looked at the rest of his life as if he were looking out over a cliff and into the empty sky, with nowhere left to go, nowhere to turn and nothing behind him except the trail he had used to get there.

Vince packed up his work and stared at it for a moment, contemplating whether or not to take it back to the hotel to finish or leave it for tomorrow. He then whipped around, grabbed his black leather briefcase from beside his large oak desk, flung it up onto the papers he had been working on and threw his cell phone inside. He then closed it up and walked abruptly out of his office down the hall, keeping to the right and towards the elevators without looking back.

*

The next day back at the office was much the same as the one before it, and Vince was fairly certain, as he had decided the previous day, that it wouldn't get any different in the future either. This is what he had to look forward to. For the rest of his life, this was just about everything he'd be doing from now on. Or maybe not, life was, as he had also noted earlier, constantly changing. Maybe it would take another unexpected turn. He hoped against it however, figuring that he was better off with boredom than another round of everything that had happened lately. What he didn't know was that unseen events were already set in motion that would change his life forever. There was no way for him to know at this moment that what had been started at eleven o'clock on that fateful night was far from finished.

The usual daily business took place yet again and Vince had survived it still hoping, despite his previous conclusion that it wouldn't, that life would get better; that there was indeed something to look forward to. There had to be, even if there really wasn't, he would imagine there was something, anything, to keep him going. How could he function otherwise? His lunch was boring and just as full of the mindless chitchat everyone at the office seemed so fond of. Finishing up the day's work, he tossed the files into his black briefcase to take with him, reached inside one of his pockets and plucked out his cell phone. He gave Micah a quick call to confirm dinner with him, Trey and Dave.

"Yeah man we're all set for tonight, I went ahead and made reservations at d'Avignon for four at seven. I know it's not exactly Trey's favourite place but he's always calling the shots," Micah said when Vince had asked about the game plan for the night.

"That's perfect. We go to Canal too much lately, I'm getting sick of it," Vince responded.

"Yeah same here. Anyways bud I gotta let you go. I'm meeting a client in about fifteen minutes across town," Micah said abruptly. "Apparently this guy's too important to leave his own house so I have to haul my ass over there every time I need the smallest thing. Do you believe it? Gotta run. I'll see you at seven," and with that, he clicked the phone off.

Vince added some more of the never ending pile of paperwork that had been accumulating on his desk lately to his briefcase and moved out of his chair and through the door out of the office. He had to go back to the suite for a while to work some more, take a quick shower and change out of his work suit into a more dinner appropriate suit before heading out for the night.

Once the elevator hit the lobby and the doors opened to the dark marble flooring, Vince was on the phone again to hail a cab back to the hotel.

Within minutes, a yellow cab came screeching to the curb and Vince hopped inside and called out, "711 South Hope Street."

Without a word, the cabbie took off into the fast moving traffic without taking any noticeable vehicular precautions. He sped past other cars and weaved in and out of lanes where other motorists were obviously moving a little too slowly for his taste. He pulled up to the hotel in front of the two storey high panelled glass and red brick pillar entrance and merely tapped his finger on the meter to indicate what Vince owed him. The fare came to $7.13 and Vince threw him a ten, grabbed his briefcase that seemed to be a permanent fixture on him lately, opened the door and disappeared inside the hotel lobby.

Upon arriving at his room, Vince threw the briefcase along with his navy jacket onto the bed and went into the bathroom to take a shower that wasn't needed for anything other than mental decompression. Afterwards, he stepped out of the bathroom draped in nothing but a white terrycloth towel that hung off his hips and wandered over to the bed where he opened the briefcase and stared blankly at the enclosed contents.

'Screw that,' he thought. He'd done enough work for one day and had just managed to relax from it all. He wasn't about to dive back into the source of his exhaustion just yet. He grabbed a simple black jacket, a blue striped shirt and a dark red tie, finished working a small amount of moulding paste into his short, dirty blonde hair and left for dinner.

He hoped that a night out with the guys like old times might help loosen the increasing tension that had formed between him and his friends at the firm since his promotion. A good dinner and some laughs might make everyone see that he wasn't a different person now and would hopefully get things back to normal.

It had momentarily occurred to him that it was beyond absurd that *he* was the one trying to save the friendship and hoping to display some form of humbleness after *he* was the one who just had his wife murdered. He considered how inflated their egos must be to unofficially demand this of him during *his* time of crisis so they won't feel belittled. He brushed it off, like he usually did, as their immaturity and considered the possibility of finding new friends. As it turned out, new friends were closer than he knew, as were new enemies.

*

Vince found himself eating yet another gourmet meal and trying to ignore the never ending banter about where the hottest club to be seen at was or which restaurants to visit, the only slightly interesting things his friends talked about anymore were girls. But even this was reduced to mere numerical rankings. After everyone had finished their drinks and slapped their credit cards down without placing much credence on the total, they parted ways. Normally Vince might have gone to whatever club they would be visiting but he wasn't in the mood.

"You sure you don't want to come man? We're going to Census, it's pretty decent, and lots of hot chicks," Trey asked one last time as the others stopped in their tracks and looked back, hoping Vince would change his mind.

"No, it's ok. I have to see my psychiatrist tomorrow and I don't really want to be hung over on her chair," Vince responded with a laugh.

He wasn't lying about actually having a shrink but he was lying about having to see her in the morning. He really had to go back to the hotel and get some work done, but he didn't want it to seem like that was all he ever did. And he *definitely* didn't want to squander any progress he'd made with them tonight towards making them think he hadn't changed at all since his promotion by blowing them off to go work.

"What? You're seeing a psychiatrist?" Trey asked, genuinely shocked, as if he hadn't considered the possibility of someone who'd just had their wife murdered wanting to see a counsellor.

"Uh, yeah, I didn't mention it cause I didn't want you guys to think I was crazy or anything," Vince responded a bit embarrassed.

"That's ok man, we know you're crazy," Trey laughed, indicating to some degree that he hadn't completely changed his opinion of Vince, "But don't say I didn't warn you!" he finished as he coolly lifted a finger towards Vince while turning back around to go to his car.

"Yeah, yeah, you always say that," Vince called.

"And still, you never listen …" Trey called playfully as he leaned down into the driver's seat before taking off.

A minute or two passed after everyone had left before the cab he had called arrived to take him back to his suite. He was using cabs now because even his Porsche had crapped out on him recently and he couldn't be bothered with the rental the body shop provided for the week or two it would be 'out of commission'.

Plus he actually rather enjoyed not having to drive around the cluttered city, especially in the wake of everything he'd gone through. It was really nice to just relax and he didn't mind the waiting a few minutes because there were always cabs around, so it never took more than a couple minutes anyway unless it was raining out. He hopped into the back seat and soon found himself back at the large, mostly glass hotel. He was already tired and wanted nothing more than to go upstairs and fall flat onto the bed and just sleep there like that, spread eagle and fully clothed, but he had work to finish up.

He paid the fare and set one black leather clad foot then the other onto the cement. He turned his head to face the entrance which was warmly lit from inside. The orange light shone through into the darkness of outside and softly illuminated the drop off area. He closed the cab door and walked towards the revolving entrance to the hotel on the right side of the walkway before he heard someone say something to him from behind as the cab slowly pulled out and back onto the street.

"Hey! You Vince Torres?" he heard from behind him.

Vince turned to see three men, two black guys and one white guy wearing grey hoodies and slouchy jeans standing on a sidewalk about twenty feet away, much closer to the street than the hotel.

"Yeah ... who are you?" Vince asked more confused than ever.

But before he got an answer and just after he finished asking the question, one of the men, he couldn't remember who, it happened so fast, pulled a gun out of the large front pocket on his hoodie and shot at Vince three times, hitting him twice. The gunfire cracked in the air as Vince felt the metal shards enter his body and was overcome with shock that disabled most of the pain he should have felt. He fell to the ground and heard a lady screaming from somewhere near the street as the three men took off running.

Lying on his side, his body went numb, but he could feel the blood puddle that was forming around him. He fell into a sort of daze as the lady who had screamed rushed over, whipped out her cell phone and dialled 911. Quickly, another older man and some other people had gathered around but Vince could only recognize their blurred images moving around slightly as they talked urgently to one another about what they should do before Vince succumbed to the heavy feeling and lost consciousness.

Chapter 4 – *Aconitine*

Vince's eyes fluttered open to the groggy sight of bright white lights. Had he died? A more enthusiastic effort at opening his eyes revealed that no, this wasn't anything close to eternal paradise or the pearly gates - it was a hospital. His vision was still blurred and he couldn't feel much of anything except for a slight sensation of being suspended in air. A side effect from whatever was pumping into him from any one of the numerous intravenous tubes that were winding their way out of his body, no doubt.

He actually didn't feel that bad for having just been shot three times. Or was it two? He glanced down and saw a large bloodied gauze over his left shoulder below his collar bone and a quick look under his hospital gown revealed another bloodied gauze taped onto the right side of his mid-section. 'That one probably did some damage,' he thought. He was oddly at ease with the injuries themselves, but the cause afforded no such mental comfort. He hadn't died, so that was a plus, he wasn't buried six feet under somewhere ... but why had he been shot? And who shot him? Panic set in quickly as he realized if he wasn't dead, then whoever it was that tried to kill him would probably try again.

It was at this point he noticed three other blurred shadows standing and talking behind the curtain that was pulled around his bed. He coughed a little to let whoever was out there know that he was awake. He figured if they were here to kill him, they would have done it already and even if they hadn't yet and they'd just gotten here, he had no hope of escaping anyway. Upon hearing the noise, one of the figures moved towards him as the rest turned to look. It reached forward and drew back the curtain to reveal ... Micah's worried face. A wave of relief overcame both of them upon seeing each other. Vince was thrilled to see his friend and Micah was happy Vince wasn't dead or in a coma.

"How ya doin bud?" Micah asked treading carefully.

"Not too bad actually for having just been shot two times," Vince stated. "And the large amount of whatever they've doped me up on doesn't hurt either," he finished, to which Micah laughed slightly.

The rest of the curtain was pulled back and they were joined by Trey and Dave as Micah pulled up chairs for all of them.

"So ... do you know what the hell happened?" Vince asked hoping against all odds that they would provide him with some sort of plausible answer.

"No, we thought *you* would have known what happened. You were shot, obviously, but we don't know by whom ... does it hurt?" Trey asked in that sort of senseless way of his.

The other two glared at him.

Then Dave turned to Vince and said, "We don't know what happened, Vince ..."

"It's been all over the news though, everyone seems to think its gang related," Trey piped in handing Vince a couple of newspapers.

It didn't make sense to Vince why everyone had assumed it was a gang related shooting seeing as he wasn't affiliated with any sort of gang ... Vince looked down at the papers and willed his fuzzy eyes to focus but they couldn't, although he could still make out the titles and the bold headlines. The Los Angeles Times read,

J.P. Crane Partner gunned down by gang members. Is a drug war brewing in the office as well as the streets?

Vince scoffed and pulled out a copy of The Morning Star from behind whose headline read,

Los Angeles gang seeks revenge for death of one of their own!

Vince's eyes widened and focused a bit more intently now. Well at least somebody knew what was really going on. He didn't actually have any proof to back up his instinct but it did make sense. Maybe that Jamie guy was a member of this unknown gang. But then why hadn't the police told him this?

"That's who it was!" Vince near shouted, pointing to the paper. "It must have been! That Jamie ste ... uh ... stern ... um ... Whatever the hell his name was, must have been one of their members and now they're trying to kill me for killing him."

"Ok buddy, I think you're taking the newspaper headlines a little too seriously," Trey stated as he yanked the thick folded copies out of Vince's right hand.

"No, No I'm not! It all makes sense," Vince insisted.

"Then why wouldn't the police have told you this?" Micah retorted.

"Well maybe they didn't know, or maybe ... shit guys! I have no idea but I know that's what happened. Why else would somebody try to kill me? And that means they won't stop! I've gotta get out of here!" Vince said a little too enthusiastically in the minds of his loyal friends.

"No, you need to stay right here," Micah said with a stiffening tone. A tone that revealed exactly what Micah was thinking; 'You're overreacting. You've blown everything out of proportion in your head.' Vince wasn't having it.

"Then why did someone try to kill me?" Vince asked now a little frustrated and accusatory. The look on Micah's face turned from seriousness to a display of emphatic confusion.

"I don't know Vince; you're a partner at J.P. Crane, who the hell knows. Maybe you or the firm wrongfully let a murderer or rapist go free and now somebody wants justice or maybe someone else wanted that job and hired a hit man ... Maybe it was Cameron. Or maybe they simply thought you were someone else. It could have been anything," he said, dramatizing his soliloquy with hand gestures and facial expressions.

"No, because whoever it was knew my name. Why is this so difficult for you to believe? It's the *only* logical answer to all this," Vince stated rather flatly hoping to convey the simplicity of his argument without any hysterics so they wouldn't think he was overreacting.

He didn't bother to let his friends know that he thought their suggestion that Cameron was behind it was a legitimate one because he just knew that what the paper had said was right. He didn't need another explanation.

"Look, all I'm saying is that's only *one* of the possibilities and there's no need to get worked up over something that isn't certain yet. Ok? Just get some rest, we'll talk to the police about everything and let you know. In the meantime, don't panic." Micah's reassuring tone was enough to settle Vince down to the point where he could at least feign tranquility.

As his friends left the room, he thought maybe he should relax a little. He was in a hospital after all, and if anything were to happen, if anyone actually managed to get by security and everyone else without being noticed, the nurses and doctors would be able to tell if his health was in any sort of rapid decline. Besides, the drugs that were probably being pumped into him by the gallon were taking their toll. He felt dreamy and light but most of all, comfortable.

'This is nice,' he thought, not knowing if it was the drugs or if it was maybe the endorphins kicking in as some sort of post-trauma defence. He lay back on the fluffy white pillow and tried to fall asleep, still wondering how this could have happened to him. Staring up at the blank ceiling, he felt hopeless. He relaxed a bit, closed his eyes and tried to fall asleep.

*

Vince found himself back inside his house in the Hollywood hills. It was great to be back but everything seemed different. The house wasn't quite the same. He couldn't put his finger on what it was but he knew it, he could sense it. The surroundings had changed too. The glass structure now allowed no view of the skyline in the velvety dark of night anymore. All that he could see out that large wall of a window that once peered over the glistening city, was black nothingness. And although he didn't know how or why this was, he also didn't feel particularly interested in investigating this oddity.

An almost undetectable haze filled the air now. Moving towards the front of the house, he noticed that, unlike the glass wall to the rear, the front window did in fact still provide a view of the street. The area outside now also housed a multitude of glass and white concrete ... townhouses? Yes, glass townhouses now lined the other side of the street that he lived on. 'How odd,' he thought to himself.

Looking out one of the windows at the front of his house, Vince could see people coming and going from each one in a similar fashion to a supermarket where the ever revolving door constantly let people in and out.

He travelled back down the right side of the main hallway to the living room and sat down on the white sofa. Somebody must have cleaned it. There were no blood splatters on it anymore and the glass coffee table that had been shattered by the corpse of the intruder that killed Vanessa was now in perfect condition. They must have found an identical replacement when he was staying at the Sheraton. This place seemed so far away to him now, not like home. Looking out the panoramic windows, everything was black to him and he couldn't see anything.

He sat there for a while longer in the dimmed light that came from a single, new triangular lamp resting on the end table beside him. For some reason, he wanted to try and get into one of those town homes. He wasn't even sure why he had the urge, but he did. He had to do it carefully though so as not to get caught breaking and entering. There was something in there that he wanted, *needed*, pulling his mind towards it like some sort of magnetic force.

He got up, started down the hallway and suddenly found himself standing on the sidewalk in front of the glass row houses. He thought about it and didn't remember the walk over. These people looked like they weren't home. To be honest, it didn't look like anybody actually *lived* in any of these. He climbed the stairs to the front door, opened it and slowly entered into the space which was surprisingly enclosed.

Only the front of the house was glass and even that seemed to be an illusion. The room was filled with a soft orange light and decorated like the whole thing was deliberately set up in a fashion so as to allow you to be able to sleep anywhere you like. Low to the ground, large spacious couches that looked more like giant mattresses and giant decorative pillows were everywhere, piled stylishly and a few potted palms finished the space. At the back of the room was a spiral staircase that led up to the second level with doors to other rooms along the length of the open walkway above.

He had an overwhelming urge to see what was up there. He made his way over to the stairs and stopped at the bottom. Two candles were lit at the top of the stairs, one on each newel post where the railings ended. To the left was another small case of three stairs that led up to a shorter hallway that gave access to three rooms. The room directly to the left had even more soft orange light emanating from behind the open door.

Vince stood and contemplated where to go and decided to see what was in the illuminated room. Just as he started to make his way up the flight of stairs, he heard a noise. There was a soft bang and a ruffled sound coming from inside his destination room. Shit, someone *was* home! He sped back down the couple stairs he had ascended, out the door and back to his house, which was much farther down the street than he remembered He ran past a few completely disconnected looking people along the way whose eyes were glazed over and who didn't seem to notice him at all.

The haze in the air had grown to all out fog now and by the time he made it to his front door, he could barely see his own feet. He opened the door, went inside and sat on the floor in the foyer at the base of the stairs in a bit of a panic as the adrenaline rushed through his body.

Slowly, three figures appeared at the door and began banging on it incessantly. 'Oh shit,' he thought, 'someone knew I was there.' They banged louder and louder and Vince could feel his pulse racing as fear tore through him like a bolt of lightning. Slowly, a small bead of sweat ran down his forehead and he wondered what to do. 'Run!' he finally decided, and barrelled through the hallway back into the living room where he could see more figures standing outside the glass walls and peering in through the large window in the kitchen.

They had no eyes, no mouth, no nose; no real features at all actually, just an overall human like shape. A thousand possibilities ran through Vince's mind but he didn't have time to figure out what was going on. The invaders had already broken through the front door and the ones that had been simply gazing in at him from the windows at the back of the house managed to make it inside in the small fragment of time it took Vince to look at the ones coming towards him from the front then gaze back again. He ran back into the hallway where they had trapped him and began grabbing at him relentlessly.

The rest of the incident was fuzzy to Vince, he didn't know what was happening or why. He couldn't see much of anything. Maybe he had been clubbed or drugged, but he was groggy. He tried to fight back but they didn't seem to be doing too much more than constantly grabbing at him and trying to drag him around. The grey figures jumped and pushed and writhed around him and although he didn't feel like his life was particularly in danger, they definitely wanted something from him. He kept trying to push them away but they wouldn't go. In his peripheral line of sight he caught a glimpse of a dark shadow in the corner that was sitting motionless as they continued their grasping. Then finally, out of nowhere, they ceased and disappeared before Vince had realized they stopped. He opened his eyes to see what they were doing but they had already completely vanished from sight.

Vince sat on the ground, helpless, with his back against the wall and it was then that he noticed a dull pain encompassing the top of his head. He reached up wearily to touch it and instead felt a deep incision all around the top of his skull. He normally would have panicked but he didn't seem to be able to at the moment. He reached up with the other hand and grabbed the top of his head with both hands. He pushed on one side and felt the very top of his skull shift over slightly. They had cut all the way around, through the bone and left the dislocated part sitting where it was before, on top of his head.

There was next to no blood, just a small drip or two down the sides. They had cut the top of his head loose and left him there to die. He sat still wondering what to do and decided not to move in case something went wrong or he fell over, which would have been disastrous at this point. He sat on the floor in the hallway calling out and waited for what felt like an eternity for someone to help him but nobody came.

*

Slowly Vince awoke and looked around with fuzzy vision. He could make out that there were machines to the left of him and a curtain draped all around the bed he was lying in. The hospital! He sprung to semi-consciousness a little quicker and pulled out his hand from under the covers to feel the top of his head. He reached up, hoping he was alright, but half expecting not to be, and ... nothing. Nothing was there; no cut around the top of his skull, no blood, nothing. It was a dream; it must have been a dream. But it seemed so real. Remembering back, it all felt very real but it did seem like he was in another realm suspended in time and space.

Why was he here then? A quick survey of his body revealed the blood soaked bandages below his left shoulder and on his abdomen. 'That's right,' he remembered, 'I was shot.' This almost seemed like a relief to him after what he'd just dreamt.

Before he could think or do anything else, the curtain was hastily pulled back from around his bed and two uniformed officers stood looking at him with what could only be described as pity. The shorter and stockier of the two spoke first.

"Son, do you know where you are?" he asked slowly as if he thought the words weren't going to register with Vince.

"Yes, I'm in the hospital," Vince replied with a bit of a snide tone.

"Do you know why you're here?" the taller officer asked in a deep voice that seemed to perfectly match his large build, piercing eyes and chiselled jaw line.

"Yeah, 'cause I was shot," Vince answered again with not a bit of frustration at being treated like a moron, "But I don't know why *you're* here."

Of course he did know why they were here - somebody gets shot and the police are bound to show up sooner or later, but they clearly thought he was either drugged or an idiot anyway.

"We're just here to ask you some preliminary questions while the police at the hotel examine the crime scene. We were hoping you might have a description of what the assailant looked like."

"AssailantS," Vince corrected.

"There was more than one?"

"Yes, there were three actually, they were all wearing grey hoodies which seemed sort of odd, the one who shot at me first was about 6'1", black and had some sort of snake tattoo around his left wrist and the other one who shot at me was ... uh, wait ..." Vince couldn't actually remember what had taken place but was desperately trying to spit out answers in rapid succession so as to not sound like the doped up moron they clearly took him for.

"The other one who shot at you ... what did he look like?" asked the taller of the two who had recently taken to standing still, taking notes.

"Well, um, actually I think it was just him who physically pulled out the gun and shot. I don't know what the other two came for."

A look of cognition overcame the officers' expression as he said, "Thats right, we've already had ballistics run tests on the two bullets they removed from you. They were indeed shot from the same gun, and the officers who initially investigated the scene only found three shell casings." It was a small, although mostly insignificant comfort to know that he wasn't going crazy, that he *had* remembered what happened, but why was it starting to sound like they were testing him? "So can you give me a description of the other two attackers?" the officer continued.

"Um, yeah, one of them was white, about 5'11", dark hair, I don't remember what colour his eyes were but he did have a bit of a prominent nose. Kind of like he had been hit with something but I don't really remember the details exactly."

The second, still un-introduced officer standing back looked up from his notepad briefly.

"And the other one was about the same height, black and wearing the same thing as the other two ... wait maybe he wasn't that tall, I don't know exactly," Vince continued.

"Was there anything else that made an impression?"

"No, not really," Vince replied.

"Any articles of clothing that stuck out or seemed out of place to you?" the officer asked pointedly, his eyes now focused on Vince's.

"Well there was a sort of handkerchief thing that I saw one of them had hanging from their pocket as they left but I had already been shot by that point, I wasn't exactly focusing on their choice of attire ..." Vince's answer came out curter than he'd meant it to.

The officer leaned a little closer in his chair, put his hands together casually and waited for Vince to provide the rest of the answer he was looking for.

"Was it green?" he finally asked, apparently not having much time to sit and watch Vince try and figure out what he was waiting for.

"Yeah, I'm pretty sure it was. Why does that matter?" Vince asked as his eyes darted back and forth between the two men hoping to catch a glimpse of the answer they seemed to not want to provide.

"Well son, that matters because it means the people who shot you were members of the Daravians. You heard of them?" he asked frankly still maintaining full eye contact.

"Yeah I know that, it's in the paper already but I didn't know which gang ..." Vince was wondering more and more why this conversation was resembling an interrogation instead of a sympathetic visit to collect a description of his attackers.

"So let me ask you, why would these people want you dead?" he asked, cutting Vince off, "and I suggest you speak now because we can't help you if you won't help us ..."

"They want to kill me because I killed one of their members I guess. I don't know for sure but that's the only thing that makes sense," Vince stated as calmly as he could after having been gunned down and then interrogated on top of that. He knew where they were going and he was not amused by their accusatory tone.

"You owe them any money? Was it about drugs?" the officer asked as he loosened his demeanour a bit. Vince looked at him with a mixture of confusion and disgust.

"No, I just told you it's probably because I killed one of their members or whatever you're supposed to call them!" Vince answered becoming increasingly frustrated at their apparent lack of listening skills or the fact that they clearly didn't believe him.

"You mean Jamie? The guy who broke into your house and murdered your wife a while back?"

"Yeah, that guy." At least they were *starting* to comprehend what he was saying.

"So how do you know that Jamie Stetson was a member of the Daravians?"

"I don't, but that's the only thing that makes sense to me. I read about it in the paper this morning and realized that's probably why I was shot out of the blue and for no reason."

The black clad uniformed officers exchanged a slightly suspicious look at Vince's reply then looked back at him and said, "Well, you're right. Mr. Stetson was a member of the Daravians. He wasn't on any specific job, probably just petty theft for his own personal reasons.

"Within hours after the story was featured on the news, they all went ape shit; started shooting at the building you were brought to for questioning. Someone even threw a Molotov cocktail through a window in the right wing. Burnt the entire room down but it was contained. You didn't happen to notice any of this going on while you were there?"

He looked at Vince for an answer, or even an expression that signified he knew what he was talking about. Nothing. Vince racked his brain trying to remember back to that night. He didn't remember any shooting or even any fire alarm. He wasn't even sure where in the building he was that night and how far away these alleged incidents might have been.

"No ..." Vince replied simply, slowly, as if he himself wasn't even convinced of the answer he'd just given. He looked back up to the officer who was still standing, "This happened while I was there, inside the building?"

"Yes it did. But I guess you were too traumatized to notice. This shooting is most likely a continuation of what they started at the station. Although to be honest, I'm absolutely shocked it took them so long to try again ... it's been a few months now."

Vince nodded sombrely taking it all in as if he actually hadn't considered it before. The attacks at the station were news to him but he already knew it was them who had shot him. Now that he thought about it, Vince vaguely recalled a faint ringing while he was at the station but had passed it off at the time as some sort of trauma-induced tinnitus. It must have been a fire alarm from when the fire was started.

"Yeah well, I'm surprised it took them that long too then I guess, seeing as they must have known who I was ..."

The officer sighed and continued, "We're gonna get these descriptions you gave us back to the station so they can start compiling a suspect list. In the meantime, you get some sleep and we'll let you know if we come up with anything."

He stood up and patted the second officer on the shoulder as they both disappeared out the doorway and into the hall. Vince could only describe what he was feeling as sheer disbelief. Two un-introduced, un-welcomed officers had just barged into his hospital room, interrogated him for being shot and then abruptly left without sharing any further insight into the situation.

And worst of all, didn't seem to care that he'd almost been murdered. They didn't even seem to ask very many questions about facial or bodily features or anything. Once they had confirmed the green bandana thing, which apparently meant that they were undoubtedly gang members, they seemed to give up on the situation. As if to say, 'We've got bigger things to worry about than another attempted murder by a gang and there's not much hope to finding out who it *might* have been that shot you anyway so we're gonna call it a night.'

Vince normally would have been seething by now but he was too dumbfounded. He sat for what must have been a half an hour going over every bit of the abrupt arrival, conversation and departure of these two officers who hadn't even given Vince their names. Yet another sign of just how uninterested they really were in this case. After considering this, another question occurred to him; 'if they knew that this gang was after me, then why didn't they give me some sort of warning or try to help at all?' He figured it was again, probably due to their lazy decision that nothing could be done against an entire gang anyway and so they just left it.

Vince looked over at his IV's and pushed the red button a few times to release more of whatever that glorious liquid inside was and grudgingly did what he was told, and knew he was supposed to do, and tried to go back to sleep.

*

Vince awoke in the night in a cold sweat. He felt horrible. 'What's happening? Where am I?' The same thoughts jumbled around in his head every time he woke up somewhere he wasn't used to. He felt nauseous and tried to think. It didn't take him long to remember that he was in the hospital but he didn't remember coming in for this - he had been shot.

Suddenly there was a burning sensation in his mouth and an odd sort of numbness he'd never felt before almost like a dental freezing but with a sort of needle like sting to it every once in a while. It spread from his mouth to his face as he gasped for air wondering what was happening. His heart started to pound. 'This is it,' he thought. 'I've overdosed on whatever is in this IV and I'm gonna die.' Right then, his heart monitor on the machine beside him started flashing and beeping in that same unnerving fashion it did in those hospital shows when someone was going into cardiac arrest.

A nurse rushed in and yelled for someone to grab Dr. Stenwick. Trying to look around the increasingly blurry room and stay conscious, Vince saw the doctor come rushing in, white lab coat flapping behind him as he ran.

"Tell me what you're feeling," he said instantly, not wasting any time.

"Um, burning in my face and stomach, I feel sick, my mouth and face are numb I, uh -"

The bile rose to the back of Vince's throat and he threw up all over the front of himself and onto the white bed sheets. The doctor checked the heart monitor and audibly worked through several possibilities and finally deduced that this was symptomatic of aconitine poisoning. 'What the hell is that?' Vince thought.

"Get me 3 mg of atropine!" he yelled to the nurse who was coming through the door. She ran out of the room and quickly brought back a small vial and handed it to him along with a syringe designed to be implemented into the IV system.

Vince felt his body going into some sort of shock, and upon hearing that he had been poisoned, started to panic. His heart pounded against the inside of his ribcage so hard, he thought it might just break free. His muscles cramped and he was sweating profusely by this point; hot and cold flashes were coming and going like an oven door being opened and viscously shut again in front of him. The sweat ran down his forehead and soaked his hospital gown. His body began to ache horribly and he actually felt like he knew he was going to die, that it was too late for any sort of treatment. The pain in his stomach could be equated to that of dry heaving for hours on end and his lungs felt as though they were tightening and filling with fluid, disabling him from taking the deep breaths he was desperately trying to inhale.

"You two get the activated charcoal ready," Dr, Stenwick yelled again at the two nurses. He pulled the syringe out of the plastic wrapper, plunged it into the vial and drew up the liquid inside. Tapping it and pushing it into Vince's IV, he pushed down on the plunger until about one third of the liquid vanished into the drip. Vince instantly felt his heart stabilize significantly. He still felt nauseous and the burning sensation creeping under his skin but somehow had a sense that he would be fine.

What had just happened? The two nurses returned to a now delirious Vince and begun the preparations to pump his stomach as Dr. Stenwick looked utterly relieved that he had guessed correctly and not a little proud of himself. Had Vince been looking, he would have seen the woman that was secretly watching from outside the door quietly slink away, but he wasn't. Instead, Vince sat and endured the horrible pain of both the after-effects of the poison and the pump knowing that he had to endure it and trying not to think about it too much as he stared up at the empty ceiling.

*

"So why are you guys back here?" Vince asked the two officers who had taken a seat beside his hospital bed as he reached to take the coffee they had brought him.

"Well Mr. Torres, we need to have a talk with you, a rather difficult one," Stan answered. Stan and Rick had officially introduced themselves this time and even though they didn't exactly seem any more interested or invested than the last time they had come, they did at least give their names this time, their first names no less. "Some people who belong to the same gang as the ones who shot you in front of the hotel were the ones who tried to poison you," Stan continued.

"Now don't worry, a nurse saw two young men leaving your room right before you started going into cardiac arrest and called security with a description. They caught them just as they were trying to leave and had an empty vial of aconitine on them, which is a poison that works by interfering with the heart, and a hypodermic needle which wasn't opened, so they must have actually dumped the toxin in your mouth," he slowed down hoping he wasn't giving the news too fast. "Anyway they were arrested and are going to be tried for attempted murder. And don't worry, there will be an officer stationed just outside your room at all times from now on."

Vince was still uneasy about what had happened even though he hadn't been at all surprised. He knew they would try again and even told his friends they wouldn't stop.

"Yeah thanks, but I told everyone this before and nobody believed me. Nobody listened!" Vince stated rather annoyed.

"We know you did son, and we should have listened to you, but the main thing is that you're safe ... for now." His words were indicative of something worse that was to come as he stopped for the first time and expressed a bit of sympathy for Vince, looking as though he were a doctor who was about to tell a patient they had a terminal disease.

"For now?" Vince questioned, raising both eyebrows.

"Yes, For now. Because of the complexity of this case and the fact that you aren't a witness to anything and are unable to provide a testimony in the courts, we can't place you in the witness protection program."

"Why not? I testified against the guys who shot me ..." Vince almost yelled.

"Yes but describing one Caucasian and two African American men in hoodies and jeans isn't exactly enough information to put out a warrant let alone put you on the stand. And you said you don't really even remember their faces right? You were probably in too much shock," Stan grudgingly explained.

Vince was on the verge of tears he was so angry. Why wouldn't anybody help? Being a lawyer and understanding the ins and outs of just about every situation, he of course knew what Stan was saying to be true but it didn't matter to him at that moment. He sat near seething as Stan continued his explanation.

"Even if you could remember and testify and we managed to charge them, they'll be put away and someone else will try and finish what they started. It's a very unfortunate situation you've been put in, but there's really very little you can do. We think your best option, for your own safety, is to leave Los Angeles, to go somewhere far away from here where they'll never know you've gone. You're in way over your head on this one. I'm sure you've got family elsewhere in the country right?"

"No," Vince replied dolefully, realizing that as much as he hated to think about it and as much as he already knew he would have to do this, Stan was right. They had tried to kill him twice now and had almost succeeded both times. What if next time he wasn't so lucky? He sat and stared into space for a moment longer before Stan interrupted his trance.

"Well it's still your best option. Arrange for a job somewhere in New York maybe. There are lots of legal positions out there. It's not really safe for you here anymore. And going back to the witness protection program, even if we could get you into it, it would still mean you have to move, and then you don't have a choice as to where." He stopped and tried to look Vince in the eye but Vince was still staring blankly at the end of his bed. "Do you understand son?" he asked after not getting anything in the way of facial expressions.

"Yeah I understand," Vince replied with dour enthusiasm as the sad reality set in.

"Alright, good. Have a talk with your boss and see if he can get you something at another firm maybe. I would imagine you were going to sell the house anyway, after what happened. This will be a good chance to get away from it all, put it all behind you and move on with your life. Start over, it's the best way," he added as a last touch before getting up from his chair and patting Vince on the shoulder as he left, leaving Vince to sit alone and deal with his thoughts.

After many, many phone calls, one to Patrick (who'd willingly agreed to get him a job anywhere he liked and was willing to pull some strings for him), a couple to his real estate agent and lastly, to his close friends, Vince was all set to leave his life in Los Angeles behind. All his friends, all the memories, good and bad, all the tragedy and this entire chapter in his life would be forgotten as he started a new one in Denver.

Chapter 5 – *The Enlightenment*

The sun shone way too brightly today. Like a bear that had just come out of hibernation, Vince couldn't stand the strong rays that were symbolic of happiness right now. When nothing is right, a bright sunny day just seems to make it worse, almost as if to say, 'You're alone in your misery.' Entering the bulk food store after getting out of his car, Vince looked around for what he needed.

The store was fairly large with an open style mid section where the rows of containers only reached shoulder height so that one could see across to the other side if need be. Directly to the right were the cash registers and at the very back, a wall extended over the right quarter of the store to form a small but very accessible enclave. Vince wandered through the aisles and picked up a few things here and there.

His life had returned to a somewhat normal stage. He was far away from all three incidents now and was fairly certain he was safe, although he knew he could never escape the void feeling he constantly bore now. Nothing would ever be the same but it was as normal as it would ever get for him. He had quit his job some time ago now and had started working for a smaller law firm here in Denver. His life had changed dramatically but still it drudged on, lazily like a tired horse forced to carry its last load before being put down, only Vince didn't have the hope of escape by being put down like they did.

He had significantly downsized his living conditions even though he had reaped a sizeable benefit package from Vanessa's life insurance, both personal and through the marketing firm where she worked. He also still pulled in enough money to maintain an almost equal version of what he had in L.A., but he just couldn't be bothered. He now inhabited a two storey apartment right downtown. It was an ultra-modern styled place, similar to the house he had long tried to forget, but much smaller, and without all of the glitzy extras that come with a coveted Hollywood hills locale. The apartment also boasted a fairly enchanting view of the downtown lights and buildings thanks to the floor to ceiling windows all over the space. This still didn't compare to the majestic panorama of the Los Angeles skyline, but it was close enough for him now. He knew subconsciously that he had chosen that pad because it hugely resembled the lost home he was trying to forget, but this paradox in thought did nothing to stop the feeling of wanting to regain at least some of what was taken from him.

He wandered through the aisles some more in that persistent dreaming daze he spent most of his time in lately, before noticing some commotion going on outside. Looking out into the sun drenched light of day through the large glass windows at the front of the store, he saw a woman in her mid twenties with straight blonde neck length hair, wearing a tight brown leather jacket and pointed heel boots standing over an elderly man and looking down at him.

Her face was not visible as her thin hair dangled over the side of her face that would have been exposed to everyone inside the store. A couple of other people in the store stopped and looked to see what was going on. The woman yelled something inaudible at the man, to everyone's shock, as a fairly well built man in a black tee shirt and sunglasses came and stood beside her.

"What the hell is going on out there?" someone yelled from a couple aisles over as the unknown woman again yelled something inaudible at the cowering man on the ground.

The next few minutes happened faster than a lightning bolt rushing to the ground but seemed to go by in slow motion to Vince's overly dazed, under stimulated mind. To the screams of everyone in that large store who had turned to look, the woman pulled a nine millimetre seemingly out of nowhere and shot the elderly man in the head. The guy beside her bolted into the store flailing a gun of his own and ordered everyone to get down. He spotted Vince immediately and started toward him.

Vince, once again shocked into overdrive mode, got down beneath the unit he was standing behind and quickly crawled around to the side then back behind another unit and another. He only glanced back when making the quick turns around the red and yellow units to see where this newest of unknown attackers was. The one time he did get a brief glimpse of him, he saw the man only pushing people around and telling them to 'get the fuck out of his way'.

Vince finally made it to the back section where the small stretch of wall created an enclave as he saw the vicious woman come through the front doors and head straight for him. Vince turned the corner and pressed his back against the wall, breathing heavily. He was trapped. There was no way out from here and she had a gun. 'This is it,' he thought, feeling that all too familiar racing of his heart as if it knew it would be the last few minutes it got to beat and took full advantage of the opportunity. He closed his eyes momentarily and exhaled, praying for something to help him.

Immediately upon opening them again, he spotted a fairly large hammer and some nails that had been left there by some store maintenance person while putting up some new shelving. Dumb luck if there ever was any. He grabbed the hammer and pressed his back against the wall again, this time not in fear, but with complete fury. He felt the anger rise in him until he could hardly contain it. He felt bad for the old man who had done nothing that Vince could see, but get in their way. They weren't going to get away with it.

Had he been in a better frame of mind, the clicking of her high heeled boots would have clued him in as to where she was long before that lock of blonde hair came whipping around the corner. Vince grabbed the hand she held the gun in with his and drove the hammer full force into the top of her head with the other as the gun went off. She dropped to the floor, hammer stuck in her head with a small trail of blood running down her cheek from her right eye. Of course, he didn't realize how much force he must have struck with in order to do what he did, all he could do was stand over her once again void of all empathy for the ruthless woman, glaring down at the corpse through hollow eyes.

It didn't take much longer for her accomplice to come rushing around the corner to see what had happened. As he took a brief second too long to glance down at his bloodied partner in disbelief, Vince, standing still and ready with the gun he had grabbed from her lifeless hand, shot him in the forehead.

*

Another round of those all too familiar questionings at the police station. Although it was clear to everyone involved that it was self defence, especially given Vince's recent past, the officers in charge of the investigation persisted in their never ending inquires. This was getting old. Even the questions themselves hadn't changed from the first time Vince had been forced to endure this. 'What time did this happen?', 'What were you doing and where were you at the time of the incident?', 'Have you had any dealings with the assailant prior to the incident?' etc. Vince sat and answered their questions much more coherently than the last time and wondered if there was any way he could put his voice on auto-answer.

"So, how are you feeling about all this?" Ashton asked him, the first question that wasn't on his requisite list.

"Fine, I guess," Vince responded with a fair amount of normalcy and his attitude a little uninterested in the seriousness of the situation.

"Are you having any regrets or unsettling feeling about having killed someone?" Ashton persisted.

Vince wasn't annoyed by this, as it seemed to be a genuine concern for his emotional state as opposed to an interrogation or an accusation, so he answered as honestly as he could.

"Well, I'm not thrilled about it, but it's not like it's the first time I've killed someone either. I'm fine ... honestly ... And they deserved it, they killed that old guy for no reason at all!"

"Alright then, I think you're ok to go now if you like, if we need anything else, we'll give you a call, and please, do the same should *you* need anything," Ashton said, shooting him a sympathetic look and patting him on the shoulder as he got up to leave.

The officers finished taking the last of their notes and physically indicated that Vince was allowed to leave by opening the door for him. He was more than happy to take them up on their offer. In fact, his aloofness towards the entire situation raised not a few eyebrows in his direction. After all, he was a grieving widow; at least he was supposed to be.

This time around was different in the fact that his utter lack of compunction towards the severity of the event didn't come as any sort of shock to him, as it had the last time. Vince thought about it briefly but concluded that he was completely justified in his actions, even if those actions had included murder whether it was self defence or not. He couldn't comprehend the fact that he had killed yet another person, or perhaps he didn't want to. Either way, it was a slippery slope he was travelling on and he didn't even know it, as he was not plagued with guilt or even self questioning about his lack of it.

"He seems pretty cool about the whole thing," remarked one of the more burly officers about Vince as they stood and watched him walk out the front door and into the daylight.

"Yeah he does, doesn't he? Maybe he's just gotten better at hiding what he feels. I mean c'mon, wouldn't you? Ya can't blame the guy," Ashton responded, giving Vince the benefit of the doubt and they both sighed in agreement as they sipped their coffee and got back to work.

Vince strolled along outside in the bright light feeling much better than before he had been attacked for reasons not entirely clear to him. It was at this moment that he truly realized he would never be left alone. They would not stop, not until he was dead. He had come to this conclusion before in the hospital as well, but this time they actually sought him out after he moved across the country!

With that thought, Vince's semi-contented feeling vanished like spilled water evaporating on a hot driveway. They had found him. The shooting could have easily been passed off in his mind as gang allegiance, he had killed one of theirs and they in turn would kill him, same thing with the poisoning at the hospital. This time however, he was purposely tracked down in malicious intent. They were officially 'after him'. This thought, though unsettling at first, gave way to a more solid and focused frame of mind. If they were to seek him out to this extent, they would never stop, so in his disconnected mind, there was only one thing to do now. He must kill them before they kill him.

Self preservation fused with the wrath of being personally attacked and his late wife victimized by these people to produce the most potent mix of emotions Vince had felt since that horrible night. He had made up his mind now much faster than he had about anything in his life before and suddenly a wave of contentment washed over him once more.

He could picture everything he needed to do in his mind and started forming a game plan. He was now crossing that line that he was never sure existed in the first place. He was about to raise, or lower himself, depending on how you look at it, to their level of morality. He was now the one setting out with malevolent intent. In his mind, he found himself fumbling with these things while at the same time convincing himself that it was not at all the same situation. They were the villains in this equation and everyone else looking at him would certainly agree. This was simply self-preservation, not revenge. That makes it ok, surely it does. And even if it was revenge, it's still completely justified.

At that moment, he could begin to see his future unfolding in a new way. He had to figure out how exactly one would 'go after' an entire gang. How exactly would he do it and where would he even start? He didn't know but he decided he still had some time to figure it out. Another huge question that presented itself was what to do when it was all over, but that didn't matter right now. That particular mystery was the last of a series he had to focus on.

There was a peculiar feeling to having everything you love taken from you with only one goal left in sight. The sheer lack of loyalty to anyone or anything except oneself raised a powerful sense of freedom that can overcome, accomplish or attain anything but at the same time bound you to a life of little meaning. Nevertheless, it felt exhilarating.

With these revelations coming to light in his mind's eye, Vince continued on home fully content now. A small, mischievous smile stretched across his face that would have seemed out of place to anyone who knew what he'd just been through. Walking in the middle of the sidewalk and taking in the abundance of beautiful scenery around him, the world had come alive to him again but in a whole new way. A way he had never experienced before but knew would have scared him, had it not been for the events and bizarre insights into the human psyche of the last few months.

*

With newfound plans for the next little while in his life, Vince worked out a strategy. After the elation of coming to a supreme enlightenment such as the one he just experienced had worn off, the reality that Vince had no idea how to go about this new course of action set in. He would need help.

He would also need to get the hell out of Denver, but in secrecy this time, not like when he left Los Angeles. He had made calls to his boss, real estate agent, all his friends, and told each one of them where he was going. While he couldn't imagine any of them deliberately informing the murderous thugs that he was headed to Colorado, there was no doubt in his mind that they had told *somebody*. This somebody in turn told somebody else and they told somebody else until the entire west coast knew of his relocation destination.

Not this time. He would secretly sell the condo, get up and move. This time he wouldn't tell anyone, not even his closest friends. He hadn't actually made any friends in Denver yet anyway so it wouldn't be difficult. 'Maybe I'll contact them when it's all over,' he thought to himself, half knowing that wouldn't happen for a number of reasons and half hoping that it would someday be over and he would actually be able to return to the life that was taken from him.

He had come to the realization several times before now that life for him would never be the same. It would always have a deepened yet empty sense to it and he would no longer be nursing the cozy illusions that he would be able to live the perfect life he had before Vanessa was murdered.

He looked into a couple of records he kept from old phone books; friends from law school that he'd known, friends from various other places and even friends from high school. There was no one in his immediate mind that he knew would be able to help him. 'Am I in way over my head?' he wondered as he stared blankly into space. 'Yep, of course I am, but they are the ones who attacked me and sent orders for my assassination. All of them from the highest up all the way down the ladder.'

They had beaten him and thrown him to the ground in hopes of killing him but instead he ended up banished from his own home. 'Of course I'm in way over my head but I was in over my head from the start. I wasn't given a chance and they kept trying to put me down, to keep me there in death, so death will come to them instead now.'

Vince looked back up and focused again wondering why he was still trying to talk himself into the fact that he *had* to do this. He was right, they were wrong. So what if he had it all and still wanted more? Who doesn't? That's no reason for fate to treat him as badly as it did. He was sure in his mind that that was Jamie's exact justification.

At this point, he was physically, emotionally and psychologically beaten down. Damaged in an irreparable way, unable to experience the most rudimentary aspects of life and he needed help to raise himself physically, mentally and strategically in order to destroy those who attempted to destroy him. He would not stop until they were all dead. Vince called the only other person on earth he knew he could trust and asked if he could come stay with him for a bit while he sold his apartment and to help him out while he did his research.

"Jake, hey man its Vince."

"Holy shit man what's up? I haven't seen you in forever! I'm so sorry to hear about Vanessa and the attacks. I hope you're alright. Did you get the card and flowers for the funeral? Sorry I couldn't make it ...""

"Yeah I did -" Vince started but was cut off.

"I sent them to your office but I'm not sure they forwarded it to the right place and all ..."

"Yeah I got it man, and thanks, it meant a lot but I *really* need your help right now."

"Sure, anything ... What do you need?" Jake asked sounding a little concerned.

"They came after me again. Somehow they found out that I moved to Denver and they came after me ... in a bulk store!"

"Shit, so what are you doing? You need to get out of there!" Jake insisted.

"Actually, that's why I'm calling," Vince stated then paused for a moment before continuing with the same nervousness he would have asking someone to donate one of their organs, "I was wondering if I could stay at your place until I can sell my condo here and manage to buy a new one in New York."

"Definitely!" Jake said enthusiastically. "Anything you need just let me know."

"Thanks Jake, it would really help me out a lot," Vince said, relieved. "I was actually also wondering if you could call in some favours to help me find out everything I need to know about these people so I can find them?" Vince continued.

"Why do you need to find them? ..." Jake asked as silence prevailed on the other end of the line.

There was no way to logically explain 'why' to someone who hadn't been the victim of their brutal attacks. No way to express the urgency in the fact that if he didn't go after them, then they would continue to come after him. Jake could never fully grasp the concept of everything Vince had attempted to convince himself of in the recent past. He himself wasn't completely sure that this was the right thing to do, even for his own safety. He didn't have the energy to present a huge explanation however, so he simply stated the obvious.

"Why not?" Vince said flatly. "It's not like I have anything to lose, they've already taken everything from me and if I don't kill them, they'll kill me anyway."

"Yeah but how are you possibly going to kill everyone in a gang? There's probably thousands of them."

"Not all of them, just the head guys, the leaders or whatever you call them," Vince responded.

"What? How? You have no idea how that kind of stuff works. You're in way over your head. Do you even know how to shoot a gun?"

"Well first of all, you say 'I have no idea how that stuff works' like its composite aerodynamics or something. And secondly, yes actually I do know how to shoot a gun. I spent two summers at a military academy during high school ... didn't I ever tell you that?" Vince asked as his face twisted into a bit of confusion as if Jake could see his expression over the phone line.

"No you didn't, but have you ever actually killed anyone? I don't think so - *they have!*"

"Wrong again bud, did you really read the papers or just the headlines? Actually, I think they put that I killed the first guy in the headlines too ... and I just killed the two people who attacked me today."

The other end went silent again for a moment before Jake spoke up, "Well, even still, they have a lot more experience with this kind of stuff man, it's their job! I say you just get out of town, change your name and keep it that way."

"If I change my name, they'll still find me," Vince stated. "Besides, I think they deserve it. I need to do this. If you don't want to help me, I'll understand, but if you do, I promise they'll have no idea of your involvement. I'll come stay there, sell the condo, buy a new one in New

York, do my research then buy another place in L.A. *after* I'm finished and no one will ever know I was even in New York."

Jake sat and thought about this for a moment then said, "Well man, you gotta do what you gotta do ... but don't bother going to all that trouble buying a place here when you'll just be selling it in a bit anyway. Just stay here until you need to go back. I seriously think you should reconsider though. You're gonna get yourself killed."

"Yeah that makes sense, and the possibility of getting myself killed seems to be the situation either way," Vince responded trying to convey the fact that this really was the best option as he leaned down and cupped his hand over his right eye to hold his head up. He looked down at his lap and noticed how tired he was. Jake must have sensed it.

"Look bud, just get some sleep until you can fly out here tomorrow. We'll figure everything out when you get here, alright?"

Vince nodded even though he knew Jake couldn't see him and sighed.

"Yeah, I'll call you when I get there"

"Alright, just take care of yourself. I'll see you tomorrow sometime."

"Ok, I'll talk to you later," Vince said before replacing the receiver to the base.

He sat and thought for a moment. Did Jake have a point? Of course he did, but Vince already convinced himself that he was going to do this and nothing would stop him now.

He pulled off his dirty clothes and threw them on the floor before climbing into bed. As he lay there, he went over how he was going to accomplish the immense task ahead of him. He would get the ticket to N.Y. tomorrow and figure it all out there.

Chapter 6 – *Collateral Damage*

Upon arriving in New York, Vince followed Jakes instructions with relative ease. 'Why does everyone find New York so difficult to navigate?' he wondered. Maybe it was just the fact that he was naturally good with directions. Even in the dark of night he could instinctively tell where North, South, East and West all were in comparison to wherever he currently was. He didn't actually have to know where to go seeing as he had hailed a cab to get there anyway. It was a fair distance from La Guardia airport to Jake's apartment on the Upper East Side. Still, he somehow knew exactly where to go after exiting the airport. Compared to Denver International, La Guardia was fairly easy to find his way around, significantly less interesting, but easier to navigate through the hordes.

Weaving through traffic wasn't as easy for the cabs here as it was for the cabbies in Los Angeles. At one point, Vince sat in gridlock for 15 minutes without moving. He didn't get too upset about the wait though; he wasn't in any sort of rush. Jake wouldn't be home for a while and nobody was expecting him to be anywhere, but he sympathized with all the people who worked in this city and had to endure this kind of traffic. How did they ever manage to actually get anywhere on time?

By the time they arrived at Jake's apartment, Vince was exhausted. Probably some form of jet lag he figured. He still removed his own bags from the trunk and took them up to Jake's apartment. Even as tired as he was, for whatever reason, he just couldn't ask someone to take his bags up for him. Jake had given him his access code to the building before he arrived as he would be at work until about 5 p.m. tonight and Vince's flight to New York landed at 1:15 p.m. He let himself in the front door, checked in with the concierge who Vince had been told would be aware of his arrival, and headed into an elevator to go upstairs.

"29 please," Vince said to the elevator operator as he lugged his bags into the small enclosure and the suited man attempted to help by taking one, which Vince refused.

He pressed the 29 button which lit from behind as they started to whisk upwards. Vince looked down at the wood panelled floor, his mind already a thousand miles away. He got off the elevator, thanked the operator as he politely refused help again.

"No, no that's alright, I've got it. Thanks anyway."

"No problem sir," the elevator operator said as the doors shut in front of him.

He walked down the middle of the grey coloured hallway and suppressed the urge to take a breather on one of the ornate benches lined against the wall at a couple spots along the way, figuring that if he were to stop, Jake would probably find him passed out there upon arriving home. When he finally made it to Jake's apartment, he punched in the second access code Jake had given him, turned the handle and walked in. The foyer was bigger than he had expected and was laid with beige tiling. To the left was a large round mirror divided into four equal sections by dividers running top to bottom and side to side. Attached to it was a note that read;

Hey Vince, I've done up the guest bedroom for you. It's the second last door at the end of the hallway to your left. You can keep all your stuff in there; the closet's empty. Make yourself at home and help yourself to any food you can find. There might not be very much because I usually eat out but help yourself anyway. Other than that, if you need anything just call down to the concierge and they'll help you out. I'll see you around seven because I'll be getting a drink after work with Rebecca.

-Jake M.

Vince held the note to his side and looked over and down the hall to try and locate the room he'd be staying in. He kicked off his shoes, picked up his bags and started down the middle of the hallway towards the spare room.

Pushing the door open, he looked in and again was impressed with the size of the space. As far as he knew, New York was one of the most expensive places to live in the country, if not the world, and you normally get a lot less for what you pay than elsewhere. Vince knew Jake had a good paying job and all, but he still expected to walk into somewhere significantly smaller than this. Probably no cockroaches, ancient appliances or anything like that but he still figured it would at least be smaller than this.

There was a queen sized bed to the left and at the back, a large window that had a view of a couple taller buildings nearby. He walked over to it and looked down at the people on the street. 'They look like ants,' he thought. Walking over to the doorframe, he grabbed his suitcase and threw it beside the bed and headed back into the hall to find the bathroom which was on the other side and two doors down.

Vince walked in and unenthusiastically pulled off his clothes. He needed a shower, if for no other reason than to relieve the acute exhaustion that had taken over his body. He turned on the hot water and sat there momentarily breathing in the steam before turning the cold dial a bit and stepping inside.

After the long and luxurious shower, Vince decided it would be a good idea to get a head start on his research, even though he had no idea where to start. Making his way back into his room, he untied the four extra large suitcases that had been bound in two's so he could carry them up to Jakes apartment in one trip. He propped one of the leather giants onto the bed and opened it, pulling out a grey Zegna cashmere sweater and his favourite grey Dior homme glen check pants and set them onto the bed while he continued drying himself off.

He placed the large leather suitcases that most of his belongings had inhabited for a while side by side and sat on the bed, pulling the soft sweater over his torso, then the pants.

Vince eventually worked up the energy to wander into the kitchen in search of food. Making himself a quick sandwich and not even really being in the mood for much else, he then turned his hazed attention to the task at hand: finding out who these people were. The shower and the lunch were small attempts at procrastination; he was starting from scratch here and he knew it.

Back in the bedroom, a mediocre effort at searching through the tons of clothes and other wares he had brought with him produced his sleek, white laptop, which he immediately took into the living room and set on the coffee table.

Looking at the blank screen, he sighed and wondered yet again where he would start with something like this. He assumed the first step would be to simply Google the gang name and see what came up. Opening the page, he typed in 'Daravians' and clicked 'search'. Immediately, a plethora of sites dedicated to the infamous group popped up onto the screen. The first site was Wikipedia of course, and this seemed like a reasonable place to start. Vince clicked on the link and read carefully.

The Daravians had been started in L.A. in the 1960's by Roy Jenkinson, a high status crime boss during that period. Unlike most other gangs that perpetrate petty theft, burglary and robbery of liquor stores, The Daravians were started as a more sophisticated crime machine, much like the Italian Mafia and committed crimes of much larger scale (for the most part) such as extortion of businesses, highly choreographed bank robberies and most importantly, drug trafficking. This was where the majority of their funds were derived from.

They pretty much had a monopoly on every major drug being sold on the west coast from marijuana to heroin, ecstasy to crystal meth, cocaine to prescription painkillers, the latter two being the gold mine for them. The vast majority of their drug money was made off their own cocaine farms and plantations in Colombia and from large intercepted shipments of prescription painkillers such as oxycodone, hydromorphone, hydrocodone and morphine, among others. They would also extort doctors for a smaller, more constant, stream of the schedule two drugs.

Vince scrolled down further and found an estimate that the highly organized gang contained an astonishing 30,000 members in California alone and had smaller bases in most other major cities throughout the country. There was no way he could even come close to killing all of them. Only in complete secrecy and disguise would he be able to exact his revenge on the head guys and slink away to his next target undetected. Those at the top would certainly begin to suspect that they were on someone's hit list but it was imperative that who he might be was not broadcasted at all.

For the most part, the Daravians were there to cash in on the changes in the drug trade over the decades, carefully choosing which ones to invest in as its popularity soared which only served to further increase the status of that particular drug. The 60's were overtaken by hallucinogens such as LSD and PCP. Then into the late 70's, cocaine sales skyrocketed and the gang leaders of the time quickly invested in their own 'farms' in Colombia. This would provide them with not only a monopoly on most of the cocaine being consumed by the entire west coast but also give them influence over quality control which proved greatly beneficial as they had garnered a reputation for providing the highest quality coke on the market.

This trend continued into the 80's, earning the gang more money than they had seen since starting out and eventually crack overtook the trend of the 'hip' drug to do at the time. The cocaine plantations proved again to be supremely useful as the cocaine they had been manufacturing for years needed only one more refinement process to produce crack.

The money they made and saved due to their largely expanding fields in South America allowed the members to spread to other cities and expand their turf in Los Angeles as well, becoming more violent in turf wars. They did however, more often than not, win. It was at this point that the gang was divided up into multiple 'sets' and leaders assigned to each one. Three sets had formed in Los Angeles and two other sets were only run out of Los Angeles and mostly controlled their members in other large cities throughout the country.

By the early 90's the gang had dominated the criminal underworld and had become heavily involved in trafficking of illegal arms from which they also earned a tidy profit. The switch in favourability from crack and cocaine to heroin at this point did little to slow them down as they had managed to keep up production and established ties with traffickers from China and the Middle East in order to keep a constant supply.

The fact that they did not have their own heroin plantations didn't hinder them at all because of all the money they had made (and were still making, although not as much as in the late 70's and 80's) from cocaine production. The other means that they had built up while raking in the cocaine money such as the illegal arms trafficking and extortion of businesses also helped keep them in prominence. Several powerful members had also joined during the cocaine golden years and began funnelling funds into their market, always reaping more than they had sown.

Aside from the drug money, business extortion and illegal artillery trafficking, members also made large sums of money from highly choreographed and strategized bank robberies, always choosing banks from out of state and being careful not to hit too close to home.

Several distinctive symbols and signs were associated with the Daravians and Vince studied the pictures of the hand gestures carefully. The colour green had always been their trademark but the green bandana use had waned in recent years due to severe police crackdowns on gangs in L.A. They were now usually more secretive about it and unless someone flashed a hand gesture or other symbol showing their allegiance, Vince was left with no immediate way to identify their members.

Vince read on and on, noting everything he possibly could but failed to find anything on the gangs leaders. That information would probably be sufficiently more difficult to procure than how they rose to power in the world of crime. This, Vince concluded, would take a lot more extensive research and personal favours from friends to locate names. Hopefully someone could get them by pulling up any sort of criminal record these people inevitably had. Maybe the police had also formed some semblance of a hierarchy of the gang's infrastructure. Vince had a flashing moment of foreboding while thinking about how much he was up against but pushed it out of his mind, as he did with everything he didn't care to think about.

It would not have been outside the realm of possibility for Vince to be researching this topic for the next couple of years in order to attain all the answers he needed, except he had only about two or three months to do it in. Not necessarily because of any official time limit but more because he couldn't afford to stay in one place for too long. He had already decided that he wasn't going to change his name - at least not his first name. He'd be damned if they were going to take that away from him too.

Vince sat back in the sofa and his eyes began to feel very heavy. Half lidded, they refused to stay fully open or even widen in the first place in order to stay that way. The body numbing exhaustion in his legs that he couldn't tell if it hurt or felt relaxing, had taken over again. He wandered back into the bedroom and fell onto the bed but managed to crawl between the sheets before succumbing to the debilitating, all pervasive fatigue.

*

A stabbing pain went surging through Vince's body, a side effect of being shot in the abdomen where it had hit some sort of nerve, as he tried to pull himself out of bed. The pain lasted only a moment or two and gave way to a numbing sensation and inability to get much use out of his legs for a few minutes. The doctors had said that unfortunately, this would most likely be a lifelong problem to which there was no cure and he was given a prescription for Percocet. This, of course, was absolutely useless seeing as the pain only lasted a moment then vanished, and the drug would take a little over an hour to start working anyway.

Vince reached one arm up and grabbed the top of the headboard but rolled too far over and fell onto the ground which hit him like a ton of bricks. Feeling the cold wood below him, he reached up again and pulled at the bed frame to yank himself into a semi-sitting position, his legs still sprawled out across the floor.

Just then, Jake and Rebecca walked in to find him sitting there. 'Shit,' he thought, hoping against all odds that nobody would ever see him like this. It was especially annoying that this would be the first time he'd seen Jake in years and he was currently twisted about on the floor of his guest bedroom. They both gasped and were quickly overcome with worry.

"What happened?" Jake asked furtively, looking at Vince's legs and rushing over.

"Just a bit of nerve damage, sometimes I get a pain in my side then numbness in my legs. It's really not a big deal," Vince responded in a clear voice with no indication of being under stress.

"Sounds like sciatica," offered Rebecca, joining Jake on the other side of Vince.

"No, it's from the gunshot wound; apparently it nicked a nerve or something. Actually, I've only had this happen twice but the doctors said that no meds traditionally work to cure it."

"Shit man, does it hurt now? Can we help you?" Jake asked warily eyeing Vince's contorted legs.

"Yeah, it only hurts for a second though then it goes away. I just can't move my legs so that'd be great if you could just make sure I don't fall," Vince responded.

Jake grabbed Vince under the armpit and pulled him somewhat upright while Rebecca pulled at the other side of his body in assistance. Vince slowly moved his wobbly legs into a semi-standing position as Rebecca and Jake kept him upright.

"You alright bud?" Jake questioned, looking a little calmer than a few minutes earlier.

"Yeah, yeah, just need to make sure I don't fall again," Vince said as he took a few clumsy steps towards the door.

It was as if both of his legs had been asleep for a very long time and he couldn't gain control of them. He knew the annoying loss of sensation and strength would vanish in a minute or two but it seemed like forever. One step, two steps then his right leg gave out slightly but Jake and Rebecca stopped him from falling and continued to guide him all the way to the living room until he could stand easily on his own again and felt comfortable having them let go. It didn't take long, and Vince explained this to them again in a bit more detail upon their insistence that he sit, but he was fine now. Their worries had ceased after much pleading on Vince's part for them to stop worrying and that it was no big deal. After the last of everyone's anxieties had passed, the happy reunion occurred.

"It's so great to see you again bud!" Jake exclaimed.

"Yeah it's great to see you too! It's just too bad you had to come home to me flopping around on your floor," Vince joked, "I see you're doing pretty well for yourself here ..."

"Yeah well being a top attorney at Sullivan and Cromwell certainly has its advantages."

"I guess so ... and how long have you two been seeing each other?" Vince asked, gazing at Rebecca who had started staring off into space and had tuned them out.

"Who me?" she asked looking around.

"Unless Jake has another girlfriend we don't know about," Vince responded as kindly as possible, trying to sound funny instead of sarcastic.

"Oh well we've been dating for about ... uh ... five months, right honey?" Rebecca answered as she glanced over at Jake for affirmation. 'Not the brightest bulb in the box,' Vince concluded.

She was on the taller side around 5'11" and had dark red hair, not bright red like a natural redhead, but definitely coloured and was fairly pretty although she had a sort of lacklustre quality about her. 'Maybe it was her seemingly witless nature,' Vince thought. This actually surprised him quite a bit as Jake was a pretty good looking guy and not really one to take to someone as apparently vacuous as Rebecca.

After receiving confirmation from Jake that, "Yes, they had been dating for about five months now", she politely excused herself by mumbling something about having to meet up with some of her friends downtown. Maybe she was just one of those affluent girls who have nothing better to do than go out and spend their boyfriend and or husbands money while popping Xanax or Valium like they were skittles. 'This could possibly be the reason for her odd behaviour,' Vince rationalized as he watched her leave, still fairly certain that nobody could naturally just be like that.

"It was nice to meet you," she said just before closing the door behind her almost as if she had forgotten to say something.

"Really nice meeting you too," Vince called back as she resumed shutting the front door and left. Just then, without meaning to and without even knowing that he'd done it, Vince turned and looked at Jake questioningly who must have known what he was thinking.

"She's actually a lot of fun ... you shouldn't judge a book by its cover you know," Jake insisted.

"Yeah but if the cover lacks a certain finesse, then that's usually a pretty good indication that there won't be much inside either ... and you must be thinking it too seeing as I didn't say a thing ..." Vince stated semi-jokingly and almost laughing.

"Your look said everything," Jake returned as Vince threw his hands up in mock surrender and dropped the subject.

A moment of silence followed that indicated both parties knew something more serious needed to be addressed, and Jake spoke up.

"So how exactly do you plan on doing this?" he asked, eyebrows furrowing.

"I really don't know yet, but I know I have to, and I know I'll need help."

He looked up at Jake as he took a seat on the large grey sofa.

"So what? You're just going to kill every single one of them just because they killed your wife? I mean, it's terrible what happened to Vanessa, it really is, but you have to think about this logically. Every rule in the book says you won't win this one ... and even *if* you do manage to kill all the leaders ... what then? Someone else will step up and take their place. You won't stop them."

Vince looked down at the floor and tried not to express the anger that was growing inside him. There was no way to explain to Jake that success was his only option, he could not and *would* not accept failure. What Jake was saying wasn't overly terrible but the way he was saying it was almost patronizing. It was as if he were a child being reprimanded for something stupid they hadn't even done yet but had expressed an interest in doing. Only he wasn't a child and this wasn't an idiotic idea. He was an adult, full grown and capable of making his own choices and this plan was necessity.

Even though Vince knew he was right; that someone else would inevitably step up and take their place, he also knew he would be able to be safe in the world. If he could do this, then he wouldn't have to spend his life running and hiding and following what everyone else told him. He had listened to other people his whole life, led blindly astray by what everyone else thought was best for him and look where that had gotten him. If he didn't do this, he would regret it and live in fear every day for the rest of his life.

No. Nobody was telling him how to run his life anymore. What did they know about his situation anyway? They weren't the ones who'd experienced it. It's easy to pass judgment and criticize other people and tell them what's best for them when it hasn't happened to you. They weren't the ones in his shoes. This blind devotion to the 'rules' is what had held him back from doing what he felt was right and being himself all his life. They could throw as many obstacles and as much 'logic' his way as they wanted but it wasn't going to work. He would do whatever it took to do things his own way and he would make it work.

"I need to do this," was all that Vince could utter, looking at the space on the floor between Jake and himself with half open eyes.

Jake looked at his friend sympathetically now, realizing that he wasn't going to convince him otherwise. It hadn't made sense to him from the moment he heard Vince say those words, but in a way he did understand; a way he couldn't describe and apparently, neither could Vince. He stood there for a moment going over how he was going to possibly help his friend with this.

Vince sat and thought too. He himself wasn't sure what his first step would be in this seemingly impossible mission he was undertaking. At least everyone was on his side in this situation. The police, the newspapers, the country that was shocked by the headlines of those newspapers ... they all took his side in the matter and could probably be enlisted for help with the issue as well. 'Yeah that's right; I'll have plenty of help for this. Nobody wants to see the bad guys win,' he thought to himself again and again.

The police could pull up records, arrest anyone Vince decided not to kill and help him find the vicious people at the top of the criminal ladder. The newspapers would create publicity in his favour and they would be backed up by a sympathetic America. Hell, pretty much the whole world would sympathize with him given they knew about the previous situation. He may even garner pieces of information from helpful citizens. His friends would help him out now by providing a place to stay and research material. They would all help him defeat his enemy in one way or another. Of course no one on the outside would be able to know who was committing these acts of vigilantism, but they wouldn't need to. Only after it was all over could he reveal that it was him and everyone would understand.

With renewed hope, Vince sat upright, looked at Jake and insisted that they call it a night. They could talk more about the subject in the morning. Jake, even though it was only about 9 p.m. but feeling his own eyelids beginning to weigh more than they had a few minutes ago, wearily obliged. Vince knew that he had a lot more information to collect but the most difficult part, their names, would be revealed to him soon enough.

Chapter 7 – *Aliases*

Vince walked out of his bedroom in a house that he had not lived in for 18 years. He hadn't taken a glance out the window and instead passed by it and went right into the bathroom. He picked up his facial cleanser, dabbed a quarter sized portion on his fingers and massaged the thick exfoliating liquid all over his face, feeling the small beads gently scrape his skin as they rolled around on its surface. He rubbed it everywhere, over his nose, up his high cheekbones onto his temples and just under his chiselled jaw line. A bit of the acrid solution got into his right eye and he flinched slightly in pain. Keeping it closed so as to not get any more of the cleanser into the delicate mucous membrane; he relied on his left eye to observe his actions and to find the tap to turn the hot water on. Splashing the warm water onto his face, he could actually feel all the dead skin washing free and the pores opening to be able to breathe once more.

He looked up into the mirror, right eye still stinging from residue even though it was still being held shut, and wiped his face dry with a the grey towel that was hanging off the edge of the counter. A few seconds later and a few attempts to re-open his eye to give it some air proved to be successful and it was only a minor irritation now even though it was still bright red.

He walked out of the bathroom and schlepped down the middle of the hallway towards the stairs that would take him down to the main level. As he placed his foot on the wooden floor, the cold boards creaking a little under his weight, he wandered into the dining room and gazed out the all glass garden doors.

'What the hell is going on?' he thought incredulously to himself. A smoky haze had filled the air and reduced visibility a bit. Like fog, but somehow it didn't seem like fog; there was a different consistency to it. It was at this point that Vince noticed the tiny flimsy thin grey flakes falling gently from the sky like light snow. '*Ash?* Why is ash falling from the sky?' Vince wondered with growing concern as he stood rooted to the cold wood underfoot. Closing his eyes and rubbing them intensely, wondering just how much damage that facial scrub had done to his vision, Vince knew he had to be wrong.

Upon opening them again, he glanced out the large glass doors again and realized that his eyes did not, in fact, deceive him. There really was ash falling from the dark grey clouds that hung overhead. He rushed over to the door and pressed his hands against the warm glass. Thunder cracked and a lightning bolt raced amongst the thick clouds in the distance from which the ash fell.

He opened the door and stepped out onto the deck in his bare feet, feeling the burnt dust under his flesh like a thin layer of flour. Running over to the end of the wraparound deck that provided a view of the backyard and expansive forest behind it, he looked into the sky as more lightning flashed silently between the suspended clouds. To the far right, smoke billowed gently into the air from somewhere behind the trees. Vince's heart surged. What was going on? He did a slow 180 and noticed a few more spots where smoke reached from the earth high into the sky along the horizon.

Looking back into the forest he realized that a few trees and random branches were missing, the burnt ends and surrounding foliage were smouldering slightly. It seemed as though a few random trees had spontaneously combusted and disappeared leaving nothing in their place. He could hear faint screams in the distance mixed with sirens and horns. Cutting a wide trail in the ground bound ash with his feet as he moved, Vince walked back to go inside the house where he figured he would be much safer and spotted one part of the pair of shoes he had set out the night before.

One shoe was completely missing and had left a burn mark along the side of the other shoe where it had sat. Picking the lone sneaker up, which had cooled down by now, Vince stared at it and for some unknown reason, suddenly knew exactly what had happened. There must have been some sort of spontaneous energy surge or electrical imbalance in the lower atmosphere that simply caused random items to vaporize into thin air. He set the shoe down and went inside to see if the news would coincide with his theory.

Turning on the TV, the bizarre occurrence had been plastered all over every station. It seemed the entire world had been affected, and it wasn't only inanimate objects the 'random atmospheric surges' had vaporized, it had taken people too. Millions of them actually, and the entire world was in a state of complete chaos. Vince was overcome with an intense feeling of foreboding but remained calm. It was all too much to comprehend but it was happening and there was nothing he could do except worry that these raging energy surges would strike again and take him without him even realizing.

'Would it be painful?' he wondered, 'or would it simply be too fast to notice, like a nuclear explosion?' He figured it would most likely be pretty painful; even though it would probably be very quick, being burnt up never feels good no matter how fast it is. Had he been more coherent and a little less traumatized, he probably would have been able to pay attention to the reporter that prattled away on the screen looking equally as terrified as he was.

Vince turned around to face the front door where the doorbell had been ringing incessantly without him particularly noticing. He ran over to the wooden and frosted glass door and attempted to peer through it but could only make out a shadow which moved quickly away. After a second, Vince opened the door and noticed the figure moving speedily through the haze of the thick air until eventually; they vanished from sight not far from the house. It was much too indefinite for Vince to even make out the gender of the unknown person but it didn't really matter, a prankster was the least of his worries.

Turning to go back into the house, he looked over at the mailbox and noticed a white envelope sticking out of the top. He pulled it from its place in the black metal mailbox that hung upon the red brick wall, gasping and almost dropping it to the ground upon seeing the crimson stained bottom. It was addressed simply 'To you'. He closed the door and brought it inside. He could feel that there was a small object in the sealed envelope and opened it up slowly. He stood ready to throw it if, in the rather likely event, something particularly grisly came out. He saw a piece of white paper which he pulled out and read without investigating further as to what else might be in there.

We have them. They will die if you don't comply.

'Comply with what?' he wondered frantically, this newest of disturbances not doing anything to ease the intense worry that plagued him since witnessing the freak occurrences outdoors. He peered further into the oversized envelope to the bottom and almost vomited upon seeing a severed finger inside with a ring that he immediately recognized as a co-worker's by the trillion cut diamond still attached. It had obviously been left on so Vince could identify the digit as being from someone he knew. Heart now racing a thousand beats per second, Vince threw the envelope onto the nearby granite countertop as he gasped for air.

*

Vince woke up staring at the ceiling of his guest bedroom in Jake's apartment. 'It was just a dream,' Vince thought again. He was always half aware of this fact at the time of the strange occurrences but that didn't prevent them from relaying a hefty emotional toll onto his subconscious.

Whatever he had *felt* in his dreams, if they were as severe as this, would stay with him for at least a few hours and he would be unable to shake the good or exceedingly negative feeling. Oftentimes, he momentarily forgot what it was that was making him feel the way he did so intensely for a minute or two. Upon remembering that it was only the aftershock of a particularly horrid dream, he would at least be able to force himself to remember that it wasn't real. A lot of the time they felt more real than anything in reality, but he still realized nothing had actually happened that he needed to be concerned about.

This time, he was doubly comforted by the fact that Trisha, the owner of the trillion cut diamond ring, had died a few years ago in a car accident. There was no physical way that someone could be holding her hostage.

He pulled himself upright in the bed as the pain shot down his legs again. He waited those few horrible seconds in agony until the pain gave way to the numbing sensation. He figured he could simply wait out the entire episode safely atop the mattress, but he would never learn to overcome it that way. He grabbed the top of the bedpost and pulled his body around so he could attempt to push his legs off the side of the bed. Grabbing his right leg with one arm, he heaved it over the side until his calf hung perpendicular to his thigh, then the left leg. He looked over at the night stand that sat beside the bed and laughed when he saw the two silver crutches propped up against the wall on the other side of it. Jake must have figured he might have another 'episode' and thought ahead in case he wasn't actually there to help him.

Reaching over as far as he could, Vince stretched out his fingers in the direction of the crutches but they were just a bit too far away. With a small push of his torso further than it apparently wanted to go, he tapped one of them with the end of his middle finger, knocking both metal helpers into his reach. Wrapping his fingers around the white grips and securing the ends into the floor, he attempted to lift himself up but fell back onto the bed. 'Better onto the bed than forward,' he thought. A second attempt proved more fruitful and he lifted himself to victory.

He forced himself forward with his metal stilts and tried to make his shaky and unsteady legs do more with each step. One step down with the left foot and his leg collapsed under him. Another try with his right leg worked slightly better, crutches still affixed to his arms just in case. By the time he made it out of the bedroom and into the hallway, Vince was pretty much walking by himself.

Passing by the bathroom, he paused and looked back at it then turned around slightly and headed inside. There were enough sturdy objects around now that he could use his hands and arms to navigate his barely functioning legs through the bathroom. He placed one hand on the marble countertop and removed the only garment he had on after getting out of bed; his boxers, with his other hand. He pulled them down inch by inch like an amputee with one arm, over his toned thighs, then his calves and over each foot, switching sides after they wouldn't descend any further in one direction and back again then tossed them onto the floor.

He made his way over to the bathtub and ran the warm water, passing his forearm under it and adjusting the dial until it was the perfect hot, but not scalding, temperature. Sitting on the side of the white porcelain tub, he reached over and grabbed the large wood basin Epsom salts were kept in, took some out and threw them into the water. He wasn't really sure how they worked or if you were supposed to put them in before or after the water was drawn. He didn't even really know what they did in the first place but had heard they were good for a bunch of health stuff, so he used them anyway.

Immediately, the water in the tub began fizzing. He put his legs into the bath one at a time, and then slid the rest of himself in, cringing slightly at the burn that ran up his skin as it made contact with the hot water. He leaned over, grabbed the basin Epsom salts were sitting in and thrust it back into its empty hole on the shelf just in case he forgot later and Jake was the anal type. He wasn't sure, so better to just do it and not piss him off.

He slipped further into the warm water and could actually feel the salts working to relieve tension and spasms in his leg muscles. Again, he wasn't sure how they worked, but it felt a hell of a lot better than anything he had tried before, so he just sat back and relaxed.

*

"So did you find anything yet?" Jake inquired taking a seat beside Vince on the oversized grey sofa he spent most of his time sitting upon while researching on his laptop.

Staring at the screen intently as if he'd come across a new nugget of information that mustn't be lost, forgotten or interrupted, he responded simply, "I need more."

"I figured ... you just started," Jake responded with a laugh, "but have you hatched a game plan yet?"

"Yeah sorta ..." he responded arbitrarily, eyes still glued to the screen "I got quite a bit of reading done but I still need to do a lot more."

"I know, I'll see what I can get for you ..." Jake said. He didn't want to interrupt Vince's train of thought but also wanted to know how Vince possibly thought he was going to manage it. "So, how are you gonna do it?"

"Well, I figured I'll go after the lowest ranking ones first; there are five leaders from what I can gather. There have actually only been five leaders since the mid 80's even with all the expanding they did after that. I guess they just keep rotating after one dies or something."

"So how are you going to find them if you don't even know who they are? I can't ask any favours from my buddies at the police station until we at least know who we're after."

"I know, I know, well actually, I did find out that the leaders don't go by names. They and everyone else in the gang refers to them by some sort of gang name or alias or something," Vince responded, still trying to do two things at once and answer Jakes questions while maintaining his reading.

Right then he came across a newspaper article from approximately three years ago about a similar incident as the one that happened to him. The man's name was Blake Williams and the thugs had killed his girlfriend at their house, he came home to find one of the intruders who hadn't left and shot him. He had gone about business as usual for a while and was attacked by three members while walking to his car after work. He actually survived; they had intended to kill him but apparently didn't do a very good job. He ended up in the hospital for a little over three months.

Oddly enough, nothing happened after that for over a year. Then one day they came again although he managed to fight them off with a piece of pipe he had wrenched out of one of the attackers hands and even beat one of them to death as the others fled. He went to court, served a year in prison for manslaughter and when he got out, changed his name to Richard Haliday, moved to Georgia and began a new life. Six months later and just when he was beginning to feel like his life was getting back to normal, they had found him somehow and finally finished their attempted revenge plot. He was shot point blank right outside his house on a bright sunny morning.

Why someone would include the weather details was beyond Vince but he sat stunned as he read nonetheless. The situations were undoubtedly remarkably similar, although, up until this point at least, had different outcomes. He was now reassured in his decision that he had no other choice and felt for one fleeting moment that he was perhaps on the right track, decidedly not following in Blake's footsteps. These people clearly only understood extremes, so that's precisely what he would deliver.

How many other times had something like this happened that he wasn't aware of? How many more people like him had been caught in their vicious cycle? They were just ordinary citizens going about their lives and all of a sudden, out of nowhere and for no reason at all, were plunged into darkness and chaos. Blake's story wasn't *as* innocent as the papers made it appear however. The reason Blake's girlfriend had been killed was because she owed them money as a result of her incessant gambling. Still, it seemed a little extreme, and Blake was innocent in all this but ended up the one who was forever sentenced to live out his life in fear. Vince tried to pull his attention back to Jake who was patiently awaiting the rest of Vince's explanation.

"I'm sorry, what was I talking about?" he asked apologetically for ignoring Jake who had been doing anything he could to help him and who was actually engaging Vince in conversation about his plans now instead of telling him how much of a stupid idea he thought it was.

"You were saying something about how they go by some sort of gang names."

"Oh right, yeah they do and they're highly unoriginal too, like they were out of a cheesy 80's flick ..."

"What like 'Master Kwon' or something?" Jake asked, laughing a bit at the possible absurdness Vince was about to bestow upon him.

"No, No, nothing like that ... it's not a kung fu 80's movie ..." Vince started. "There's The Knife Fighter, The Marksman, The Pimp, The Dealer and get this, Lord Deulsus," he said, looking at Jake wide eyed as if to say 'do you believe this?'

"WHAT?" Jake nearly yelled, quite taken aback, contorting his face and wrinkling his slender nose in a mixture of confusion and disgust, "Seriously?"

"Yep ... I guess they just name themselves after what they do, or what they do best, or what they're in charge of ... I'm not really sure."

"Well what the hell does the last one do then?"

"He Lords," Vince laughed. "Your guess is as good as mine Jake, maybe he just came up with some stupid mystic name that he thought sounded cool ... for being crime bosses, these guys sure sound like they haven't got enough brains among them to fill an eggshell."

Jake snickered for a second, still unable to believe that these people actually expected to be taken seriously before launching himself to his feet and walked over to the fridge in the kitchen that sat across the living room directly in front of them. He opened the sleek appliance and produced a bottle of Molson Canadian.

"Want one?" he asked Vince motioning the bottle towards him.

"No thanks," Vince answered. "Molson? Where'd you get that anyway?" he asked eyeing the cold dark glass bottle Jake grasped in his right hand.

"A buddy of mine has a condo in Toronto so he brings it back for me whenever he goes. Canadian Beer is so much better, I don't drink it very much but after trying it, I just couldn't drink American beer anymore. It tastes like water."

Vince's eyes widened and brows rose up in an expression that said, 'I don't really have any idea what you're talking about but I'm going to agree anyway,' and turned back to his research. Heading back over and taking a seat beside Vince again, Jake looked as though he just thought of something brilliant and interrupted Vince again,

"Hey man, I've got tickets to see Philip Selur live next Thursday night. Wanna come? We were supposed to take Rebecca's mother with us but she cancelled because of some crazy emergency with her dog ..."

Vince looked over questioningly with another raised eyebrow and said, "Who the hell is that?"

"He's a violinist; he plays all sorts of songs. Well not just him, he's the focus and the lead and all that good stuff but he's got a small orchestra that plays the backups too. Rebecca was dying to see him now that he's back in New York and so was her mom but I guess just not as interested in it as she is in that dog. Don't ask me what sort of emergency lasts a week and a half that she can't come all of a sudden, but hey, I'm not complaining."

Vince looked at Jake, one eyebrow still reaching up his forehead. "Um, alright I guess. So I'm going to be your third wheel huh?" he asked with a playful tone that indicated he was serious about what he said, but didn't really mind.

"No, no, just think of it as a gathering of friends."

"Yeah, two of whom are dating and the other one who is not - that's a third wheel!"

"Whatever, do you want to come or not? It'll help you take your mind off of all this, you're gonna drive yourself crazy."

"Sure," Vince said, giving in and realizing that Jake had a point. He had been so focused on his investigation lately that it was all he did or thought about doing. "Where is he?"

"Philip Selur lived the street down from here and in the building that's right next to this one actually, but I think he's moved to the Upper West -"

"No, no! Where's he *performing*?" Vince interrupted, looking at his friend incredulously, wondering what was going on inside his head that made him spurt out random, unconnected answers like that. "Why on earth would I be asking about where he lives?"

"Oh, I'm not sure actually, Rebecca has the tickets."

Vince thought about pursuing the conversation further to maybe shed some light on why Jake knew where this guy lived but not where they were going to see him perform in less than two weeks, but decided against it. Mostly because he had other things he needed to do and couldn't be bothered with the charade. He would go with him to make him happy and certainly to take his mind off his revenge for a minute but he wasn't sure either attempt would prove fruitful.

This plan of his was all he could think about lately and he didn't see an end in sight, even if only for an evening. As he rose to his feet each morning, this was all that was on his mind until he went back to bed that night. Not necessarily because he was obsessed but because he had a lot of work and research to do before even setting out on this gruelling task.

He had to admit, he did seem to have a certain curiosity about his findings. There was something about this world of crime, separated from reality indefinitely, which intrigued him. To live in constant fantasy where the only goal is to acquire as much as physically possible with little concern for the means to such an end, fascinated him. How did real people actually do this? How do you live in a world completely separate from the one you are pretending to live in? They may physically live on this planet in theory but metaphorically, in their mental state and lifestyle, were galaxies away. How did they explain the source of all their income to the government? They surely had houses that they had to pay for. Wouldn't *someone* be on to them? Or maybe the government doesn't really care unless they're officially caught doing something illegal. 'This may be the case,' he thought, considering the fact that they were running a multi-billion dollar industry. Billions of dollars is billions of dollars to the country whether it's illegal or not. Pretty good business in any case. Who knows?

In either case, there was still plenty he needed to know about the infamous gang and he knew he had to continue on if there was any chance he was to defeat them at their own game.

Chapter 8 – *Mysterious Meeting*

In the following two weeks, Vince continued his research and sent Jake to ask his friends at the Police station if they had any information on the gang at all. He found bits of information here and there on various websites and began assembling fragmented lists, descriptions, locations and any other pieces of information he could possibly use as well as a lot he probably wouldn't ever use but jotted down just in case he should need it.

Vince came across a site dedicated to the gang by unknown members, probably people lower down on the totem pole, which actually provided quite a bit of useful information. It gave a bit of info about the two other 'sets' throughout the country that were part of the gang 'conglomerate' so to speak and even details about where in Los Angeles they were run from.

The two outer L.A. sets were divided, fittingly, into northern and southern sects. The major northern cities that housed many gang members were New York (shit), Detroit (big surprise there), Chicago and Baltimore among a couple other cities but these four were the ones with significantly higher numbers. The southern parts listed Miami, Atlanta and Houston as their highest in Daravian populations. This information wasn't blatantly displayed upon the site but hidden amongst conversations in posts, descriptions and newspaper articles members had posted as some sort of trophy.

By the time Jake had come back home from his own day of research and fetching documents, Vince had gathered a lot of the last of what he needed aside from their names and where exactly they could be found.

"Hey, how'd it go?" inquired Vince, setting down his pen and sitting back in the large couch.

"Actually, really good, I had to pull in a lot of favours but I got just about everything you need. I guess it shouldn't surprise me that every one of them has got a record, but it does. And they know who's who too. Apparently when you actually manage to become a crime boss you don't keep it to yourself."

"What? They know who the head guys are?" Vince asked wondering why they hadn't arrested them yet if they already knew who they were and what they were doing. He asked as much.

"Well actually they have arrested them, but they can never really be physically tied to anything so they make bail and well ... bail."

This figured. The police knew who these people were and still refused to *really* do anything about it. On the other hand, they must be trying or else they wouldn't have attempted to put them behind bars so many times, but why didn't it ever seem to work?

"So what'd you find out?" Vince asked as nonchalantly as possible in an attempt to make Jake believe that he really wasn't obsessed with the topic.

"Well you were right about the five leaders and you were right about their 'code' names," Jake said casually as he walked over, took a seat on the couch next to Vince and looked down at the papers he had either been given or had collected notes on. He looked over the filled out pages momentarily as Vince waited eagerly before he spoke up again.

"The bottom guys are the ones they have controlling the non-L.A. groups, those two 'sets' you mentioned ... they're led by Rick Denache aka 'The Knife Fighter' and Troy Daunton who's known as 'The Marksman'. I guess they somehow manage to run all the out of town groups while still staying in L.A ..."

"Did they give you an address for either of them?" Vince asked eyeing the sheets Jake held in his hands.

"Yeah, here's all the info they had on them," he said passing a small pile of papers to Vince from the top of the stack.

"Thanks and what about the other three?"

"Well The Pimp is next up on the ladder and his birth name is Andre Lepore. He controls the smallest of the L.A. sets and runs all of the prostitution rings the gang owns. The next guy up and pretty much second in command is The Dealer. They actually have next to nothing on this guy, including his real name, so I can't really help you there. The head guy, this Lord Deulsus ... *his* real name is Miles Le Veighton. They've got a bit on him but he's pretty evasive and never really stays in one place for very long."

Vince looked over Miles' background after Jake handed him the rest of the papers. Evasive fellow indeed. He really hadn't stayed in one place for more than six months or so and had changed his 'real' name four times that the police knew of, while still keeping his Alias as well. He had lived in Malibu, Palm Springs, Baltimore, Bal Harbour, Manhattan, Nantucket, Bel-Air, Washington, Sagaponack and seven separate locations within the actual city of Los Angeles. Those were just the last of his residences inside the country. He had also bought, lived in then sold estates in Bourges, Prague, Rio de Janiero, Toronto, Berlin, Paris, Bordeaux, Vancouver, Florence, Tokyo, Luxembourg City, Zurich, Sydney and London. How he had actually managed to purchase properties in *so many* countries whilst being a crime boss was beyond Vince, but he was oddly amused by this fact. It seems money really does talk. Or maybe there was some sort of art to being involved in the criminal underworld.

Every time there was too much knowledge about him or ties too close to him and any criminal activity (which happened a lot, hence the multiple uprootings), he simply up and moved, oftentimes changing his appearance and name as well before resurfacing somewhere else in the world. 'How did he know when they were getting too much information on him though?' Vince found himself wondering. It wasn't set out in the file in black and white but he could see a pattern in the moves Miles chose to make and the time at which he chose to do it. He had managed to make it to the top of this nasty world and even further, managed to control it a lot of the time from halfway around the globe ... and without being caught. His lieutenants must have known where he was and knew to carry out his instructions, but why did Miles feel it was necessary to leave the country, let alone the main city, his gang resided in so often? Maybe it actually made it easier to run a large, multi-faceted criminal organization from abroad, or maybe he simply enjoyed travelling.

Being away from the epicentre of a gang must certainly have its benefits like not being harassed by the peons within the gang, and maybe he created this elusive persona to deliberately surround himself with mystique, making him more of a deity to be obsequiously obeyed than a mere human. Being viewed as a mysterious entity as opposed to a man must certainly make getting those lower down to follow him much easier. Scare everyone enough and never reveal any genuine information about yourself and people are sure to listen and do as they're told, most likely even without any real consequences for not doing so.

He would most likely show up for a few random events, to which nobody would ever be sure he was attending, and off somebody for being disloyal or interfering with the gangs (or his) intentions to keep everyone thinking that he may show up at any minute. 'Interesting mind set this Miles guy has,' Vince thought. This also wasn't outlined in black and white of course, but again, Vince could see a pattern unfolding as he read through Miles record.

'Who should I start with?' Vince pondered as Jake, who by this point noticed Vince now had his blinders on once more and could only see the task directly ahead, excused himself for some lunch then work that needed finishing.

Going after Miles first would certainly send the greatest message to the gang members as well as catch him by surprise. However, Vince could also very well be caught by surprise himself. Seeing as he had no idea where this guy was at the moment, let alone know about or be able to anticipate any tricks he may have up his sleeve, Vince reconsidered this course of action. The next logical conclusion was to start at the bottom and work his way up. That's the way everything else in life goes so it seemed only rational that this should play out in a similar fashion. Yes it would give ample warning to the higher ups but Vince didn't really see any other option. This way he could also collect missing pieces of information on the other, more elusive members from the other leaders who were sure to know *something*.

He decided he may as well start with The Knife Fighter. Vince riffled through the stacks of paper and produced, Rick Denache's file. It wasn't nearly as long as Miles or even The Pimp's file but it contained enough information that Vince could use to hunt him down. His last known address was 524 Wharf Crescent, Malibu, California. 'Hmm, maybe this will be more fun than I thought,' Vince found himself thinking. Malibu … he thought he'd be travelling to a secret spacious apartment in the Los Angeles underbelly, not Malibu. This really shouldn't have surprised him. Leaders of such an affluent gang were sure to have money themselves.

From the list of crimes and other notes mentioned in his record, Vince deduced that Rick seemed to be a bit on the stupid side when it came to the big picture. He didn't have a clue on how to handle such obstacles as the need for nationwide predictions on how the gang should prepare for the world events influencing their operations. Things like new legislatures in weapons standards or the government's requirement of artillery and weaponry that was handled by the gang were a completely foreign concept to him. He did however, have surprising precision and acuity involving which immediate moves would produce the greatest return for those members under him. It was as if he were sort of like a knife himself, sharp and precise on one side but blunt, dull and useless on the other. He obviously must have still had great value to The Daravians as a whole though or else he wouldn't be leading one of their sets.

Rick was 31 and had a steady girlfriend, Lydia Trull who had been living with him at his beachfront estate. He had risen to his position simply by working for the weaponry division in his set in Atlanta. He proved himself as being able to strategically incorporate ideas for international smuggling and promoting the use of specific artillery that was most financially rewarding for his gang members. As a result, he was made second in command of the set by the former leader, Jason Donahue and moved out to Los Angeles to have more broad control of the influence over the arms division.

It was only two months after he had been promoted that Jason was assassinated by a much smaller rival gang and Rick assumed his role as leader of the 'southern set' that Vince remembered reading about and pretty much controlled all of the non L.A. groups below the Mason-Dixon Line. He himself had managed to hold onto that position for the past seven years after wiping out a sizeable chunk of the rival gangs members who were associated with Jason's assassination using a series of raids. This was not who he had to worry about now, as Vince would be the one removing him from his position and he would have no idea it was even coming. This thought was oddly comforting.

To actually see in writing everything these guys had to go through to get where they were in the gang, and to know that Vince was the one who would bring it all crashing down around them, warmed his heart. This time *he* would be the one destroying everything they'd worked and killed for.

Next on Vince's list was The Marksman, Troy Daunton. Troy was 33 years old and his personal life was rather normal when compared with the rest of the leaders. He had a wife named Theresa and two sons, Adam, 13, and Steve, 11, who all lived with him in his estate at 142 Laughland Rd. in Santa Monica, California, another nouveau-riche suburban sect in the G.L.A.A.

This was unbelievably easy. Vince couldn't believe that he actually had the physical addresses of these guys in his hand; 524 Wharf Cres, and 142 Laughland Rd. Vince began to wonder why nobody else had tried this before him, but then he remembered that the papers he was holding were not public information displayed in every newspaper, they were confidential police files that were painstakingly obtained through many friends of friends pulling strings and calling in favours. He briefly wondered again how Jake had attained the files in question but decided not to push his luck and ask.

Vince then began to wonder why the leader known as The Marksman wouldn't be put in control of the guns and weapons division of the gang's profitability. The police files didn't directly answer this little riddle but did hint at a reason why. Apparently the weapons side of the gangs business wasn't in very much need of greater control seeing as it didn't produce anywhere close to the massive cash flow as the drugs, prostitution rings or business extortion. Therefore this leadership job was given to someone newer and lower down in the hierarchy. Vince couldn't really figure out what exactly it was that gave The Marksman seniority over The Knife Fighter considering he wasn't much older and had only been affiliated with The Daravians about a year longer. However, Vince wasn't sure how large gangs worked in the first place and police reports never make any mention of the internal politics. He therefore was left without an answer. Not that it mattered though, it really was a trivial piece of information.

Vince skimmed through the other files but didn't pay very much attention. Mostly because he knew he didn't have much time. He glanced at the tall wooden grandfather clock's round golden face, the light from the outdoors glaring on the metal, and tried to make out the time. It was precisely 3:00 p.m., almost time to start getting ready. Vince hadn't forgotten about the Philip Selur show but he did momentarily think he could squeeze in a bit more work before reconsidering, deciding instead that it would be far more productive to get dressed appropriately and have something to eat.

He was in an odd sort of way, looking forward to the show. He had never been a big fan of orchestra or chamber music but something about the idea right now implemented soothing and relaxing thoughts into Vince's overworked psyche. He would actually be able to relax for a bit and enjoy a night out, something he hadn't done in a very long time. He set the papers into a neat pile on top of the white laptop and headed into the kitchen, signalling Jake who was outside on the balcony behind floor to ceiling sliding glass doors. Jake nodded and pushed back off the glass railing, heading inside to get ready for their night out as well.

"Yeah, at seven," Jake said into his phone as he walked through the door and clicked it off.

After dinner, Vince had gotten changed into a sleek black tuxedo complete with a grey silk tie and French cuffed poplin. Affixing the grey and black cuff links to his shirt he called out to Jake from the dimly lit bathroom, "Hey man, are you ready yet? We still need to pick up Rebecca ..."

"Hold your horses bud, we don't need to leave for another half an hour," Jake called back from somewhere in the recesses of his cavernous bedroom where he was surely stressing over what he was going to wear or what he could actually get away with wearing.

"Yeah, if you want to make it there right on the dot, you really should be early, it's not like a movie theatre where you can just show up whenever you want, it's the Palazzo Rucelli," Vince replied, hoping to convey the rather simple fact that the doors do *not* open back up once the concert had started with his tone.

Once Jake had finished adorning himself in his own black tie attire, he stepped into the hallway and leaned against the doorframe to the bathroom as Vince spritzed each wrist with his Prada Infusion d'homme and a small spray of something else overtop.

"Why are you mixing them?" Jake asked looking a little sickened at the thought. "And why don't you just spray one then rub them together instead of trying to avoid spraying it on *both* sleeves?" he added, noting Vince's struggles with his cuffs.

Vince looked over at him casually.

"It's Ambergris; it deepens and blends the cologne. Plus, it's a fixative, so it'll stay longer. And I'm not rubbing my wrists together because you're never supposed to do that, apparently it bruises the fragrance."

"It what?" Jake asked, his face again contorting into extreme confusion. Confusion mixed with brusque agitation was perhaps the most cultivated of Jakes expressions.

"It bruises the fragrance; it breaks up the top, middle and base notes and smashes them together so you get the wrong mix of smells instead of the natural development as it sits on your skin."

"What are you a cologneologist or something?" Jake asked playfully, laughing slightly at Vince's excessive knowledge of cologne.

"No, uh, Vanessa taught me that actually ..." Vince said softly as he bowed his head a bit trying not to think about it. "And you pick up on things like this from people who actually have taste instead of rich trash who ramble on and on about how much class they have when they really have no idea what they're talking about half the time," Vince shot in as an afterthought to try and mask the disheartening direction the conversation was heading in. Jake appeared amused instead indifferent, which is what Vince expected him to express about proper cologne application.

"So that's why your cologne always smells like it suits you ..." Jake stated clearly either not detecting or simply ignoring Vince's obvious desire for a change of topic. He seemed to be more intrigued and impressed with this information Vince had relayed instead of annoyed so Vince softened a little considering Jake was either genuinely interested or was just trying hard to keep the peace.

Vince and Jake continued to make small talk about the upcoming show and partly about Rebecca and whether or not she would even appreciate the subtle genius of Mr. Selur and his music. That is, until she was ushered into the car with them, then the conversation was purely performance related. She had actually managed to make Vince chuckle a bit with her observations of Jake's own attempt at subtlety. As Jake exited the car, his eyes immediately fell upon a woman in a short shirred cocktail dress walking down the street. He then quickly turned back to Rebecca and, quite surprisingly, she picked up on the small transgression.

"Go on dear, do ogle whomever you wish, don't let me stop you!" she hissed before prancing inside in her long cream coloured ball gown and leaving Jake looking a bit bewildered.

Just then, Vincent noticed a fairly well built man with dark hair and piercing green eyes lurking by the door who had been watching them before Vince's eyes met his own. He certainly wasn't here to attend the concert, judging by his choice in attire; he looked fit for a night of clubbing. Vince looked to Jake for a split second in hopes of catching a glance that indicated Jake knew him as well.

"Go ahead, I'll be right behind you," Jake insisted. "Gotta sneak a smoke while Rebecca's inside," he finished, giving a falsely mischievous chuckle.

Vince looked at him tentatively for a moment. Then, without even glancing at the stranger who was now pretending to be ignoring them with his face turned, Vince strode up to the doors. He opened it under the pretence of going inside but quickly snuck off to the side where he would be able to see if Jake met with the unknown man from behind a small outcrop of decorative glass. Just as he had anticipated, he saw Jakes figure meet with the dark haired man a moment later. Vince watched him hand the guy an envelope.

"There it is. Thanks," Vince barely heard Jake say over the noise of the street.

"No problem. Just don't tell him," the dark haired guy with blazing green eyes replied.

Vincent barely had time to wonder what all that was about before Jake started walking towards the doors. He quickly escaped inside and bolted further ahead in an attempt to not appear as though he were eavesdropping. 'Why on earth was Jake sneaking around to talk to that guy? And what was in the envelope?' Vince wondered. Perhaps he was paying him for something. 'Maybe Jake was paying him for helping secure the documents that he gave to me,' Vince thought. But then why would the guy say, 'Don't tell him'?

Jake caught up with Vince inside the foyer and Vince decided not to ask him. It quite possibly could have had nothing to do with Vince, but that wasn't the feeling he got. In either case, Vince wasn't going to find out by asking Jake. If he had lied in order to simply meet this guy, he wouldn't be honest about what was in the envelope if confronted, nor would he simply disclose what they had been talking about. It was Jake's business and he had already helped Vince so much; he wasn't going to ruin it by confronting him. Vince let it go with the hope that whatever it was, it wasn't some form of sabotage or anything else with malicious intent to hinder Vince's plan.

The Palazzo Rucelli was spectacular in every sense of the word. Vince had heard of this place from various friends and publications, all of whom fawned over the expertly imitated interiors but seeing it in person was a whole other ball game. The entire interior was done in the best of renaissance style in everything from the art that graced the walls to the magnificent carved dark mahogany tables detailed in gold gilding. Even the ceiling had been painted in some areas as if it were an homage to the Sistine Chapel. Decorative golden sconces hung upon the walls and illuminated small sections along the hallways and enormous foyer. The entire place was as magical as it was grand even if it was all an illusion designed to look like the real thing right out of Italy.

The concert itself was the only part of the evening that rivalled the majestic opulence of the Palazzo that contained it. Philip and his orchestra unequivocally mastered the works of Antonio Vivaldi, Rachmaninoff, Tchaikovsky, Beethoven and Bach among others including a particularly spine tingling rendition of James Horner's 'Rose' from the film Titanic.

The grandeur of the evening was unmatched by anything Vince had experienced to date and left the crowd eagerly murmuring amongst themselves afterward. This night was the first in a long time that Vince remembered feeling completely peaceful and he thought about the violent past and to-be future only once during the whole show. The ride home, or more accurately, back to Jake's apartment was as unobtrusively elegant as could be expected. As Vince finished removing his clothes for the night and slid between the sheets, he briefly wondered if plunging himself into this violent world he had been studying would be the utmost in moronic ideas. A moment of thought on the subject quelled the illusion spawned by such a peacefully regal evening and Vince fell asleep perfectly content with having had the experience of the day and with what he had to do next, which was in stark contrast to the day's events.

*

The next weeks proved to be much more productive after already having the names of his targets and having all the background information he had gathered. Vince figured that normally in this type of scenario, he would need to capture a lower member of the gang and torture them relentlessly until they yielded completely and produced the answers he hoped for. Or at least that's how it happened in most movies.

Luckily, this did not seem to be needed now, because he wasn't sure he would have been able to do that, and Vince wondered if it all seemed too easy and perfectly set out. The last time he thought something was perfect, that something being his life, it was turned inside out and upside down. He should have known that all good things must come to an end but blindly believed that his own little fairy tale truly would play out forever. Real life simply wasn't like that. He wondered momentarily just how messed up this newest of endeavours could get and decided he didn't particularly care, as long as everyone was 'tended to'. He had to be able to overcome any obstacle, solve any problem and push through for what he wanted.

He didn't hesitate at what he had to do but rather embraced it now. It must be done and even though he couldn't see what may lie ahead, he could see what needed to be done first; the things right in front of him. He needed to head west and re-locate to Los Angeles. From there he came and now back he would go.

Vince had kept a pretty low profile while in New York doing all the research he needed to do so there wasn't really anyone to bid adieu, except for Jake who had helped him back onto his feet and onto this new path. It was of course Vince's choice but Jake had helped in every way he could and Vince was deeply appreciative. In that last week he had made plans to move back to L.A. and start his rounds of self served justice. He had bought a condo in West Hollywood with the money he had from his sold properties, first the house in L.A., then the condo in Denver. He didn't touch any of the money he had saved or the money from any one of his multiple investments, and still had tons left over from Vanessa's life insurance.

He expressed his gratitude to Jake for all his help and giving him a place to stay while he collected all the information he needed and of course, for his moral support, by treating him to dinner at Le Cirque. Vince also surprised him with two bottles of vintage champagne, one bottle of Dom Perignon, and one bottle of Moët et Chandon. Jake had decided to use one for himself, and promised that the other be opened and celebrated with once Vince had successfully carried out his plan and arrived back.

Of course, this last part put a bit of a strain on the idea of a celebratory party considering it wasn't certain that Vince *would* succeed or return alive. It was highly likely that this could very well be the last thing he ever set out to do. But, Jake accepted the notion anyway and offered to drive Vince to the airport the day of.

As they pulled up to the side of the road near the airport where Vince would depart from New York, Jake reached into his pocket and produced a bluish green crystal.

"Here, I want you to have this," he said handing it over to Vince who took the crystal in his hand and couldn't help but feel some sort of connection to it, as odd as that thought was to him. "It's Azurite; I found it digging around a cliff up at my cottage when I was 20. It intrigued me right away when I found it and I always kind of thought of it as my good luck charm. After all, how often do you find something like this while digging around in the dirt?" he continued with a bit of a laugh, probably feeling a bit stupid for believing in a good luck charm and admitting that he carried it with him for so many years. "Hopefully it'll light the way for you," he finished, a look of sincerity taking over his expression.

"Thanks Jake, it really means a lot to me, and if it's been good luck for you, then maybe it'll help me out too," Vince said trying to not make Jake feel uncomfortable for actually believing in this. "And after it's worked for me, I'll bring it back to you," he finished with a genuine smile.

One bear hug and another round of 'good luck' and 'thank you's' later and Vince was out of the car, bags at his side and looking west towards La Guardia airport once more. The afternoon was slipping into evening and the sidewalk ahead of him was drenched in golden rays as Vince headed forward on his path towards the sun.

Chapter 9 – *Well Stocked*

Los Angeles had a new feel to Vince now than it did when he left. It was now no longer home, but his own Oz or Wonderland. Like a dream land in which he was desperately seeking something out instead of living. He had moved into his West Hollywood condo about a week before and even though he had lived in the area before, he still needed time to get used to the city and scope things out. It had seemed to him that he hadn't stayed still for very long ever since Vanessa died, which is exactly how it was. The fact that L.A. was now to him only one of those many moves was partly true but in reality he had spent a lot of his life there *before* the incident, so why did it feel so foreign?

The condo he now resided in was different in style from his former abodes. This time around, Vince went for more of a plush and luxurious setting as opposed to the cold, unwelcoming and stark although extremely chic modern decor and architecture he had chosen in the past. Immediately upon entering, there was a foyer with large mirrored closets flanking each side. Directly ahead was the large living room with floor to ceiling windows and sliding door onto the balcony. Vince had requested that the apartment be left fully furnished seeing as the last thing he needed to worry about was decorating and actually having to go out and purchase furniture and appliances. The previous owners happily agreed, for a price of course, and only insisted on keeping some rather important artwork and other sentimental pieces. One item they had left that Vince found rather interesting was the high polished Mahogany edged table with tiger wood centre that gave off a waving sheen as you moved by it.

Vince walked down the centre of the hallway to his right in search of his new bedroom. Seeing as he was living in New York when he'd purchased the condo, he hadn't actually seen it in person but the realtor did provide multiple pictures as well as a virtual tour and Vince knew that the building itself was in an excellent location, so he trusted it. The only thing it didn't show was the master bedroom which he found very strange. He was told it was because the owners 'didn't like people viewing their most private of rooms' and thus refused to post it, showing the other bedrooms instead.

He had almost expected to walk into something very bizarre or outlandish considering their apprehension in showing it, but it didn't let him down. The king sized bed was once again done in rich earth tones and looked so fluffed and comfortable that he would be happy to sleep for the next three weeks straight in it without getting up. The closet was also enormous. This was actually useful seeing as he would indeed be unpacking his clothes this time instead of keeping them in the giant leather suitcases they had been crammed into for the past little while.

Vince set the luggage down close to the closet and wandered over to the ensuite that sat right beside the entrance to another smaller private balcony. This one gave a view of the hills instead of the panoramic view of the city, the immediate surrounding area *and* the hills in the living room.

Going back into the bedroom, he took a seat at the foot of the oversized bed and began to go over his action plan yet again in his head. Seeing as they wouldn't be expecting it, he figured the first two targets would probably be quite easy to sneak up on. After that though, it was sure money that the other three or four leaders would begin to catch on and make military esque efforts at tracking him down. How would he escape it then? They would be sure to have people watching at all times. How would he even make it back to the car without being seen?

Vince's thoughts were rudely interrupted by the raunchy gurgling of his stomach. He hadn't eaten since he left Jake's apartment because airline food, and it wasn't even food as he understood the definition, teetered on the edge of making him physically ill. He felt the grumbling continue for a moment more before deciding, upon tasting the acrid aroma that rose from his throat to coat his palate, that he had to satisfy his hunger. Accompanying the sour taste in his mouth was now hunger pains he either didn't have or hadn't noticed prior to this moment.

He'd reached that point where you are actually so hungry that you feel like you're full. He knew, to the contrary however, that he would regain his appetite after making something then eating a small portion of it. Almost like teasing your body into thinking it's interested in whatever edibles you've set in front of yourself. With this notion in mind, he readily prepared a healthy helping of French toast, toasted to golden perfection. As it cooked his stomach told him no, just as he'd predicted, but then succumbed to the nutrition after being given a sample of what was to come and he downed the rest of the butter seared bread topped in golden syrup in close to one mouthful.

He walked back over and fell down onto the couch, laying back in it and letting one arm and one leg hang over the side. At this moment, he had fallen into one of his sporadic bouts of depression that consumed him from time to time for no apparent reason, like a true neurotic. He wondered what the point of everything was. If he succeeded, what was the point? What would he do? Work up to something? He knew now from nothing more than life experience that all good things must come to an end.

Nothing can get too good before it is inevitably destroyed, and likewise, nothing can rise to greatness without the fall afterwards. Rome, Versailles, Greece, Egypt ... all rose to prominence in the extreme to which they were capable, only to have it all come crashing down around those who had built it up. Left behind to live in the great devastation were those poor souls unfortunate enough to have survived the travesty. That fate could possibly be worse than simply being taken by whatever disaster, war or revolution that destroyed everything they had worked for to begin with.

Everything ended this way as far as Vince could tell. Life becomes death, light becomes dark, flames become ashes, grandeur becomes shambles, lively crowds become desolate spaces haunted only by memories of what used to be, and great cities become barren ruins. 'Beautiful things grow to a certain height and then they fail and fade off,' he remembered reading once. He tried to ignore his negative thoughts and in such an attempt, got up, took a shower and listened to music that always put him in a better mood. After finally realizing his petty attempts at improving his mental state were futile, decided instead to go to bed and simply wait for tomorrow, hoping it would be better. He walked into the bedroom, removed his clothes, placed them on the cream puckered bed stool at the foot and crawled beneath the plush comforter after shutting off all the lights and focused his attention on trying to get some sleep.

*

Twitching in the bed and rousing into semi-wakefulness, Vince drifted in and out of his perpetual alternative dimension. He certainly spent enough time here and even during the most morbid of occurrences, usually found it quite enjoyable to escape from reality. He never realized that he was dreaming directly but the underlying feeling that he wasn't awake was still there. Tonight was no exception to his experiences of a pleasurable nature. The only problem was forcing his body back to sleep so he could return to his dreamland. He had heard of restless leg syndrome and was experienced in handling it after a couple run ins with it himself, although hardly enough to diagnose him with anything out of the ordinary, but tonight it seemed to be in his arms.

The palace was all white and inside were white and rose, blush or salmon pink clad women and men of regal stature. Vince looked around and basked in the strong light that seemed to emanate from every surface. Stairs were everywhere and he stood in one 'hallway' only separated from the grand rooms surrounding him by giant white marble columns. In each room there were massive chandeliers that flared tens of thousands of glistening crystals from their point where they touched the ceiling to the widened square base.

He woke up again to the violent twitching and contorting of his body between the sheets. NO! Go back to sleep. Go back to sleep. Go back to sleep!

Looking over into another room there flashed hundreds of different coloured triangles like the streamers in used car parking lots, a multitude of varying shades of yellow, red, blue, green and purple that danced and spun out towards him in the same fashion as a pinwheel. They spun in free form, not suspended by anything as they rotated in a hypnotic style. A golden table sat beside the whirling wheel that he turned to look at after a moment of watching the hypnotic and elusive colourful pinwheel. Just as he turned his attention to the console pushed against the side of a flight of white stairs, the cameo painting of a man dressed in the height of Victorian fashion above it came to life, turning his head to look at Vince.

Thrusting himself to the edge of the bed, coverless, trying to freeze himself into another state, he somehow sat motionless with great, uncomfortable restraint, waiting to slip away again.

A woman walked by him in the illuminated hallway, the only one of the hundreds of beautiful figures in the entire place that dared to wear black. The long fishtail gown that had multiple folds of blush rose coloured silk spattered with peach coloured morganite stones over the bust flowed and whirled as she stood, majestic in her stance as if posing at a fashion show. The staircase at the end of the hall behind her looked like an interesting route.

The cold of the fan didn't do much and he was twitching and flailing atop the bed once more. Ok, so the best thing to do when you have restless legs is to go for a walk ... so restless arms ... go do push ups! That's it! Down onto the ground in a flash, he counted one, two, three, four ... all the way to one hundred and crawled back between the sheets.

Looking ahead again, past the columns he could see that there was a very large space that went down a few stories of white palace rooms if one were to wander too far past the cylindrical mammoths. Vince walked between two of the tall, massive marble giants and over to the edge of this opened space to peer down. Beyond the vacant space and encompassing it were the stairs. They went every which way. Upside down, upside right, diagonally, vertically and horizontally, and looked as though most of them led nowhere except to more stairs. Loads of people came to and from the white rooms chatting eagerly to each other and laughing. Vince was excited at the thought of exploring this intriguing palace. The white marble tiles underfoot were warm and glowing.

Awake once more, Vince thrashed his anxious arms around in the darkness in hopes that they would give up. No such luck. He sat still and figured that his body would have no choice but to obey and he could return to his exciting paradise. He focused all his energy into remaining calm and not moving, the same way one ignores an itch that sooner or later, disappears, and could feel his body starting to respond. Looking to the North then directly down to his feet, he sat motionless in the dark and forced his mind and body to quiet itself with little luck until he looked back up into the grand room in front of him and realized he hadn't moved from this general area since he'd arrived at this wonderful place. Placing one foot forward, then the next, he made his way slowly into one of the cavernous spaces behind the pillars that was big enough to be a ballroom and was, like everything else, glowing white from every surface. A large mother of pearl vase that held bundles of milky white roses sat upon the golden table in the middle of the giant room surrounded by the white columns. He walked toward it and reached up to touch an unopened blossom and upon doing so, pulled back when it started to unfold, yielding the beautiful cream petals into the light.

*

He turned his body around and saw daylight staring back at him through his bedroom window. Shit! He'd hardly slept at all. Why couldn't he stay in his own little world? Everything there was brighter and more beautiful. He knew that now, of course as opposed to the night when he was supposed to get sleep, he would be able to rest peacefully for a few more hours.

Vince pulled his surprisingly rested body, for only having approximately three hours of actual sleep, from the large bed and strutted over to the bathroom while mentally envisioning what the next move towards his goal would be.

After finishing his morning routine, he pulled out the files he had collected from Jake. Who would be his first target? He had actually already decided that his first opponent would be The Knife Fighter, aka Rick Denache to those outside the gang. 'I wonder if he's French,' Vince thought unnecessarily to himself. Looking down at the file he read aloud, "524 Wharf Crescent ... Malibu. Well that's close enough."

Walking into the middle of the hallway, he made his way back to the living room and took a seat on the large soft sofa. He thought for a while about how he should proceed with his plan. Should he play fair and give them a chance to defend themselves? They didn't give Vanessa a chance. Or him for that matter; they attacked him after getting out of a cab, while *incapacitated in the hospital* and in a food store with no warning and seemingly no chance to escape. Besides, they would probably have the upper hand anyway seeing as this 'killing people' thing was sort of their job.

However, it took Vince only a minute to conclude that he couldn't lower himself to their level. He had to at least give them a chance. Yes he was setting out with murderous intentions to exact his revenge, but he would not, *could not*, be as unscrupulous about it as they were. Otherwise the point would be defeated. He knew that this of course put him at a much greater disadvantage considering they were highly skilled in the 'art' of killing people, but he still couldn't do it.

Back in the bedroom, Vince pulled out the new suitcase he had bought from under the bed and placed all the weapons he figured he'd need in it. He had to visit quite a few different weaponry dealers in order to avoid suspicion that would surely arise from the purchase of *that many* weapons of varying kinds all within a couple days. He had gotten everything he thought he could need though. Looking over the case, he surveyed his wares; the small black browning 9 millimetre, the glock, the silencers, the elongated sniper rifle, the black and silver magnum Lone Eagle with a perforated tip and the various loads of ammunition.

After reverently eyeing each piece, he lifted the top tray to reveal the lower section of the case that contained all the knives he had selected. Looking down at the impressive selection, he wondered which one would be best to bring to an attempted assassination of the undisputed master knife fighter on the west coast. Vince picked up a unique model of tanto knife only about a foot long and pulled the handle slightly away from the sheath to reveal the blackened blade inside. Next he picked up a black handled hunting knife and looked at his reflection in the shiny blade before replacing it. Lastly, he pulled out the black cord handled hawkbill blade and replaced that as well before deciding on the hunting knife. He thought about it again and also removed the black tanto knife and a small black pocket knife to bring as well, just in case. 'What could it hurt,' he figured. He set the blades on the bedside table before riffling through the closet and selecting a simple black V neck top, grey pants and a leather bomber jacket to wear as he hunted down his first target.

Chapter 10 - *The Knife Fighter*

The plan was flawed and he knew it. But he couldn't formulate another one that made more sense without intensely frustrating himself. He had scoped out Rick's house once before today, so he knew the entry plan by heart. The front was guarded by security just behind the solid front gate at all times so the only way to the house was by entering through the neighbour's yard. This presented a challenge in and of itself, not only because of *their* gated property, but also because the two yards were 50 feet apart in altitude. Vince would somehow have to make it over their gate and up the 50 foot precipice, which in all fairness, still had some very scalable sections, but was still a daunting task nonetheless.

The other option would be to swim in from the ocean without being seen. This wasn't actually a problem, even with the nearest public entrance to the shore being about eleven hundred yards away. However, the cliff that stood between the shoreline and the yard looking much more dangerous than the one adjacent to the house *was* a problem.

Vince looked around squinting in the sun soaked California day and placed one hand in his pocket to remove the keys to his newly purchased Jaguar XJ220. A fairly old car by most definitions but it still looked much more modern and über luxe than a lot of others he had seen. He walked into the parking garage in his building and made one final check to see if he had gathered everything he needed before hoping into the svelte vehicle and speeding off towards Malibu.

Driving up the curvy lane that led to Rick's house, Vince sped up a little in hopes of not looking like he was casing the joint and parked several houses down the street in between various other cars. Walking calmly in the middle of the suburban sidewalk towards 524 Wharf Cres, the palm trees provided perfect shade against the blaring summer sun. Vince glanced slightly to the right at the large solid iron gate flanked by large stonework pillars that sported the number 524 as he passed by down the sudden hill towards the neighbours.

Standing in front of the neighbours wrought iron gate, that indicated they were far less paranoid than Rick, with his solid stone and iron shield that provided no view to the yard, he realized there was no time to stand and stare or make sure nobody would see him. He must jump over now and so he did, leaping up and grabbing hold of the top of one of the stone pillars separating the wrought iron in sections with his hands and pulling the rest of his body up and over the fence. He hadn't thought about it until right now but it was a good thing they didn't have barbed wire up there.

When he had driven by before, he had looked through the vast stretches of wrought iron into the yard. He knew that if he kept to the right, he would be pretty much invisible to anyone inside the house due to dense tropical shrubbery. And that was only if anyone in the house were even home let alone paying any attention to what may be transpiring in their yard. Most people would be at work and any kids would most likely be in school right now anyway so Vince was fairly certain that he wouldn't be seen by anyone.

He weaved his way through the trees with large leaves and sorted plants before he came to that monster of a hill he was sure would provide him with the most debilitating climb of his life. Looking north, up at the wall of earth, he could see the top of the cliff like mound that looked much closer than it probably was and sighed slightly before carrying on.

The first 20 feet or so wasn't too bad as it was a fairly shallow slope but after that, it got tricky. Vince grabbed hold of the large rocks that jutted out from the side of the earth. Next, he moved to secure his footing in the near vertical slope. He climbed up a bit further before a bit of gravel under his right foot gave way and he slipped, leaving him hanging onto the grungy moss and dirt covered rock above him with both hands for dear life. He was about 35 feet up now and falling would mean severe injuries if not death, not to mention a whole lot of criminal charges and police haggling as to why exactly he was attempting to make it onto a gang leader's property.

His heart raced in his chest as he tried to blindly reunite either one of his feet with a ledge or crack in the rocky wall. His fingers were getting raw and the fiery pain shot from the tips of his fingers down his hands to his strained forearms and back again as he tried to hold on. He tried now to literally just climb up the rock seeing as whatever placement his foot had been in or on before had now apparently vanished. As his foot slid down over the dry dirt covered rock, it came upon a small crack that he used to stabilize himself.

He sat for a moment trying to calm himself before remembering that he was out in broad daylight scaling a cliff onto someone else's property with a public street not too far away. He continued up with minimal problems before he reached the top. Peering over the edge, he tried to figure out where he would proceed to next. Because the front of the yard had been cased in, Vince wasn't able to get a look at it in order to figure this part out when he passed by it on the road.

The house was a rather large Mediterranean style estate in the shape of a large U from the back with the pool situated between the two stretches of building on either side. He spotted stairs on the far left outstretch that led up to a terrace, presumably situated outside a bedroom. 'That's perfect!' Vince thought to himself. But it was quite a large yard with much less greenery to hide amongst than the neighbours had. There was no other choice, he had to just make a run for it and hope that none of the guards, or cameras if there were any, saw him.

He pulled himself up quickly and bolted towards the stairs, passing the pool from which the scent of thick chlorine soaked into the air. At the bottom of the stairs, he pressed his back against the wall and looked up. Nobody was racing onto the balcony after him. Nobody coming whipping around either side of the house yet ... He shuffled over a bit towards the all glass double doors that led from the bottom level of the house onto the concrete pool area. Leaning slowly over and peering inside, he noticed nobody was there either. 'Maybe I should just go in here,' he thought before recanting. 'No, if there is anyone monitoring the house, they're most likely to stay on the main level, besides the hole from the glass cutter would be easily noticed by any of the guards walking the yard.'

Starting slowly up to the balcony, he put one foot in front of the other onto the yellow concrete and brown tiled stairs until he was about halfway up and realized he should move quickly here as well. Anyone in any of the back rooms on the upper level would be able to see him venturing up the flight of stairs. At the top of the landing he raced toward the glass doors that lcd to a bedroom, as he had previously surmised. Looking inside, he could see that nobody was in the room at

113

that moment. He glanced through other windows across the way and down on the lower level and didn't see anyone walking around there either. 'Have they all gone on break or something?' he wondered. Or maybe he'd actually timed it right and nobody was home.

Vince pulled out the small glass cutter from his pocket and etched a hole just big enough to stick his hand inside in the door near the handle. Reaching his hand inside, he grabbed randomly at the other side hoping to find the lock and almost pulling his arm out to reposition it before he connected. Flicking the knob back and turning the handle, the door opened with Vince's arm still through the hole and almost threw him back onto the ground. 'Shit! How stupid am I?' he reprimanded himself. Yes, it was his first attempt at breaking into someone's house but common sense should have told him to remove his arm from the hole *before* he opened the door ... 'Something to note for next time,' he concluded, deciding he couldn't afford to get too upset with himself right now.

Placing one foot onto the caramel coloured hardwood and closing the door as quietly as possible behind him before locking it, Vince looked around the opulent room. It was done in a similar style as his own place right now. Thick brown curtains draped back on brass rods, plush oversized bed and intricate wooden end tables all set against brilliant earth tones. Walking over to the bedroom door and looking out into the hallway, Vince could see down to the next level over the spiralling and twisted wrought iron banister on both sides of the walkway. He looked down over one side then the other, still nobody there. Directly across the hallway that opened to the lower level, there was an actual hall that judging by the structure of the building, ran through the midsection of the house and around to the other side of the U shaped back half.

There was a tightening in his chest accompanied by a sort of light headedness that he hadn't experienced before. It was surely the physiological response of his body to the fact that he was in a place he had no business being in as well as the fact that if he were to be caught, he would have little to no chance of survival. Not to mention that he himself was there to kill somebody. Every aspect of this little venture was new to him and it was thrilling and terrifying all at the same time. He figured he would simply shoot the guards after he killed Rick because if he came home to find his staff dead, he wouldn't need to be a rocket scientist to know something was up before Vince sprung his surprise visit on him. On the other hand, what if they heard the commotion during Vince and Rick's fight and came to his aid?

It was at this point that Vince realized that no alarm had gone off upon him entering. 'That's odd,' he thought. However, he quickly passed it off as Rick figuring there was no point for mechanical security when he had hired actual guards. Guards, who would probably be in and out of the house, if for no other reason than to go to the bathroom, and would set off the alarm anyway. And seeing as none of them had come after him yet, Vince figured there was no silent alarm or cameras either.

Deciding it unwise to stand about in a gangster's house he had just broken into like a frog on a lily pad, Vince looked around briefly for somewhere to stay out of sight. The closet he opened the double doors into was actually a rather large walk in with an ensuite at the end. 'This is perfect,' he thought, closing the beige doors behind him and eyeing the expansive bathroom at the back of the closet.

The thoughts jumbled around inside his anxious brain. How do I do this without the guards coming to help him? When exactly is he going to be back? How am I going to get away afterwards? What if someone sees the hole in the door? Some of these questions he answered immediately after pondering on them. If they noticed the hole and came in, he would simply shoot them. The silencer would certainly come in handy there ... but what about when he had to make his getaway? He couldn't go back the way he came, figuring he would sustain serious injuries if he leapt off that cliff and down to the neighbour's yard. He would have to go out the front gate. Well, may as well just shoot them at that point. Rick would be dead by then and they'd have guns too, so it would still be a fair fight by any definition.

'That's all good and great but how do I stop them from interfering with our fight?' Vince thought over and over again in a superfluous attempt to produce a suitable answer. Maybe he could somehow coax the guards into some place where they could be locked up after Rick got home and saw them on duty but *before* Rick knew that Vince was there. That idea was out seeing as he didn't have the luxury of roaming around the house to scope out possible holding stations. Maybe he could just shoot the guards after Rick got home and before he discovered that Vince had broken in. That was it. It might be difficult to manoeuvre downstairs and outside once the time came, but he could do it.

With this new revamped game plan now formulated in his head, Vince wandered over to the bright creamy marble bathroom. Incidentally, the window to the outside provided a perfect outlook over the driveway that curved from the front main entrance to the large, tall sliding solid iron gate that led to the road. The guards were standing right behind this gate. 'I guess that's why I could hear people talking as I passed by on the sidewalk,' Vince recalled as he took a seat on the toilet after closing the lid. Keeping one eye on the guards through the sun soaked window to his right and the other on the darkened area closest to the closet doors, Vince sat and waited for The Knife Fighter to come home.

*

The moment finally came sometime after dark and Vince had begun to wonder if he would slip off into a slumber and be woken by gunshots at his own body upon being discovered by Rick. 'That moment was sure to arrive soon,' Vince thought moments before he saw Rick's Cadillac Escalade pull through the sliding gate. He leaned intently over the window and watched to see what would transpire. It was indeed Rick who stepped out of the expensive SUV and walked up to the front door. He turned around and waved to the guards who in turn, started towards the side of the house.

Oh shit, he knew something was up. Or maybe the guards *had* informed him that someone broke in and were waiting for him to get home when he could deal with Vince himself and they would simply back him up. He thought about running to find somewhere to hide but changed his mind. After what felt like a lifetime but in reality was only about a minute, Vince witnessed lights on the driveway before a small black car emerged from behind the house, heading towards the front gate followed by another slightly larger silver car which he could make out as a Chrysler 300.

'Holy shit!' Vince thought in sheer exhilaration at the realization of what was happening. The guards were leaving! They were waiting for Rick to get home and now they were leaving! Dumb luck if there ever was any, as the only thing Vince hadn't yet figured out was how to efficiently prevent the security from intervening in his assassination.

It took quite a while for Rick to venture upstairs, only to wander back down after what seemed like a mere use of the facilities. Vince momentarily considered waiting until he came back up but realized there was no point and that it was only his nerves holding him back. 'What, am I gonna sit here like some vengeful amateur who never has the guts to actually do anything?' he reprimanded himself. He started slowly making his way through the stretch of closet lined in an amazing array of suits, to the double doors leading back to the bedroom.

His heart pounded in his chest as his sweaty hands closed around the brass handle and slowly pushed the door open into the quiet darkness. It was one thing to imagine going through with his plan and actually doing it; the nerves never played into fantasy but in reality they came around full force. Looking around, Vince tried to see if anyone was waiting or watching. His eyes were accustomed to the dark now and he could make out the general outline of most things in the room and distinguish what they were.

Creeping slowly towards the open concept hall, he gazed down below to see if he could catch a glimpse of Rick, whom he knew for a fact was the one that stepped out of the Escalade because of the photos that had been provided in the police file. He stood about 6'1" and had a rather muscular build, often wearing clothes that showed off his cultivated physique and sported short brown hair which he usually wore plain without any styling. Around his neck, several necklaces could usually be found, from which hung dog tags, a white Italian horn and a Russian seal, and he always wore an all black oversized watch on his left wrist.

'What exactly did Jake say to the police to let him take files on top gangsters' home with him?' Vince wondered again, for no apparent reason at all other than the fact that the files were the reason he was here now.

The sight of Rick walking down below, although quick, was enough to make Vince jump back in an effort to not be seen. His heart was pumping much faster now as he headed quickly around the corner to the closed section of the hallway. He slowed considerably as he descended down the stairs, sweaty hands sliding along the cold metal railing. Placing his feet firmly on the tiled floor of the area just outside the kitchen complete with a brown tiled island, Vince stood motionless in the dark, surrounded only by the light left on in the living room to his right.

Vince started towards the direction of the soft yellow glow that melted onto the brown and yellow surfaces among the room. Looking around, there was no apparent evidence of anyone else being home. He hadn't yet made a sound even though he felt as if the thumping of his heart would emanate throughout the spacious home and somehow alert Rick of his arrival. And if that didn't do it, he was sure Rick would be able to feel the tension in the air. Vince had sometimes experienced this when Vanessa had walked into the bedroom while he was sleeping to ask him an important question. It was almost as if he could sense her coming and would wake up mere seconds before she actually reached the door.

Just then a small noise behind him sent Vince whipping around to see Rick, looking as shocked as he'd ever seen anyone in his life. The time played out in slow motion in Vince's mind and even at that delayed pace, he couldn't force his body out of the path of the large wooden spatula that Rick had grabbed off the island in those short few seconds.

Time returned to its normal pace the second he felt the blow to the side of his head that sent a wave of pain ringing through his skull, and almost knocked him to the floor. Blocking Rick's next swing with his forearm, he shot back with his fist, striking in the jaw. Rick fought back and continued for a couple seconds, flailing, swinging, missing, blocking and connecting before he hoped over the island to the other side, grabbing a shiny butcher knife on his way. Vince picked up one of the two wrought iron stools with a wooden seat that was sitting beside him just in time to stop the large sharp piece of metal that had been hurled at him in a rapid fashion.

He looked, momentarily shocked that he'd actually blocked it, at the blade jutting out of the wooden top before he launched the entire thing over the countertop as Rick opened a drawer for another blade. Rick had ducked just in time before the heavy stool went crashing into the kitchen appliances behind him, sending pieces of plastic, utensils and shards of glass from the coffee maker flying into the surrounding air.

Rick emerged from behind the island wielding a large steak knife and waited for Vince, who had also removed his large hunting knife from its sheath by this point, to make the next move. His eyes were focused and fierce, pupils drawn to a fine point behind which was nothing except extreme concentration and fury. Vince wasn't expecting him to speak but he did.

"Who are you?" he asked in a slightly raspy voice, never taking his intense focus away from Vince.

"You know who I am," Vince responded, locked in the stare down.

"What? I have no fucking idea who you are! What are you doing here?"

"I'm here to kill you, genius, just like you killed my wife then tried to kill me! ... and failed! THREE TIMES!" Vince all but shouted, his blood now boiling with rage in his barely contained hostility.

"Oh, you're that guy from the papers! That wasn't me you moron!"

"Your people and your commands."

"My people, NOT my orders! I don't decide everything they do; if they have a grudge against someone they don't come running to me for permission."

"I. Don't. Care!" Vince stated coldly, striving to convey his animalistic intent.

"So what, your plan is to kill me? Ha ha! Do you know who I am?"

"Yes I do and even if I didn't, I really don't have anything left to lose, *that* you can blame on your people if you like!"

"You won't win this," Rick said with a smirk.

"What makes you so sure? You guys have tried to kill me three times already."

"Yeah, one difference though, you weren't facing off against me," Rick replied, never once letting his concentration slip.

"The point is that you - they - have tried. Which actually brings me back to my last point; someone had to send orders to track me down.

119

The first two tries could have been just the peons, but the attack in Denver was mandated."

"So what if it was? You think you're gonna beat ANY OF US?! You're out of your mind."

"Damn right I'm out of my mind."

"Well, then you're an idiot for even TRYING!" Rick emphasized as he whipped a second blade from behind his back at Vince.

He had felt the buildup of energy and the looming attack almost in time to move out of the way before Rick lunged across the granite countertop, blade in hand. The smaller blade stuck in Vince's shoulder and instantly sent a fiery pain down his left arm. He was still quick witted enough to lift the remaining stool up from the ground as Ricks head slipped quickly between the rungs and his arm that wielded the other blade thrust the knife towards Vince's body.

In a flash moment, Vince glanced down at Rick still gliding forward before pulling back down on both legs of the stool with a force that permanently removed the connection of Rick's skull to his spine, sending a loud snapping noise instantaneously echoing throughout the room. The large blade fell from Rick's hand that hung over the edge of the counter and clashed onto the floor as crimson spots that leaked out from under the stool started to dot the mustard coloured tile.

Vince sat momentarily in shock at what had just transpired. He had done it. His first target was dead. He had actually beaten the Knife Fighter in a knife fight. He had pictured it going quite differently when he thought about how it would play out before today, but he had done it nonetheless. He imagined they would cross blades and slash each other up before someone proved victorious. However, now that he considered it a little more, he realized that something as deadly as a knife fight couldn't possibly last very long. Hell, even samurai's only fought for seconds before someone inevitably fell.

He loosened his still tight grip on the metal stool legs and slowly lifted it away from the corpse. Setting the blood covered seat down to the side, he studied Rick's body for a second. His head hadn't actually come clean off or even close to it, but rather hung lifeless over the side with a bone visibly out of place beneath the surface of the skin at the back of his neck. The blood that had covered the floor had come from a cut on his throat, surely caused by the edge of the stone countertop upon being slammed into it.

Vince reached down to retrieve the dagger he had dropped, replaced it to its sheath in his pocket and simply walked towards the front door, leaving the crime scene behind without guilt or regret. He actually felt quite the opposite now. Exhilarated, powerful and relieved. He hadn't felt any of these in a long time but rather their counterparts. Now is the time. He had conquered his first major opponent. That amateur fear and anxiety had come and gone and he was now in high drive mode with one thing permeating through his consciousness: to kill the rest of them. It wouldn't be easy; they would surely hear of the Knife Fighter's demise within hours and hype up their own security as well as probably attempt to launch some form of counter attack. He knew all this but he still couldn't shake the feeling that it would somehow be a lot easier now that he had overcome the first of his obstacles.

Removing the small blade from his shoulder with as quiet a yell as he could and a makeshift bandage later, a simple push of a button opened the front gate and Vince strode back out onto the sidewalk once more and headed towards the sleek futuristic jaguar parked down the street. He closed the silver door behind him and sped off into the night, knowing the next battle was somewhere close ahead.

Chapter 11 - *The Crash*

Lying on his side, face pressed into the plush pillow, Vince squinted open his right eye to the rays of sun beaming through the glass door that led to the small balcony off the side of his bedroom. Pulling his incredibly refreshed body from the bed, he wandered over to the door and stared out into the daylight. It was absolutely beautiful outside. Not a cloud in sight and as he slid the glass door back and stepped outside he was overcome with the hot wave of the sun and wind that brought with it the sultry scent of tuberoses that grew all over the neighbouring yard uphill. There was something intoxicatingly carnal about their smell. It was indeed something to behold and not too often experienced by most, but he was blessed enough to wake up to their heavy aroma saturating the air every morning.

Vince looked over the hills that reminded him, for whatever reason, of his hot trip to Italy and the slopes past Sulmona, how the groves ran down the side of the mountain like the beads of sweat that had started to run down his chest in the immense summer heat. The city looked vibrant today as well, with not a stitch of smog hanging overhead. Every aspect of the surrounding atmosphere was fresh and alive, perfectly mirroring his mood.

He tried to think of what his next move would be but his elated state barely allowed it. He wasn't yet sure if any of the other leaders had heard of Rick's demise by now but it certainly would be helpful to know. The only thing he could think of right at this moment that *might* provide him with an indication was the news. Walking back inside, down the middle of the hallway and into the living room, he flicked on the flat screen.

Flicking through the channels, he looked down at the large new bandage he had applied to his shoulder upon arriving home the night before and realized that that crazy polysporin really did work miracles. He felt no pain at all and his shoulder didn't even appear to be any sort of damper on his health or movement. After a few minutes watching CBS news, Vince finally came across what he was waiting for.

"31 year old Rick Denache, one of the alleged leaders of the notorious gang, The Daravians, was found dead in his Malibu home today, the victim of an apparent invasion and brutal attack. It is unclear at this point who may be responsible for this violent act of rumoured vigilantism but the police are on the scene and ask that anyone with information contact their local police department. We'll keep you updated with more as this story unfolds," the pretty but vanilla blonde onscreen finished narrating as the focus shifted to the latest Lakers game.

Vince pushed himself up off the couch after flicking the channel and headed back into the bedroom to get dressed. There was only one thing to do next and there was no point wasting any time trying to figure out how it would all unfold.

*

Vince hopped into the sleek silver machine once more, feeling on top of the world. Double checking that he had everything he needed, he reached under his bomber jacket and felt the handgun with silencer attached stuffed into the left side of his pants and reached into his jacket pocket to produce the blackened Tanto knife. He knew the small pocket knife was still in his shoe because it was starting to really annoy him. He took a deep breath and mentally prepared for the next fight before speeding down the road once more.

As he pulled onto Laughland Rd. from Sussex Dr., he glanced at the gates for the numbers. The house to the right, hidden behind dense tropical shrubbery read 371. He was still fairly far away from 142, about halfway there though. He watched the numbers descend as he drove along the surprisingly busy street that was currently lined with cars at 11:00 in the morning despite being a suburb. As he neared his destination, he pulled into one of the few empty parking spaces on the palm lined street. 11:00 on the dot actually, he realized as he looked down at the copper coloured roman numerals on his brown leather strap Cartier.

Just then, through the windshield he noticed three black Cadillac's pull out from one of the gated estates. He looked at the number on the gate beside him, 146. A quick count down four driveways revealed that the three mysterious cars were indeed departing from 142 Laughland Rd. The thoughts raced through his mind a million miles a second. Do I follow them or just stay here? What if they see me following them? If I do follow them, what do I do when we get to wherever it is they're going? If I stay here how many people will see me before they get back? It's significantly busier here than on Rick's street. Will he have tightened the security guarding his house after last night?

It took him about just as long to make up his mind and he pulled out from between the lineup of cars on the side of the road after them. He continued mimicking their stops and turns at a safe distance through the winding roads passing through the hills to a rather remote location. After a while Vince began to wonder a bit more pressingly, where exactly they were going and when they might stop. He figured they were probably somewhere just north of Brentwood by the time the vehicles slowed and pulled one after another into a large gated compound.

The area was completely desolate and had only trees surrounding the abandoned and broken down factory. Vince pulled up next to the gate long after everyone else had driven in. They had not seen him due to the fact that he had stopped higher up on the twisted road that ran in a large S figure through the hills and overlooked the area with minimal forest to allow a pretty good view. He had of course waited until he watched the last tiny ant like body vanish into the concrete rubble building before he got back in his car and started after them. Vince had stopped along the side of the road upon seeing the factory down the hill through the clearing because something told him he should simply sit and watch, which proved to be rather useful considering they would have noticed him behind them on this particular stretch of road.

Quietly opening the slim door and carefully closing it behind him, Vince stepped out onto the gravel driveway just behind the large concrete gate. The air was hot and heavy and even though the factory looked as though it hadn't been operational for over twenty years, the thick scent of chemicals and hot asphalt penetrated the air. It was as if they had been infused into the grey concrete rubble that was strewn about the expansive empty yard and seeped slowly into the atmosphere.

Pressing his back against the rough rock of a gate, Vince worked up the nerve to steal a glance around the corner through the opening in the wall the others drove in through. No guards, that's a good thing. Again, like at Rick's house, he figured he had no choice but to dart towards the building as fast as he could, so that's exactly what he did. Legs sprinting towards a blank spot without any windows on the building, he leapt over large broken pieces of grey concrete multiple times as he went, never sure if his leg or foot would snag one and send him tumbling loudly to the ground.

By the time his back was pressed up against this new slab of rough rock wall, his breathing had increased tenfold. He was also overcome with surprise at his own agility for being able to hurdle the large stone roadblocks without any difficulty let alone avoiding landing flat on his face or severely injuring himself. He took a moment to pant and catch his breath, while noting that there was actually a stabbing pain in his shoulder that indicated he hadn't been *entirely* cured by the magical ointment. He looked around to make sure nobody had spotted him on his two hundred yard sprint and was now coming after him.

Nobody coming out and aimlessly wandering around yet either. At this point Vince wondered if this could be a trap. He actually found it pretty difficult to believe that a *gang leader* hadn't noticed a car following him and his entourage ... especially through the more remote areas and also considering he wasn't exactly driving an inconspicuous vehicle. He had done his best to stay as far away as possible while keeping them in sight but still ... Maybe they were actually busy or focused, who knew? If it were a trap, he would certainly find out in a couple minutes and he had come too far now to turn back.

Creeping around the corner until the longer stretch of the broken building was in sight, Vince fumbled slightly over debris scattered about the ground. Moving steadily towards one of the open windows, Vince made a careful move to look in. It wasn't what he expected. Still run down, still desolate and gutted but the floor to which the large busted out window peered over was that of the basement. The whole place had been stripped of the main floor and the only place to go once inside was down. He wasn't sure how they did it, they must have all travelled to this lower level but where were they now? They weren't visible from this angle. 'Well at least that explains why nobody saw me racing over here, I may as well have just walked and saved any possibility of injury,' Vince thought.

One eye on the ground as he inched forward trying not to fall over or make any sort of noise in the rock piles, Vince worked his way to the next window in an effort at a better view of where perhaps, they may have ventured to. By the time Vince reached the next window, voices were emanating from further down the building, much farther. Looking down at the portion of wall to his side and wondering how he was going to navigate through and over the post-apocalyptic looking area ahead, he carefully strode towards the mumbled yelling voices. As he passed each opening in the coarse grey stone wall he carefully peered inward in hopes of getting a view of Troy.

Nearing the second last window, Vince began to wonder if maybe he had passed them. The voices had stopped a while ago although he did not hear anything to indicate they had gone too far but there wasn't much place left for them to go from here so he must have passed them somewhere along the way. The clicking of artillery echoing from down inside the factory from a very close range brought his mind back into focus. He knew he was right beside them now. Kneeling down and pressing his body to the hot ground, he shifted over until he was directly below the windowsill where he could view all that they were up to. The voices were much clearer now.

"This isn't going to last. I already told you fucking idiots to double the order. Why does J.P. always send you shitheads to do his dirty work?"

There was no way for Vince to know for certain but he just had a gut feeling that the voice he just heard belonged to Troy aka The Marksman.

"Don't give me that shit, he's a busy guy ... you know that we just deliver the goods and collect the payment, we don't got dick all to do with whatever else you two discussed."

"You better believe you have 'dick all' to do with our business seeing as you're the ones sending it in for him because right now I'd be ready to blow his brains out all over the side of that wall ..." a pistol clicked into stand-by, "and considering he's not here, that leaves you two that I have to have this conversation with m'friend."

Even though things were obviously getting sketchy inside, Vince worked up the nerve to raise his body up and to the side of the window

126

just enough that his left eye could watch carefully over all that was happening below, keeping the rest of his face hidden behind the wall. The man Vince knew to be Troy from the police photos was currently pressing a handgun to a dark Latino man's head who, amazingly, was showing no signs of distress. 'I guess this is just business as usual for them,' Vince figured.

Troy had aged quite a bit since the mug shot that had been taken of him and he now sported an almost completely shaved crew cut as opposed to the slightly long, sloppy mess of a do that he'd had in the picture. However, Vince could certainly still recognize his distinguishing features like the slightly contorted upper lip and right eye that were either some kind of birth defect, which was very possible considering how minor the differences were, or the result of damage from a fight. He had managed to maintain the same average build in those years and wore a brown leather motorcycle jacket and black pants.

"So I'm gonna ask you ONE MORE TIME! ... Where's the rest of the coke?" Troy yelled.

Just then, one of the guards looked up to see Vince gazing down at them through the busted window.

"HEY!" he shouted as he quickly raised his gun and shot, sending fragments of pumice like stone shooting out from the wall beside Vince.

Vince looked back in for one split second to get a shot at Troy but he only gave one hostile flashing glance back at Vince before taking off running full speed back towards the front of the building.

Vince pushed himself up off the rocky ground and started to sprint towards the entrance to the building as well just as a mess of bullets bombarded the edge of the window. They hit with such force and numbers that they actually blew bits of the wall out from around the sides. Once again, hurdling over the pieces of rock at full speed, Vince ran as fast as humanly possible back to the front of the building.

Each time he passed a window, Troy made an effort at shooting him, the bullets actually making it through the window and only *barely* missing him, which was severely impressive considering that both he and Troy were bolting full speed and looking straight ahead. Vince wasn't actually watching but there's no way Troy could have been running that fast *and* looking to the side in order to have that good of a shot, he must have been blind shooting, or maybe not.

They were definitely keeping up with each other and Vince knew that once Troy made it up to the ground level and out into the open, he didn't have a chance in hell of surviving to tell the tale. Troy was after all, 'The Expert Marksman' and Vince still had a 200 yard dash towards the road before he could swing around the solid stone wall of a gate and either be able to hop into his car and speed off or wait for Troy to follow.

Breaking back out into the light as the building ended beside him, Vince miraculously found his way again over the large stone hurdles and simply waited to be shot in the back of the head in midair as he hopped over each large pile of stones.

There must have been something to cause quite a delay in Troy reaching the ground level again. It wasn't until Vince had literally been inches around the corner of the gate that The Marksman burst out into the light from the empty, darkened doorway and sent a bullet into the wall beside him.

In a lightning quick second, Vince considered the possibility of staying there and waiting for Troy to come around the corner or driving off. Deciding that if he stayed, Troy would definitely come, but so would his machine gun wielding minions and he wouldn't stand a chance, Vince pulled the door to his car open, jumped inside and took off. As he quickly passed the opening in the gate, he could see a black Maserati Quattroporte he didn't notice driving into the place, weaving its way through the piles of stone at full speed. 'He must have come before everyone else,' Vince realized. That would explain why Troy hadn't noticed Vince following him - because he wasn't, he was following his goons.

Pressing the gas to the floor and shifting the car into gear, Vince sped off as quickly as he could knowing that Troy would soon catch up, but still not knowing how exactly he was going to kill this guy let alone not fall prey himself.

Sure enough, one look into the rear view mirror revealed the black car that came speeding out from behind the gate and roaring up behind him.

Winding as quickly as possible through the twisting roads in the forested hills, Vince could feel Troy blaring towards him. Once on a semi-straight stretch of road, his suspicion was confirmed and the black sports car came up behind him faster than light and pulled up beside him. A shot through the tinted window sent Vince swerving and although still alive, barely managing to keep control of the car in the high speed chase. What was he going to do? There was nothing *to do* except keep going. Then the crazy bastard pulled up fast again and slammed into the passenger's side, knocking Vince off kilter once more.

Vincent cursed fluently to himself while trying to regain control before whipping around the next turn.

The black Maserati loomed forward again, crashing into the side, then again and again, finally making Vince lose control of the wheel and then one more violent, jolting, whiplash inducing slam to the side of the silver Jaguar sent the car off the road and down through a forested hill. Vince knew he was about to die. There was no chance of surviving this. He had had the good sense to buckle in his seat belt upon getting into the car but that wasn't going to help now. Trees and branches lashed against the windshield one after another and Vince cringed, holding on for his life as he waited for the car to slam into a tree trunk and instantly kill him.

If that didn't kill him, then Troy certainly would. There was no way out, he had lost. His heart pounded faster and faster and he could actually feel the hot blood coursing through his body in tune with its rhythmic thumping. Right as Vince opened his eyes, he made out the edge of the cliff that sped towards him. Gripping the wheel with all his strength and believing these to be his last few seconds to live, he almost slipped off to sleep in calm relaxation as if he were embracing the inevitable. Taking off over the earthy edge, the car dropped down and upon hitting the ground head on, toppled sideways onto the roof and shattered the heavy glass. Pieces of broken glass flew up into Vince's face as he clenched his eyes shut. Suspended upside down, in the air, it wasn't until after the eardrum bursting crash that Vince realized he had only fallen about 15 feet or so.

Blood dripped from a cut on his head and left hand onto the glass covered pavement that was now showing between the slightly dented steel frame of the car, and he smelled smoke, poisonous smoke. Like that of burning rubber or chemicals. He would have simply sat there and waited for the car to explode and kill him except he wasn't injured at all as far as he could tell. Pressing the button to the seatbelt, it came whipping off from across his chest and he fell to the pavement as carefully as he could manage. He crawled out the windshield, glass cutting his palms as he went.

He had forgotten about The Marksman until he was standing upright, and seeing an opportunity to live, Vince ran to a stretch of earth that would be easier to climb up than the miniature cliff he had just fallen off of and made his way up and back over to where the car sat in shambles not more than twenty feet away, just in time to see the black car come blaring around the corner in the distance.

Vince ducked behind some shrubbery and watched from behind the thick mess of branches and leaves. The Maserati slowed slightly but showed no intentions of stopping completely as it crashed into the back of his demolished and flaming car. 'This guy is nuts,' Vince realized, seeing more pieces glass go flying and flames shooting higher as the Maserati backed up, revealing horrible scratches and deep dents in the front of the car. The door opened slowly and Vince carefully pulled out the silenced handgun from its fastener, attached to his belt and pointed it in Troy's direction.

He waited in baited breath as Troy set one foot onto the pavement then another and pulled himself from behind the shiny opened black door, holding up a gun of his own towards the driver's side of the upside down Jaguar. Inching closer and closer to see if he had indeed killed Vince, Troy leaned down to take a look through the intact tinted drivers' window. Right then, Vince took aim and fired, sending a small stream of blood rushing through the air from the back of Troy's head as he fell to the ground.

There were no words to describe the sheer ecstasy he felt at this moment. He had just knocked off the second target on his supposedly impossible to complete hit list of gang leaders. The Marksman was dead. Unlike Rick, he had no idea who Vince was or why he had come after him but he fought the fight no less, and rather ruthlessly. Still, he fell to Vince, just as he vowed. Vince was starting to believe that nothing was impossible as he replaced the gun to its holder with a wide smile. There was no time to reminisce however, as Troy's lackeys would soon be following. If they knew where they had both sped off to that is, but better not sit around and wait to find out.

Vince jumped down off a lower part of the tiny precipice and landed harshly on his feet, sending a jolting pain through his legs and knees. He coughed for a second as he wiped his dirty hands on his pants then got up. Troy's body lay lifeless beside his now destroyed very expensive car, but it was worth it. He had been so close to death and yet never felt so alive. Leaning down into the Maserati Quattroporte and closing the door, Vince settled into the black leather and drove off down the middle of the road only looking back once as his former vehicle erupted into a monstrous explosion of flames, metal and shards of glass.

Chapter 12 - *The City of Angels*

Via rodeo proved to be the perfect unwind to all of the anxiety and stress of the past week and a half. The tiny strip of pedestrians only cobblestone European Mock-up Street that sat diagonally off of Rodeo Drive and connected to Wilshire Blvd was actually all Vince needed to ponder what his next move in this epic tale should be.

Vince had been utterly shell shocked at the strategy being played by the remaining leaders. In all rational thought, he had expected a full on war. An epic battle between good and evil that would end The Daravians reign of tyranny over the country or in a simpler finale, end Vince's own tale of revenge, but it never came. He expected them to send troops and assassins or maybe even come after him themselves, to infiltrate every level of his life and turn it upside down ... not so. They made a move that still left Vince reeling a week and a half later as well as left him wondering yet again what his best course of action would be. It hadn't been exactly crystal clear before, but this certainly didn't help his insight into the near future. Maybe *that* was the ultimate goal of their shocking decision.

The remaining leaders, in a show of either cowardice or strategy, Vince still wasn't sure which of the two options it really was, had dispersed themselves across the country. Well, he wasn't certain that they were even still *in* the country but it would seem rather illogical to leave the nation that housed all their members. He knew that the man he had already decided he would go after next, The Pimp, also owned a townhouse in New York City somewhere and although the building's exact address escaped him at the moment, he would be able to find it in the police reports he had kept.

As for the other two, he had no idea where they could be at this moment and wasn't sure how he would get to them either. There wasn't a snowball's chance in hell of actually locating Miles, considering his pathological aversion to remaining in one place for more than a fortnight. The Dealer, however, might be easier despite not having a name or a face to Vince. The future was hazy, as if he were squinting at it through half shut eyelids unable to fully open them just yet to reveal the entire scene before him. He could see where he needed to get to but the obstacles that stood between him and his destination as well as the path to get there remained a mysterious blur.

With this knowledge and his mind's examination of the situation, Vince decided it wise to focus on The Pimp and only The Pimp until he was taken care of then decide what to do about the others. Indeed, he was still perplexed by their decision to move as well as the fact that nobody had yet come after him. This unusual occurrence alone told him that it was strategy, and not fear, that prompted their abrupt departure from their home town. It had been a week now since Troy had been shot in the head by 'An unknown vigilante who is seemingly relentlessly seeking out top leaders of the notorious Los Angeles based gang, The Daravians,' as the newspapers and news reporters so aptly called him.

Vince also considered the fact that one of Troy's guards or understudies or whatever he was that had tried to shoot him, had seen him at the factory. He, in theory could have provided the police with at least a vague description of what he looked like. That is, if he were actually dense enough to go to the police, considering who he was. What he *could* have done however, was informed someone within the gang and provided them with a description. They could have had armies after him already. Why then had nobody attacked him? Vince brushed it off as one of those unanswerable questions, coming to the simplest conclusion possible; that he hadn't actually seen him at all and therefore *had* no description to provide to his fellow comrades. He also figured that if they hadn't come by now, then they never would, at least not in the near future.

For now, it seemed Vince had stumbled upon a situation that allowed him to roam the streets of his favourite city once more without fear and completely worry free. It had been a long time since he had been able to do this and he had forgotten just how magical a place it was, like the land of fairy tales. Standing just inside the two large white Italian pillars at the curved front of the building, Vince looked around the large boutique for a moment. There was an island section of curved white wall in the middle that accompanied the curving staircase to the second level. A small circular platform that held upon its surface three mannequins dressed in cocktail dresses in shocking blues, butter yellows and sequins, sat at the bottom of the stairs, fitted into the curve.

Walking across the dark glossy floor, Vince found his way to the men's department and started scoping out some new outfits. He had never liked shopping, in fact, he despised it but he was in a sort of lazy, comfortable mood that prompted the sauntering through boutiques on this hot and beautiful day. He picked up a dark red French cuffed poplin in a medium; a size he knew would fit, and continued on. Along the way he rounded up a few more dress shirts, including a black silk shirt with white trim of which he bought two because he liked it so much, and a couple interesting cashmere sweaters. Turning down numerous offers for a fitting room, Vince purchased his items and headed out of Versace, back under the mid day sun.

He passed by Bulgari before backtracking and deciding to venture into the über chic looking stone storefront. He had seen artwork done by Guido Mocafico for Bulgari featuring various pieces from their Haute Joaillerie line strewn about and amongst piles of different fruits. Most notably a collier necklace with brilliant and pear cut diamonds darting downwards into cherries and an Asscher cut diamond necklace wrapped over whole and broken lychees. His favourite however, had been a yellow gold diamond necklace featuring a pendant with an enormous cardinal red sugarloaf cabochon cut ruby surrounded by blue sapphires that was perched regally atop luscious fruit in complimenting dark blue with a red centre.

Since witnessing those creative displays, Vince had been intrigued by the brand but had not yet ever visited one of their locations. There, he picked up a multi-dial futuristic black watch with a faceted tungsten band that he spotted below the sparkling glass showcase. The next stop was Dior Homme, a personal favourite. Reading the time, 1:37 p.m., off his new watch was difficult due to the sun glaring off the slick black face with multiple dials going every which way. He had about an hour to kill before his appointment at Bijan for 2:45 which he had made a couple of days ago.

He decided at this time, to use the rest of this beautiful day to go out and get some things he needed or simply buy whatever he saw that he wanted, then go out to dinner with himself and top it all off with a visit to the beach. Dior always had interesting articles for the closet and this trip proved to be no exception. He had found a pair of oxford style black and white wingtip dress shoes with perforated holes that he immediately needed to have. He also spotted a jacket with zippers, stitching and patches of leather on the torso under the arms, a white poplin with black satin trim along the collar and down the front with multiple horizontal black satin stripes on the cuff, and a newer version of his favourite grey glen check pants. A paramount way to pass the extra time he seemed to have on his hands right now.

The appointment at Bijan was pretty much what he had expected. A stately, well put together salesman escorted Vince around the yellow shop as they hovered over the shiny white marble floor and ascended the staircase above which hung a large red and clear crystal chandelier from the coffered ceiling. Together, they selected more poplins, dress pants a couple suits, one of which featured a very light butter yellow jacket and white pants, and ties from behind closets with perfume bottle handles that each housed their own colour scheme. He purchased a pair of black dress shoes as well as 3 pairs of socks to go *inside* the shoes at $50.00 each, something he thought was ridiculous but did anyway figuring he might not ever be here again. There was definitely a reason this place was considered the most expensive store in the world. The undying service and attention to detail were bar none.

Afterwards, while wandering along the sun soaked, decadent green palm lined Rodeo Drive under a brilliant blue sky he watched his reflection pass by in the glass store fronts chopped up by white stone. As he made a couple trips to the car to unload his merchandise, Vince briefly started to think about the leaders again. The fact that they had all skipped town and not sent anyone after him most likely meant they were most likely formulating a strategy or some elaborate trap, but what could that trap be? The possibility that they had all just simply left at the same time for 'business obligations' after two of their co-leaders had been murdered was very slim to none. Or maybe they all had really expected Vince to come after them and figured if they split up, then at least he couldn't pick them off one by one.

He had scoped out The Pimp's address at 40 Beverly Park prior to his attempt at a break in about a week ago now, which judging by the scale of the estate, was most likely going to be a much more daunting task than getting into Rick's house. There were no cliffs to be scaled, but the sheer size of the place indicated that there was going to be much more security, gang leader or not. When he had arrived there however, he was greeted by a deserted manor. He had looked into it further and found that the estate was actually up for sale and it was this curious finding that spurred his realization of what had happened. A few hours of frighteningly simple research led him to similar findings regarding the other two leaders. He wondered briefly if anybody would be able to pull up the amount of information on him that he had just gathered on the remaining leaders and their travel plans. It took him only a moment, however, to remember once again, that he had confidential police documents the general public were generally not privy to at his disposal.

As useful as the police records had been to him, they were of no more use in finding The Dealer or Miles. There was no other indication of where they may live or where they may have gone. In fact, the only reason he knew that they had left the city was because of a frenzy of blogging comments on the gangs' fan pages that had helped Vince to get a lot of his information on them back in New York. Apparently the pages were indeed supported and followed, at least in part, by actual members and the comments were blazing from page to page with speculations as to where their respective superiors had disappeared to. 'Speedemon42' suggested that they had all taken off to Colombia in order to maintain or secure the cocaine plantations they owned, while 'Daravillian7' insisted that they had travelled abroad at the prospect of investing in a newly formulated drug discovered somewhere in the middle east. There were hundreds of suggestions at where they may have gone, each as unlikely as the next, and some that were downright absurd, such as having gone on a fly fishing trip.

There was no way for Vince to even guess at whose theories may be correct so he decided to stick to what he knew for fact - the police reports. He had wondered momentarily how it was possible for there to be fan sites dedicated to such a notorious gang without incriminating anyone who dared to admit they were members, but decided that the police probably had as much difficulty deciphering fact from fantasy or plain delusional lies posted therein as he did.

The second his foot landed on the floor behind the glass and steel door and he smelled the aroma of steak and other various gourmet dishes being prepared, he forgot about it entirely. All former contemplation on their motives or where they had travelled to dissipated from his mind without a trace and he was free from the thoughts that gripped him once more. His stomach on the other hand, offered no release from *its* wrath. Now inhaling the wonderful aroma of simmering wine and fresh herbs and spices, Vince became acutely aware that it was now 5:15 and he hadn't so much as eaten a single bite since breakfast.

After being led to his table, he sat content with himself and picked up the leather bound menu. There was hardly any noise in the large room at all as if the tables and dimmed frosted glass light fixtures soaked up a lot of the sound. There were people talking though; one hostile looking couple were sneering in each other's directions and whispering urgently. Another couple that were seated two tables down from Vince were talking to each other in a passionate lilting French accent and looked as if they'd just walked away from the altar and started off on their honeymoon here on the Pacific coast. The two couples looked remarkably similar but were conjuring vastly different energies that manifested in their attitudes.

The Pellegrino and lime was a surprisingly perfect refreshment for Vince's parched throat. The heat outside was another element Vince hadn't particularly noticed until walking into the air conditioned room. Although he despised the cold, the mid day, early summer sun had taken its toll as the hours passed. The corn crusted baby calamari on a lemon white wine sauce was sheer heaven. It was cooked to perfection in that way only talented chefs were able to achieve where the calamari isn't rubbery or stringy.

The next appetizer, the lobster timbale with saffron mousseline and parmesan tuile, was even more impressive. The saffron gave a rather unique flavour to the delicate lobster meat that seemed original without being ostentatious. A filet arrived in a cabernet reduction sauce with an enormous baked potato and various vegetables that Vince loathed almost as much as the cold but ate anyway because they were healthy. A small gravy boat full of extra cabernet sauce completed the dish. He ate leisurely, savouring every orgasmic bite as if it were his own last supper. The entire meal had been a perfect addition to an already perfect day.

Sipping the last of his Chianti from the elongated glass, Vince glanced over to two striking women at the bar on the other side of the room. The one had on a short black sequined cocktail dress and the other a flowy white chiffon dress that created a beautiful contrast against her tanned skin where it sat just across the top of her thighs. Both looked remarkable as they sat, legs crossed atop their respective barstools and sipped their martinis. The slightly thinner of the two picked up what looked to be something resembling a Lindor chocolate off a plate and daintily ate it. The other woman, deep in conversation with her friend, followed suit and slightly squinted as one of the mousse filled chocolates exploded in her mouth.

Vince sat for a while longer pretending not to watch them as he waited for the cheque, even though they were only turned halfway towards him as they talked to each other and probably couldn't see him even if he *was* full out staring. Laughing at something, the girls exchanged drinks, probably to sample whatever the other one was drinking but Vince still couldn't figure out why girls did that. They would switch shoes, bags, makeup and apparently drinks with each other and yet most probably wouldn't be caught dead drinking out of a public fountain or filling up a cup with tap water from a bathroom. No, it's not exactly the most sanitary thing to do but neither is putting on someone else's shoes or sharing makeup that inevitably collects bacteria or sipping each other's drinks (and the backwash that goes with it). 'Oh well, maybe it's a girl thing,' he figured.

After paying and filled with renewed vigour, he headed back outside and tried to figure out what to do next with this most perfect of days. The heat hit him again like a wave and he remembered he had already decided on the beach. No better way to end the day than lounging around on the hot sand and going for a swim. Well, beach lounging was more of a mid-day sort of thing to do before dinner or an event in the evening but when one *has* no event after dusk, it's the unparalleled, blissful finishing touch.

He headed home quickly to drop off his newest wares, grab a quick shower and change into something more sand and water appropriate. Afterwards, Vince hopped back into his newest car and headed off, down Sunset Blvd. towards the Pacific. He had ditched Troy's Maserati into the ocean after getting back and purchased a new, less pretentious, more reserved style BMW. Still luxe, still superior and still more than adequate, but not as obviously flashy and also not quite so detrimental to his account should he demolish it.

He parked the car and removing the towel, flung the small travel bag over his shoulder before shutting the door and noticing two bikini clad blondes walking towards the distant shore and looking back at him over their shoulders. He smiled slightly and the girls exchanged a light laugh before continuing on. Vince crossed the road and stepped onto the sand which he knew was exceptionally hot, not because he could feel it on the bottom of his feet, but because he could actually feel the heat emanating up to his calves. Sand dispersing under his rubber soles as he walked, he laid out his towel and set the small bag down beside it before removing his shoes and sprawling out on the towel. He pulled his shirt off and tossed it to the side as he surrendered to the glorious golden rays beaming down from above. He placed his tinted shades over his eyes before shutting them and slipping into nirvana.

Warm wind carried on the sea as waves crashed in the distance and the voices of people around him grew louder and faded away again as they passed. He could still see the golden glow from behind his closed eyelids as he felt every muscle in his entire body relax in a way they hadn't been able to for quite a few months now while Madonna's sultry voice rang in his ears. He could feel the beads of sweat forming on his torso as his skin heated up and a tan started to form. Turning to lay on his stomach in order to expose his back and not burn the front, Vince wasn't sure he would be able to get up any time soon he was so comfortable.

He had inadvertently slipped into a blur and the time passed until the sun hovered just above the horizon. Vince constantly flipped from side to side and tried not to fall asleep, occasionally sitting up to take a drink from the blue water bottle or check out the passersby. The sky above the water had turned a ruby red colour with flashes of yellow amongst a couple of clouds in the distance as the breeze came in strong from behind him.

Vince got up and looked around. He had actually, against all efforts, fallen asleep and was now one of the only people left on the sandy shore. Walking towards the water in the west, he gazed at the setting sun, the most beautiful thing he had seen in a long time, as it soaked the mountains to the north and the buildings behind him in golden light. Like El Dorado, the city of angels was illuminated and bathed in gold, the last of the sun's rays reflecting brilliantly off every surface and gleaming against the glass of windows.

The water at Vince's feet was warm as he kneeled down before the glowing gold light that shone against him to retrieve a seashell that was wavering between his feet in the tide. As he waded into the water, he was entirely refreshed, washing away all the sweat and sand particles that had gathered on his body. Once out far enough that the salty water lashed gently against his chest, he dove down into full submergence. Breast stroking under the surface with the water rushing against his face, Vince felt completely at home. There was nowhere in the world he would rather be at that moment. Every detail of the day had played out perfectly against the perfect backdrop.

Breaking the surface to the golden dusk with new life, he floated softly in the current, staring at the horizon as water rushed then slowed to a drip off the top of his body. He let his legs float up in front of him and started treading hoping that he wouldn't fall asleep here too as that would be disastrous. Nothing else at all mattered now. Every worry in the world had been washed away and for a moment feeling reborn under the golden sunset, he briefly considered giving up his quest for revenge, preferring instead to live forever as he was now. Only he couldn't.

Even if it were mentally possible to retain his current euphoric state, physically, it was beyond impossible. Eventually, whether the remaining leaders were formulating an attack in their absence or not, they would return if Vince did not pursue them. They wouldn't let it go even if he could. They had already proven that they would stop at nothing to see him dead but now, with two of their co-elite murdered by him, there wasn't any possibility of a sudden onset of amnesia amongst them. Vince wondered if they were even aware that it was him that killed Rick and Troy or if they even guessed at it without having any proof. Who knew?

Just as he was walking back onto the beach from the water, the perfect little interruption to his decidedly negative thoughts smiled at him then passed by in a red bikini, heading directly towards where he had parked. 'Time to go,' he decided as he quickly packed up his belongings and clumsily pulled everything along behind him. He walked towards his car as quickly as he could in order to catch up with the little blonde vixen, but trying not to look like he was chasing after her. As he retrieved the keys to his new BMW, which happened to be parked two cars over from the one she was currently loading her own beach wares into, he looked over at her and smiled. Opening the door and tossing the bag in the back seat he turned to her.

"Hey …"

Bursting through the door pressing Rachel against the wall as he passionately engulfed her neck with his tongue, the faint taste of saltwater and perfume still on her tanned skin, Vince's excitement increased tenfold. Rachel grabbed at Vince's back and slightly dug her red nails into his flesh as Vince led her to his bedroom. He picked her up and all but threw her onto the top of his bed below the diamond shaped mirror on the wall. Both of their hormones blazing at the speed of light, he leaned down and kissed from her neck down past her breasts to her naval then back up again as he ran his hands up her smooth legs. She raised her head slightly to kiss him and looked directly into his eyes for the first time. He in turn, stared back intensely before running his hands up her thighs again and they continued their night of passion.

*

The lake water was warm and very suitable for swimming. Vince looked around at the trees that lined both shores on either side and realized he must already be in the middle of the lake which was much longer than it was wide. Five other people were swimming around nearby that he knew were 'with him' even though he wasn't sure how he knew them. Maybe they had been friends from a long time ago. He swam through the water for a while staring out at the shore and the docks while his 'friends' frolicked as they followed behind him. It was then that he and everyone else saw it and stopped in their spots, slowly treading water.

"What the hell is that?" asked one of the guys behind him.

"What I'd like to know is what it's *doing* here?" replied the dark haired woman from beside Vince.

Everyone sat there trying to figure out why there was an enormous staircase jutting up out of the middle of the lake at least fifty feet into the air. As Vince and his entourage gathered around it, everyone was goading each other into actually getting up on it and jumping off into the lake. Looking up at the side of the odd contraption, Vince saw a monster sized jet sitting atop the flight of stairs with the words 'LARTSA STAR TRANSPORT' printed in large red block letters along the side. It was almost as if the stairs led up to the door to the jet. 'Lartsa must be the name of the county or country we're in,' Vince figured, even though he had never heard of it. After a blink of his eyelids, the jet was gone however and he realized it must have been a momentary hallucination. As everyone was carrying on, Vince hopped up onto the floating platform at the base of the stairs without a word. At this angle, he could see a second flight, only about a quarter as high as the first, veering off the wobbly inflated platform.

"Come here! Look at this!" Vince said to his friends.

They swam around the other side to see what he was talking about and then continued daring each other to jump off the smaller flight if they were too afraid to jump off the larger one. Nobody stepped up so Vince started up the higher set of stairs, which he would admit was slightly scary seeing as it looked much more difficult to reach the top, but figured it would surely provide for a better dive once there. As he set his first foot onto the stairs they began to wobble under the weight of his body. Struggling to keep the stairs from toppling over with each step, he made it about half way up.

The next thing he remembered was not hitting the water, but rather being in a small field surrounded by small ten to thirteen foot pine trees. They discussed the fact that they needed to go *somewhere*. The group from the lake wandered through the sparse forest as the trees got taller. Eventually after a ten minute walk or so, the ground was becoming much less muddy and uncomfortable underfoot. Vince and his clan came upon a large clearing at the end of which stood an old seventeenth century Scottish dark grey stone mansion.

They were at the back of the estate and could see the main square shaped centre of the building that stood three stories high with the last top row of windows jutting out from the slanted rooftop. Tall rectangular windows encompassed the building on the lower two levels and directly in the middle stood a slightly outstretched section that rose up to the roof, topped off with a triangle pediment. Several short, fat chimneys jutted out of the roof and from the far left side stood a smaller two storey circular section connected to the main house as if it were an attached guesthouse.

Walking along the perimeter of the yard, they headed around towards the front, all the while staying behind the trees that lined the edge of the yard so as not to draw any attention to themselves from anyone that might be inside even though the house itself looked rather desolate. Coming up to the front, they walked quietly, reverently past a couple of the large columns to one of the side doors.

Vince pushed open the door that looked as though it hadn't been used in quite a while. Stepping inside, there was a smell of old rich decor, the scent of splendour that came from silk tapestries and upholstery that had gone slightly to seed. As odd as this thought seemed to him, considering there was no official smell of an old rich building, it was sort of fitting. As if the thick brocade curtains, rich silk damask upholstery and oak flooring, cabinetry and furniture had started to release the slight scent of decomposition. In the middle of the living room to the right hung an old chandelier with just a few visible cobwebs, all collecting dust and sitting in the eerie grey glow of daylight that seeped through slightly dirty windows.

Even though everything was old and unused, with the exception of the chandelier, most items were still fairly clean. Just down the short dark mahogany panelled hallway ahead the daylight shone into the kitchen which was much larger than most people's den, bedroom and bathroom put together and even though he could only see a portion of it through the doorframe he still got a pretty good idea of its girth.

Vince turned to his left as two of his comrades went ahead into the hall to check out the kitchen. At the bottom of the staircase were two half rounded columns on either side pressed against the wall that were made of veined marble in a slate blue colour. Vince wasn't sure where it had come from as he had never seen stone in that colour but it was stunningly elegant nonetheless.

Climbing the stairs and stopping momentarily at the window on the landing half way up, Vince looked out at the general nothingness of a front yard. An empty three tiered fountain sat in the middle of the circular driveway that was surrounded by a small stretch of yard and very tall coniferous trees. He then turned to his right and continued up the other half of the stairwell that would put him on a path towards the back of the house. After reaching the top Vince wondered what he was really doing there in the first place.

The other person that had remained with him was now continuing down the wide wooden hallway alone. Vince let him go though, figuring he'd rather be alone anyway. He walked forward himself, shoes clicking against the hardwood floor and decided to head down an even shorter side hallway. To his left was a bedroom in which three people were standing, backs to the door and talking quietly. Vince passed it without a thought and continued down the middle of the corridor to the bedroom at the end. There was a long dark wooden dresser pressed against the left wall. The head of the bed was pressed into the far right corner putting the bed on a diagonal slant in the room and had a potted palm plant in the vacant triangular space behind the headboard.

Suddenly realizing that the people he had just passed were not anyone he came into the house with he panicked. 'Shit! What do I do?' he thought frantically to himself. 'Hide down behind the bed until you hear them leave,' he concluded quickly. Vince quietly rushed over to the other side of the bed and crawled down onto the floor in order to not be seen by the mysterious people should they come walking out of the other room.

A voice came from behind him as he pressed his body against the floor. It sounded soft and peaceful, not at all like an accusatory tone he would have expected upon being caught trespassing in a seemingly abandoned mansion. It also sounded vaguely familiar; he turned around, looked up, and had never been more shocked in his young life than he was then when he saw Vanessa standing over him in a flowing cream dress.

"What are you doing down there?" she asked quietly.

Vince was stunned into a non-response and even though he should have been overcome with joy at seeing his wife again he was more confused. Climbing to his feet he grabbed her in his arms and kissed her. She seemed very interested in seeing him as well but also sort of distant like she wasn't really there. She looked more like a hologram and her spunky personality had been replaced with a peaceful, genteel and very well rested, if not a little detached, nacreous luminescent aura.

"What are YOU doing here?!" Vince exclaimed upon overcoming his shock and wanting to know where she'd been or how he was even in her presence right now.

"I've been here for a while ..." she responded not showing any of the surprise or disorientation Vince was exhibiting.

"No, you're dead. I saw you; I closed the casket at the funeral!" Vince said slightly exasperated not only at his own apparent confusion of the facts but also at the thought that she hadn't told him she was here now.

"Dead?" She asked looking a little alarmed, the first show of emotion since their reunion, "no, no, there's no such thing."

"What?!" Vince nearly yelled as he choked on his words and began to cry slightly. "What are you talking about?"

"There's no such thing as death," She responded calmly. "We just travel from place to place. You've been deceived," she continued in her new gentle voice.

"What? So am I dead now too? Is that why I'm here with you? Oh my god that must be who those other people were too ... they must have died at the same time as me!" Vince asked the questions but in his mind had already concluded that's what had happened.

145

"No, I told you, there's no such thing. We just go from place to place."

"Then I must have died if I'm in your 'place' now," he said trying to convey the simplicity of the situation.

"Come here," Vanessa said ever so peacefully as she motioned for Vince to follow her over to the long dark wood dresser. There were several pieces of heavy yellow gold jewellery upon it including thick necklaces and rings, some plain, some encrusted with diamonds.

"Take whatever you want," she said looking at the pile. Vince only wanted to be with her but he knew she meant to take some of the jewellery so he reached out and grabbed a random handful of the precious metal objects.

"There. Now what?" he asked clasping the jewellery and looking at Vanessa's radiant face and thick wavy brown hair. Her eyebrows rose as she looked first into Vince's eyes then down at his hands in a sort of 'well ... look at it ...' expression. Vince glanced down to find that the small pile of valuables he had been grasping a second earlier had disappeared. Utterly shocked, he looked down at the dresser to find that the pile that sat upon it mere moments ago had also vanished into thin air.

"See," she said, "we just move around."

"I don't understand! What do you mean by that? Move to where?" Vince asked eagerly still wanting to know if he had actually died despite whatever she wanted to call it.

"We're all on different planes. Same place just different plane," she answered with an expression one would see upon the face of someone who'd just convinced a blind person that they could see. Only he couldn't, he still had no idea what she was talking about. It must have shown because she looked slightly crestfallen as her expression faded to one of humble disappointment.

"You'll understand someday," she said and Vince couldn't help but feel like there was something about her that he no longer connected to. That *she* was the one who didn't understand. At this moment he began to feel like he genuinely would be without her forever; that they simply didn't connect anymore. He didn't care though he simply wanted to be with her again even if it was only for a short time and even though they didn't seem to understand each other anymore. He sat for a moment with her in blissful silence putting aside their differences in perspective and simply enjoyed each other's company. That was the last thing he remembered.

*

When he awoke, duvet comforter pulled halfway down his topless torso, he rolled over to Rachel only to find that she, like Vanessa, was no longer there. The spot where she had been lying was still slightly indented and covers pulled fully back. Vince lay back down and thought about the dream. He realized now that this had been the first real thought he had given to her since she had been killed. This was the first of all his fantastical and obscure dreams that she had visited. She did seem to be quite different though, not quite the same person as she was before. Her demeanour was calm, peaceful and almost patronizing. As though she knew something he didn't. As if what she had told him was some sort of infinite knowledge that she gave up on trying to relay because she figured he simply couldn't grasp it.

She had been exceptionally pleasant and nice enough but he detected an undertone of exasperation nonetheless. He had almost felt as though they had grown apart in what seemed like a century of lonely nights since she left and there was no way to go back to her now. The golden ring that he noticed still encompassed her finger in his dream somehow now signified their separation as opposed to their union and he couldn't stand to think about it anymore. He pushed it out of his mind though, realizing it was just a dream and that it wasn't really her and that he also couldn't afford to waste time dwelling on it.

Rachel had obviously only partook in the previous nights frivolity with the intent that it be a one night stand. 'Wasn't it the guy who was supposed to lose interest after finishing?' he thought, staring at the ceiling, figuring he'd met someone who might actually be worth keeping around. But she was gone. It wasn't more than twenty seconds later however and the feeling of abandonment had gone as well, so it must have been for the best. He knew the next thing he had to do, so not having Rachel there and having to try and explain his situation made things a whole lot easier.

After his morning routine he retrieved the police reports Jake had given him on the other side of the continent and studied more intently his next target's profile - The Pimp. He hadn't expected to knock the first two targets off his list so quickly or expected the rest of the remaining leaders to skip town after he had killed Rick and Troy and thus only really remembered Andre's address in Los Angeles.

Skimming through until he found the residence area of the script he read that The Pimp's, aka Andre Lepore's, primary residence was at 40 Beverly park in Beverly Hills, CA; information that was now rendered useless. He also owned a luxury townhouse in Manhattan's Upper East Side at 8 East 62nd Street. 'These guys must have a shit load of money,' Vince thought to himself. There was no description or picture of the townhouse but there wasn't any conceivable way, given its zip code, that it was at all cheap. And judging by his estate here in L.A., Andre didn't seem the type to settle for second best. Most people would consider themselves lucky to reside in either of those humble abodes. Not The Pimp though, he needed both of them.

More than any of the other leaders Andre was responsible for the gang's extortion of businesses. This was his main source of personal income aside from the gang's international prostitution rings that he ran. They started from the epicentre in Los Angeles, extending through larger cities in the Midwest and all the way over to the next largest group - New York. 'This would explain the location choice of his two houses,' Vince realized as he read.

Andre was known to be a bit of a maniacal character as far as Vince could deduce from the carefully worded police reports. He was the suspected, although not convicted, murderer of another local pimp in Los Angeles. He had reportedly given the victim a 'smiley' where the other intruding pimp was made to bite the curb before Andre kicked at the back of his head. Apparently he had done this while laughing hysterically and firing shots into the night before spray painting the word 'antag' in red paint on his back. He was clearly crazy as a cootie bug in a shit heap by this point but everyone obeyed him nonetheless. Vince had found this bit out on that ever-reliable site dedicated to the gang he had used back in New York, the stories online coinciding with details in the report.

148

He was also very manipulative and much sharper than given credit for. He had somehow managed to convince a number of police officers to turn to a life of crime while under investigation and during the multiple times he had been interrogated by police. He had gotten them to supply him with information on other pimps he considered competition while providing any bits of information he had on them to police. Simultaneously, he was slithering into the minds of the accusing officers to turn them and their opinion in his favour and thus, minimizing his role in any criminal activity.

During one police questioning, he was quoted as saying, "We are the gods that decide what you will and will not do. You do not see what we see and therefore cannot act in your own best interest and because of this we must be the ones to set your path."

Vince's face wrinkled in confusion as he read Andre's words that continued to unfold to produce the most bizarre dialogue he had ever heard.

"You and I are like one, the same we are, you take and I take, I give people what they want and you try to stop people from attaining their desires. You only do as you're told because the price is good, but should that carrot on the stick in front of you disappear, then you begin to see things from my perspective and you will understand that we all have it, and we don't want to let it go."

Vince personally did not see what was so enamouring about this lunatic's banter but the creep did manage to convince many officers that he was not so bad and that they too would commit crimes in time, which eventually, a lot of them did just as he told them to. It didn't make sense to him but like most things in life, seeing something on a screen, reading it in a report, hearing about it from someone and actually witnessing it were vastly different in magnitude.

He decided not to confuse himself further with the emphatic ramblings of this maniac and shut the reports. He didn't need to read anymore anyways. In a few short days, after he had enjoyed a fear and tyranny free L.A. for a bit more, he would jet off to New York to find The Pimp. Vince sat atop his plush bed and fondled one of his rifle's extra compartments as he thought about how he was going to do it.

He had thought about this same thing before going after The Knife Fighter and The Marksman. Time had already passed and Vince still felt as though it happened too quickly and easily. But that was how it happened whether he thought it too simple or not. Reflecting on that thought he realized that he would never know what was going to happen until the time came and the task was upon him. The cards were dealt and the revolution was coming. He could make out that it was there, a distant mirage in the desert, but it was impossible to see it clearly until standing right next to it.

With renewed confidence in his abilities and a more optimistic outlook, he got up and went about planning another perfectly peaceful day. It was perfectly normal to not see it all and know it all right away but he would come to understand everything he needed to in time. It was obscure and scary now but all the pieces of the puzzle would fall into place. All he could do was try to emerge from the elaborate maze of confusion victorious. And the way to do that was by simply heading out after the next person on his list, Andre Lepore, The Pimp.

Chapter 13 - *Sighted at Monduc*

New York was just as he remembered it from his younger years. Not so much the same as when he was here last at Jake's apartment; the time then was full of questions, research, confusion and fury. Things were brighter now. In one way this was quite literal because it was summer and the dampness of spring was no longer upon him, but also because he himself had changed towards the brighter, both in his mood and his intellect. Things were more obvious to him now and he was able to start to see pieces of the puzzle. His confidence was boosted now in a way it hadn't been for a while.

The air and his mind were clearer. He now had a sense that this was possible even though all odds were against him. Seemingly following suit, everything else was also fresh and exciting to him now. The trees were in full bloom, leaves spread out to soak up as much of the glorious sun as possible and the summer air breathed new life into his revitalized mind. Walking down Lexington, Vince simply observed the passersby. They were noisy and rushed here, everybody always had somewhere to be and apparently very quickly, as if their lives themselves were hinged on their punctuality. L.A. seemed to be more leisurely, like it didn't really even matter whether they made it to their destination at all let alone on time. Perhaps they believed if they moved too quickly they would burst into flame in the heat.

Vince had decided to keep his condo in Los Angeles because he loved it and he loved Los Angeles. It was really that simple. He wasn't going to be intimidated or pushed around or told what to do by someone he'd never met before, had never even seen or otherwise had any tangible proof even existed in the first place. It could have been a facade either by the real leader or by the police to make it look as though they were on to someone. That would certainly explain why they hadn't made any arrests yet and how Miles was able to be so impossibly elusive, popping up here and there like a whack-a-mole.

Upon seeing the building looming ahead of him, in which he would take his first real life look at The Pimp, Vince's thoughts dissipated from his mind like smoke in the wind. The building's exterior was rather ordinary, just a plain modernized glass front with white backboard and lights. Nothing out of the ordinary for New York, being one of the most innovative and progressive cities in the world, this was rather tame. The stairs up to the front were simple stone but ascending upon them into the building were New York's fashion elite. Most were dressed in summery floral print chiffon mini dresses, cocktail dresses and even one guest decked out in a brown mink coat and mesh fascinator with black feathers swooping down over her right eye. 'That must be rather uncomfortable, why would someone wear fur in the summer?' Vince wondered before passing it off as the fashion crowd's eccentricity.

Climbing up the stairs and into the building, Vince found himself standing amidst a sea of the aforementioned eccentric fashionista's. It seems the people outside were merely a preview of the main attraction past the front doors. One stunning lady, whom he recognized as Daphne Guinness, had blonde hair that incorporated black streaks in a very elegant, and not at all punk way, was wearing a miraculous example of futuristic couture. She had on a black long sleeved mini dress covered in black and hematite crystals that glistened as she walked daintily on sky-high pewter Mary Jane platform heels that were scooped out from the back.

Everyone else in the place was either an extravagant example of fashion as art, like she was, classically classy or just downright boring and dowdy, which really surprised him. Maybe they were just more focused on the fashion in front of them instead of *on* them, who knows. It really was an odd combination of people and even though nobody quite matched that avant-garde beautiful weirdo in the black dress, a lot of people had on their bodies some of the craziest stuff Vince had ever seen in his life, only they didn't orchestrate it as well as she did.

Vince had gotten a pass to the show from Carl, one of his friends in Los Angeles that he had gone to law school with and now worked for the advertising agency that handles all of the marketing for 'Monduc', the name of the label that was showing its fall/winter collection here. Taking the very privileged front row seat he didn't have a hope in hell of getting without Carl's connection, Vince looked over the runway as crew members swept and lightly polished the floor. The long white runway ended at the back with escalators going up and down, to and from an upper level that Vince couldn't see from this angle but that either led to another bunch of guests or backstage. Each stair had a flattened white top and was lit from underneath to appear as though the stairs were ascending to and descending from heaven in mid air. The rest of the space was simple with one row of pocket lights in the ceiling above the walkway.

Vince looked around for a man he would recognize as The Pimp. He had heard for whatever reason that The Pimp frequented these events, the shows for Monduc in particular. He most likely had shares in the company or something and thus, he came to them every season. This rumour was actually confirmed by unofficial information he had collected on Andre during his last tenure in New York.

The lights dimmed after about half an hour with Vince having no luck in locating this man and simultaneously wondering what was taking so long to get the show started. 'Maybe he wouldn't be coming this time,' Vince thought. Fast paced hip hop/club style dance music, the exact kind Vince hadn't expected to play at a fashion show, boomed from overhead as the first vibrant platinum blonde descended the escalators, frozen in pose.

Her arm was outstretched with her hand raised in a neoclassical pose, chin jutted up and the other hand perched dramatically on her hip. Her feet stretched upwards in high mirrored platform heels. She wore an incredibly tight mini dress with next to no top aside from the multiple strands of faceted metal beads that hung across her bust and left random strands hanging down past the hem. They flung carelessly as she hit the floor and came to life, strutting enthusiastically towards the end of the white path before her. The next model came down upon the moving stairs also frozen in pose in a white and silver streaked metal bustier laced up the front by crystal encrusted chains while the bottom flowing chiffon skirt embroidered with spatters of crystal and metallic beading hung silently off her hips. She was positioned in a way that she held an empty bottle of Grey Goose upside down above her open mouth until she too hit the floor and jutted forward as the first girl came back. Upon reaching the escalators going back up, the first model once again locked into position upon hitting the self-ascending stairs.

Vince watched as the amazing futuristic parade unfolded before him overflowing with metal, crystals, chiffon, organza, silk and even some LED lights that contrasted against each other perfectly in an incredibly artsy yet beautiful way. The show itself reminded him of winter and freshly fallen snow, looking like dew drops had stuck to everything then frozen before having a chance to fall or melt. The colours on the other hand were definitely summer tones with ninety percent of the collection being white and only miniscule amounts of black, grey and blue or pink, accented only by crystals, broken mirror fragments and metal.

Just as a girl in a slate blue dress passed by on the runway, Vince noticed a tall black man in a grey fur coat making his way to his seat with a much younger girl attached to his arm. He knew instinctively that it was Andre but the large coat and sunglasses made it impossible to be sure. From then on all other aspects of the show he had formerly been enjoying faded into the background as Vince eyed his target. He put on his own Prada shades in order to disguise the fact that he was intently studying The Pimps every move. The decadently clad futuristic women moved hastily between Vince and The Pimp, long legs ending in heels that seemed to melt into the ground instead of clacking upon it creating blurred visions back and forth as they went. It was exceptionally cool in the room and Vince wondered if it was just him or if the label was trying to literally set the mood for the upcoming frozen season which was still about four months away.

After the parade of thin girls in weird outfits had ended and had adequately managed to fill the attendees' heads with ecstatic delight, Vince managed to keep one eye on the man he presumed to be Andre. He didn't look like the maniac he sounded like in the police reports, at least not from afar. As the spectators of the show headed backstage to congratulate the designer, Vince caught a glimpse of the man in the grey chinchilla coat removing his sunglasses, proving unequivocally that he was indeed the man Vince had been seeking. There was no real reason for Vince needing to see this man before trying to assassinate him aside from the satisfaction Vince would get in knowing he was on the right track.

154

With this newest of confidences Vince decided to forgo the backstage party where Andre would inevitably spot him and most likely piece some sort of connection together between him and the Los Angeles assassinations. Vince had already heard in the short amount of time he had been in New York, on the news of all places, that Andre would be hosting some sort of party at his townhouse tonight. Vince was astonished at how blatantly the media spread information on what people were doing. Do they not know who he is?

It was like any other mini discussion topic on that channel, much like thousands he had heard before. How many of these other events and fundraisers he had heard about casually on some station were being attended or hosted by mobsters or gang leaders and he'd thought nothing of it except some other rich person throwing another charity fundraiser or institute ball?

Had he not known better, Vince would have assumed the same thing about this event as he did about all those others but when The Pimp's real name was mentioned, it caught his attention. Nobody said anything about him being a crime boss however. In either case it provided him with easy info on The Pimp and a way to easily get inside his house. Sure, there would be a guest list of some sort but that didn't matter, the fact that somewhere in the vicinity of hundreds of people would be entering and exiting his house was instrumental in easy access.

Vince headed back to his luxury suite at the Waldorf and passed by a woman shouting "Tim, Bus! Now!" to her child whom apparently did not wish to board the same bus as his mother. A group of gay guys were excitedly chattering about something that registered at the time but escaped him now as Vince contemplated how he was going to get in undetected, loads of other guests around him or not. Upon arriving at his room halfway down the hall Vince opened the door and immediately felt an overwhelming desire for sleep, deep sleep. It had come out of nowhere and hit him like a ton of bricks.

Maybe it had something to do with the build up of anxiety at seeing Andre, subconscious or otherwise, that had risen and risen and now that it was over gave way to the body's genuine physical need. Walking sloth like through the small foyer and elegant sitting room Vince wandered into the bedroom. Normally the light yellow striped

155

wallpaper, rich damask comforter and beige octagonal printed floor would seem soothing but in Vince's over tired mind appeared only unnecessary. All he wanted right now was rest and it really didn't matter if it was in a cardboard box or 500 thread count sheets. He removed his clothes down to his briefs and hung them in the closet before closing the curtains and crawling between the plush, comfy and slightly cold, sheets and falling asleep so quickly that had he been able, he probably would have thought to check for a dart in his neck.

*

The ground below him was cold, hard and damp. The few spots of cushiony moss below him were hardly enough to make lying on a rock even remotely comfortable. Vince opened his eyes slowly, still blurred from being shut for so long and realized he must have passed out from something he didn't remember. Squinting past his own eyelashes, he gazed into the dark of the forest. A forest unlike the ones he was used to in America. The large trees, twisting vines, luscious shrubbery and hot heavy air brought him to the realization that he was in some sort of tropical location. Where crickets normally would have chirped there were strange buzzing and clicking noises that were most likely made by some sort of frog or other small animal. 'Where am I?' he thought desperately to himself.

He slowly pulled his body from the moist ground below, realizing much too late that his aching muscles and bones wouldn't properly allow for this sort of movement without at least a few minutes preparation and he almost fell back to the ground as he tried to move himself into a standing position. His dark jeans were ripped at the knees and part way down the calf of his right leg. The tee shirt he was wearing also bore a great rip along the right shoulder.

There was a terrible pounding in his head as if someone was continuously taking a hammer to it and he reached his hand up to touch it and felt something wet and sticky. Pulling his hand back down to get a look at it, he realized it was his own blood. He felt around the top of his head some more searching for the source of the crimson stain but couldn't locate any actual injury from which it stemmed. 'It must have just been a small cut,' he rationalized, recalling that even the tiniest of head injuries can bleed for hours on end.

Still faintly dizzy, he looked around and didn't recognize anything but it also didn't seem odd to him that he had no idea where he was or how he had gotten there. Then there was a faint noise like the beating of a drum in the distance straight ahead of him. Considering that he was lost in a foreign and most likely sub-tropical jungle judging by the dense sticky air, Vince figured he may as well follow the noise until he at least came across some sort of civilization that could tell him where he was.

Pushing through the thick brush and large foliage, Vince made his way over logs and under low hanging, twisted branches covered in some sort of light green moss that smelled of an earthy, almost pungently relaxing odour. Vince jumped on the spot in shock as he heard an animal getting mauled in the distance and most likely eaten. This was enough to make him move a little faster even through the thick shrubbery. The only light that lit his path was from openings in the canopy that permitted the moon to peek through the leaves.

He knew it would take a minute or two for the unknown predator to consume its prey but didn't know if there were any others around or if it would simply change its mind and come after him instead. Vince was running by now and large leaves with surprisingly sturdy stems threatened to slow him down just enough to make him dinner for the savage animal. His heart beating faster and faster, he didn't even realize the beating of the drums getting louder and louder until ... he tripped over a branch or uprooted tree and landed face down on another rock. Shit! He was going to have one hell of a collection of scars and bruises from this little outing. That is if he hadn't jumbled his skull around enough to make himself completely brain dead by now.

He looked up again, groggy from the abuse Mother Nature had bestowed unto him. The yellow light of fire south of the cliff he was on was the only thing visible at first. Opening his eyes wider he noticed he was at the *edge* of the cliff. Not a very high one, but a cliff nonetheless that probably would have killed him had he tripped a mere ten feet further ahead than he did. He shuffled forward a bit to get a wider view of what was going on below and gazed down quietly into a large pit where eleven or twelve tall torches were lit and stuck into the ground in a giant circle that encompassed a mass of dancing tribal denizens.

There was one more fire, a bonfire, in the middle of the giant circle and in front of it sat a middle aged woman who appeared to be the chief judging by the large coloured feather headdress and multiple beaded necklaces she wore. Everyone danced around her as she sat motionless, eyes closed and not uttering a word. The beating of the drums stopped and everyone in the circle began some sort of high pitched screaming and shrieking that sent chills up and down Vince's spine. Normally a festival or whatever was going on below should have sounded like a joyous event but the tone that carried the shrieks and cries in the unknown language was indicative of something much more sinister.

Two out of the group of dancers walked up to the chief and yelled something at her in the aforementioned foreign language. Her eyes opened instantly and began to bulge frighteningly out of her head with a severity that looked impossible. She rose slowly, staring into space and uttered something incoherent in what could only be described as a wicked and raspy voice. Everyone burst into excitement and once again resumed their dancing and drum banging.

The two natives that had walked up to the chief grabbed at her head from both sides and hastily pulled at the top making the line that had gone around the circumference of the top quarter of her skull separate. The two men quickly removed the top of her skull to reveal her throbbing pink brain as the still alive chief sat completely still, eyes closed again and not paying any attention to the small amount of blood that ran down her forehead. Everyone erupted into ecstatic roaring once more as Vince's stomach churned and waves of nausea overtook him. His heart started to pound in rhythm with the ominous beating of the drums as the whole scene began to slip into a surreal hazy setting.

The chief woman opened her eyes again to reveal the bulging whites and veins that looked as though they might pop and shouted. The whole scene got louder and louder. The fire blazed more wildly and the beating of the animal skin stretched over the drums increased its decibels with each pounding. Vince knew he would be sick but he couldn't move. All the members of the tribal cult were still jumping and dancing around enthusiastically, the central woman knelt down, head held upright. The muscles in her face strained and pulled the corners of her mouth into a wicked open mouthed grin as everyone continued their primitive dance around the woman to be worshiped.

Chapter 14 – *A Familiar Taste*

Vince jolted upright in his bed covered in sweat but not panicking. He had known the entire time that it was just a dream but he couldn't escape it and it *felt* so real! He lay back down and stared into the dark for a few minutes more before trying to slip off into another deep sleep. One where he hoped he would not again become trapped inside another violent dream such as the one had just had, like a prisoner inside his own body, and quickly lost consciousness.

He was still somewhat nauseous from the trip into his alternate universe when he awoke the second time and climbed out of bed. He could already tell that this was going to be one of those dreams that caused an underlying sense of foreboding all day in which Vince would constantly find himself having to reassure himself that everything in *real life* was actually going good right now and that there was no need to worry about the momentary unidentified stressor.

Trying to force the thought out of his mind as he showered and got dressed, he briefly reminisced about how far he had come already. The distance to his victory was shortening and it all seemed to be happening at the speed of lightning. Just as it began, the lightning bolt reversed back into the sky just as quickly as it had hit the ground. A smouldering circle remaining in the place where it had struck and leaving the face of the earth forever changed by the descent of that bright electric force of nature. Just as he reminisced about the speed of which this epic tale had been slipping by, so too was the day and time before his next strike. As it was, he was now standing across the street from Andre's townhouse gazing up at the magnificent structure.

A true glory, the building's exterior was majestic and impeccable, dimly lit by pocket lighting underneath twisting cypresses and tucked under outstretched sections of limestone. The entire front was done in the aforementioned stone and curved slightly outward. There was a small stretch of stairs that led up to large mahogany double doors with two lit windows situated on either side. Above that sat a balcony in front of another set of tall double French doors, covered by Austrian curtain. The limestone facade continued up in 5 stories and looked positively regal in its stance, but also a little ominous.

A soft, rather unobtrusive noise of a private band and chatter came wafting out from inside the glowing interior. Vince had apparently lucked out and came late enough that the doorman was no longer expecting anyone. Seeing as the party started at 7:00 p.m. and it was now 11:00, this seemed perfectly appropriate and understandable even though Vince hadn't expected it and had spent the past few hours wracking his brain in an attempt to devise a strategy to get into The Pimps home.

People sauntered out lazily and probably quite drunk to pull on a cigarette or maybe to simply escape seeing as most of them were just sitting there without any apparent reason for leaving the party. People also entered without hesitance and as the door opened Vince caught a brief glimpse inside to the loitering crowd in the lobby. There were certainly a lot of people here. Nobody would know he had come in uninvited and he certainly dressed the part for a fundraiser in a simple black tux and white mandarin collar button down shirt, decidedly forgoing the bow tie for no reason other than comfort. He absolutely hated anything too close around his neck and even when wearing ties he would keep them loose in a sort of deliberately casual way unless he absolutely had to for work.

He walked up to the stairs and climbed them before slightly procrastinating to open the door, not sure what to expect but ready to take the plunge. He barely had time to try and foresee what he would encounter before he found himself standing on the other side of the door, watching the glamorous crowd in silence. This was absolutely *not* what he had pictured when he thought of a party, extravagant fundraiser or not, that was being thrown by a man who had infamously called himself 'The Pimp'. There were no scantily clad women prancing around in feather boas, clear plastic sky high platform heels and large gold bamboo hoop earrings, hanging drugged off their master's arms or congregating around each other cussing each other out and making a scene.

No, not any of that, these people were more refined. More so actually than the nouveau-riche people at any party he'd attended in Los Angeles. They all donned elegant gowns instead of the more sexy mini dresses everyone in L.A. seemed to be so fond of, making the 20 something year old women appear as though they were actually much more mature than they probably were. The silk charmeuse of their dresses shone in drapes and folds, twists and ties or very luxe chiffon, taffeta and sequins covered most of their bodies and fell gracefully to the floor. If Los Angeles styles were to be summed up in one word it would be 'sexy', whereas here people seemed to go more for the refined old money look.

The jewellery followed suit and many people had a more impressive display upon their necks, fingers and ears here. Simple lines and stately diamonds glistened from the dramatic and more often than not, rather enormous pieces. One beautiful brunette who occasionally showed off long slender, tanned legs from the thigh slit in her floor length cream coloured gown wore a stunning array of cascading cabochon cut emeralds and diamonds around her neck that danced in flashes under the soft light of the crystal chandelier overhead as she moved. To the immediate left was a white marble staircase with a black wrought iron railing intertwined with leafy gold designs stretching all the way up. Directly in front of the staircase landing on the opposite wall was a large white marble fireplace that reached up three quarters of the wall and was flanked by floor to ceiling mirrors.

Right in front of him, sitting carefully atop the white marble tiled floor was a golden easel with a cream coloured board that displayed 'American Social Health Association' inked in black cursive script at the top followed by the hosts name, Andre Lepore, names of the chair men and women within the charity and a list of benefactors. At the bottom was simply the time and date of the fundraiser.

Well, that cleared the air for Vince now as he had already forgotten it was an AIDS benefit he was currently attending. This simple etiquette always observed on such an occasion surely saved Vince from certain embarrassment in the near future when he would undoubtedly be asked why the charity meant something to him. If he wasn't even aware of which charity exactly he was there to support, he would look like a remarkable fool in an attempt to lie as smoothly as possible, which usually does not go so well when you truly don't have the slightest clue what you're talking about.

Vince silently made his way through the chattering crowd towards the rooms in the back, trying to be eloquent but feeling as if he stuck out like a sore thumb. Hopefully, the fact that he was there by himself wouldn't draw even more attention than was necessary. It was hard to do given the grandiosity of the event surrounding him but Vince had to try and remember he was there for a reason. Not to party or socialize but to knock one more name off his list. He felt more like he was at a gathering of Parisian aristocracy than a fundraiser thrown by a pimp. He walked into a well lit yellow painted room with bronze sconces placed on the wall between pieces of art being auctioned off for the fundraiser.

The room situated a couple back from the main foyer was also filled with party goers dressed to the nines. People around him mingled and discussed various things amongst themselves. Vince couldn't help but feel slightly lonely, finding himself wishing for the first time in a long time that Vanessa could be with him. Everyone else in the room had someone else whom they knew from some prior engagement and were able to comfortably accompany each other around the party without having to feel like an outsider. The waiters carrying the flutes of champagne and hors d 'oeuvres on golden serving trays were probably the only other people who didn't know another soul in the room. But even they probably knew each other and made fun of the particularly outrageous or amusing guests behind their backs in the back room that they disappeared into to get more drinks.

Of course people smiled gracefully and seemed quite friendly as they passed by or gave a subtle nod of their head in acknowledgment upon making eye contact with Vince. But he still didn't know any of them personally and wouldn't be able to produce a single one of their names if mandated by the president himself. At this point the reason he had come, the reason he had done all of this in the first place, raced back into his consciousness and his loneliness turned to anger. Stopping in front of a large vertically erect painting, he glanced down at the plaque in front of it.

It was titled, 'Jardin Hypnotisant' by Victoire du Chandré. Vince looked at the painting again and had an immediate attraction to the piece, noting the fluid nuances the artists brushstrokes undertook to produce this piece of work. It was an interesting rendition of a forested walkway with a certainly mystical tree that bloomed in white orchids. Lush bundles of lavender flowers stemmed from a bush on the ground and the dense and varied green shrubbery played against the twisting brown branches of the focal tree to the far right of the painting. Three subtle moons hung in the minimized sky, almost hiding behind some of the tall shrubs on the left side of the painted path, one right behind the next.

The whole thing looked as if it were taken right from a slightly blurred and undefined dream. Not any of his own of course, this seemed much too peaceful, but someone else's dream perhaps.

"Beautiful isn't it?" The delicate voice that came from behind him still managed to shock Vince even as she walked up to take a spot beside him seamlessly joining her words to her actions in apparent admiration of the piece. "I love the way she plays with mysticism and still manages to portray it all as rather natural looking. Almost as if these imaginary things could be found in some far flung corner of the world if one searched long enough."

"Yes, it's rather elusive looking isn't it?" Vince noted in feigned interest, for he was looking now not at the painting, but at her.

She was wearing a long tight mermaid gown constructed completely of black organza with a thick black satin hem at the bottom that had black sequined embroidery densely enveloping the bottom of the gown and becoming sparser as it rose up showing off her perfectly toned legs. The top of the dress was simple, long sleeved and belted at the waist with a simple black body suit covering the necessities under the sheer organza.

Her radiant blonde hair was done up in an exceedingly elegant sweeping bun that looked much more New York socialite than librarian, which of course made sense seeing as that's exactly what she was. From her ears hung elegant briolette cut rubellite and diamond earrings and an impressive cascading necklace to match, much like the girl with the emerald necklace except a raspberry red colour. Vince usually thought matching necklace and earrings looked cheap but this was extraordinary. Her makeup was shadowy yet still light looking, completing her dynamite ensemble.

'Definitely high society,' he decided, 'and stunningly beautiful.' The gown was definitely a couture piece. Not the *word* couture that's casually and carelessly thrown around by people speaking merely of anything bearing a high end label, but the genuine article. One of a kind, hand crafted at an atelier in Paris, custom tailored from multiple fittings, using only the finest, most luxurious and exotic materials and definitely well into the five figure price range. Vince was certain this was Dior couture actually as he had seen it in one of their shows. She had made some pretty major changes to it like the satin hem along the bottom and the embroidery was vastly different indicating that she had indeed *bought* the dress rather than borrowed it.

The jewellery was most likely Haute Joaillerie as well, although it's pretty hard to tell seeing as there's no real definition of what it must actually entail to be called 'Haute Joaillerie'. Outfit and jewellery aside she was gorgeous. Those extremely pricey and extravagant clothes did not overtake her in any way as she carried herself perfectly and gracefully in them. She wore the articles, not the other way around, which was difficult to do when one is donning an outfit costing hundreds of thousands of dollars. She had perfectly plump red lips and piercing blue eyes that gleamed from within as she glanced over at Vince slightly with a smile before returning her decorous gaze to the topic of discussion.

"This piece would be a perfect addition to my collection," she stated casually, longing after the oil rendition.

"You're a connoisseur of art are you?" Vince asked somewhat playfully.

"Well I don't think that's the most appropriate word for it, more like a hobby," she replied humbly before continuing, "... or a continuous interest."

"I see. It's actually a continuous interest of mine as well although I don't own any major pieces."

"Well, maybe you could start tonight," she said lifting the svelte champagne flute she had been holding to her red lips and delicately taking a sip.

"Ha ha, yeah maybe ..." Vince responded, realizing her efforts at promoting the auction. She must be involved somehow.

"Oh, I'm sorry, I haven't properly introduced myself, I'm Olivia Duchardé," she said extending her free hand in a somewhat spontaneous introduction.

"Vince Torres."

"Vincent, that's a nice name," she replied trying to sound polite.

"So is Olivia," he pointed out, "and Duchardé ... as in Harvey and Ruth Duchardé?" he asked, realizing the name sounded familiar.

"That's right," Olivia answered, confirming his suspicion that she was a member of the real estate Tycoons family.

He was also fairly certain he had seen her in the society pages of the New York Times more than once, although she was much more beautiful in person. Vince rather smoothly relayed a cool disinterest in her wealthy family in an attempt to not come across as star struck or attracted solely to her money. He wasn't of course, seeing as he hadn't known that upon initially meeting her and even if he did, he was more interested in their conversation anyway.

"I've heard a lot about the developments your company is doing here in Manhattan and I've got to say I'm impressed."

"Well thank you but it's not my company, it's my fathers," Olivia replied, "I'm actually in Law."

"Really?" Vince inquired, "So was I."

"No kidding, what firm?" Olivia asked looking interested and curious at this newest of common factors shared by Vince and herself.

"J.P. Crane and Associates in Los Angeles actually, I was a partner there but I've retired."

"Oh my, why? You're much too young to be retired. You actually look much too young to be a partner too for that matter. Is it your family's business or did you just pass the bar when you were eleven?" She asked coyly, eyeing Vince as she again took a sip of her Cristal and looking genuinely intrigued.

"No it's not, it had no affiliation with my family, and yes, I do seem too young don't I? In truth, I was too young, but I worked hard and I guess I just got a break," he laughed, trying to elude the question of why he was now 'retired', fearing he had already divulged too much information about himself.

"Really, well good for you. Actually that's why I'm so interested in the firm I work for as well. It has no ties whatsoever to my family's business so it can't be said that I didn't work hard for my title or my job ... you didn't tell me why you're retired though," she pointed out after a moment. He had hoped against all odds that she wouldn't ask that question again but it seemed there was no escape from this one.

"Well, I'm not exactly retired in the sense that I've worked long enough and now I'm finished. I retired because there was a death in my close family and circumstances prevented me from continuing my job there," he finally told her, still trying to avoid going into too much detail.

He didn't believe Olivia was part of the gang but as much as it didn't seem like it, it was still indeed a party hosted by one of the leaders of the gang that had repeatedly tried to kill him and there was no telling who could have been listening at that exact moment. He had to remember that fact and not to let the bedazzled party or jet set crowd distract him from the reality that he was there for one reason and one reason only.

"Oh I'm terribly sorry to hear that. So what are you doing now? Or are you actually retired as in not going to be pursuing another career path?"

"Well no, I'm not done working just yet but I still haven't decided what exactly to do next. I'm kind of using the break to find something in my field that I can really work at and build it up once something does come along," Vince said as Olivia nodded in understanding, earrings swaying back and forth as her head moved slowly.

"Well, Vincent, I feel certain that something perfectly tailored to your situation will present itself in due course," she responded almost a little too quickly with a smile reminiscent of the Mona Lisa.

Just then, a uniformed gentleman approached from behind Olivia and after he politely apologized for interrupting, discreetly informed Olivia that there was an urgent call for her that she would need to take in the parlour upstairs when she had a moment.

"Oh, alright I'll be right there," she said to the older man before turning back to Vince. "I'm sorry; you'll have to excuse me. I need to take this call," she said apologetically, "It was a pleasure to meet you Vincent and hopefully we'll run into each other again in another life."

This sparked his interest, why in another life? Why not in this one?

"The pleasure was all mine Madame Duchard é," Vince responded.

"Oh no, call me Olivia, please, that's my mother's name," she said with a slight laugh.

"Ok, it was lovely meeting you Olivia, take care."

"Same to you, Au Revoir," she lilted in a slight French accent he hadn't noticed before as she departed, following the stately butler into the crowd.

Vince looked around for a minute before deciding he really had nothing else to do at this party anyway and headed back towards the foyer, climbing the staircase to the second level of the party. Others came up and down the stairs as well and all the lights on every level were lit when Vince looked at the house from outside, so there would be no reason it would be considered odd for him to venture up there. The second level was much like the first one except with more of a 'homey lounge' feel to it as opposed to a gathering area.

Vince thought better of joining the people here and having a seat, instead carrying on to the left and down the middle of the hallway to the next room towards the back of the house. He had a mission and he still wasn't sure how he was going to accomplish it. This place was huge and he wasn't even sure he'd ever find The Pimp let alone get enough of a chance to kill him without being seen by a plethora of spectators. Then, of course, he would have to figure out a way to escape back down however many flights of stairs he had made it up to get to The Pimp in the first place. Clearly he had overlooked the fact that Andre was probably counting on there being numerous witnesses should Vince, or anyone else try to kill him when he entered the party.

Vince passed by more quiet rooms along the way, each of which seemed to be pre-designated to a set group of people as hardly anyone got up from their spots and moved around or mingled. It seemed as though the ornate gilding on the walls and along the railings held some sort of supernatural power that prevented too much movement of the guests that Vince was somehow able to circumvent and move about freely amongst the trapped frozen crowd. At the back of the townhouse, which was rather long, there was another large lounge area with a continuation of a smaller staircase that led back downstairs and up to the next level. Vince started up them in confidence hoping to convey to whoever may be watching that he was indeed allowed up there, when in actuality he was not. 'Say or do anything with enough confidence and people will naturally believe you,' he recalled from management training.

If the first level of the house was more of a lobby/foyer and housed the display and the second floor was more of the lounge area consisting of multiple 'living rooms', then the third storey was definitely the entertainment level. The main room which was at the back of the estate was a bar and billiards with three pool tables complete with ivory pool sets, racks of cues and scoreboards affixed to the wall. The bar stretched out along the far right wall and ended at the window that overlooked what must be the backyard. The bar was extremely sleek; a glass countertop hovered slightly above a blue light that ran along its length to appear as though it were floating. A few empty pint glasses of Guinness sat amongst martini and highball glasses, that hadn't yet been cleaned up by the bartender, sat on top of the counter. A few people were perched on the high stools in front of the bar either sipping a drink of their own, waiting to be served or watching one of the games of snooker that were taking place.

The gilded sconces on the wall between the racks of cues illuminated the upscale bar scene and the few seemingly dream inspired paintings that hung on the wall. Halfway across the far wall there was a painting that looked like an orb of light shining suspended in mid air and surrounded by wisps that curved and hugged the glowing ball. The other painting depicted some obscure scene in what looked to be an ancient palace. Large stone pillars and stairs set the stage for some form of festival or party where the attendees lounged around decked out in white chiffon or purple satin and lay strewn on the steps. The fanned tops of reeds scattered in the bottom left hand corner in an apparent river and a goat peered out at the water. Grapes sat on platters and wine spilled and stained small areas on the stone floor red. The whole thing was done in a way that the elements of the painting almost blended into one another with little distinction yet still managing to accurately depict the items within.

Vince only had one of the skinnier knives he could find and a 9 millimetre he had somehow managed to conceal in his pants under his jacket on his person. He knew from various friends that the police could tell who was packing by the way they walked and their overall body language. If the police could do it then the other various gang members that were sure to be in attendance certainly would be able to tell as well. What could they do though? If he was concealing weapons and they could tell, they still wouldn't necessarily know what he was here to do. He could be security or in the gang himself for all they knew, or maybe he simply liked to carry a gun for peace of mind. In either case they couldn't simply open fire on him at an AIDS benefit anyway.

The next room he passed by in the middle of the hallway was a media room, proving correct his theory of the third floor being the entertainment level. In it, a movie was being screened in which a young brunette was brushing past party goers wearing gothic Victorian outfits and elaborate Venetian masks in a dazed light. He briefly noticed a small dining room as he walked by and wondered what exactly it was doing there as he continued down and found himself at another set of stairs sooner than he had expected.

He started up the staircase that was at the front of the house, making his way quietly up the marble risers, noting that nobody else was moving between the third and fourth floors. The fourth floor was yet another level of lounge areas but significantly more open. The entire level was separated only by small half walls finished off by white pillars that stretched from the top of the half wall to the ceiling. This was precisely where the lavish party started to look more like something he would have expected from a man who calls himself 'The Pimp', as if there were no other.

The women here dressed in a more inappropriate manner and showed much more of themselves than the women downstairs did. Legs stretched out over the arms of couches as women lounged around and sat on one another. A few were permanently attached to their phones, texting, talking or whatever else they may have been doing. One girl in a fully sequined mini-dress pranced around in 5 inch heels chatting to just about everyone and seemed to either be high or just highly social.

The whole setting was actually rather simple and not a bit plain compared to the decadence that played out downstairs. Almost as if Vince had opened a door and stepped from an opulent benefit party in one part of the towering townhouse, to a much more laid back gathering atop it all.

One of the girls here, not women, was actually wearing a jean jacket. Then there were the few men in the room, some in the same tux getup that Vince was currently sporting, but most in larger sweaters than actually needed for their body size and high end logo track pants. It was all a little difficult to comprehend. Was this where everyone went to relax and get out of their ball gowns or was this really just a more 'homey' part of the party reserved for very close friends or 'business associates' of Andre's? He wasn't sure but he figured the fifth level of the house would only be bedrooms and maybe a bathroom or two so there was no sense in going up there in search of the infamous pimp.

Taking a seat on the comfy looking sofa next to him, Vince tried to take it all in, again to no avail. Maybe this was where he kept his 'girls' so the other guests could have their party. If so, then Andre must be back *downstairs*, mingling with other New York elite. He decided to wait it out here anyway and listened to everyone around him while at the same time pretending to be doing absolutely nothing. This played out rather smoothly since nobody had particularly noticed he had shown up in the first place. The small crowd of dressed up trashy girls next to him proved his suspicions with their endless banter about who was currently having the most difficult time with their pimp, referring to them more like a corporation than a person and who had recently overdosed and died alone and cold in the streets.

As Vince sat and stared blankly into space, taking in every sorrowful word that escaped their mouths, he couldn't help but wonder if he was different from them, and if so, why? Their world seemed too far away to him even though in reality it was currently seated on the same sofa he was. It still didn't seem like any of this could be real to him. Any fool can see they're falling, so why couldn't any of these people realize what they were getting themselves into from the start? He wondered if he was possibly getting himself involved in something that would consume him at some point down the road.

As he was deciphering these and other thoughts, he noticed Andre way at the back of the room wearing his usual grey chinchilla fur coat again. 'Classic pimp material,' Vince thought snidely to himself as he tried to remain calm and figure out what to do. There was nothing *to* do except to simply get up, walk over to him and see what happens. He lifted himself from the spot on the couch and started towards his next intended target, not knowing where the next few minutes would take him.

Vince wasn't sure if Andre saw him or not due to the fact that he had his sunglasses covering his eyes, like a surprising amount of other people in this room, but he got up and left the room before Vince had made it halfway to the other side. Considering how long of a room it was, Vince decided to forgo any attempt to chase after him as that would only lead to disaster. "Where the hell is he going?" he mumbled to himself. But he couldn't chase Andre right now. Instead, he chose to sit on top of one of the multiple plush sofas in one of the many seating arrangements around the space.

The little cove between two small sections of wall that he had tucked himself into was perfectly quiet with only one other couple mumbling to each other on the brown leather couch next to him. There was a golden clock with a glass dome over top on which the minute hand passed the XI roman numerals on the face. Vince had no idea where Andre had gone to or when, if ever, he would return but there was time anyway. Nothing else at that moment mattered besides Andre.

At that moment, however, Vince noticed that a blonde woman in a jean mini skirt and shiny silver tank top entered the room and instantly took a liking to Vince. She flashed him *that* look and played coy for a moment before strutting over. She was striking in her own 'look at me, I'm a hooker' sort of way and Vince couldn't help but notice her as well. She continued eyeing him in a sultry manner as she placed one leg in front of the other in his direction until she stood over him in pose then plunked down into the vacant seat beside him. 'Not one for subtlety or wasting time,' Vince thought silently to himself before speaking up.

"Who are you?"

"Who are you?" She asked playfully pointing a freshly manicured finger at him before pressing its tip to his chest.

"I'm Jake," Vince responded. Who cares if he gave his real name? He was certain she didn't give a damn what it was anyway.

"Well Jake, I'm Adriana," she said tilting her head to the side and letting her straight blonde hair fall over half of her very lightly freckled face. She kind of reminded him of Bridget Fonda when she played Melanie in Jackie Brown. She looked *a lot* like her actually and the more he looked at her, Vince began to wonder if it *was* her.

She looked at him from her remaining eye and asked, "So what's a guy like you doing at a party like this?"

"What, you mean I don't look like the type to attend a Charity benefit?" Vince asked.

"No, I meant a party like *this* ..." she emphasized as she motioned around the room with her head.

"Oh, actually I didn't know this was a separate party," Vince said. "A mutual friend of Andre's invited me to the benefit and Andre said it was alright. I figured it was for a good cause, so I came."

"Oh did he?" She looked down and away momentarily almost in a sort of daze before continuing, "That still doesn't explain what you're doing *here.*"

"What do you mean *here*?" Vince asked getting slightly perturbed by her beating around the bush.

"In *this* part of the party ... where his business people hang out," she added after her failed attempts to make Vince pick up on her subtle indications that this was indeed Andre's separate party for his 'workers'. Of course, Vince figured out what she was trying to get at but kept playing dumb or indifferent so as to not provide too much insight into his true intentions and she wasn't helping his frustration by constantly making some sort of underhanded hint. Any lie, any deception, any hidden agenda could be covered and muddied by misdirection of any sort, so he used that to its fullest potential.

"Well Jake, I'm glad you're here anyway," she said as she looked away again almost as if she was drunk or stoned and trying to follow some imaginary thing she kept seeing. Or maybe in all fairness, *was*

173

seeing and just had a delayed reaction to its motion. She looked back at him and into his eyes.

"I guess you're one of his business partners or something huh?"

She was making less and less sense by the minute.

"No, just an acquaintance," Vince said as Adriana leaned in and kissed him, again proving her impatience and inner sense of urgency for whatever reason. There was a taste in her kiss, her lips. It was there, he knew it was and it wasn't alcohol. A tingling sensation left itself on his tongue and lower lip after she pulled away, a taste of bitterness with a powdery nature. Then the slight burning came, coupled by a gut feeling of foreboding.

He pushed Adriana off of him as hastily as he could while trying to remain calm. It was poison. That was it! It was the same poison in fact, which the other gang members who snuck into his hospital tried to use on him. Adriana fell over in a clumsy fumble. That's why she had been acting so strange! She herself had been feeling the intoxicating effects of the poison she had coated her lips with. The layer of lip gloss between her lips and the potent botanical toxin apparently wasn't enough of a shield her completely; just enough to *maybe* not kill her.

What was it called again? Aconitine, from Monkshood, that's it! Vince had looked it up after his incident in the hospital and knew it could be absorbed by the body through the skin and therefore even more readily through mucous membranes like the tongue and lips. He also recalled reading that Atropine from the nightshade family of plants would counteract the toxic effects. This was exactly what Dr. Stenwick had ordered the nurses to retrieve the night he had been poisoned. Where the hell would he get that now though? There was no time to go running to the local greenhouse and start munching on the shrubbery found therein.

Right then, Vince spotted Adriana's metallic clutch that he had been too distracted to notice her leave on the glass table in front of them. He grasped at it in hopes that she brought some sort of antidote to use on herself. He glanced over at her momentarily feeling as if he should help her too but she was too far gone herself now to realize what was going on. Even though Vince could see that she was losing control of her body, she would probably be fine eventually. Especially if someone thought she was overdosing and called an ambulance. He on the other hand got a full, unguarded, concentrated dose and would begin to lose control of vital functions in a matter of minutes. Rifling through the bag past lipstick and pills and loose cash, he came across a small sample vial of Chanel No. 5 that held a dark brown liquid inside which was definitely *not* Chanel perfume. He grabbed it and darted up towards the stairs to the lower level where he remembered seeing a bathroom as he passed by.

Racing down the stairs he ran into the dining room he remembered seeing and grabbed a glass and a salt shaker off one of the tables much to the shock and confusion of the few guests left dining. There was no time to be concerned about what everyone else thought or how strangely he was acting. He stumbled down the hallway and burst into the bathroom, now starting to feel the body crippling effects take place, thrusting the glass under the tap, jamming the nozzle on full blast and dumping salt into the water.

The second it was full, Vince gulped back the salty solution and tried to throw up. No luck. He could feel the beads of sweat running down his forehead and the back of his shirt becoming soaked with sweat. He jammed his finger at the back of his throat and immediately felt the bile rise instinctively. He emptied the contents of his stomach into the white sink with one heave after another as the chunky bits of stomach fluid vanished down the black hole in a swirl with the running water. After he felt he had adequately relieved himself of all that he could, he pulled the vial out of his jacket pocket and dumped it in his mouth hoping it was indeed some sort of backup antidote Adriana had brought and not perfume or worse - another poison.

The liquid was disgustingly bitter and almost made him vomit again with its pungent, bitter and leafy taste. After resting his head in his arms for what felt like an eternity of pain and discomfort, there was a moment of relief where he realized that the worst was over now and he could breathe again. He would need another few minutes or so to regain his strength and mental state of normalcy and calm, but overall he would be fine.

As his racing heart began to slow, he raised his bloodshot face from its spot between his arms and became filled with indignant fury. That bastard had tried yet again to kill him and by ruthlessly using one of his own girls whom he could have killed in the process. Gripping the cold granite countertop with one hand, he rose to his feet and stared blankly into the mirror at himself for a moment. His reflection did not deceive him but it did not provide, what he considered, an accurate depiction.

The calm surface and good looking facade only hid something more, something only he knew about and realized now why. Because it was not visible to the eye, for it was a torment of the mind that haunted him. Lying latent at the base of all that he did, it was there. Only to surface once every so often like some sort of mystical creature that a very select few had been privy to witness and seemed a myth to everyone else who believed it could not be so when presented with a summary of the facts at face value.

Pushing open the door and walking as tall as he could down the middle of the hallway, Vince purposefully marched back into the 'trashy' crowd at the party deliberately looking for Andre and not wasting time feigning interest or manners towards anyone who was not him. Adriana had vanished from her spot on the floor, probably gone to a restroom herself to purge any toxin before it took too much of a toll on her. Seeing that The Pimp was not in the room and infuriated at the events of the last few minutes, Vince pressed forth through the crowd towards the back of the room where he found another flight of stairs leading to the next level. It should have been assumed that Andre would be downstairs mingling with his honoured guests but he had disappeared into this back half of the house that only led upstairs and considering the fact that he had sent someone after Vince he would probably be waiting.

Ascending one carpeted hardwood step after another, Vince climbed up towards the next battle ahead. Entering the darkened hallway of what was sure to be the bedroom level, Vince looked towards the end of the hall. There was no one and nothing in sight. A couple of doors were open and he knew he had to be careful crossing them as anyone could be hiding in there and waiting to follow him out into the passage and strike. Moving slowly, body tilted to the side in a defensive manner, he continued until he came upon the first opened door.

The carpeting rolled down the middle of the hallway provided perfect cushioning to move silently through the dark. Peering slowly inside the first open door frame, Vince saw that it was indeed a bedroom. There was no window, which seemed odd to him, but being in a townhouse that's probably quite a normal occurrence for rooms that aren't towards the very front or very back. The plush four poster bed had about twenty pillows piled on top of it and the thick down comforter hung below sheer curtains that were pulled back around the bed. No person in it, on it or otherwise in the room though.

Continuing on, Vince passed an elaborate golden rococo style console with a matching mirror hanging above it. The perfect opulent decor to be sitting in a five storey townhouse on the Upper East Side but still a little odd because it was the only thing sitting in the hall save for the few simple, unlit lights attached to the ceiling.

After checking the other two rooms which were also vacant, Vince continued, wondering where exactly Andre had disappeared to. Turning around a slight bend that led to a small continuation of the hallway Vince came upon a white wooden staircase that led up to white painted wooden double doors. Something inside him squirmed. As if he were in a dream far away and somewhere he should not be, there was a moment of discomfort that he was not accustomed to as he sat and stared up at the door. The feeling that accompanied the chill running through his body registered somewhere in between déjà vu and fear mixed with mysticism and confusion.

An inherent resistance kicked in and for a minute or two he seriously considered turning around and going home. Something here was very, very wrong. This seemingly normal area appeared to have nothing wrong with it but his instinct told him otherwise. The small space seemed to be a world away from the glamorous party going on downstairs. He felt the further he went up towards the top of the house, the more the scene he found himself standing in the centre of was displaced from reality, almost removing itself from the physical world entirely.

He decided he had come too far to turn back now. Indeed, there was no turning back. Two of the gang's leaders were already dead and even though the journey was becoming increasingly difficult and surreal, he had to continue. 'Fear is only in our minds,' he reminded himself, 'Do not let it take over. They use it, they feed off it to trap and enslave you.' It had almost worked already and they hadn't even really harmed him yet, proving the power of the fear they were able to conjure and impose on their victims. 'Domestic terrorists,' he thought. Refusing to give in, to fall victim to them, he started up the stairs against his better judgment, to challenge the ideal they imposed. Vince had not seen a sixth level from the street and he did indeed see the spindled rooftop so where did this staircase lead to?

Pushing open the doors he realized that there actually had been another level. How had he not seen it? It was right there and he was standing in it now. It was quite simple and brightly lit by fluorescent bulbs that made the small room leading outside glow white. Large doors that faced the back of the house looked out over the rooftop terrace. There was nothing leading towards the front, to any area he would have seen from the street, which he figured is why he didn't see it.

Opening the door and stepping onto the dark stone patio, Vince looked around for Andre. About fifteen feet ahead was a small set of three or four stairs leading to the slightly lowered level of the rooftop terrace. The entire area was nothing more than an exceptionally large space with multiple seating arrangements, the very back being vacant ground as a sort of dance floor. Two tops of an olden style English street lamp sat on either corner at the very end and provided the only light other than a few very small lights underneath spiralling potted cypress trees placed around the roof.

It was so dark and empty, in fact, that Vince almost didn't notice Andre sitting at the farthest couch towards the end. His back was to Vince and he sat facing the opposite direction, looking out over the terrace at the glittering city. The short brown hair on top of the back of his head was all that Vince could see rising above the backing of the chair he was calmly seated in. There was no doubt he was waiting for an inevitable confrontation.

Vince moved closer and closer, always keeping one eye on Andre to make sure he didn't move from his spot on the chair. Pulling up behind him, Vince moved around to the side as Andre sat motionless. As he came to the point where he could see Andre's front, his heart raced in his chest. He never knew what to expect next or what these people might do. It was comparable to approaching a rabid dog or a mentally unstable inmate. This time, however, his target and enemy sat still, glass of brandy in hand and said nothing as his dark shades covered his eyes. Vince almost began to wonder if he had died of some sudden onset of a rare disease or simply had a stroke or heart attack given his current motion and expressionless posture. Until he spoke that is.

"Well well well. What do we have here?" Andre said coyly as his head tilted slowly upward to look Vince in the eye from behind the tinted Gucci glass. "Why dontchya have a seat ma man?"

Was he serious? 'Ma man?' Where had he learned to speak like this? Vince had to try and remember that this guy was a lunatic and not listen too closely to what he said, so full of trickery was his endless banter.

"You," Andre said, pointing one finger at Vince while the others gripped the fat brandy glass, "you a tricky guy. You good."

Vince could only sit and listen. Lunatic or not, he wasn't making much sense. And even if he was, he hadn't provided Vince with much of a question to which he could respond.

"You're the one they put down aren't you? They said you'd be back, *he* said you'd be back. I didn't believe you'd get up to our level again, or down to our level, see that's not the way I view it. You think you're so above it, above us? Nah."

"Who are you referring to?" Vince finally asked not able to take the senseless rambling for much longer.

"You! You the one that killed Jamie, yes? That two timin', low life guy. That was you, correct?"

"Yeah that was me. What are you trying to get at?"

"Well, everybody knows why you're here and so do I. It wasn't supposed to happen that way, you were supposed to be dead m'friend," Andre responded, finishing off his diatribe with a maniacal laugh at his own apparent comic genius. He then tightened up a bit and leaned in. "They all said there was no way you'd get here, this far ... you! That's you they say that about. You s'posed to die now four times but we still don't get you. You made it here though, to this place. Rick and Troy; that was you wasn't it?"

"Yes," Vince answered coldly, not wanting to give The Pimp any ammunition.

"Yes yes yes yes yes ... That it was. I knew it, I said to myself, 'Self, that's gonna be bad news bears for me someday'." He sat silent for a moment as a wide smile emerged, "Nah, not for me, for you! I must say it's impressive, but I don't wanna kill you ..." There was another moment of silence in his narrative but Vince knew he wasn't finished "... you should work for me."

"Work for you?" Vince asked in shock and now mentally confirming that this man was completely off his rocker.

Finally being able to speak with Andre, he understood now what the police reports were talking about. His ramblings were completely senseless but for some reason, sort of enamouring. It seemed as though there *may* actually be some sort of substance to what he was saying but he was too crazy and couldn't word it properly and thus left you wondering if you listened a little longer, that maybe you could decipher it. Vince also noted that he *sounded* much more deranged than he looked.

"And you did try to kill me actually!" Vince pointed out.

"Nah, nah, nah, that wasn't me. I was right here ..."

"Your girl, that means you!"

"No, No, see this is your problem ... you're gettin' shit confused now. You thinkin' left is right and right is up and that I tried to kill you ... No! That bitch out of her mind drunk, I don't have no control over what bitches be doin' down there. No, no, we two, we're too much alike you and I. Yes we are!"

This was getting stranger by the second and Vince began to want to plunge a knife into his throat now not so much out of revenge but to make him shut up. That slightly amusing factor had somehow slipped away.

"The same?" was all that he could mutter in his post-poisoned, overstressed, infuriated and confused state of mind.

"Yeah man, we the same. You gotta do what you gotta do and I gotta do what I gotta do. We're instinctive. Not like the rest of these dullards, nah, we know. We're together in this. Those other people ... they only good now because they got what they need. They're blind. Try bein' on

180

the streets and you'll steal. They don't know how it is, that life aint perfect. Think about it. If they were told 'Ok, you can kill this plant or you don't get to eat a carrot today' what you think they gonna do?"

Vince stared and tried to keep the sheer confusion he felt inside from surfacing into his expression.

"They gonna kill it and eat it, no big deal! Same thing for a chicken or a cow, they gonna kill it, same deal. But then tell em to kill a person because they gonna kill you if you don't and no, no, no! Nobody gonna believe you until that bullet's heading' straight for their brains, see? It's all in the working. It's gonna happen, you see it. People gonna try and kill you and you gon do something 'bout it." He sat back and took a sip of brandy before setting it onto the armrest of the chair and continuing, "Now tell em you're not gonna eat until this person or that person meets with an unfortunate accident ... *then* we'll see what happens, how long it takes for that bullet to go spinnin' through their skull. Eventually, they gon do it, but only once they *feel* it. Me and you, we don't need that, we see the need and we commit. That's that. They need some pushin' to make those decisions and come to our level, all the while sitting back and calling us crazy. They crazy too, they just ain't pushed there yet."

"I'm nothing like you. You're a murderer," Vince said rather calmly considering the rage that was building inside him.

"Oh, I see, that's what makes you better than me huh? Well by my count, you've killed let's see, one, two, three, four, five! FIVE people already!" he said, holding up the fingers as he counted like a pre-schooler. "That's five more than I killed to get to you!"

"You know that's not the same! You sent people after me. I either kill them or I die."

"Yes, that's what I'm sayin'! You kill them cause you need to. But I didn't send them to kill you anyway, I wanna help you."

"*Help me?* How? ... and you *did* send them after me. You sent one of your own girls after me TONIGHT!"

"Nah, I told you, she was doin' that herself. She gets drunk and there ain't no tellin' what she gon do."

"So she just tried to kill me for no reason, do you really expect me to believe that?"

"Well you gon believe what you gon believe but I'm tellin' you, I'm the truth. She ain't got nothin' to do with me. I don't want her to get ya but I ain't got no control over what them crazy bitches gon do once they get an idea in their crazy little heads."

"So, she just had an elaborate plan to poison me because she was drunk or something?"

Vince was asking the questions and saying the words but he knew he didn't need to and even as he spoke, his questions dripped with sarcasm. He knew that Andre was lying. Any fool could tell that, nothing else made sense, not that he had to question common logic ...

"Yeah man. I don't want her after you. That's why I got her for ya," he said looking back over his left shoulder.

Vince followed his gaze and saw Adrianna's limp body tucked contorted into the corner where the small stretch of cold stone stairs met the lower level they were currently standing on. Her eyes were hazed and cold from behind the clear plastic bag that was draped over her head and secured around her neck. Vince's heart raced as he realized *just how crazy* this man really was. It had hit him a few times before now but hadn't really cemented in his mind until now. Why did he kill her? Did he really kill her out of some sort of retaliation for her attack on Vince? No, he probably killed her because she *failed* in her attack on him. Was that it?

"See man, I got your back."

He was lying. He had to be.

"Why did you do that?" Vince asked rather flatly. There was no need to explain the simplicity of the question other than exactly what it was - a question as to why he had murdered another human for nothing.

"I didn't do it. I dunno who did it but I said I got your back. She ain't gonna try and kill my new lieutenant."

"New lieutenant! Do you even understand why I'm here?" Vince asked now becoming simply frustrated at this man's idiocy.

"Nah man, you came here 'cause you think I did something I didn't do! I ain't got nothing to do with it. It's between you and the big man, not me."

"It's between me and all of you that decided to murder my wife then try and kill me!" Vince almost shouted.

"Nah, see you're confusin' yourself again. It's got nothing to do with me. Me n my click, we just chill, we ain't got nothing against you."

"I don't care," Vince stated no longer interested in this little game of 'I'm so innocent'. It had almost worked for a fraction of a second but now it was getting excessive and contradictory. He was there for one reason and one reason only.

"C'mon man I'll prove it to ya," The Pimp said extending a hand, angled more for a slap and a friendly hug than a handshake.

Vince, a little apprehensive, had nothing left to do; no more words left to say, no actions left to consecrate. So, he leaned forward a bit to grab The Pimps hand and prepared himself as he actually made a (feigned for the sake of curiosity) motion of compatibility towards this utmost of enemies.

As he grabbed The Pimp's hand to shake it, deciding to forgo any further benevolent embracement, his hand was jerked forward and his body pulled into a knife The Pimp had retrieved with the other hand and was extended upwards. Twisting around and narrowly missing the severed edge, Vince elbowed Andre in the face, breaking his nose and sending blood oozing out of his flaring nostrils that almost blended against his dark skin.

He loosened his grip on Vince's hand and Vince took the opportunity to jump back a bit. He retrieved his own knife from the holder from his inner jacket pocket as Andre stumbled to his feet, staring out at Vince from one broken lens on his sunglasses. His eye was stark white in comparison to its centre and surroundings and revealed nothing but demented rage. The two glared at each other for a moment while circling round before The Pimp lunged forward with a swing as Vince dodged it and sliced the back of his arm as it passed him.

"AH! YOU! I told you, you not gon win ma'fucka," he yelled as he jumped spastically at Vince again with another swing this time connecting his blade with Vince's collarbone.

Vince let out a roaring scream, the stinging pain shot up his neck as the metal scraped the bone slightly below his skin and blood trickled down from the wound staining his cut open jacket and white shirt.

Focusing his eyes back on The Pimp, he would not lose concentration, this man would not win. He had the disadvantage of being totally deranged, there was no way Vince was about to lose all he had worked for to this guy. Not now. The Pimp sat across from Vince breathing heavily as he hunched over slightly in position to attack. Vince stepped back a bit as Andre inched forward. Keeping their eyes locked on each other's, they both waited for who would attack next.

Andre was the first to flail his blade in Vince's direction. Vince grabbed the attacking hand, thrust it to the side and punched The Pimp in the face three times with his empty hand before he writhed lose and fumbled around to get away. Grabbing the thick stone railing at the very back of the house with one hand and pulling his glasses off to wipe the blood away with the other, Andre looked as though he wasn't quite sure what was going on. Vince saw the opportunity and lifting his thigh sideways he kicked The Pimp in the jaw sending him flying back and tripping over the waist-high railing. The crazed scream that was released actually sent a chill up Vince's spine as he heard The Pimp's body smack the cement six storeys below.

Vince slowly made his way to the edge where Andre's blood soaked hands had left a stain mere seconds ago, and peered over the edge. Lying contorted on the ground below, Vince couldn't see everything in the dimmed light of the backyard but he could make out the red pool that grew around his head on the concrete patio signifying he was in fact dead and not merely crippled.

The irony of the situation didn't escape him. The Pimp had helped to throw Vince out of his home and now it was his turn to be thrown from his house. Vince, remembering there was still a party full of people downstairs that would find The Pimp's corpse any second, turned around and started for the door that would lead to the stairs going back down as fast as he could. Even with this thought that should have struck severe anxiety into him, considering he was six stories away from getting out before somebody who had inevitably heard the scream would find Andre and call the police, Vince was deliriously ecstatic. He had knocked another name off his list. This was almost too easy and he had to remind himself to keep his ego in check and not to get overconfident. Yes, he had managed to kill three leaders of the most tyrannical and notorious gang in the country but they could easily have a trick up their sleeves.

184

Rushing back down the stairs, flight after flight, Vince tried to keep the smile that was threatening to emerge off his face and his head down as he hastily passed by other partygoers. Some noticed the blood on the cut of his jacket and whispered to their friends but Vince kept calm and continued on, pretending nothing out of the ordinary had happened or was currently happening. Now that he had killed The Pimp, the next person to find would be The Dealer, but how? He had no information on him at all and no leads. It would take a miracle at this point to locate him; a miracle that he had no idea was right around the corner.

Vince managed to make it down to the main marble foyer and out the doors without a single incident before he heard someone scream from within the recesses of the ground level just as the door shut behind him. 'Perfect timing,' he thought. Knowing full well why they were screaming, he felt no need to linger and thus, continued onward on his journey as nonchalantly as physically possible while trying to escape the gruesome scene he had just created.

Chapter 15 - *The Axis Allies*

Vince walked along a familiar street from his high school days looking around for something. He wasn't sure what, but something. Suddenly in the dark of dusk he saw one of his old friends, Sasha, in the distance walking towards him on the sidewalk. She was wearing her usual jeans and club style shirt combo with a pair of flats and had her blonde hair down and straight. Vince started walking towards her and knew she could help him find whatever it was he was looking for. The sky emanated a dark purplish red hue from the already set sun behind him in the distance and directly opposite, behind Sasha, the sky was dark and dotted with stars that hung in the powerful glow of the full moon.

Vince increased his speed to cover more ground than she did seeing as they would be going back in the direction she was coming from anyway.

"Hey, what are you doing here?" Sasha asked upon joining paths with Vince.

"I'm looking, come on lets go."

"Where are we going?" Sasha inquired somewhat nastily as Vince continued past her.

"We're gonna find that house!"

"Oh, ok ..."

Sasha walked beside Vince on the sidewalk. The direction they were headed in was the straight line they took on their way to high school when they were younger. They passed silently by houses and side streets until they crossed over a flowing river, the sound of the trickling water running into the quiet night. They stopped for a moment and looked down into the blackened water at their reflections in a calm spot on the surface for a bit then continued on.

"Here it is!" exclaimed Vince, pointing at a house to their right. It loomed in the darkness and Vince stood beside Sasha for a moment staring at it from the sidewalk. He walked over the grassy yard to the front door that sported a brassy number 11 upon the old white painted wood and opened it. Inside was a medium sized room that took up the entire front half of the house and had a single half staircase in the middle of the back wall leading to the upper level of the back split.

There were two beds built into the back walls on either side of the staircase with thick brocade curtains draped over the sides of the openings. There were no windows but many elaborate paintings. One painting depicted the waning moon casting a soft dreamlike light over a church and the tiny sleeping village surrounding it. On the opposite wall, there was a painting of the waxing moon illuminating the space behind thick clouds above a massive city.

Both were very well done in an excessively dreamy yet realistic tone. There was another painting of a simple red triangle on a white background with a bottle of olive oil and a fresh sprig of juniper atop a white slab of alabaster situated in the middle. Golden statues were placed around the room tucked discreetly on tables. The most intriguing was a lady lying on a rock reaching up into the air that was placed just underneath an antique lamp which rested on a table that sat below a golden antelope head affixed to the wall above it.

Vince motioned for Sasha to follow him and crossed the room to go up the stairs. He placed his foot on the first step then the second and was three quarters of the way up when he heard Sasha behind him ask, "Why are we going up there?'

"Because we need somewhere to sleep," Vince responded trying to ignore her increasing state of agitation.

The second level of the back split house was only a half a flight of stairs higher than the lower level and was decorated in light and dark blue tones. There were no rooms, only beds built into the walls. Each were accompanied by thick dark blue curtains that were pulled back to show the mattresses covered in soft silk bedspreads.

Looking ahead, Vince noticed the soft light of day coming through the only window in the entire house at the end of the hallway and started towards it. He made his way past the cavernous bedding arrangements and stopped three quarters of the way to the window. He turned around and noticed that Sasha wasn't following him but instead stood still at the other end, waiting.

"I don't want to go. I don't want to sleep here! There's nobody here and this place creeps me out!" she said, exasperated.

"Well, where do you suggest we sleep then?"

"I don't care, let's just go back home."

Vince looked down for a second and decided she'd just complain the whole night if they stayed so he started back towards her and once outside again, they headed back in the direction they had come from.

As they continued back down the path, there were various obstacles that weren't there before, and everything seemed to be disintegrating around them. The bridge crossing the river had decayed and lost a lot of its wooden pieces, leaving Vince and Sasha trying to jump over the empty spaces. He leapt across one opening and landed a little too harshly on the other side causing some pieces of old wood to fall down into the blackness of a hole, not the water that he remembered being beneath the bridge before.

As they hopped over fallen trees and manoeuvred through crumbling walls they came across a fifteen foot glowing ball that appeared to be a very small star that had fallen out of the sky and had burned itself halfway into the ground. The light that emanated from it was just enough of a glow to light their way for the next little while. About halfway back, they noticed a group of other people coming from all directions and going the same way, the full moon still shining its light from behind Vince and Sasha.

They decided to follow everyone else since they were already going in that direction anyway. To the left of the sidewalk there was a large hill about three quarters of the way home where everyone had congregated and was watching something across the street to their right. Across the two lane road, there was nothing except a large clearing between two dense groups of trees. 'What was everyone looking at?' Vince wondered to himself.

"Want to watch?" he asked Sasha.

"Yeah, I wanna see what it is!" she exclaimed, showing the first signs of excitement she had all night.

They found an empty spot in which to sit on the hill amongst their fellow spectators and waited for whatever everyone else thought was going to happen. Sasha soon grew impatient waiting.

"What's taking so long?"

"I don't know," Vince responded as calmly as possible to avoid agitating her further. It didn't work though and she tapped someone in front of them on the shoulder rather uncouthly and demanded to know exactly what was going on.

"They're gonna show us something that will help," the stranger replied, which didn't answer Sasha's question at all and instead left her looking pissed off and confused. Vince sat and looked through the trees waiting for whatever was going to happen, the thin air allowing near perfect vision across the way.

Suddenly, out of nowhere and with no warning whatsoever, from the wide pit behind the clearing in the trees an enormous explosion of flames came roaring up into the sky. Everyone in the crowd gasped as the enormous flames billowed up into the night and faint screams from within the blaze mixed with the blaring climax of Orff Carl's 'O'fortuna' as it began playing.

"Sors Salutis et virtuosi," The flames continued to rage upwards as the music grew louder, "michi nunc contraria! EST AFFECTUS, ET DEFECTUS SEMPER IN ANGARIA!"

Then, just as fast as they came, the flames and music that had terrified everyone watching from the hill, halted and through the clearing between the still alive trees was a perfectly clear, smokeless view of downtown Toronto. The tall buildings glistened in the night with the CN Tower to the far right of everyone's view between the trees. Vince and the other citizens fell quiet as they all gazed up at the sparkling city.

Just then, it was revealed to all who were sitting on the hill that they were in fact in the newest, most technologically advanced movie theatre. The ground below them seemed to melt away, turning into seats and the space between the trees revealed itself to be the screen on which they would be viewing whatever movie it was they were all waiting to watch. 'A most impressive illusion,' Vince thought to himself. Even Sasha was sitting on his left side now instead of his right where she had been moments earlier. The outside aisles glowed green along their length and a large green drawn star spun around upon the screen as a preview while the movie was waiting to start.

*

Vince awoke in his suite back at the Waldorf Astoria. A smile came across his face that was at present half buried in the plush white pillow.

The summer sun's rays peeked in through the crack in the curtain, reminding him that it was going to be a good day. Last night he had accomplished phase three of his five point plan and he couldn't feel better. He felt invincible. His dreams provided a nice escape to another world, like an obscure vacation where he was never certain whether he would be thrust into an unpredictable realm of darkness or find himself wandering through an intensely bizarre sub-reality like last night.

Each one felt like an extension of his life in the real world and even though they seemed to have no connection to the real world in any way shape or form, they served to fuel his ambition and ideas while forging new perceptions. He never took them seriously, but they were certainly amusing enough and provided creative entertainment he knew he wouldn't be able to find anywhere else, even in the best, most vivid movies.

Other people constantly told him that they could never remember their dreams or that they were either horrible or boring and next to nobody said that they remember dreaming in full colour. Even the people who did constantly remember their dreams and felt it necessary to share, usually had dreams that closely mimicked their real lives with only one small thing being out of the ordinary like a relatives changed persona or the size of their house. Not too many people, to his knowledge anyway, created full blown separate worlds in their heads full of vivid imagery and intense yet random plot lines. Vince had been astonished to learn that this was not normal and when he thought about it, he realized they had only really began to increase in their inertia after Vanessa's death. He wouldn't allow himself to think too much about why that was however.

He pushed back the heavy down filled comforter and pulled his warm, half naked body upright. His clothes were tangled on the floor and he hadn't yet disposed of the bloodied shirt and jacket. 'I should probably get on that in case the police show up asking questions,' he reminded himself. The room was slightly cooled, though being a native of Los Angeles, the heat of the New York summer didn't bother him.

He walked through the lounge area into the small kitchen which was actually just the other half of the sitting room and turned on the coffee maker. No point in being disrupted by room service just yet. Grabbing the porcelain handle, he led himself into the seating area and plunked down on one of the beige seats with carved oak trim, sipping his morning beverage.

His mental checklist was becoming shorter and shorter. The Knife Fighter, The Marksman, and The Pimp were all dead now and he only had two leaders left. Past the halfway point, he had overcome many of the obstacles they placed in his way and yet it still seemed to be going along too smoothly. The surprising part was how easy the leaders were to kill. As if all the hype about their status was more challenging to compute mentally and defeat than the actual entity in the flesh.

They invoked fear in their subordinates and the nation alike but when it came right down to it, when all the illusions had dissipated and all the obstacles they had conjured were removed, he realized that there really wasn't anything to be feared. He was after all, the same physical being as they were; made of the same elements - the same flesh, the same bones and the same blood.

The ringing of the old fashioned golden phone with ivory coloured base interrupted his thoughts and he set his coffee on the glass table in front of him as he reached for the receiver.

"Hello?"

"Good Morning Sir. I have a call for you at the front desk. The man refused to give his name but insisted it was an urgent matter, shall I connect you?" the concierge's voice was decorous and obsessively proper but it came through in Vince's mind as subtle as a bomb. Had they found him already? Should he pretend he wasn't there and simply leave? It must be them! It has to be. His heart raced behind his ribs, pounding against them rhythmically as he tried to mutter something coherent.

"Yes, um, sure, that's fine," he stuttered, figuring if it were them, they would be waiting outside for him to either leave or come back anyway, so he obliged.

"One moment sir," the concierge said before the line clicked over and Vince heard ringing on his side, 'Was it supposed to do that?', then a voice on the other end.

"Hello?"

"Hello, who is this?" Vince asked immediately.

"A friend. Is this Vincent Torres?" the voice asked nervously and Vince got the distinct impression that this man was actually as anxiety riddled as he was himself to be speaking with him, so he answered honestly.

"It is. Who is this?"

"You don't know me but I've heard about you and what you've been doing."

Vince was shocked into silence. His escapades had certainly found their way into newspaper headlines the world over as well as on TV. The reporters never failed to mention who it was that was actually being killed along with their notoriety, as it was sure to be big news. What nobody had mentioned or even made any logical guesses at, let alone figured out, however, as far as he knew anyway, was who was committing these acts of vigilantism. How did this person, whoever they were, know it was Vince's endeavours that were making front page news? He decided to play it cool, figuring this person either already had concrete evidence because they were involved in the gang themselves or they were fishing for an answer to confirm a guess they had made.

"What exactly are you referring to? I've been working a lot lately."

"I mean your attacks on the Daravians' leaders. I know it's you that's doing it. Don't worry though, I want to help you," he added quickly.

Realizing that this person most likely did have evidence considering their persistence Vince had only one very logical question left.

"Why?"

"I can get more into that when we meet. I'm not sure it's safe to talk on the phone."

"When we meet?" exclaimed Vince, noting that this person hadn't really provided him with any information about himself in order to gain his trust at all yet and already assumed Vince would meet with him. "Well, you've already said a lot here man, how much worse could it get if you told me who you are?"

"Fine, fine, my name's Tony but I'm not telling you any more until we meet in person."

"And what exactly makes you think I'm going to do that? How am I supposed to know this isn't a trap?"

"Well, if it were a trap, I obviously know where you're staying; I would have just come over there and attacked you before you knew any better."

He had a point. Even though he would only have to call the front desk and ask to be connected to Vince Torres to confirm this was where he was staying, he wouldn't necessarily know what room. But The Daravians had found him in a bulk food store in Denver; a hotel room surely wouldn't pose any challenge to them.

"Alright then, where do you want to meet?" Vince asked with few options left. Even if it really was a trap of some sort, he would just misdirect them and take them down as he did the others. 'If I could overcome three of the leaders already, then these goons would surely be no problem. Especially seeing as there would be no need for dramatic small talk to distract me,' he thought, recalling The Pimp's maniacal narration from the night before.

"Central Park, there's an entrance from 5th Ave that will lead to a small enclave after about a ten minute walk. There you will find a small wooden gazebo, can't miss it. Meet me there in half an hour."

"Alright, but try anything and you do realize there would be witnesses at this time of day, so don't be stupid," Vince said, leaving out the small detail that he would be armed even though he figured it was pretty much a given.

"Yeah, see you in thirty," Tony said as he clicked the phone off.

This was certainly interesting. Vince had run out of resources to locate and kill the two remaining, and by far the most elusive, of the five leaders. This stranger might help, no matter how small a help it might be. He had to remember not to get his hopes up too high but this person had chosen a spot open to public perception to meet and this indicated to some degree that he was serious in his intentions to do nothing more than talk. Vince had his usual list of requisite uncertainties flood his mind once more after hanging up but there was no time to reconsider. He had very little time to shower, get dressed and make his way to the park. Deciding to forego the shower as he didn't have the luxury of time, he tugged on a pair of black dress pants with a grey acid washed cardigan over a white dress shirt, threw his knife in his pocket and headed out the door.

The rays beamed into Vince's eyes and he reached for his Versace glasses to shield them. The strong sun provided a feeling of contentment as if everything was now going his way, but it was a bit too much physically for his eyes to take. The tinted glass provided hazy relief from the rays. He rushed down and crossed over when he got to 5th Ave. He saw the entrance to Central Park that he assumed 'Tony' had mentioned, not because he had actually described the wrought iron gate pushed open between two red brick pillars, but simply because it was the closest entrance to the park from his hotel. Walking down the middle of the paved path, Vince kept an eye open for someone who looked out of place or suspicious.

The lush leaves suspended from heavily barked branches of the large oaks lining the path provided a spotted canopy overhead and freshened the air from that in the heart of the bustling city, like he had stepped right from city to forest in another world. Dappled sunlight danced on the path before him as the leaves moved in the breeze. Without even realizing how far he had come already, Vince looked up to see the wooden octagonal roofed gazebo that 'Tony' had mentioned; only it was empty.

He looked at his watch, becoming slightly more nervous. It was 3:17, precisely 25 minutes since Tony had called. Vince looked around for someone he might recognize or looked like they were waiting for someone from a safer distance. There was nothing, just people out for afternoon walks with their partners, dogs or children. He walked up the small path that led to the wooden structure with dense greenery behind and above it, up the three steps and sat on the far side so he could sit and look out over the path from which he came.

He waited for a few minutes watching diligently over each person that passed, wondering if any of them would turn around and approach him. Had he been stood up? Glancing through the crystal on his wrist, he read 3:26. Maybe he was in the wrong spot. Just then, a black man, whose body language betrayed any thoughts Vince had of someone on the attack, came around from behind the gazebo out of the forest. He rounded the corners of the structure with his head down, started up the stairs and sat beside Vince with his hood over his head, not uttering a word.

Seeing no other reason for this oddball's appearance, Vince looked at him and asked rather blatantly, "Are you Tony?"

"Yeah," the man replied, head still bowed and face barely showing.

"So then, you know who I am. Let's get to the point; what did you want to talk to me about?"

The African American man reached up and removed the hood, revealing a slashed scar extending from his upper left forehead down over his right eye and onto the far side of his right cheek in a diagonal line as he pulled the black material from his head. 'So that was the reason for the hood,' Vince thought. The expression on 'Tony's' face was not as timid as his body language had implied but rather quite angry and teetering on the verge of seething. He looked up at Vince and spoke.

"I want to help you."

"Yeah, you mentioned that on the phone, but why? Who are you?" Vince asked.

"Well, my names not actually Tony, its Bale ... Bale Sharpe," Vince's expression revealed that he was already aware of this and Bale continued, "And to put it simply, I'm a former member of your favourite group of people."

Vince was more shocked than he had been in a long time. He had been expecting a police officer or an ex-officer who had been removed from duty after taking on the gang or at the very least, a victim of the gangs brutality who happened to be holding information on their whereabouts. Not a member, but wait, he said *former* member ... why? How does one become a former member? Wouldn't they kill him? He wondered this, but had a more important question to ask.

"So, you didn't really answer my question. Why do you want to help me?"

Bale breathed in deeply and calmed himself slightly before replying.

"I've known about you from the beginning." It was Vince's turn to be the one in a state of utter fury as well as confusion. "The night Jamie went to your house, he told us he found some new millionaires house that he could hack into because of the pin pad on your front door. I told him not to do it, that it wasn't an official job and that he would get in deep trouble if he went through with it behind the leaders backs ..."

Vince interrupted, "Why would that be a problem for him? You guys are gangsters ... aren't you supposed to do shit like that?"

"The lower guys can do petty shit like that pretty much whenever they feel like it, yeah, but we had to obey strict orders. The only attacks, jobs or whatever that we were supposed to carry out were specific orders or requests from the leaders." Vince looked confused yet intrigued as he realized that these people may be more highly organized than any thoughts he had previously entertained. Vince watched Bales expression change slightly as he continued, "Anyway, Jamie went behind their backs. At first, the leaders and other members blamed you for simply murdering him. I knew, of course, that he went behind their backs, so I told Andre and Rick and they lost it on us; said we turned on them and compared us to a guard dog gone bad or something ..."

"Wait, wait, wait ..." Vince interrupted again, "Us? ... who's us?"

"Me and my ... group I guess you could call it. It's nothing official so there's no real name for it but we sort of work freelance for the leaders doing stuff they want done whenever they want it done. We're all tight though, so they blamed all of us for being in on it with Jamie. The heat was going to come down hard on them because all of the press that Jamie's little escapade had caused, and they were pissed. In addition to that, the entire gang was in an uproar over you killing Jamie, so they made us, and you, the scapegoat ... that way the members were mollified while simultaneously putting a target on all of our backs without having to offer up any cash for the hits."

Vince had never imagined anything like this had taken place without him knowing.

"How did they make everyone believe that I was the one to blame for Jamie's death when he was the one who broke into *my* house and killed *my* wife first? And come to think of it, how did they blame *you*? You had nothing to do with it whatsoever ..."

"I dunno man, possibly cause they're the ones that everyone listens to, or maybe because they're just good. I really haven't got a clue."

"So, wait a second, you said 'us', where are these other people? Did they get killed by the other members?

"Nah man, we all made it. Luckily we found out what they were up to before they got us. The leaders let us go so someone else would do their

196

dirty work, as usual, but they didn't count on us figuring it out. We got away but we were struck from the group obviously, and chased out of our own homes. Just like you ... now do you see why I want to help you?"

"Yeah I guess so ... so what's with the scar? Is that from one of them when they tried to kill you?"

"No, Miles did that when Andre told him about Jamie and the fact that I knew beforehand."

Vince shot Bale his best emphatic look and briefly thought about everything he had just heard, trying to internalize the politics within the gang that he had been completely ignorant of. Not to mention the fact that he was surprised there were politics within a gang in the first place. These people tried to stop this Jamie guy from coming to his house and somehow actually ended up getting blamed? He also didn't realize until right now just *how* manipulative these people were and concluded even more so, that he had been doing the right thing to rid the world of them. Another random, probably mute point crossed his mind. Why did the cops say Jamie was a petty bottom feeder within the gang's hierarchy when Vince asked about him the night Vanessa died? He decided to ask Bale as much.

"Because man, they didn't know about us or what we did in the gang at all. We just carry out orders for the top guys. I don't have a criminal record at all actually and one of the other guys has a pretty similar one to Jamie's, little things here and there but nothing major."

"Oh ..." Vince looked down at his lap, believing what Bale was telling him. The pieces of the puzzle were starting to fall into place now. Little bits of missing information were unfolding and starting to yield the bigger picture that was still blurred, undefined and unfinished, but at least there was a general idea formulating, waiting to become clearer.

"So, how do you plan on helping me if you're no longer privy to their inner workings?" Vince asked, thankful for the loyal ally with a common goal but still left wondering how he could be of use given his outcast status.

"Power in numbers my friend." A dramatic answer indeed, but it lacked an actual plan.

"That's not really very much," Vince stated hoping to not come across brash or ungrateful.

"You may not think so, but that's what's really going to help you. I have information on The Dealer and Miles from before they kicked me out and with the help of my friends, we should be able to find them for you. We've been with you all along you know ..." Vince looked at Bale from his lap questioningly as Bale continued, "We were the ones who placed the sympathetic cops on your case so you weren't imprisoned after killing their assassins. We were the ones who sent the security guards after the people who tried to kill you in the hospital and told the nurse and doctor what they had poisoned you with. And we were the ones who got one of our friends, who happens to be on the police force, to provide *your friend* Jake, with all the criminal records you needed. You didn't think all that stuff just happened by chance did you?"

"Well I guess not. It did strike me as kind of weird that the doctor only took one guess at which one of the hundreds of possible poisons they had actually used. And I never did understand how Jake convinced an officer to just hand over confidential police reports. I just figured he was really persuasive or maybe I was just lucky."

"There you go, it was us, not luck ..." Bale said with a laugh, lightening up a bit now that Vince had become more receptive to him and his help. He also probably felt much better having explained the situation as it actually happened.

"So, you said your friends weren't killed either, where are they?" Vince asked eyeing his new ally who he knew would be instrumental in his victory over The Daravians reign of tyranny despite the fact that he had just expressed disbelief in Bale's capability to help.

"Actually, they're right there," Bale said, pointing to a group of three men and a woman, walking towards them in long strides along the path from deeper in the park.

Vince hadn't been paying much attention to the endless parade of people passing by on the path in front of them and these people didn't look like gangsters of any sort. They just looked like normal people, one in jeans, some in slacks and the woman, who was actually quite pretty in a sort of natural and intellectual way, was wearing a suit. The four strangers walked up the stairs towards them in perfect synchronization. Bale looked at them and nodded in salute.

Vince instantly recognized the man with dark hair and blazing green eyes. He stepped up, wearing acid washed jeans from which hung a gunmetal coloured chain, a simple white dress shirt with rolled up sleeves and a triangular tattoo on his forearm and was introduced as Mathias Mason.

"You were the one waiting outside for my friend, Jake, and I at the Philip Selur show," Vince remarked.

"Yeah, I was," Mathias responded with a small smile.

"So, then it was you who got him the police files he gave to me," Vince pieced together aloud as Mathias stood, silently nodding. "What was in the envelope he gave you?" Vince asked, recalling that he would have already had the files by that point, so it probably wasn't blackmail or a bribe.

"A cheque," Mathias responded before pulling out the same envelope, now folded, from his pocket and handing it to Vince, who looked at him questioningly. "Here it is. I didn't cash it; I just needed him to think I was only helping you for money so he wouldn't start asking questions. I didn't want him to tell you we were helping; we thought it best to stay behind the scenes until the time was right."

"Well, Thanks," Vince responded with a smirk, which Mathias reciprocated and nodded in acknowledgment.

The woman was the next to be introduced, wearing a solid beige skirt suit with a baby blue satin blouse underneath that perfectly offset her slightly darker skin tone and brown hair. She looked him dead in the eye, extended a hand towards Vince and gripped his hand firmly in her shake to let him know without a word that she was not to be undermined simply because she was a woman. Even though he picked up on her subtlety, the thought would have never even crossed his mind to think of her as somehow less human or less important because of her gender.

"This is Aurora Deloris," Bale narrated to him. "You have her to thank for tipping off the nurse as to what they had poisoned you with in the hospital."

Vince nodded as Bale had done in acknowledgment and said, "Well, thank you very much, Aurora. Nice to meet you, I'm Vince."

"I know," Aurora said with a bit of a laugh, reiterating the fact that they had indeed been there all along and therefore already knew who he was. Recalling this fact, Vince now felt extremely calmed by the notion that they had always had his back. He felt like he belonged somewhere for the first time in a long time and became instantly fond of his new allies.

Next, Bale introduced Sheldon and Parker Thayer, brothers who were both wearing slacks and dress shirts with bold stripes on them. They were obviously adopted brothers because Sheldon was black and Parker was white, although they did look like brothers in every sense of the word other than that. The confusion must have been sensed by Bale, who went on to explain that Parker was indeed adopted. Together with Bale, they were the perfectly unrecognizable group.

Mathias, the most well built of the group with a lot of similar features as Vince besides the bright green eyes and dark hair, sat on the other side of Vince and reassuringly said, "We're with you all the way."

Sheldon and Parker, the duo Vince had already figured out were inseparable, nodded in agreement. They looked a little robotic and left Vince wondering if they always thought, acted, dressed and talked the same way until Parker spoke up.

"They've tried to kill all of us," he said in a deeper and much more intelligent voice than Vince had pictured, abolishing any fleeting thoughts of half-wittedness or mechanical behaviour he had previously harboured. "But we're going to do everything we can to make sure you kill them and not the reverse."

Vince was overjoyed at the unwavering support and apparent spontaneous loyalty displayed by these relative strangers. He, for whatever reason, had a feeling that they were each a long lost best friend and that he had known them all along, even though in reality he had just met them. The sense of strength and power in the group combined with fiery ambition as well as one common goal ignited an overwhelming feeling of comfort. He truly believed there was no way that with the help of these newfound friends, he could not accomplish his goal. Even if they ended up giving Vince nothing more than moral support, he would know in the back of his mind that he was not alone, that he was not the only one scarred, literally and metaphorically by this notorious group and that he would never again be alone. They would always be on his side and they would follow him until the very end.

Bale glanced over at Vince as the others sat down on the benches around the octagonal structure and said to him exactly what he had already concluded, cementing his optimistic view, "We'll help you. We'll follow you till the end and together, nothing will stand in our way. The first order of business will be to kill The Dealer, and it just so happens we know where you may be able to find him."

Chapter 16 - *Unexpected Encounters*

Amsterdam. How did he *not* know that a gang leader referred to as 'The Dealer' would retreat to Amsterdam after his split from their base in Los Angeles? Vince had officially received the exact details about where he was staying from Parker, who had been closer to The Dealer than the other members of Vince's newfound comrades and was therefore privy to information most others weren't. Although Parker had no idea where he had a residence in Amsterdam, he did know the name of the nightclub that he owned. It was generally assumed that next to nobody knew where The Dealer actually lived, seeing as he was the most secretive leader of them all. He was not quite as elusive as Lord Deulsus, but much more secretive. In all reality, the only people who would know are people who *need* to know where he lived such as personal assistants, his chief lieutenant etc.

These new friends had something in common with Vince and it felt good to have other understanding, similarly aimed people around to support and help him. They had been run out of their homes and forced into this fugitive like state of living, just like him. Unlike him however, they were also rejected and thrown out of their gang, essentially for helping him. Much in the same way schools expel delinquent children, only they hadn't really done anything wrong at all and Vince had never belonged to this same 'school'. He had something more precious torn from him, lending him a more aggressive perception whereas they had the insider perspective.

The club which Parker had informed him about was actually only one of a series that he owned throughout Europe and the United Sates. The flagship club, Esqué, was here, in the heart of the red light district. He had also told Vince that this club was near a hotel in which they could stay, 'Luxury Hotel Sofitel, The Grand' which was along the Oudezijds Voorburgwal near Damstraat St. It was perfect, the club and the hotel as well as anything else they could need would all be within walking distance from each other and all along the same canal.

On the day Vince awoke in his suite in the sinful epicentre of the city, the air outside the windows of the long thin room was hazy. Being the end of summer, most of the trees outside were still green while others, most likely due to their own growth cycles rather than the temperature, had already lost all of their leaves. The tree just outside the window closest to his bed was a prime example, bare sticks and jagged branches jutted up towards the sky, darting through the haze.

Vince pulled himself from bed and wandered over to the wide pane of glass and stared out over the street and silent canal. With the heavy fog that hung in the air preventing a clear view of anything, the scene had a sort of dark romantic quality about it. Little cobblestone streets lined with trees that sat right along the still water's edge, a tiny bridge with black wrought iron spindles curved up into the air in the middle and descended onto the other side of the canal. Matching black iron street lamps dotted the space between the trees on the road and next to nobody wandered or pedaled their way past Vince's hotel down below. The hotel wasn't very high and he was on the fourth floor so he could still see down to the street even with all the fog. It was almost as if the fog came in, overtook all activity and left a post-apocalyptic scene on display for those left behind as it went.

Aside from the general feel of the day, there was a sense of ecstasy accompanying it. He was here now and about to embark on his venture to find his fourth target. He wanted it so bad he could taste it and was now so closer than ever.

What had occurred to him at this moment was the striking resemblance of his life at the moment to a children's video game in which the player has to fight his way through multiple levels in order to achieve what he wants and win the game. He had fleeting fantasies of his entire life as if it were a video game that was being played out by someone, somewhere on a screen in front of them and the rather unsettling feeling that his fate and entire destiny were wholly in the hands of this unknown person. His own higher reality, the real reality and not the virtual one he was trapped in. Maybe he himself was his own higher reality, playing out his actions in accordance to his own thoughts on another dimension. Suddenly fearing his mind had wandered too far into fantastical theology, he pulled his thoughts back to the issue at hand. He had found The Dealer, the man he never thought would be traceable, with the help of his new followers, and now must carry out 'operation execution'.

He walked towards the bathroom in his little abode that was a much different style of room than in America; it was quite long and thin. There was only about eleven feet from the foot of the bed to the wall lined with windows overlooking the street and canal. It looked as if the seating arrangements within the room had to be tediously thought out in order to accommodate everything into the awkward space. Nearing the in-room phone placed on an antique end table, Vince took a seat on the large grey suede sofa beside it and dialled his friends in their own rooms. 'Where the hell are they?' Vince wondered, while soon after remembering that they said they would be going out for lunch. They had even asked Vince to join them, which he politely declined due to some serious jet lag he needed to sleep off. His body had been deprived of sleep for such a long time now that it almost felt normal to never get any shut eye. So, the first chance he got, he took it.

He would have thought that being in a strange country that also housed, in very close proximity to himself, a gang leader that had tried to assassinate him would be the utmost in unnerving sleep exercises but this was not so. It was actually quite relieving to be in a city out of the country where nobody knew who he was and could not get a hold of him. Also, having five new former gang members befriend him and take up his cause didn't hurt in the relieving of anxiety either.

Vince had actually slept right through till 3:35, which was precisely five minutes after the other five had reservations, although he didn't know where. It didn't occur to him until now that it seemed like a bit of an odd time to make reservations for lunch or for dinner if that's what it was. He didn't dwell much on it though. He had a good feeling about these guys and his gut feeling, especially when it came to appraisals of character, was never wrong. Even when he had been fooled by people in the past, they proved his original inclination right sooner or later and there was still an underlying sense he got from them that all was not as it seemed.

While thinking about how he was going to keep himself entertained until they all got back, he realized he was in the centre of the most infamous red light district on earth. He laughed out loud to himself at his own dim wittedness. He had actually been sitting around for a good 15 minutes trying figure out if there was anything he could do in this

204

town by himself before he had to head out to The Dealer's club later that night.

He pulled out his laptop instead of simply going downstairs to find someone to mess around with. It was probably safer than going out and wandering around the city and risk being seen by either The Dealer or one of his many subordinates, although nobody else seemed to have a problem doing it. He wasn't sure they knew what he looked like or who he was, but he wasn't *unsure* either, so he decided to play it on the safe side.

Scrolling through, he found a site, Mismatch, which provided instant hook-ups. All you had to do was turn on your webcam and join in the chat room, look through the pictures that were more like miniature live video feeds, and if there's someone you like, speak up and hook up. If not, then move on. Enabling the site to access his information and declaring he was over 18 years of age and agreeing to enter a site containing sexually explicit material, Vince turned on his webcam and entered the chat room.

He didn't realize he had been holding his breath until the first older woman with breasts hanging in a leopard print bra, scraggly hair and pink nails came on and blew a smoke ring into the camera at him. He ignored the invite as fast as he could and kept scrolling down the list of live video feeds. Another much cuter girl came up on the screen as an attempted contact. 'Damn, these people are quick, they sure don't like wasting time do they?' Vince clicked the confirm button and right away she was off and running.

"Hey sexy, where are you at?"

"Sofitel, The Grand," Vince replied back, "You?"

"Prague ... where did you say you are?" asked the slim brunette who was wearing a black lace top just low enough to reveal the perfect amount of cleavage.

"Prague? ... I'm in Amsterdam," Vince said.

"Ha-ha, you need to select the city you're in or it's just gonna send you live video of *everyone* that's logged on all over the world silly," she replied back. She didn't seem mad, a little disappointed yes, but not particularly mad.

205

"Oh, ok thanks. Sorry about that," Vince replied back but she had already clicked off and left the conversation. Wandering over to the descriptive part of the site that was left up he did manage to find, in plain sight, the location tab where he selected 'Netherlands' in the tab then 'Amsterdam' in the sub-tab. It had seemed weird to him that there were *that* many people online at this very second in Amsterdam alone but he passed it off as that just being what they do here. Just as the majority of the windows disappeared and gave way to one full rearranged screen, the number of pages shortened from 680 to 14 and a tab titled big_hammer22 came up. Vince looked at it and realized it was a guy. With a bit of curiosity and probably to tell this guy he had the wrong person or perhaps that he was barking up the wrong tree, Vince accepted the invite and immediately a message popped up.

"Hey, what's up?"

"Not too much, what did you want to talk to *me* for," Vince wrote back.

"I dunno, cause you're here,"

'Well, that's a confusing answer,' Vince thought before remembering that this site really only had one reason for existence and that was to help people get laid. He knew this but he was mildly intrigued nevertheless.

"Ok then, what are you up to?" Vince asked figuring it wouldn't take this guy long to get to the point if he was anything like the last two people he'd encountered on here.

"Not too much, what are you doing today?"

"Nothing right now. Why?"

"Wanna meet up?" the guy asked.

"For what?" Vince asked, playing dumb only to procrastinate. It was an interesting thought to fool around with another guy but he had never really had any real urge or even an opportunity to act on it.

"To hook up man ..."

"Oh, sorry ... I'm not gay," Vince responded, deciding suddenly that he didn't want to go through with anything and feeling a little ashamed and embarrassed for even contemplating doing it. He felt like he just wanted to get away now, to just log off and forget about the entire thing but he didn't, he stayed on for a moment too long.

"So ... neither am I ..." the message that popped up on the bottom of the tab read. Vince immediately typed back.

"So why are you on here looking to hook up with guys then?"

"Because man, don't you wanna give it a try? That's what these sites are for. It's completely anonymous ... obviously you do or you wouldn't be on here ..."

"Well actually I just accepted it to see what you were going to say ..." Vince snapped back, surprised at how honest and yet, at the same time, dishonest, he was able to be with this stranger.

"Uh-huh. There's only one reason anybody comes on this site."

"Yeah I know ... look man, I don't know about this ..." Vince replied, hesitantly giving in to this guy as well as his own curiosity.

"It's normal to be nervous. Is this the first time you've done this?"

"Yeah."

"Mine too bud. How old are you?" he asked obviously not taking much time to read Vince's profile that, as brief as it was, still included his age ...

"27."

"Same! That's pretty cool, and you're in Amsterdam right now too? Where are you at?"

"Sofitel The Grand Hotel."

"Oh man, that's just a few streets away from me. I could walk to you. What are you doing right now?"

"Nothing," Vince replied honestly even though he still wasn't completely sure about doing this. He still hadn't even checked out if there were any hot women close by, but then again, this guy was obviously really into him and he was close. And Vince now had a rare opportunity to try something new with someone he would never have to see again and therefore avoid an awkward grocery store reunion.

"So, you wanna meet up now?"

"I guess so, but what are we gonna do? Or where are we gonna go? I've got other people here," Vince lied to get out of bringing a stranger back to his hotel room. He was incredibly nervous. His palms were sweating and his fingers left moist marks across the keypad as he typed. He didn't even know how it was going to work or how they would decide who took what position.

"Well, we can come here then. Nobody's home other than my roommate but he lives upstairs, we'll stay down here in the basement bedroom."

"The basement? What if he comes down?"

"He won't, just don't scream."

"Ha-ha, yeah I guess so ... Then you can't either," Vince joked back, in an effort to loosen up despite being as exceptionally nervous as he was and even with the unbidden chill running through his body. He had managed to uphold a normal conversation through the odd bodily functions and the fact that he was considerably aroused by the thought of taking a bite of the forbidden fruit.

A lightning bolt flashed across the conversation box as Vince minimized it to check something completely irrelevant on Google. After a second, he clicked it back open and another large lightning bolt instantly struck the conversation box back up into the middle of the screen.

"So where do you wanna meet?" the guy asked.

"Well, I don't even know your name yet bud ..." Vince replied back, now having a bit of fun

"It's Brayden ... and what's yours?"

"Jason. So that settles that then, how about you tell me where you are then I'll come over there?"

"Sorry bud, I don't tell people where I live over the internet."

This was odd considering he'd troll this apparently horribly invasive internet looking for random hook-ups but he wouldn't give his address even when they would be going back to his place.

"Well, you know where I am. Why can't you say where you are? We're going back there anyway," Vince pointed out to Brayden just in case hadn't even really considered it or had just forgotten.

"I know, but I'd prefer to meet you somewhere then we'll come back here."

"Fine," Vince said not really giving a damn and not wanting to spend the next four hours arguing, "where do you want to meet?"

"There's a spot on the bridge on the canal your hotel is on, I don't remember if there are more but I know there's one right in front of your hotel. How about we meet there at say ... 4:30?"

"Sure, sounds good to me ... Oh, do you have condoms and all that?"

"Yeah, I've got a couple here," Brayden replied.

"Alright, good. I guess I'll see you in a bit."

"Yeah man, can't wait," Brayden replied back before the lightning bolt struck again as Vince closed the window and logged off.

4:30, that left Vince less than half an hour to shower, get dressed into something a bit more appropriate than a robe and get down to the bridge. He could feel his excitement rising. It was certainly intriguing if not a little intimidating. This would be the first time he had ever done anything like this at all. He had thought about it and figured it was Ok because he had heard somewhere that everybody has thought about it at least once. All that aside, even if he had wanted to act on it before now, he never had a legitimate opportunity. As he got into the steaming hot shower and let the relaxing water run over him, it was all he could think about.

*

He stepped into the slightly cool air still filled with heavy fog, feeling the tiniest molecules of moisture seep into his lungs. The room upstairs was rather dry, but he hadn't noticed until this moment how much. The bare twigs of the tree that stood in front of his window pierced through the thick fog down at him and up into the dark sky. One of the old fashioned street lamps lit the small space between another, fuller tree with a soft yellow light. Vince wasn't sure where Brayden would be coming from in order to try and watch, and even if he did know, he wouldn't have been able to spot him coming through the ground trapped cloud.

He walked up to the bridge he presumed to be the one Brayden had mentioned, sauntered up to the middle and leaned against the railing, the sound of water and dirt slightly crunching and splashing underfoot with each step. The thoughts raced around inside his head. What is it going to be like? Will it be like having sex with a girl or are guys more aggressive? How long do other guys usually last? What position will Brayden want to take? Will he want to be on top or on the bottom?

The questions, while valid, were unnecessary. As Vince tried to calm himself, he reminded himself that it's not really a big deal. More blown up in his head than anything else, like the elaborate facade of fear and power that the gang leaders built around themselves that did nothing more than conceal the absence of substance. This was much the same thing. There are millions upon millions of people out there who do this probably close to every day. What was he so scared of?

Just on cue to interrupt his thoughts and save him from his own irrational mind, Vince spotted the outline of a man walking towards him through the dense fog. He could feel the muscles around his throat tighten as he swallowed and pretended not to be watching. As the still blurry but visibly well built man strode towards him and turned to walk up the bridge, Vince glanced down at his watch. 4:34, almost right on time. This must be him. The man approached and his body language was telling Vince he was headed directly towards him and not actually across the bridge. He could make out a face by now. He had short brown hair, brown eyes and a chiselled jaw line topped off with a slim nose. His glance darted in Vince's direction before turning back ahead and at precisely that moment, his body language also shifted back towards the other end of the bridge they were both currently standing on. 'What?' Vince thought to himself. 'That must not be him; he must still be on his way.'

Vince had no idea what Brayden looked like from the neck up and fully clothed. Seeing as the video was focused on his torso and the little pixilated picture he provided just enough of a view to determine that he wasn't horribly disfigured, Vince had no real proof that this was him. But he could feel the tension that was thicker than the fog as he passed by without a word or even the usual nod in acknowledgment that strangers give each other when crossing paths on the sidewalk.

He could have been wrong though, maybe it was tension he himself was feeling and maybe it was wishful thinking. Maybe it actually wasn't him and the real Brayden would show up soon and probably not look as good as this guy. No, that probably wasn't him, it couldn't have been him. He was the one who was so interested online and Vince really couldn't see his own physical features being the reason for someone to continue walking. Trying to find a state of self induced reassurance, Vince kept his eye open for anyone emerging from the fog as he watched the would-be Brayden walk over to the other side and up the canal a bit before having a seat on a bench under one of the street lamps between the trees.

Just then, another masculine figure moved forth in the fog on the other side of the river. That had to be him. 'He's just late ... that's all,' he reminded himself, trying to keep the thought of being stood up out of his mind. The manly figure strutted towards him still, passing the only side road between where Vince had originally spotted him and the bridge Vince was on. 'Yes! That has to be him. I knew he would come,' Vince concluded, a smile finally emerging from the worried frown he had been sporting for the last few minutes. Vince watched as the man neared the opening of the bridge, trying not to look as if he was waiting too eagerly ... and then passed by it. 'Shit, that wasn't him either. Where the hell is he?'

Vince sat and waited for another ten minutes, getting more and more anxious with each passing second. He looked over to the bench where the first guy had gone and sat down. That had to be him, it *had* to be. He had subconsciously known it before but didn't want to believe it. Why? Why did he just keep walking? It didn't make any sense. He was the one that was so gung ho at the idea online and *he* was the one who wanted to meet up right now. Why then did he simply keep walking? Maybe he just got nervous or something. Vince glanced back up at the bench and saw that the guy was still sitting there. Against all good judgment to simply leave and forget the whole thing ever happened, he started towards the blurred shadowy figure on the bench not even sure of what he was going to say when he got there.

One foot in front of the other, Vince kept his head down, focusing on the moist cobblestone beneath his feet as he moved and glancing up occasionally into the dense air dotted with random lights and empty branches. As he neared the bench, the guy he presumed to be Brayden had his face buried in his hands for a second before he looked up.

"Hey, are you Brayden?" was all Vince could say to him, not wanting to look like a complete lunatic if it wasn't and not wanting to sound accusing if it was. If it was, he was clearly already having problems with the idea.

"No," the anonymous guy responded, his answer coming out with the tone of confusion at the question mixed with a bit of defensiveness

211

which made it utterly impossible for Vince to tell if he was lying or not. For a lack of evidence, Vince had only one thing left that he could mutter.

"Oh, Sorry."

He looked at him one last time and even though he knew it was him, there was nothing he could say or do. Even if it was actually him, he was quite obviously having a great deal of trouble wrapping his mind around this rather mute concept in person as opposed to over a computer screen. What was the big deal? Yeah Vince himself had been nervous but that wasn't going to stop him. Yeah he had wondered if he could really go through with it or not, but in the end, he must have just been more comfortable with it and himself than this guy was. Furious, even with the points he had just made to this guys defence in his head, he walked back to his spot on the bridge and began pacing, wondering if he should just go back and say, "Look bud, I know it's you, now get over whatever little problems you have and let's go," or if he should just wait in case he was wrong.

As he was leaning most anxiously against the railing on the bridge again, he realized without a shadow of a doubt that the guy whom he had confronted was indeed Brayden when a cab pulled up and he jumped into it. Probably so that if he left, Vince couldn't chase him down to see where he went. 'That's great,' Vince thought to himself simultaneously realizing that nobody else had even come into such a distance that he could see them through the fog in over ten minutes.

He couldn't believe he'd just been stood up. He tried very hard to wrap his mind around the fact that it probably had nothing to do with him but instead 'Brayden's' own insecurities but he couldn't do it, he still blamed himself. 'Was I not attractive enough? Did I smell funny? Did I look at him in a manner that scared him or made him uncomfortable?' The questions raced through his livid mind and he realized just how indignant as well as inadequate one person could make someone else feel simply by not acknowledging them.

Hastily, he bolted back down the slope of the bridge towards his hotel. He stopped three quarters of the way across, and remembered that he was in the red light district in Amsterdam and turned back around, continuing across to the other side. He figured there was no need to drag out a bad day and no reason he couldn't still have some fun. He passed by the countless small storefronts in the post-apocalyptic scenery of thick fog and desolate streets. He hadn't really realized how dark it was at 5 o'clock in the afternoon until it dawned on him that the street lamps are light-sensitive and only come on at night time. They weren't all on, but enough were to make him appreciate the unusualness of the situation.

Just then, walking a hundred miles an hour and before he could stop to realize how far he had come, Vince looked up into the beaming red light beside him. He had actually forgotten how close he was to the literal red light district until it was staring back at him in a white bra and red lace panties. He stopped for a moment and eyed her long smooth thighs and calves stretched out behind the gleaming glass. He opened the door and found himself walking down the middle of a red lit hallway with translucent doors where you could make out silhouettes of people enjoying each other's company.

He found it odd that there wasn't even an attempt by this establishment at a receptionist's desk, and having never been to a place like this before, he almost felt like he was intruding, but then decided that's probably just how these places were. He walked slowly by each door, some quiet with nobody apparently behind them, some a bit louder than others and yet still more simply displaying a women's svelte silhouette writhing in front of a light to cast a shadow on the door.

He picked one and turned the handle, much less nervous here than he was while on the bridge and found himself standing on the other side in a room he felt like he shouldn't be in before he had time to consider what was happening. A beautiful woman with long blonde hair that looked to be of eastern European descent was standing on the opposite end of the room. As she spoke, her beautifully captivating and sultry accent proved he had guessed right about her ethnicity.

"Hey you," she said playfully as she lifted one leg up to cross it over the other while taking a seat causing her white panties to shift slightly. A little cheesy, but who cares.

"Hey, um, the door was open."

213

"That's ok, come in and tell me what you like," she responded seductively as she stood back up.

She turned around to reach for her glass of water, revealing perfectly round, tanned cheeks peeking out from underneath and behind the lower regions of white lace. Vince removed his leather bomber jacket, dropped it on the floor and walked over to the bed she was standing beside, propping one knee up on it. He placed his hand on her thigh and ran it gently down and back up her smooth skin.

She turned around and he grabbed her with his other hand and pulled her in to kiss her. She reciprocated with a warm strawberry flavoured embrace before she moved to his neck, her light hair falling over her right eye as she looked up at him with the other that was heavy lidded and darkly lined. As she removed his shirt and pressed her lips to his chest, he ran his hands up over her hipbones, over her curvy torso and didn't think about being stood up at all. What his mind offered no respite from, however, was the uncertainty of what was coming next; his confrontation with The Dealer.

Chapter 17 – *Mass Exodus*

Vibrant noise, blinding lights, overwhelming scents of sweat and spilled vodka, the slight taste of smoke that seeped into the hot air and into his lungs as he breathed in. All these things seemed to hit Vince like a ton of bricks as he stepped into Esqué, the club where his newfound allies told him he would be able to find the man aptly known as 'The Dealer' and whom would hang back out of sight in case Vince needed their help and would stay there until Vince left as well.

The club was immaculate in design and theory. Mirrors and glass composed about 90 percent of the wall space. Curved mirrors, druggy smoke, strobe lights and wildly dancing people certainly gave new meaning to the term 'smoke and mirrors'. Especially when combined in these proportions. The checked pattern of the glass floor was perfectly offset by the large sleek steel bar with a black marble top along the side of the wall at the back of the club. Bottles of premium spirits glowed on glass shelves behind the counter illuminating the immediate surrounding area just enough for the people sitting down for a drink to be able to see exactly *what* it was they were drinking. Should they be sober enough to care ...

In a separate room to the right side of the club and removed from the main floor by a single translucent white chiffon curtain, was a smaller area completely filled with white curved sofa's and beds that were pushed against the back walls in a row. The sight of this, even though nobody was *currently* making use of the beds, made Vince feel slightly uncomfortable. He figured it was a good thing that he could still feel unnerved considering that mere months ago he would have been too shy to even set foot in a place like this let alone doing so with the intention to kill one of its inhabitants. He rationalized that to some degree, this still made him human.

The entire club flashed and bounced for a minute or two as Vince stood there, taking it all in before he realized he was the only one standing still in the hustling epicentre of it all. Making his way through the dense congregation of partygoers, he took a seat at one of the tall bar stools lined up against the large gleaming countertop. He stared straight ahead into the blue light for a while as his mind went blank and entered into a brief state of lucid day dreaming. He then came back to reality and casually placed his elbows on the bar counter and folded his hands together.

Normally, having to wait this long for a response from the bartender would have pissed him off immensely but tonight all Vince could focus on was the task ahead of him. It was almost as if someone had, during one of his bizarre dreams, placed metaphorical blinders on him which remained as he awoke, turning him into an ambitious and driven killer. Each time he went after someone meant a whole new set of challenges, obstacles and traps, all of which he would have to overcome while constantly looking over his shoulder. For anyone else, he assumed this would be a great annoyance, but he had started to enjoy it, to thrive on it. Looking back he wasn't sure how he ever lived the boring, one dimensional life he had before all this. Yes, he missed Vanessa terribly, but the majority of that hurt had long since transformed into something else which he could not identify.

He sat for a while longer still before finally shouting, "Can I get a grey goose on the rocks," to an unresponsive bartender who was at present leaning over the edge at other end of the counter talking to a younger guy sitting in front of her.

Even though they were far enough away that Vince couldn't hear them it was obvious that they were flirting with one another. He wouldn't be getting his drink, or even so much as a glance in his direction for that matter, from her for a while. Just as he was debating simply getting up and going to find this dealer guy, another man, tall and fairly well built with dark hair wearing a white dress shirt and black vest walked over and slid a lowball glass filled with ice and a clear liquid at Vince from the other side of the counter top.

"Thanks," Vince said with a bit of surprise in his tone lifting the glass slightly in a salute and taking a sip.

"No problem," replied the man behind the counter who was obviously another bartender he hadn't seen.

"She gets that way sometimes; she takes a sudden liking to some new guy just about every night and then just sits there flirting with him until her shifts over."

"Yeah, then what?" Vince asked with a slight chuckle and a grin.

"Well, then she probably takes them home and rips off their head," the bartender responded jokingly.

"Which one?" Vince asked with that ever-present smirk, deciding to go along with the light attitude.

The bartender laughed for a second as he threw the black hand towel that seemed to be every bartenders indispensable tool over his shoulder and said, "Touché m'friend." He then casually extended his hand over the counter and introduced himself as, "John."

"Vince," he replied, shaking his hand ..." So, if she's such a slacker why don't you fire her?"

John laughed for a second before answering, "Because she's *my* boss."

"Oh, that sucks," Vince replied with a bit of sympathy.

"Tell me about it. I do everything around here and I can't say shit to her."

"Well, isn't there someone else above you that you could speak to? I mean if it's that bad then I would imagine someone would do something," Vince asked fishing around a bit hoping he may, however unlikely, reveal who The Dealer really was. Vince had been briefed on what he looked like but not his real name and this guy may have some idea what it was considering he worked for him.

"I would if I had any idea who owned this place. Apparently he's a very low key kinda guy, doesn't like to attract too much attention. I guess owning a club like this though, you gotta be like that," John replied.

'Shit, he either doesn't know anything or he won't say anything,' Vince thought to himself as he gave another smirk before taking a nonchalant sip. He decided to keep digging in a non invasive, more curious way.

"So you guys all have no idea who you're working for?"

"Well, we all have our theories, but nobody knows for sure. Personally I think it's this Russian guy who always comes in and spends all his time in the V.I.P. room and doesn't speak to anyone then leaves ... and he's always wearing sunglasses which I find kind of unusual," John let out in a low whisper as if he were disclosing classified information about the government.

Vince of course knew he was wrong because The Dealer, who apparently owned the club but maybe not (the extent to which their deceit ran in order to conceal themselves was astonishing to even the most jaded), was African American, not Russian. But it was highly possible that he paid this Russian guy to come in and act suspicious whenever he was around in order to hide that fact that it was really him whom they were all working for.

"Hmm, interesting," Vince said now trying to avoid the subject in case someone was onto him seeing as he wasn't getting any genuine information from this guy anyway.

"So what brings you here tonight bud?" John inquired, apparently thinking nothing of Vince's sudden onset of, and abruptly ending, inquisitiveness. "You don't really look like you fit in here, if ya know what I mean ..." he added causally, darting his glance over at a large black man on the stool beside Vince who was currently sneering at him as he pulled a small needle out of his arm which he then capped and put nonchalantly into his pocket.

"Yeah, I guess it's not really my scene. I'm ... meeting someone," said Vince, trying to not stare at the man who'd just shot himself up with smack out in the open.

"Oh, well be careful dude, this may not be your scene but you can bet that whoever it is you're here to meet knows the grounds pretty well," John replied with a look of slight worry you wouldn't expect to come from a stranger. "Dangerous world to get caught up in ... even if you're just the bartender ..." John added as he took a shot of brown liquid that Vince hadn't even noticed him pour.

"Can I get a top up over here!" shouted an older, annoyed looking guy from the other end of the bar looking straight at John and waving his hands.

"Well nice talkin to ya, take it easy bud," John said. Before Vince could respond or otherwise question his ominous warning, he was headed over towards the angry and stupid looking man who Vince noticed from his lip movement and the faint bit that he could hear had said something to the effect of 'fag bartenders' to the guy sitting next to him. Vince became infuriated at this guys ignorance and for a second considered telling John to send him over a drink after slipping some poison into it. Instead, he decided that the idiot wasn't worth his time or even his attention, since he clearly needed it more than a prissy preteen. He took a sip of his vodka and grimaced ever so slightly at the burn as it passed down his throat.

Vince hung his head to the side and noticed that a very tall, beautiful blonde had taken over the barstool beside him that previously supported the angry black guy. She was wearing red point toe heels that made her very long legs look even longer, if that was possible, a matching red mini-skirt and an asymmetrical over the shoulder black satin top. Her long blonde hair gleamed in the dimmed bar light behind and around the left side of her face, exposing the beautifully made up right half in Vince's direction. She looked like an angel atop her barstool perch as she fiddled around on her phone for a minute before looking up at Vince, who was trying not to look like he was watching her, which didn't work out as well as he hoped.

"What the fuck do you want?" she asked flatly and rather quietly considering the club was full of the sound of beating music, conversing partygoers and the occasional noise from behind the translucent curtain, which apparently had at least one couple occupying the beds since he'd seen it. Vince shot her a weary look with a slight raise of his eyebrow before returning to his equally frigid drink.

The blonde gave a slight scoff then turned to her purse and pulled out a little baggie full of chunky looking white powder. She placed a small hand mirror on the bar and dumped a tiny pile onto it. Then she began breaking the powder up into four horizontal lines. Vince knew he was staring but he couldn't help but be surprised at not one but two people openly consuming heavy drugs in a public place, nightclub or not.

"You want some or not?" snapped the leggy blonde, staring Vince dead in the eye.

"I'm fine thanks," he replied before again turning back to his drink pretending he wasn't intently watching her every move. She grabbed her wallet out of an undersized Dior clutch embroidered with Swarovski crystals, pulled out a hundred dollar bill that was rolled into a tight straw and started inhaling the powdered lines. When she was finished she threw her head back, sending her golden locks flying, mouth slightly agape and clearly enjoying the numbing sensation that was sure to be spreading through her nasal passages by now.

She looked back down at the bar top where her full martini and sparkling clutch sat, grabbed the drink, brought it quickly to her lips and downed the rest of the presumably very strong cocktail. Vince watched this unfold in utter shock at the lack of digression displayed by this deceptively beautiful woman.

"What's that stuff feel like going up your nose?" he asked rather carelessly, abandoning all pretense of enmity.

"Fucking great!" she exclaimed with a huge smile, also acting nothing like the highly aggressive person she seemed to be mere moments earlier. Maybe she had picked up on his casual tone, but more likely she was just already high.

She then grabbed her bejewelled bag, daintily wiped the top of her lip with her middle finger and quickly checked her nose for any leftover powder before leaping down off the barstool, landing firmly on the red heels that looked much too unstable to allow for that sort of movement. As she walked purposefully and confidently over to one of the black leather booths, the dangerously high heels again proved to be no challenge to her balance. She sat down and promptly began chatting with some of the other people sitting there, presumably friends but maybe not.

It was at this moment that Vince realized his head was turned in almost the complete opposite direction as his body, which was still facing the bar and holding a near empty glass. He turned back around to a position that would provide a little more comfort for his neck muscles and realized that she had left the little baggie full of white powder on the bar top next to her empty martini glass. He stealthily snatched it up as he grabbed the glass to hand back to a completely different bartender that was coming his way.

"Need a top up?" the older, slightly haggard looking woman asked as Vince handed her the glass.

"Oh, no it wasn't mine. That girl just left it here," Vince replied, motioning over his shoulder and slightly struggling for his words at first for reasons he wasn't sure of other than a momentary lapse in cognition.

"Let ya pay for her drink then left huh? Ouch," she said with a faint expression of glee as she grabbed the glass and walked away not giving Vince a chance to respond. 'A decidedly not so smart move on her part,' he thought to himself. If that had of been the way it actually happened, he could have been distraught and racked up quite a bill with other drinks to mask the pain of rejection. She, however, seemed to take more pleasure in the rejection of an overall attractive guy by an equally attractive woman, as if there was an unspoken dislike between the beautiful and the ordinary. This of course was not how he felt at all and genuinely didn't consider himself above anybody for his looks. Everyone has their strong points, immediately visible or not. Maybe someone had been overly cruel to her in the past.

He sat there for a minute in momentary shock while realizing that, attractive or not, apparently everyone is judged by the way they look, at least to some degree. He then gazed around the bustling room yet again and spotted two very large men on the other side of the club standing at each side of a door looking at him and talking to one another. The taller of the two nodded slightly and started making his way over to the bar where Vince was sitting. Placing his sweaty palms down onto the countertop and trying to look away, Vince could feel his heart starting to beat faster and faster until his whole body felt like it was pulsing in tune with the hip hop music with an entrancing beat blaring from the club speakers overhead.

The tall man with a crew cut wearing a black tee shirt stopped beside Vince, looked him up and down and asked flatly, "You here for The Dealer?"

"Yeah," Vince replied without even an attempt at an explanation as to why. What he wanted to know was how this guy knew that he was here to see The Dealer and not to just party. Vince hadn't seen so much as a trace of his crew so it was unlikely, although not impossible; that they tipped him off in order to get Vince noticed and hopefully brought to wherever The Dealer may be.

"Follow me then," he said as he turned around and started walking back to the door pushing through the dancing party people flailing about on the blue glass floor.

Vince got down from the barstool, placed a twenty from his wallet under his glass and followed the burly man through the crowd of blue illuminated dancers to the door on the other side.

"Got any weapons on ya?" asked the guy who had held his position at the door.

"No," replied Vince, trying to keep his commentary as simple and minimal as possible. The second man in the black tee shirt began searching Vince, cop style, patting him down to make sure he was not actually carrying an AK-47 or whatever it was he thought Vince might be hiding under his slightly tight fitting apparel, and stood back.

The first guy pushed the steel door open to reveal a small hallway with a set of stairs at the end of it and stood back. Vince looked at him momentarily with no response except for the expression of obvious apprehensiveness at actually having to enter this enclosed and dingy space with an utter lack of witnesses, windows or anything else that may be some sort of comfort. Unfortunately, he decided he had no choice but to step into the darkened hallway if he wanted any chance of meeting The Dealer.

He walked confidently forward, not looking back, until he heard the door close behind him and the lack of footsteps. Perfect. He was at just the right point where anybody who may be at the top of the mysterious staircase could not see him and there was nobody behind him. He quickly pulled the little baggie he had swiped off the bar earlier out of his pocket along with a couple sleeping pills he had brought with him, opened the capsules and dumped the powder from each pill into the bag. He popped the empty capsules into his mouth and swallowed them as he flipped open the lid on his slightly oversized ring, inside of which a tightly packed pile of rat poison was hidden and dumped that into the baggie as well. He re-sealed the top of the tiny zip-lock and gave the toxic mix a good couple shakes to blend everything together before sliding it back into his pocket and making his way back towards the stairs.

When he reached the top of the surprisingly long flight of stairs, he stopped in front of two more bouncer looking men who told him to empty his pockets. Vince pulled the little baggie of cocaine looking powder out first and showed it to them, followed by his wallet and a couple pieces of random receipt papers, one of which had the clubs name and address written on the back. The men looked at the small pile of stuff in Vince's hand, rather aloof for people who were supposed to be protecting the club's owner, even though they probably didn't know who it was that actually owned the place either. Finally, they opened the door after giving each other a nod of apparent approval.

Vince stepped warily into the oversized and surprisingly luxurious room which should have had a much nicer stairway leading to it than the small, dark and dirty one he had just ascended. The air in here smelled of druggy smoke, but not the same pot smelling kind that hit him upon arriving downstairs. This was more of a sticky, intoxicating scent. 'Opium, that must be it,' he thought to himself, which actually made quite a bit of sense seeing as The Dealers main narcotic of choice was heroin, which is derived from the opium poppy. He was still taken aback by the fact that apparently people still actually use opium when there's a plethora of other, more friendly and less volatile substances that could be abused.

The room itself was much better lit than the bottom half of the club. A nice bright yellow aura shone from four lamps on glass end tables that flanked each of the two large brown leather couches which faced each other in the centre of the room. Behind that was what looked to be an almost throne-like chair pushed against the wall at the back and constructed from brown leather. Two smaller chairs sat on either side of it, interspersed with frosted glass and brass sconces. 'Very nice, but a little out of place in a club,' Vince decided. He also realized that unlike most other clubs this overhead room didn't have a viewing area where the owner could watch over his loyal drunken minions.

To the left of the open space was another large room with a large bed. Damn, they sure have a thing for beds around here. That room was not near as bright but very similar in look and separated by a dark curtain that would slide along the length of the opening. A lot like downstairs, except with a little more privacy seeing as the curtain was opaque instead of translucent white, as well as the fact that there was only one bed in the room as opposed to ten or eleven.

The people that inhabited the room were not so well done up. Yes it was pretty clear that most of them had at least a little money to throw around judging by the huge gold necklaces and diamond rings on just about every finger, but they still looked tawdry.

The large black man Vince presumed to be The Dealer was sitting at the back of the room in the large throne like chair with two very beautiful black girls beside him. He himself probably accounted for half of the jewellery being worn in the room. Large rings with black and white diamonds took up the majority of his hands while a multitude of long gold chains with big diamond encrusted crosses, and what appeared to be a miniature version of a gold hubcap adorned his neck. He was wearing an oversized and very flashy brown Louis Vuitton logo shirt. To a lot of people seeing a flower and LV print on a man might make them laugh but it looked right at home on this guy. He also had on oversized black, rugged looking jeans with zippers and pieces of edgy-sewn fabric that sported yet another high end logo - Prada. Even though this one was much more subdued and only visible on a small piece of material that had been stitched on diagonally it was still there, yet another indication of how anxious he was to prove he had money.

The two women beside him were tall and beautiful, each with their own mountain of jewels glistening from almost every surface. The one to the right of The Dealer had a Prada bag slung over her shoulder as well as a very low pink satin halter top paired with an orange mini-skirt and pink canvas Gucci monogram open toe platform heels. From her ears hung those god-awful oversized golden bamboo-style heart earrings that seemed to be in every 'ghetto-fabulous' girl's jewellery box.

The girl to the left of him clearly had a little more sense about her, even though the outfit was just as skimpy. She had on a black mini-skirt, black on black Dior logo pointed toe sling backs and a wispy yellow silk top that was cut, scooped, falling and hugging in all the right places to cover up the necessities while still being very revealing. All of her jewellery was done in white gold. She wore a simple solitaire diamond pendant and diamond encrusted hoops. The two outfits they had picked were very similar in theory but one looked magnificently put together while the other just looked like rich trash. In comparison to these three, all the other people in the room, presumably body guards and The Dealers underlings, didn't make quite as much of an impression. They were all still covered with jewellery and the occasional logo spattered article of clothing but much less so than the powerhouses at the back of the room.

One man in an all black ensemble approached Vince rather firmly and said, "Take a seat. He'll be with you in a moment."

Vince looked around and noticed that a few of the eyes in the room were on him but certainly not all of them. The ones that were looking at him however, didn't cease. They kept staring with no expression at all. Vince took a seat on one of the empty brown leather couches that faced each other in the middle of the room. He would have thought there would be a great deal of tension in the room but there wasn't. The little tension that was there was probably induced by the quiet stares in his direction. He sat and watched The Dealer intently but trying not to make it too obvious. The Dealer leaned into the woman on his right who now had her legs crossed and was starring at Vince.

"Baby, get my stuff over there n treat yourselves," he said in her ear.

The woman looked at him with a slightly pissed off expression then uncrossed her legs and made her way over to the end table that was beside the couch Vince was currently sitting on. She made no eye contact with him as she grabbed a small baggie full of white powder that Vince hadn't even realized was there and sat back down in her chair beside the throne. She then reached into her black leather bowling bag that had the twisted rope and coat of arms logo in white metal on the front and pulled out a small metal box.

Upon opening it she revealed a small needle with a red cap, a spoon, a small scoop like object, an alcohol wipe, a lighter and a small vial of what appeared to be water. She placed all of the objects on a table beside her and went to work, her petulant expression disappearing in the anticipation of feeling the heroin coursing through her veins. She opened the tiny bag and scooped out some of the presumed heroin onto the spoon and mixed some of the water from the vial in with it. She then took the lighter, lit it and held the spoon over the flame, causing it to blacken underneath and the toxic cocktail within to boil. Vince watched this unfold and couldn't help but notice the irony. The spoon, probably much like her body, blackened and tarnished underneath while she was busy focusing on what was on the surface. After about

225

fifteen seconds or so, she set it down, uncapped the needle and placed the sharp tip into the liquid, drawing it up into the syringe until it was full.

After doing all this, she took a rubber tourniquet out of the box and tied it around her upper arm just above the elbow. Vince was trying his hardest not to stare at this point but it was like watching a train wreck - you feel ashamed for looking but you just have to. She then tapped two fingers on the soft spot on the inside of her arm between her upper arm and forearm, wiped it clean with the swab and gently pierced her skin with the end of the drug filled needle. Sliding it in on a slight angle, she stopped and looked down at it. 'This woman is much too beautiful to be performing this disgusting act of self mutilation in a room full of people,' Vince thought to himself. 'Maybe she's still very new to this kind of thing so it hasn't taken much of a toll on her yet, like the coke snorting blonde downstairs.'

Vince continued to watch as she then slowly pushed the plunger on the syringe down, shooting the drug into herself, taking note at how it instantly made her slump back in her seat as a glazed look cast itself over her eyes. She smiled slightly then lazily put the items in a piled, overflowing mess back into the box from whence they came and passed it to the girl on the other side of The Dealer.

Vince was in utter shock at how this made her act. He had never even seen heroin before, let alone had the misfortune to witness the effect it has on its victims. 'That's what they were,' he thought. They were victims of people like The Dealer who use it to get rich off addicts and other evil souls who use it to manipulate people into doing whatever they want the addicted person to do at any given time.

Watching the second girl perform the entire ritual simply to get high, he realized just how time consuming it was and just how much effort went into taking the drug. That's not even counting the time that these people are incapacitated while under its influence or the copious amount of hours spent trying to acquire the drug or thinking about their next hit. It genuinely was the easiest and fastest way to waste one's life. All that energy and mental focus placed on obtaining the drug, preparation to take it and time spent high simply to feed their desire, if put to actual use, could have earned them a masters degree or a promotion. Or at the very least working on improving or obtaining a healthy relationship, highly unlike the one they certainly had with The Dealer. Vince thought about all this and realized that he hadn't even witnessed the rest of the ritual yet and came to the swift conclusion that it was something he would rather avoid. It must feel pretty damn good in order to facilitate this display of dedication by its loyal followers, but still by no stretch of the imagination, from what he could see, was it at all worth it.

After they were finished and all the toxic utensils had been cleaned up, The Dealer looked at one then the other as they lay slumped over in their seats with what could only be described as a mix between a sneer and a very creepy, evil smile that stretched slowly across his face. Even if Vince had known nothing about this man at all and then seen *that* look encompass his expression, it would be clear to anyone that he was one twisted son of a bitch. He then stood up, brushed himself off and shook around in his loose clothes a little bit before grabbing the girl sitting to his right by the arm, pulled her up and hissed, "Get in tha bed bitch."

She hung her head in a drugged stupor and lazily obliged, sauntering over to the room containing the bed, pushing the curtain back and falling to her side on top of the covers. This was unbelievable. It was as if nobody had even seen Vince come into the room let alone cared that he was indeed waiting for this brooding idiot who was now leisurely making his way over to screw one of his drugged whores.

"Leave us a minute," The Dealer said without looking back and seemingly to the room at large until one of the men in black replied.

"Ye boss," he snarled sycophantically as The Dealer disappeared into the room with another malevolent smirk playing upon his face. The two uniformed men nearby closed the curtains behind him before turning back around and standing security-style in front of the dark veil.

As Vince sat there growing increasingly frustrated, he wondered if he would ever actually get a chance to so much as speak to the man he'd come to kill let alone actually do it. Was he only permitted inside for viewing purposes? It was also quite possible that one of The Dealer's thug lackeys would just shoot Vince in the back of the head. A coward's way of taking care of the problem, but The Dealer didn't particularly appear as though he were above that. Vince didn't care though, he sat for a moment more in apparent invisibility seeing as nobody was paying any attention to him whatsoever. Soon, he realized the trashy girl The Dealer had taken into the bedroom dropped the white baggie of heroin on the floor in front of the chair only a few feet away from where Vince was sitting.

He looked at it and realized this was his opportunity, so long as everything went as planned. The Dealer was obviously distracted, as was every other living soul in the room. Did they even know who he was or what he had come for? They must not have, he concluded or he'd most likely be finding himself in a very different situation right now. Moaning and panting noises came from behind the secured curtain where The Dealer was probably doing something utterly disgusting to the poor girl who undoubtedly couldn't feel a thing but had to be aware of the atrocity taking place. A flashback of Vanessa came to Vince's head and he could see his wife's slain body, lying in pools of her own blood. All the hatred, fury and wrath came thundering back into his consciousness. It was his turn for his eyes to glaze over, not because of any drug but with fire of fury hidden behind the void gaze of a predatory stare. The skin around his eyes darkened and he could actually feel the anger burning inside him.

It hadn't started this way. A few years ago he had barely given a second thought to any of the Los Angeles dwelling gangs, but now his thoughts were saturated with visions of killing every single one of their leaders and followers. After each target he eliminated off his hit list he felt an ecstasy that escalated with every new dead body. But it was short lived and soon after he found himself on the hunt once more and void of any feeling at all. Vince reached into his pocket where he had placed the tainted and poisoned coke and grabbed it in his fist before standing up and walking over as casually as he possibly could to pick up the baggie of heroin that gravity had misplaced.

Only a couple of the security looking guys noticed him get up and they stared Vince down as he moved, but didn't budge to stop him. They must not have noticed the drugs on the floor though as nobody so much as glanced away from his face as he moved or came to retrieve the small zip lock. Vince leaned down, picked up the small plastic bag and, much too smoothly for an amateur, switched the two bags in his hand before giving the tainted one back to the girl who was left behind, slouching in her seat.

She looked up at him stupidly as Vince went to hand it to her saying only, "I think you dropped this."

Vince looked her in the eyes with the best feigned sympathetic look he could muster and placed it on the small table beside her after a few seconds seeing as she was clearly making no effort to retrieve it from him herself. He then darted his glance around the room quickly trying to strategize on how to best escape if the need should instantly arise. It didn't matter though seeing as the only way out seemed to be the way he came in. Settling back down into the large brown leather couch, Vince couldn't help but to keep staring at this poor girl in the seat at the back of the room. It truly was tragic.

Without any sort of warning that he may be finished, The Dealer burst out from behind the opaque curtain like a bat out of hell, leaving the drugged girl sprawled out and half naked on the bed. He stopped and looked around for a moment as though he were confused about something before sitting back down in his chair. He then turned to Vince and stared him in the eye as he belted out, in a lazy and aggressive tone, "You the vigilante they been talkin' bout on the news right?" in more the form of a statement than a question.

"Yeah I am," Vince replied simply, making sure to stare back at him and keep eye contact as he turned to face him.

"Heard a lot about you," said The Dealer, his face loosening a little.

"Yeah well, I'd be surprised if you hadn't considering what you do and who your friends are ... were."

"Were ..." he replied slowly shaking his head slightly before a small smirk emerged on his face. "Yeah, *were* is right. They all fuckin' stupid, that's why they *were*! ..." he hissed.

"So you're smarter than them?" Vince asked, "I mean, you at least know why I'm here, if nothing else that at least gives you an advantage over your buddy Troy, but what about the rest of them?"

"Like I said, fuckin stupid," The Dealer replied, glaring at Vince before adding, "they all tried to kill you on the spot without any thought to the fact that even if it may not seem so, you may have the upper hand. Why else would you just walk up to them like everything's good?"

"So, what, you want to agree to meet elsewhere?" asked Vince, the flames of hatred still burning behind his eyes.

"Yeah mothafucka, aint you listenin'? 'sides, I don't want yo dirty ass blood all over my floor. Police'll be all ova that shit n I'll get shut down."

"Alright then ... where?" asked Vince simply, trying not to make the same mistake The Dealer was and give too much insight into his mind.

The Dealer paused for a minute, looking like the derelict that he was before responding, "The bridge out of town," he stated finally with yet another small smirk on his face that was far from going undetected by Vince.

"No way ..." Vince replied coldly. "You really think I'm as stupid as your former friends?"

"I was hopin'," The Dealer said with a slight laugh.

"Well, I'm not, you're going to have to do better than that if you want to ambush me," Vince stated with an increasingly icy tone in his voice. Knowing that simple tricks can slip their way into the equation when the victim is focused on something bigger, Vince figured he'd get him later if his little experiment didn't work. That being considered, he still had to make The Dealer believe that he was counting on him being alive to battle it out. The Dealer's face turned to stone as he said the words 'if you want to ambush me' and Vince knew at that moment he *was* going to have someone ambush him as soon as he left the club.

"So where you wanna go then pussy?" he rasped.

"Somewhere away from the cops and somewhere public. I'm thinking the train out of town, that way the winner is already on his way out of the city. We'll leave it to each other to figure out how we'll get off without getting caught."

"Sounds even stupider than my bridge idea," said The Dealer. "Sides, I'm not gonna skip town just cause I killed yo stupid ass, nobody will give a shit about you, you aint nobody 'round here ... Maybe you're a drifter who met with an unfortunate accident, who knows ..." He then paused for a moment before saying, "We'll meet at Duskins Drive, right outside of town. Walk to the end of the road and I'll be there waiting tomorrow night," The Dealer finished with an authoritative and dismissive attitude. The girl to his side looked up sombrely at him then hung her head and laughed slightly.

"Shut up bitch!" The Dealer boomed as he smacked her in the face. He then turned to look at Vince, "I told you everything you need to know now get the fuck outta here!"

Vince looked at him as he stood up, never breaking eye contact until he turned around to walk back out the door from which he came. He was actually quite stunned that The Dealer hadn't even made an attempt to try and figure out who he was. This only proved how arrogant he was in his assumption that Vince wouldn't make it to their fight tomorrow night or that he was even someone to be bothered with. This last bit infuriated Vince even further. How could The Dealer not consider Vince to be even a slight threat after he'd already killed three of the five top leaders of his gang? The two large burly men opened the door for Vince as he started back down the dingy stairs and into the darkly lit hallway leading to the main club. He passed the second set of doors and back into the grand epicentre of drunken, drugged and promiscuous partygoers.

"When he leaves the club, waste him," The Dealer decreed, looking at one of his thugs.

"Ye boss," the statuesque man replied obsequiously. The Dealer stared and sneered at the closed door for a minute longer before turning to the black clad druggie woman beside him.

"Shoot me up baby," he said with an uncharacteristically charming yet still unsettling smile. She grabbed the messy box the now passed out lackey had left on her seat and went through the grand ritual once again, tying the rubber tourniquet around his arm and cooking Vince's tainted potion in the spoon. The girl stuck the needle into his arm and pushed the plunger down, shooting the liquid of death into The Dealer's veins.

He immediately started seizing and the girl became roused out of her stupor by pure shock. She pulled the needle out as quickly as her shaky hands would let her but it was too late and he was still shaking. Foam started to ooze from his mouth as he jittered around and his eyes rolled to the back of his head. Blood was gushing out of the tiny needle prick

231

on his arm and now started to drip from the corner of his left eye down his cheek. He slumped over and vomited pale green liquid all over himself as he continued to shake. Sweat had already soaked his clothes and blood was now dripping slowly from his nose as well. Terrified into sobriety, the girl screamed with a force that shook through the building and surely curdled the blood of anyone within earshot.

The Dealer finally fell onto the floor, his lifeless body slumped over in vomit, blood and sweat with white foam still bubbling out of his mouth. His eyes remained open and rolled back with blood dripping from the sides as the little veins in them began to leak. Every single person in the room rushed over to him but it was too late, he was dead. The guards becoming infuriated and confused looked at the girl who had stuck the needle in his arm.

"You were with that guy all along weren't you?" the one screamed.

"No, No, I swear I ..." she pleaded as one of the large men raised the pistol he'd retrieved on his way over and shot her in the head, sending blood spatters all over the wall behind her and the throne like chairs where she and The Dealer sat in glory moments earlier.

Everyone in the club heard the sound of the scream and then the gunshot upstairs and broke out into sheer chaos as the drunken stampede rushed for the door, trampling one or two people on the blue lit glass. The music stopped and the thundering of hundreds of feet filled the room instead. Vince was already on his way out when he saw the two massive guards come running down and bursting through the door to the lower level as the panic stricken crowd pushed him closer to his escape. He knew there was no way they would catch him seeing as even if they had actually spotted him yet, they were still on the far side of the club and would never be able to push through that many people. He continued walking calmly but quickly and made his way to the door, joining the mass exodus of the drunken hoard out into the night.

Chapter 18 – *33 Windmill Lane*

Vince could tell well enough when he was dreaming by now and for the most part, enjoyed his little trips to his alternate plane of existence. He never started off a dream and thought to himself, 'Oh, I'm dreaming now,' however. It was more of an underlying sense that he was no longer in the physical world.

Walking atop metal plates, Vince passed through a hall composed of metal sections lit at their meeting point by either blue or red lights going right from the floor on one side, up the octagonal shaped tunnel and down to the other side. The sound of his footsteps echoed against the plated metal and made it sound as if the tunnel itself was suspended in mid air, although it was impossible to tell.

He continued on, watching the lights pass in a blur as he relaxed his eyes, not really noticing anything worth looking at and not even really wondering or caring where he was going. As he focused his pupils again to look ahead, he noticed a large black dog sitting in the middle of the futuristic tunnel with its ears perched into the air and its eyes focusing their hollow stare on him. Vince inched forward and tried to make it move by shooing it away but it wouldn't budge. It didn't look particularly nasty but there was something about it that seemed as though it would be in your best interest to not disturb it.

Just as Vince decided he had no time to try and politely get around this stubborn animal and went to shove it, he heard a voice from behind him, "Let the dog live!"

As he turned around, he saw nobody except a shadow of someone disappearing behind a sliding door into the wall he had no idea was there. He watched down the length of the tunnel for only a second before turning back to find the dog had also vanished from sight.

Vince continued onward and pressed an illuminated red triangular button he mistakenly thought was a button for an elevator to go up. Instead, it caused the large metal door in front of him to slide back into the wall and he found himself witness to some sort of gathering in an ultra modern mini-stadium. The people here looked as if they were disconnected from the world around them, void of all reaction and mentality. Before them was a large circular pool that descended down into the ground a little ways and held within it nothing more than a glowing half sphere at the centre of the concave base that soaked the inside and immediate upper air of the basin in a green light. To his side, he heard one long haired lady talking to the person beside her. He could only make out bits and pieces of the conversation though.

"... above rats, rats everywhere ... ar-ar-ar-are you going too?" Vince tried not to gawk at her apparent stuttering issue before he heard her urgently whisper to her friend. "No Sam, They're good people, all you ever hear about them is lies. Don't believe it." She paused and then continued again in a completely different direction, "I was there, in that house. I walked up to it and it just sat there. The light everywhere blinded me but I could see them coming."

"See who coming?" was the first thing Vince heard her friend ask rather mechanically.

"The randoms. They stole it!" she answered back in her unsettling monotonous tone.

He suddenly came to the realization that he had been eavesdropping on a seemingly mentally ill person's conversation. Becoming increasingly uncomfortable with the eerie direction the conversation was taking as she continued talking, sitting still as a pond as the words escaped her mouth in a robotic fashion, Vince continued on and took a seat at the back of the room. Other people came down from the seating area in a sort of trance and stopped at the large basin before staring into the light at the bottom, their eyes luminescent with a green aura for a moment as they gazed, and returned to their seats.

Vince decided to have a look at it, wondering what was so interesting that they needed to view it up close and still not sure why everyone had congregated here in the first place. He didn't feel at all uncomfortable wandering up to the centre of the room by himself considering nobody in the entire place seemed to even be aware that there were in fact, other people in the same room, almost as if they had all gone off to their own little worlds.

He stepped down and could only focus on that one thing; the glowing sphere of light. Moving towards it, he maintained eye contact and pressed his hands on the thick but short stone railing between him and the depressed basin and starred at the green ball. As his mind went

234

blank and his body rushed, his eyes seemed to soak up the energy only he could see spiralling out from its centre and suddenly found himself outside in the water.

The lagoon was clean and crystal clear. The bright blue sky and light of mid day sun provided unobstructed views of the neighbouring hills dotted with homes and cottages. Even though he was easily eleven hundred yards from any shoreline in the bay, the water was only calf deep and very warm. He looked down into the water and started picking out the oddly shaped rocks from the sandy bed and collecting them in his pocket. Up in the topaz blue sky were the blaring sun to the right and the near full moon to the left, like eyes watching over him.

'It must be about noon,' he concluded, considering the sun hadn't made it any farther west yet. Following the suns predetermined path, he gazed out over the open ocean then glanced down again to find another oddball rock. He was going to have quite a collection by the time he was done. Turning around, he looked at the mountainous land to the north and tried to locate his house amongst the green tree covered hills. No luck. 'Maybe I don't have a house here,' he thought rather arbitrarily, not placing too much credence on the misplaced property as he pivoted a hundred and eighty degrees and went back to his search.

There was a small crawfish crawling along the seabed and he reached down to scoop it up, water rushing out of his hands from either side as the tiny creature flipped around on his palm. Vince looked up to the sun directly in front of him as he felt the warm rays escape from behind a tiny cloud that had momentarily blocked their way. The rays enveloped his body and melded with the warm breeze that blew on his left side from the clear skies. He allowed the little crustacean to return to its home under the glasslike water and at that moment he felt completely fulfilled here, like he could sit calf deep in his natural oasis forever in a state of endless rejoice.

*

Vince and his crew drove along the endless stretch of tree lined highway through the Hamptons as the sun beamed overhead in the crystal clear blue sky and the air rushed around him in Bale's new Mercedes-Benz CLK 63 AMG on their way to their rental house. He knew that it was about another 10 minute drive to get there after they got off Montauk Highway. The fresh warm air and bright sun felt magnificent and Vince couldn't keep the smile off his face that was pressing his Margiela shades a little higher into his forehead than normal.

The Dealer, whose name Vince still didn't know despite police reports and former members that were now friends at his side, was dead and knocked off the list. When he thought about it, Vince didn't care that he remained nameless. The Dealer didn't deserve a name based on the display Vince had witnessed while face to face with him. What he did care about however, was how easily he seemed to be crossing off names on his hit list but he passed that off as the effects of destiny taking over and the power of good over evil. It felt amazing nonetheless and as he gazed at the green trees buzzing by in whipped flashes, he reminisced about how far he had come already. He had evaded assassination attempts three times already ... well, four if he counted the prostitute at Andre's party, and he had knocked off four, FOUR, of the five leaders of the most destructive and violent gang in America, if not all the America's.

Vince had an odd feeling that he had no idea what he was in for with the last, most elusive and powerful of them all. But at the same time he never imagined in a million years he could have accomplished all that he had up until now if he had of been asked about a theoretical situation like this a few years back. This grand journey of his was shaping up to be a serious example of mankind's power of focus and desire. Vince's exuberance in the matter kept him pressing forward in the face of death and danger in this obscure, bizarre and foreign world. It was incredibly liberating to see it was all paying off.

"So man, where's this guys house we're goin to? We've been drivin' forever," Sheldon whined.

"We're not going to Miles' house just yet or we would have stopped back in Bridgehampton," Vince responded.

"What?! So where the hell we goin' dude?"

"We're going to a rental house I got us out here ... the party's not till tomorrow night so we needed somewhere to stay." Vince paused for a second before wondering aloud, "Did you not know where Miles lived or where we were going this whole time?"

"No brotha! Nobody knows that shit!"

"Well, how did you think we found him? Somebody obviously knew …" Vince said playfully, at which point Mathias and Bale both raised their hands and eyebrows and peered at Sheldon.

"Whatever man, I aint know nothing about no Miles' house man, he's all over the place," Sheldon huffed as he crossed his arms and turned his head away from Vince and out to the road from the convertible. Vince laughed light-heartedly and looked to Bale in the driver's seat.

"I think we have to turn up here bud," he said, looking at the GPS realizing that Montauk Hwy turned into Woods Lane out of nowhere then at a bend proceeded to change its name yet again to Main street although it was still generally known as Hwy 27.

"I know that! You think I don't know where I'm goin?"

"I'm just making sure. You're not the best with directions."

"Not the best with directions? *Not the best with directions?!* What the hell man, why you gotta go and assume that? And if I'm so bad with directions then why don't you drive?" Bale shot back, half angry and half joking. It was too beautiful a day and everything had been going way too smoothly lately for any of them to be seriously angry but he still got a little ticked.

"Because it's *your* car! …" Vince reminded him of when they all started their drive from NYC, Bale insisted that 'nobody but him is gonna be drivin' his wheels.'

"Whatever man …"

Vince chuckled a bit to himself again at his group's short fuses but didn't take anything to heart at all. They drove along for a while longer before Mathias, still engrossed in the book he'd been glued to every time he had a chance and who was struggling against the wind to keep the pages down in order to actually read it, exclaimed, "You need to get off here Bale!"

Bale looked around a little frantically and Vince reminded him, "Turn right here, right onto Dunemere Lane."

"I know! ... Shit!" Bale said as he swerved across two lanes and pulled quickly into the last bit of turning lane that started to split off, passing over a bit of the divided section and almost hitting grass. Vince turned his head to Bale and even from behind the sunglasses and without him saying a word, Bale reacted.

"I know man, damn, it doesn't mean I'm not good with directions … I was distracted s'all."

"Distracted?" Vince laughed, "by what, the trees?"

"Nah man, distracted by the beautiful weather we've been blessed with …" he replied assertively as if this was a more than suitable answer that completely settled the matter, which only made Vince smirk and lean back in his seat. Bale then turned back to Mathias and bellowed, "How the hell did you see that man? You haven't looked up from that book once the whole trip!" He was obviously a little unnerved by the fact that somebody who *actually hadn't* been paying attention knew when to turn and he didn't.

"I dunno, just did," Mathias responded, still not looking up.

"Put that down man. That's like the tenth time you've read that one!"

"Eleventh," Mathias corrected, "but it's addictive. I swear it's the most interesting thing I've ever read."

"Whatever man …" Bale said, thinking he had now successfully changed the topic before Vince brought him back to it.

"Here, after Egypt Lane, Dunemere turns into Further Lane," Vince reminded, to which Bale pretended to ignore him but was caught trying to catch a glimpse of the road signs.

They passed the Maidstone club and turned right down Windmill lane. The street became smaller, only two lanes now and boasted large gated properties with large white estates and enormous cottage style homes, some hidden behind large oaks and some blatantly on display. As they neared the end of the road that stopped before the Atlantic, they pulled up to a house with a decorative stone labelled '33 Windmill Lane' and pulled into the long driveway between the two light grey brick pillars to which the carved stone was affixed. They passed slowly by the large manicured lawn in silence, the green grass creating a starkly beautiful contrast against the blue summer sky, before circling around in the large oval driveway and staring up at the large A-frame cottage style house.

"This place is amazing!" Mathias exclaimed, looking up from his book for the first time at the massive two story house with a large grey brick chimney on either side of the long estate.

"How much was this place?" Sheldon asked, hopping out of the back seat without even opening the door.

"Well, it's just a rental but it still wasn't cheap," Vince responded. He was happy that his new entourage, who had already helped him so much, was pleased with their new, albeit temporary, abode.

"Oh man, we're gonna have so much fun here dude," Mathias said, removing his shades as he tucked his book under his arm, closed the back seat door behind him and started walking towards the front door.

The house had to be at least 4000 square feet and had more than enough room for all six of them to stay in until their business here was done. Hopefully they'd also have a lot of time left over to lounge around basking in the sun and strolling down the private beach at the back of the yard later on. Only if Miles wasn't successful in killing Vince that is … He couldn't stop himself from thinking about the possibility. The others ran up and examined the deck and yard for a second after grabbing their luggage from the trunk.

"You like it?" Vince asked, arms opened in presentation.

"Ye Boy!" Sheldon hollered from the door. "You gonna open this bad boy up for us or you gonna make us wait?"

Vince smiled once again to such an extent that his sunglasses were pushed up his face a bit so that his eyelashes slightly brushed the lens.

"Hey man, when are Aurora and Parker getting here?" Mathias asked. In the week that Vince had spent with his new friends it had become apparent to him that Mathias was by far the quietest of the group. He was also probably the most quick witted aside from Aurora who unsurprisingly had a very high degree of intellect locked up in her head. Vince noticed they both caught on to a lot of little things that went unnoticed by everyone else. He was also the most caring, proving Vince's assumptions in small ways such as this; asking where the others were before getting too excited and even before Parker's inseparable brother had asked when he would arrive.

"They'll be getting here in my new car in about an hour or two … They were picking it up for me seeing as I had to be here to open the place up," Vince answered as he pulled the keys from his pocket and opened the door before stepping inside with Bale, Mathias and Sheldon eagerly waiting to be let in behind him.

"Suckers! That means we get first dibs on bedrooms! Ha ha!" Sheldon yelped as he grabbed his luggage and burst off to the right down the open hallway on the other side of the living room in search of stairs. It was right then that Vince realized not only how playful and innocently immature Sheldon was but also just *how* happy this little vacation home made them. Even though it wasn't exactly a vacation, they had probably all *seen* homes like this, probably their boss' homes, but never actually got to *live* in one, even if it was just for a week.

"How'd you manage to break up Sheldon and Parker?" Mathias asked with a bit of a raised eyebrow as he passed Vince.

"I just told Sheldon he'd get here before Parker would ..."

"And what did you tell Parker to make him ride with Aurora all the way here?"

"I didn't have to tell him anything other than he'd be alone with her. I think he's got a bit of a thing for her ..." Vince answered, not particularly looking at Mathias but also not failing to detect the subtly impressed look that emerged upon his face before he too took off down the hallway everyone else had disappeared into with his luggage.

The large den directly past the light airy foyer was opened up two storeys and was complete with three sets of large white double French doors leading out to the pool and patio in the back yard and housed a large stonework chimney and fireplace on the far right wall. The furniture was all light coloured and simple; perfectly comfortable and very New England/Hamptons style which, of course, was fitting considering that's exactly where it was. Simple lamps sat on white wicker end tables with glass tops beside the light coloured sofas.

All the others had taken off upstairs before Vince shut the door and continued on after them even though he had no idea where the stairs were. He walked down the middle of the white hallway decorated by large conch shells atop white consoles pushed against the wall before he came to the staircase.

The dark hardwood floors covered in high traffic areas by light toned carpeting was the perfect offset to the stark lightness of the house and decor. Upstairs, Vince looked all the way down the hall and as he passed by everyone else who had claimed their own respective rooms and had already begun eagerly unpacking like children arriving at Disneyland, he found himself standing before the master bedrooms opened white doors. He was fairly impressed, although not surprised, that they had the decorum to leave the master bedroom for him seeing as he had paid for the house. Walking inside, he himself was now a little awestruck.

The whole thing was stretched out and airy. At the very back was a small sitting area in a cove the shape of a half octagon with large white French style bay windows that overlooked the Atlantic. A set of double French doors on either side led out to a terrace that wrapped around one side of the cove and ended back on the other side. The large white bed with the most plush feather pillows and down filled comforter Vince had ever seen had a white wicker headboard and two white wicker and glass end tables supporting more exotic seashells and simple white lamps.

A built in bookshelf adorned the opposing wall and surrounded a large flagstone fireplace. To the immediate left of the entry was a large walk-in closet and to the immediate right was a large en-suite with white tiling as opposed to the cream carpeting in the bedroom. 'A bit girlie,' Vince thought, but exceptionally elegant, beautiful and yet extremely comfortable looking, definitely in keeping with the Atlantic/Nantucket/East coast thing the rest of the house had going on. The bathroom even had a couple small white wicker baskets full of seashell shaped hand soaps.

Vince wandered through the cavernous room and over to the cove and stared out past the balcony at the Atlantic glistening in a haze under the beautiful blue sky and blaring sun for a moment before turning back to his suitcase across the room and unpacking it into the massive closet. After a quick shower, a ritual of his once starting any tenure at a new living space and a half naked trip onto his private balcony, figuring he'd give his companions a bit of time to gawk, he got dressed again and started down the hall to find the others.

Parker and Aurora had arrived already and without a word, begun to unpack in their own rooms. It didn't surprise nor bother Vince that they had found the place by themselves or come in without any introduction and began getting settled. Vince called them all together into his room to discuss the game plan for the next day at Miles' party. They spent about an hour or so strategizing and bouncing ideas back and forth off each other before settling on 'plan A', that was not to fail, and just in case, a backup 'plan B'. With that, Vince told them to hit the town tonight seeing as it would be the last time they get to do so before their final battle, if not ever. Because after all, there's no point in living if you can't feel alive.

Chapter 19 – *The Ecstatic Masquerade*

Vince looked around the strange forested area he was standing in now. The blue sky hung overhead dotted with three moons in a row, each one looming behind the other. The leaves of the shrubbery were covered with dew droplets and the moss underfoot was slightly damp giving it a sponge-like feeling as Vince walked along the destined path towards the sun. There was a large green lizard latched onto one of the tree trunks beside him and a swarm of white butterflies emerged from the flora and encompassed him momentarily as they flew by.

Vince continued on down the middle of the grass laid path soaked in golden rays that beamed down through spots in the canopy overhead for what felt like hours. His white shoes and pants did not pick up any foreign objects or dirty themselves in any way. At one point, he noticed a unicorn frolicking in the grass of a clearing behind the shrubbery lined path and also passed by a sleeping lion without anxiety. Brilliantly coloured tropical birds watched him overhead until he came to another opening at the end of the mossy road.

This clearing was significantly larger than the previous one and through it Vince could see the end of some sort of ancient palace that led down to the wide river that separated the edge of the forest from the stone mansion. A bed of reeds sat along the other side and two white alabaster pillars upheld a roof that hung out high over the river slightly as to provide a semi-enclosed swimming or bathing area. Sheer white curtains hung on either side and left the side looking across the river exposed. Two statues were erected on the stone patio that sat at the edge of the water and had stairs descending into the quiet river. The statues depicted some sort of person, probably a former ruler of the strange land, in a seated position with one hand raised up beside them, palm facing out and the other hand holding a sceptre. Two women dressed in white chiffon sat at the edge of the river, feet dipping in.

Vince stepped to the edge of the river on his side and looked out to get a better view. It was like some sort of portal that allowed him to glance briefly at ancient life. Where, he didn't know but it led him to wonder if he himself could join them for a while. Just then, a large twelve foot black serpent like sea monster wriggled its way beneath the surface of the water past him and quickly vanished to somewhere upstream. Vince had to actually catch his breath and wondered if going into the water that housed such a beast would be a good idea.

Slowly, he placed one foot into the water then the other. He started forward becoming increasingly submerged, his white pants and shirt becoming transparent as they dampened. When he was no longer able to walk and the water had reached his neck, he let loose control of his legs from the riverbed and started to swim. The water was exceptionally warm and felt good as it rushed gently against him. Dunking his head under water and stroking his arms outward he propelled himself forward a little further and resurfaced. Now on the other side of the river, he was able to secure his feet to the riverbed once more. As he was waist deep and exiting to the stone stairs that descended into the water, he noticed that the two women who had been sitting there before had apparently left.

He climbed the stairs just as he saw a red drop fall to the stone ground below. Looking down at himself he realized that the water on his body from the river had turned crimson and thickened a bit. *'What the hell is happening?'* he thought to himself as he whipped around to see what he had been swimming in, only to find that the water gently flowing through the two lands was still clear and otherwise normal. He removed his previously white shirt and threw it to the floor where it immediately stained the surrounding area as the viscous liquid leaked off of it. The blood ran from his sopping hair down over his eye and he shut it to prevent anything from getting in. He walked forward, towards another set of stairs between two stone walls where he hoped he would be able to find a change of clothes, leaving red stained footprints behind him.

Being an ancient palace, inside the building was considerably darker. Two women, one rather short and stout, the other slightly taller and holding considerably less girth, came directly over to him. They said nothing but took one look at him and led him down the left side of the hall and into an opened room that looked to be a bedroom. It had an expansive floor to ceiling and wall to wall opening on the far side that led out to a terrace which overlooked the city. The room itself was very large as well and held an olden style dresser made of carved wood. The

244

bed against the far right wall was elaborate and done in lavish cream silk with golden tassels hanging off the corners.

The two whom Vincent assumed to be some sort of maids or royal charges, were wearing white ankle length chiffon gowns that hugged the waist and were outlined in green embroidery. They stripped Vincent of his warm, sodden clothes and wrapped him in a red silk robe that dragged on the floor and tied around the waist and quickly left, taking his wet, bloodied laundry with them. They didn't say a word and even if they did, there was probably no way he would understand them anyway. Vincent wandered over to the terrace without questioning the servants' actions and stared out at the majestic spectacle.

In the distance the wall surrounding the city was broken up by four towers, each equipped with a large bell on which guards were situated and kept watch. Vincent glanced down over the balustrade to see directly in front of the palace. Three horse drawn chariots were pulling up to the large staircase lined with green palms and burly guards in statue esque poses, the twelve spokes on each wheel spinning round and slowly coming to a stop. A few people similarly dressed as the two women who had ushered him into the magnificent room, wearing red robes instead of white, leapt off the back of the wooden buggies and walked up the giant stairs and continued out of sight.

He looked out over the massive, sparkling city for what felt like a lifetime before turning around and heading back inside. As he re-entered the room, he noticed a darkening around him. Shadows filled the room and seeped into every corner. Turning back around to look outside, he noticed that the sun had almost instantly fallen out of the sky and night was now upon him. Areas on the city wall had been lit up with the fire of torches, starting in the south and reaching up to the large mounds of earth looming over the city to the north. Turning back to see where he was and what he could discover here, Vincent noticed that the torches in his room had been lit too. The fires now blazed away, lighting up sections of the wall that were stained black from the soot of previous nights.

Vincent started towards the darkened hallway from which he entered the room, the warm stone underfoot surprisingly comfortable and natural. Setting out into the hallway, he knew where he had come from and thus, chose the other direction in hopes of finding something new. There was something here that he was drawn to, that he needed and was now a part of. There was no turning back. Keeping to the left, hand stretched out to steady himself against the wall in the dimly lit passage, Vincent came upon a dark, spiralling stone staircase from which he saw golden light and heard noise emanating from above. Deciding to travel up the stairs, he went around and around until he reached the top and stared down the corridor the sound was issuing from. Moving quicker now that he had a destination and turning around a corner to face the source of the light, Vincent found himself at a large wooden doorway. In front of it stood two leather clad, uniformed guards holding spears and wearing metal helmets with a stripe of red Mohawk like hair jutting up in the middle. They, for whatever reason, took one look at Vince and immediately opened the door for him while stepping back.

Looking down the stretch of stairs, Vincent was in shock. The most spectacular party he had ever witnessed was taking place. Two very tall clay vases sat on either side at the top of the landing where he was currently standing and held within them bundles of narcissus flowers, red poppies and water lilies. At the bottom of the stairs, people lounged and pranced around in white and gold silk robes and adorned themselves with large golden jewellery and headpieces. The intoxicating scent of sandalwood and incense filled the air and a light smoke rose from the aromatic sticks burning in hanging bowls suspended from the ceiling. A few other bowls that hung on chains from the ceiling, held within them fire to light the party.

Vincent descended the stone stairs to the bottom and tried to act as natural as possible. On the wall to the right was a stone disc the size of a dinner plate carved into pie like sections and upon which were scrawled numerous tiny symbols that he couldn't decipher. Probably another language ... and on the opposite, south wall, hung a dagger, blade pointing downward between two blazing torches. People danced about and groped each other while thrusting their bodies together in ecstatic rhythm as the music boomed from somewhere overhead at the back.

People chattered away eagerly to each other and most looked like they were either in deep conversation or surrendering to their senses.

Large golden platters held mounds of grapes and other various fruit up slightly into the air and brass goblets of wine were gripped by almost every hand in the room. Those that weren't, either sat on tables or were spilled on the stone floor, leaving small puddles of dark wine here and there. One woman sashayed past Vincent in a whirl of red chiffon as she made her way to her lover.

Everyone seemed to caress and fondle everyone else and Vincent found the whole scene intoxicatingly arousing. Two women, one of whom was wearing nothing more than an elaborate headdress and a stringed web like jewel encrusted bikini writhed against each other at one of the small seating arrangements in the middle of the room and sat beside two of their counterparts in guard uniforms, doing the same. Just then, a beautiful, decadently dressed woman walked up to Vince and smiled before grabbing his hand and leading him through the crowd.

"Come," she said as she took his hand gently. She had atop her dark hair a golden crown scattered with blue and red cabochon cut stones and wore multiple golden rings on her hands, each showcasing yet another large smooth stone in black, red, blue or deep green and held in place by filigree claw work.

"Where are we?" Vincent asked, somehow not really surprised that they spoke a common language, as he would have been earlier.

"At the Palace of course," the woman answered with a bit of a laugh. Vincent considered prying for more information but he somehow had a sense that he knew exactly where he was all along.

There were large alabaster columns around the room that held up the roof of the enclosed space with gold carving engulfing the rounded out base that each sat upon a stone plinth. Vincent could make out one of the five points carved into the floor jutting out from under the multiple seating arrangements in the middle of the room, pointing towards the back. There, sat a small bed like throne that was lifted up onto a slightly raised stage against the back wall. Torches blazed against the stone and a crocodile skull was affixed to the wall between a metal goats head and a python skeleton, also attached to the wall. The spread out bed like fixture was remarkably similar to the one in the bedroom he had come from but was draped in red silk with a gold damask pattern and golden tassels. Placed around the back of the opulent lounge area were large hunter and olive green silk pillows and decorative white feathers jutting up from behind. Two green parrots were perched on golden wrought iron gates behind the royal guests and didn't squawk but only gazed over the room in mild curiosity.

As the young beauty led him up to the area, multiple people around the room began to watch the two of them, obviously wondering who exactly he was. Or at least, that's what he had thought, until numbers of them started coming towards him and offering him various pieces of gold chains and coins, precious stones set on silk pillows and other valuable items as if he were some sort of monarch.

While all this should have confused him, he again somehow knew what was happening with a sort of sixth sense he had seemed to acquire. He decided to simply thank everyone for their generosity and graciously accepted their gifts. He then made his way up to the destined lounge area with the mysterious woman and sat atop the red and gold damask swathed throne with her. All his items were set by his feet and more gold lay around him in his royal perch that seemed it was only there for him. A few other men and women clad in red, purple, or white and gold lounged around the immediate area, petting and gently caressing each other as well. The girl then turned her deep blue eyes to Vincent and got behind him before starting to massage his shoulders.

Vincent almost audibly moaned in relaxation as he sipped a glass of wine someone had handed him and the girl's hands kneaded his back muscles into release. Two maids stood behind the area waving large peacock feathers attached to a pole to delicately fan the elite attendees. Vincent lay down on his stomach as he grabbed a small handful of grapes off one of the many golden serving platters and popped one into his mouth. The gorgeous woman continued to massage every last bit of stress out of his back. As he lay, right side of his face buried into a plush silk pillow, he relaxed completely and felt in sheer ecstasy as he watched the rest of the drunken festivity unfold from his exposed left eye.

*

Vincent drove up to Miles' estate as the tinted glass and metal top of the black Maserati Birdcage Pininfarina lifted up and he set one black leather clad foot down onto the stonework driveway at 11 Sunset Lane.

Pulling himself from the car somewhat dramatically, he handed the keys to the valet, put his arm on the small of Svetlana's back and started to escort her to the door. He had met Svetlana at a nearby club in East Hampton the day before as he usually met new girls now. She was sitting there and he went right up to her, sat beside her atop a high bar stool and said, "So, you're going to have a drink with me now."

"Oh really?" she snorted. "What makes you think that?"

"Because you want to ..."

"No, actually, I don't," she stated as she took another nonchalant sip from a frosted martini glass. The blue light from behind the bar illuminated the left side of her face as she turned and spoke to Vince. She was waiting for him to leave but he wasn't about to.

"Well, *I* want you to," Vincent stated quite confidently as he ordered a Belvedere on the rocks and, 'another one of whatever it is she's drinking,' pointing to Svetlana, who looked over at Vincent.

She wanted to be disgusted and annoyed but Vincent wasn't letting this go and she couldn't seem to read his poker face. What could it hurt anyway? If he didn't look cute enough in his fitted leather bomber jacket and his perfectly 'riche' ensemble, then the whole take charge attitude thing was sexy enough. Guys had tried this on her before but it hadn't even seemed remotely cute let alone sexy. More like they were trying to make up for some sort of multi-faceted inferiority complex by being overly assertive but Vincent seemed to really be comfortable being by himself and simply *wanted* her there.

She got the distinct impression that if she were to verbally abuse him right then and there or simply get up and leave, he would just sit silent, sip his drink and ignore her negativity, completely unfazed. This of course was how he felt. He really couldn't be bothered to be concerned about something as minute as an insult and being shut down by someone he didn't know. All he wanted was her, not her approval. If she were to leave he'd find someone else. It would be her loss. He'd already lost the love of his life anyway and he didn't really care that much about what anyone else thought.

"So, what? You think you're just gonna come in here, order me to have a drink with you and then you're gonna take me home?" she asked, now staring straight ahead into the blue light and avoiding eye contact.

"No, we'll probably have to make the requisite small talk first that neither of us is particularly interested in, grab a couple more drinks before we both realize that we don't really want to be here anymore *then* you'll come home with me and spend the night doing what we *both* want to be doing.

"Now, usually one or the other of us would leave the next morning but I'd actually rather you accompany me to a party at a friend's estate in Bridgehampton tomorrow. If you don't already have prior obligations that is ..." he added, looking at her pointedly and not really caring if she'd say 'yes' or 'screw you' and walk away, although he hoped for the former.

'Well, if nothing else, at least he's being honest about it,' she thought as she hesitated for a moment before extending her small boned hand with perfectly manicured red nails, "I'm Katrina," she said.

"No you're not," Vincent said flatly as he shook her hand, "but we'll go with that if you like ..."

Svetlana's eyebrows reached up her forehead and a few locks of radiant blonde hair fell down over half of her face from the side as she bowed her head a bit.

"So what if that's not my name ... does it really matter to you anyway?"

"No, not really, if you don't want to tell me, then that's your business," Vincent started, "but I don't see the point in lying about something as inconsequential as your name when we probably won't see each other after tomorrow anyway."

"That's true, but if it's not a big deal then why haven't you told me yours yet?"

"Vincent," he said now tightening his grip a bit in a motion to finish what she had started.

She reciprocated the grip more firmly as well this time and stared Vince directly in the eye as she said, "Svetlana."

"Seriously, Svetlana?" Vincent replied, little shocked. It was almost like he wanted to think this was just some gorgeous American girl taking on a phony Americanized eastern European accent and an overly sexy, overly stereotyped European name because she simply couldn't think of something more original. 'But why lie about your name a second time,' he figured. And besides, he could pretty much tell when someone was lying anyways.

"Why? What's wrong with that?" she asked.

"Nothing, I was just expecting Jessica or something like that," Vincent answered with a slight smirk before sipping his own drink, and noticing her raise one of her eyebrows again from the corner of his eye.

After some of the predicted small talk and taking her outside to his car, the über futuristic sleek looking vehicle Vincent was the new possessor of, she immediately relinquished the last few remaining doubts about him and gladly hopped in. 'I bet she claims she's not shallow ...' Vincent thought to himself with a grin.

He worked his magic rather effortlessly for the rest of the night and Svetlana was not disappointed. The next morning she woke up to find that Vincent wasn't nestled between the chic white sheets with her anymore. She pulled her clothes from their tangled position on the floor at the end of the bed and began dressing herself with a bit of a scoff at her own stupidity. Just then, Vincent appeared in the doorway of his ensuite, towel hanging off his hips and leaned his muscular torso against the frame while looking at her as she smiled slightly.

"So you're coming to the party with me right?"

*

The sprawling estate was too large to be seen in full from any point on the driveway or on the garden and shrubbery dense lawn that sported massive oaks and maple trees. Looking up at the entrance to the house and noticing the rays of light slipping through the leaves of the large trees, Vincent felt no fear. This was it. This was to be the culmination of a long and tiring journey. There was a lot he had come to understand during the last couple months, more than he had his whole life. There were no barriers to cross anymore, nothing to discover. He had seen and done and most of all, understood, everything there was to see, do and understand. It wasn't a void feeling however, more liberating. A veil had been lifted and he could see everything clearly now. Like the new land that had been completely discovered and awaited soon becoming a magnificent city and reigning empire. From the desolate ground, it was to rise up and become something glorious.

Long smooth stone steps led up to the dark finished house and two large carved stone sphinx's rested on either side of the path, watching out over the yard. Vincent walked past them and up to the giant mahogany and tinted glass door which he pulled open and motioned for Svetlana to go inside. Stepping in front of him in her black mini dress, she placed her black glittered face mask on as she set one tall, platform, skinny heeled Jimmy Choo onto the black and white tile floor inside.

Vincent reached down and grabbed his own facial adornment for the party and placed it over the top of his head and secured it around his light hair. It's safe to say that in all his years on earth, he had never witnessed anything close to this seductive fantasy. He had to second guess as to whether he was dreaming or not but eventually concluded he wasn't, although it could have easily been mistaken for one of his more bizarre dreams. He was now in a reality where fantasy had sprung to life and blended reality and dream together. Immediately to the right in the airy foyer, there were two scantily clad women collapsed on top of one another, limbs hanging over the edge of a large gold gilt sofa with black and white stripe upholstery. They were sporting some insanely high and uncomfortable although creative looking heels and a few more similarly dressed women were standing around chatting, exotic cocktails in hand.

The massive chandelier overhead flared out thousands of crystals from the base and worked up to a point at the ceiling from its four corners as it shone its soft light down onto the tiled floor. The intricately carved railing that ran along the curved double sided staircase with a hallway leading into another room situated between the two flights, twisted and spiralled all the way up to the centre at the top where the two landings met on the second storey. In the middle of their connection, two beams of gold painted oak ran diagonally up from each and met at the top. Half of a Versace-esque medusa face looked out over the foyer, embedded on the triangular piece of frosted glass that was held between the two beams.

Vincent looked up at the majestic handiwork as three women came bounding down the stone stairs that were carpeted in purple. One was wearing a fitted black mini-dress with some sort of mesh twisting around her arms up one side of her face and ended under a large black and gold feathered hat. The exposed eye was surrounded by solid black and red jarring makeup that was painted on to look like it was shooting out the side of her temple. The one beside her was wearing all lace. A full piece dress that covered everything from her upper thighs right up to the back of her neck, where it swooped up tucked into various spots in her dramatic coiffeur in a striking cobalt blue, complete with matching blue nubuck stiletto platforms.

The last of the strangely clad trio that followed behind them was perhaps more striking and obscene than the first two. Her dark curled and permed hair was swept up one side and was held there by an almost Egyptian looking headpiece. It reached down over her face covering her eyes, ending in dramatic jewel encrusted lightning bolts on each side. Her 'dress' consisted of red silk draped at the hips and fell all the way to the floor on one side and was also jewel encrusted at the torso that extended itself in a spiral pattern up to the bust line. This area was covered only by skin-tight, completely translucent organza that ran up to her neck and down her right arm where it ended in an increasingly dense embroidered lace pattern.

All three strutted down the remainder of the stairs and across the foyer rather naturally considering the undoubtedly constricting outfits they were wearing. Not to mention the heels that included sculpted platforms. The last, and most commanding woman smiled slightly at Vincent as she passed him and walked into the hallway that sat between the two large staircases, her darkened eyes still managing to take on incredible life from behind the mask.

Vincent had heard through the grapevine that Miles' parties generally looked like this but he hadn't imagined that it would be this strange or anywhere near this grand. It was undoubtedly fascinating and at least he had been told that *every* party is a masquerade, which given Miles elusive behaviour, didn't surprise him. Facial masks or some form of facial adornment meant to blur the distinctive features of oneself, was required on every guest, no exceptions. Aside from that, anything went as far as outfits go, 'Or more like costumes,' Vincent thought upon now seeing it all actually unfold before him.

He looked over at Svetlana who was standing in front of a giant duplicate, or maybe not, of Van Gough's 'Starry Night'. It was Vincent's favourite piece of art actually; there was something mystical and surreal about it. Like the stars just dance around beneath the moon as they watch over the sleeping town, drifting and fading, twisting and swirling into one another as they whisked their way around the skies. He walked over to her and upon hearing his footsteps slowly clicking on the tile, she turned around and smiled, obviously elated at the entire scene she was now a part of and probably never imagined she would be.

Vincent led her by the hand into the hallway the three mysterious women had disappeared into. Walking past even more illusion inducing paintings lining the walls, they found themselves in a large room, much larger than the huge foyer and stared out at the crowd. People were strewn about on large sofa's, lying on giant cushioned sections surrounding the room and either making out or massaging one another. Other people stood over to the left hand side of the room at a sort of resto-lounge looking area sipping cocktails that were as odd in appearance as their outfits.

People at this part of the party were dressed in much the same fashion as the three beautiful weirdo's Vincent had encountered in the foyer. A few wore all one colour, like red or black and simply painted over sections of their face with heavy makeup while most others fully concealed their eyes and or faces behind golden, crystal encrusted, feather swathed, lacy looking, or a combination thereof, facial masks. It was like a giant opera house gone ecstatically mad. Some of the men had chosen to go topless, barring their perfectly sculpted Pecs and abs while wearing large metal necklaces. One girl had a bra made only of loosely connected shimmering golden platelets and wore a crystal ball tucked into her blonde, up done hair that had glitter paint slathered onto it in random streaks.

None of this disturbed Vincent in the slightest. In fact, it was probably the most exciting party he'd ever been to in his life and he hadn't even spoken to anyone other than Svetlana yet. He pulled her along behind him and through the crowd of partygoers to the other side of the room where bottles upon bottles of liquor sat along the wall in a sort of free for all bar. Glasses were arranged interestingly on shelves that were sunken into the back wall and held up by carved wooden dragons. Vincent grabbed a glass and poured himself a shot or two from a bottle of Belvedere.

"What do you want?" he asked as he turned to Svetlana with a bit of a smirk at her prolonged and serious expression of excitement.

"Oh, uh, whatever you're having," she said, caught a bit off guard but still with overzealous excitement in her tone as she took a seat on a stool next to Vincent.

The room was surprisingly dark for late afternoon. The only natural light came from small, heavily frosted triangular windows around the perimeter of the right wall. Most of the other light came from various red candles placed around the room. A lot of the furniture was dark mahogany or oak and featured red or burgundy upholstery with gold detailing. Toward the back left hand side of the room lay another widened tile floored hallway lit by golden sconces. Some people came to and from it, never showing anything but sheer, almost strenuous exhilaration on the small fraction of their faces that was left.

Vincent motioned for Svetlana to grab the drink she had set on the table beside her and follow him into the black and white tiled hallway. One girl wearing large silver ball earrings and thigh high black leather boots with slits cut out of them all the way down to the ankle passed them then turned around and asked Vincent where the bathroom was. Her top lip was completely painted in black lipstick while the bottom lip had only a vertical stripe down the middle and made her look rather robotic as she spoke.

"I'm not sure actually, I'm just trying to find my way around myself," he responded to which she huffed and stormed away, almost sending her black sunglasses and large floppy hat flying as she whipped back around.

"This party is crazy," Svetlana exclaimed looking utterly shell shocked.

Vincent felt the same way of course, being in this odd fantasy-like place removed from time and space was incredibly liberating. The great maze like mansion was certainly filled with a magic essence, an unseen force that made you tide enormously with desire, always ebbing and flowing out then back in, edging further and further ahead for more. He showed little expression while verbally agreeing with her in his slight day dreaming daze.

"Yeah, like you've escaped to Oz or Wonderland or something."

"Come on; let's see what else is down here!" Svetlana said as she tugged on Vincent's arm to continue.

The next large room they came to at the end of the hallway was separated from the rest of the house by black wrought iron gates that were pulled open so no one would have to suffer the inconvenience of opening it themselves.

This room was similar to the others. The difference was that this room consisted of lots of modern looking boxy camel coloured suede chairs and couches all collected in groups around the room. Beside each one was an end table that held a simple styled lamp on it. People sat, drinks in hand, again either molesting each other or in deep conversation while the loud music played in the background.

Vincent ushered Svetlana into the room again with his hand on the small of her back, bypassing the impala head affixed to the wall above the door inside the room. An oddly shaped table directly to their right, placed against what would be the south wall, supported an eclectic collection of decorative trinkets. A large hourglass, a crystal sphere set in an intricate brass holder supported by three prongs, and a fair sized nephrite Buddha sat against the wall. Three bowls of rocks placed around the large table were set ablaze from within, flames flickering in the middle of the dry stone as if by magic. Beside those were antique crystal decanters filled with various unlabelled liquids and fanning out from this backdrop of odd collectibles were various kinds of glasses for cocktail use.

Vincent grabbed one of the crystal bottles that contained the unknown liquid and poured a glass for himself, not bothering to take a whiff because he didn't particularly care what spilled out.

"You want something?" he asked, turning his face to Svetlana who was watching the boisterous crowd so she would be aware that he was actually addressing her.

"Sure, whatever that one is," she said, turning her svelte body on one skinny heel and pointing to a short, fat bottle containing clear liquid.

Vincent poured it and she took a sip, grimacing slightly at the burn she undoubtedly felt coursing down her throat.

Looking around, Vincent noticed piles of white powder on the coffee tables and money strewn about everywhere. Why did they do that? Was it being exchanged or could these elite partygoers really not be bothered with such insignificant details as where to properly store their cash and drugs for the night? Or perhaps it was intended to be a blatant display of the fact that they don't need to care about where they put it for now because it would be recouped in an hour or two if it was lost anyway. Actually, it may take a day or two considering how much was there, but maybe not.

Vincent walked over to the closest of couch arrangements that wasn't already occupied and confidently took a seat in the knowledge that nobody here could possibly know who he was or that he wasn't supposed to be here anyway. Svetlana, who had been entranced with the entire scene, wandered over after him and took a seat as well. It was then Vince realized he must have left her alone longer than he thought because she'd already made a new friend.

"Vincent, this is ... um ..." she started then turned her head back to this new girl in hopes of recovering the name she'd either forgotten or wasn't told.

"Ashley," the young beauty finished.

She resembled Svetlana quite a bit actually. She had long, straight blonde hair that swept down on two sides in small locks with the rest pulled to the back and fixed up into a rolled bun that sprouted pieces of hair, fanned out at the back like a miniature peacock. Over her blonde hair she wore a draping gold chain and yellow rhinestone headpiece that connected at the front to a very small eye mask that barely surrounded her eyes. She wore a cream coloured mini dress that was draped at the hips and wrapped up around her torso and long black lace opera gloves. Mirrored heels that Vincent remembered from the show in New York adorned her tiny feet.

"What do you do?" she asked softly but pointedly, looking at Vincent. He turned his gaze back to her face from his distorted reflection on her heels.

"I'm a consultant for a law firm in New York," he lied rather smoothly but Ashley had already turned her attention to Svetlana.

"How did you two meet?" she asked after a moment.

"Actually we just met last night," Svetlana replied, "... at a bar."

"Romantic ..." Ashley said, looking like she was becoming increasingly bored with the conversation.

Apparently his inclination was correct because after a moment she pulled a small plastic bag containing five small round yellow pills sporting 'OC' on them out of her clutch. She removed one from the bag and set it on the table in front of her where she proceeded to shave the yellow coating off with her Amex before crushing it to a small pile of white powder and separating the pile into three small lines.

After placing the bag containing the remainder of her pharmaceutical stock back into her black Dior clutch with a peacock design in blue and green crystals, she produced a hundred dollar bill. She carried out her actions as if nothing were out of the ordinary. Vincent and Svetlana were now watching her intently. Ashley then leaned down and sniffed one line up each nostril and threw her head back in exhilaration.

"Are you in?" she asked, giggling a bit as she looked at Vincent who had been sitting back, watching. "Living in sin is the new thing."

"No thanks, it's not really *my* thing ..." he replied, recalling all too well the damage things like that had done to the two girls at the club where he met and killed The Dealer.

"Alright, more for us ..."

Vincent looked amused for a moment, wondering why she had assumed Svetlana would partake in her dangerous indulgence before Svetlana grabbed the bill from Ashley's hand, leaned down without a word and snorted the remaining line.

She then grabbed the rolled up bill, put it to her mouth and produced a flame from a cobalt blue Zippo Vincent hadn't seen her reach for, lit the end and began smoking it declaring, "I think I did it again ... look, there's still some in here!" with a coy laugh.

Vincent wasn't exactly sure what she thought she had 'done again' but looked at her, thinking this woman was the most bizarre creature he'd ever seen. He'd never met anyone this careless or free-spirited and yet so glamorously depraved, or maybe just plain crazy.

She returned his quizzical stare with one of equally sly resolution, declaring, "What? I'm not *that* innocent ..."

She exhaled hundred dollar smoke into the vacant space between them where it lingered for a while. A rush that had nothing to do with drugs spread through his body. The multi-pieced metallic and masculine monarch looking Venetian mask he was wearing began to feel like it was loosening its tight grip around his head. He wasn't sure if it was the nerves, the strangely glamorous party or a combination thereof, but he felt the same thrill and adrenaline rush as you would expect after the initial jump out of an airplane while skydiving or going down the first big hill on a large roller coaster. At that moment, he had a strange feeling accompanied by an ecstatic sensation that he was mere moments away from his next target, and possibly, his ultimate goal.

Chapter 20 – *The Garden Towers*

With renewed exhilaration, Vincent excused himself for a while.

"Where are you going?" Svetlana asked, now smoking a cigarette.

Vincent briefly wondered which was worse, smoking money that had surely been passed through the dirty hands of hundreds of thousands, if not millions of people and still had drugs on it, or an actual poisonous cigarette? He decided it didn't matter and answered her question.

"I have some business to take care of. Remember, that's why we're here in the first place? Now you behave and don't do anything I wouldn't do. I'll be back in a bit," Vincent said as he pulled his black blazer out from under one of Svetlana's tanned legs and shrugged into it in one smooth, fluid motion.

He silently noted to himself that it was a good thing Svetlana didn't actually know what he had done. He adjusted his metal mask as he strode away, leaving the two beautiful weirdo's to whatever deeds they were certain to continue in his absence.

The next hallway ahead led to a series of smaller yet still incredibly opulent rooms before entering into another large obscure room filled with party goers, still in keeping with the unwritten beautiful weirdo theme. All of this should have, in theory, seemed like a hapless mishmash of freaks in unsuitable-for-everyday clothing, but it didn't. It all flowed and melded together into a collective masterpiece. Maybe they had all visited the same stylist before this that knew who would be wearing what, and what pieces to put with what so as not to appear as the frenzied mess Vincent thought something like this should have ended up as under normal circumstances where everyone is left to their own devices.

He continued past the crazy guests; various topless men and scantily clad women making out with each other. Vincent had truly never witnessed anything like this before in his life. And to think, he had been somewhat shocked to see beds covered only by a transparent veil in a club and a woman snorting coke at the bar surrounded by people shooting up mere weeks ago. These people made the club goers where Vincent met and killed The Dealer look like Mother Theresa.

At the other end of this huge enclave, Vincent found another hallway in this seemingly endless labyrinth where half way down, one could either continue on in a straight line or turn down one of the hallways to the left or right. He walked towards the split in the hall and without thinking about it, turned to go down the left opening. As he turned the corner, he passed a few large statues, some in gold and others in carved stone, until he came to a peculiar lone room at the end of the long corridor on his left. There was next to nobody in this area of the house except for two guests and one waiter that came strolling out of one room or hallway and vanished into another just as quickly as they had arrived. Peeking into the empty room, he witnessed yet another thing he couldn't make sense of.

There was an ornate black console pushed against the farthest wall beneath an all black Rococo style mirror. On the shiny black marble surface there sat a crown placed upon a small black silk pillow. In the middle of the black and white tiled room, suspended from the ceiling, was a moderate sized chandelier composed of black metal and draped in black crystals that sparkled in the light of actual candles.

This room, even despite every other thrillingly obscure thing he'd witnessed thus far, seemed very mystical, almost spiritual and symbolic in its awkwardly lonely nature. There was nothing symbolic about it in all actuality, but it definitely had a superior vibe compared to elsewhere in the rolling estate. Maybe it was the fact that a crown, and a rather expensive looking one at that, had been left all alone in an unlocked room displaced from the main areas of the house and was still easily accessible to any whom wished to enter and steal it. On the other hand, perhaps everyone knew better than to take something from Miles Le Veighton. Stealing from the master leader of the most affluent of Los Angeles gangs, and probably the most violent in the country, after being personally invited to a party at his house, could never end well for the thief.

Nevertheless Vincent was here to kill Miles anyway, what's the harm in taking a closer look? Walking slowly over the two toned tile, Vincent made his way to the small table. The crown was certainly a marvel in and of itself. Encased in the centre of the gleaming white gold was a square princess cut diamond set on an angle with the pointed edges at the compass points. Even lying still on a pillow, the large diamond glistened and sparkled in the flickering light of the candle flames above. On each side of the brilliant rock were three rubies alternated with three sapphires cascading down in a line to sweep across the bottom of the royal headpiece.

Ever so gently, almost reverently, Vincent lifted the crown from its plush black silk pillow and placed it off kilter on top of his head then removed his shiny metal venetian mask to expose his true face and set it on the table. He stared at himself in the large ornate black framed mirror hanging upon the stark white wall that sat below a slit of a window only the size and shape of a brick from which the suns golden rays shone down onto the tile.

Mirror reflected mirror as the polished metal mask set on the table and the mirror hanging on the wall caught glimpses of everything from the crown to the chandelier, the table to the floor and the sun rays, which at this angle, cast a small rectangular shaped yellow light over his right eye. Just then, another vision came behind him in the refection - two guys pushing each other playfully through the doorframe. Vincent tore off the crown and re-attached his mask before whipping around to see the two topless, lean but muscular guys in black pants and simple black face masks stop as they saw Vincent, who sat there frozen.

"Shit dude, someone's here already."

"Sorry guys, I'll get out of your way. I don't really think I should be in here anyway," Vincent responded simply because he didn't know what else to say. The two guys straightened up a bit and stared at him with a bit of a curious expression before the shorter one spoke up.

"Why not? I kinda thought this party was sort of a free for all ... doesn't matter where you go. Except upstairs I think. My friend told me that they've got security guarding all the stairs to the second and third floors."

"Really? Oh, ok then. I guess I just assumed we weren't supposed to be in here because nobody else is around. That's usually a good indication," Vincent responded, completely disregarding the fact that he had already seen three women come down to the party from upstairs simply because he didn't want to argue and had felt a bit embarrassed about being caught trying on a crown.

"Yeah, but I think it's more likely an indication that there's nothing to do in here … or that there's no booze here," the taller, dark haired stranger responded playfully as Vincent laughed.

"Well you guys certainly thought there'd be something to do in here," Vincent pointed out jocularly.

"Yeah …" The shorter, dirty blonde one started slowly, "what is that you were looking at? Is it a fake crown?"

"Yes actually, but I don't think its fake …" Vincent said glancing back at it. "I'm pretty sure it's real."

"No way, let me have a look at it," the blonde guy said, strutting over to the table and standing beside Vincent before leaning over slightly to get a better look at the crown.

"Well you could be right …" he said. "But I have no idea how to tell the difference between the good stuff and the fake crap."

"Well you can tell because here, just off the centre of the diamond there's a fairly noticeable carbon spot. That's the easiest way to tell. Nobody's gonna make a fake diamond with imperfections in it, sometimes you can get a really good one that doesn't have them, but almost never ones this big. And even if that wasn't there, the brilliance and scintillation are different … a fake will have almost too much sparkle but still look kind of faded and not have any real fire like this one does. See how the light plays sharply inside with only a few different colours?"

Even from behind the mask, Vincent could make out the look of utter confusion in this strangers eyes as he looked at the magnificent stone then up at Vincent.

"What the hell are you talking about dude? Are you a gemologist or something?"

"Nothing, don't worry about it," Vincent started, fearing he'd come across as a smart ass, "and no, I'm not a gemologist, I guess I've just been around enough of both to know the difference …" he added quickly.

"Crazy nobody's tried to steal it yet then huh? Or maybe they just think it's fake like I did," he said, still leaning over and eyeing the jewelled crown.

"Yeah or maybe they just figured it would be highly unwise to steal something like that from someone like Miles ..." Vincent pointed out.

"Ha! That's true," he responded as he stood back and extended a hand, "I'm Derek by the way," he stated as he gripped Vincent's hand firmly.

"And I'm Ethan," said the darker haired guy who had since wandered over to have a look at the crown for himself.

"Vincent."

"So Vincent, what are you doing here?" Derek asked.

"Just came for some official business with Miles," Vincent said, eluding the truth but not really.

"I see."

"What are *you* here for?"

"We're here for the party man!" Ethan answered in a slightly cocky tone as he eyed Vincent in a way that caught him off guard for a second before continuing, "And speaking of partying, why don't you join us for some partying of our own?"

Derek looked to be perfectly on board with the idea as he too, eyed Vincent. Since the incident in Amsterdam, Vincent had decided it would be something he'd rather not do. It seemed better to him that he was stood up now that he looked back at it as he wasn't sure he would have been able to go through with it anyway. And even if he had still wanted to try it, this was not the time or the place. He was here for a reason.

"I uh, I can't. Sorry guys," Vincent said, shocked but still a little flattered at the same time. He knew he wasn't gay, but someone thinking you're attractive is never an insult, no matter who it comes from.

"Why not?" Derek asked.

"Does that bother you?" Ethan piped up coyly, possibly thinking Vincent was homophobic.

"I don't think it bothers him ..." Derek said appraisingly, guessing correctly that Vincent was quite comfortable with himself to not be embarrassed by the proposition.

"No, it doesn't bother me at all, but it's just not my thing guys. Sorry. And in any case, I've gotta meet Miles in a bit and he'll just *kill* me if

I'm late," Vincent said, again half eluding the truth. "And speaking of which, I should really get going, it was nice to meet you guys," he finished before turning towards the door.

"Well alright then. It was *really* nice to meet you too. And if you change your mind …" Derek said with a slight shrug.

"See ya," Ethan managed with a wave before turning to Derek.

"Have fun," Vincent called unnecessarily, chuckling a bit to himself before carrying on down the deserted corridors for a while and letting his mind wander.

He had no idea where he was going and just as he was beginning to feel like he was lost for the first time since entering this house, a butler of all people, walked right up to him as he turned around a corner and informed him, "Mr. Le Veighton would like to see you now."

Vincent was taken aback. How the hell did he know who he was? Was everybody in on it to the point that the bloody *butler* knew who he was and summoned him as such? Miles must have been watching him for weeks. Vincent figured he would probably have to be a pretty lousy or lazy Gang leader to *not* keep tight tabs on the vigilante who managed to kill every one of your immediate subordinates. As such, he had nothing left to do but follow the dapper servant. They walked in silence through the twisting corridors, past strange paintings of winding trees and stairs, bridges and screaming alien looking creatures until they came upon a set of double French doors.

Was this his office or something? As the butler opened both doors and stood back, motioning for Vincent to enter, he realized he couldn't have been more wrong. It was a garden, and not just any garden; the most decadent and lush Japanese garden he'd ever seen in his life. In shock and having nowhere else to really go, Vincent allowed himself to be ushered even further into this fantastical dreamland as the butler shut the doors behind him. Vincent couldn't see him but he knew Miles was here somewhere, waiting for him. What sort of crazy person sets up a meeting for an inevitably deadly fight in a garden?

Vincent looked down at the descending stone path placed between the trimmed hedges in front of him. Quite branches hung overhead and over the path leading down the slope. He walked by a small stone lantern and a larger multi-storied stone pagoda amidst the greenery. As he neared the bottom of the hill along the winding path he saw a bridge stretched out over a river, water slowly trickling and flowing over huge mossy rocks. A large tree of some species he'd never seen before encompassed the area on the other side and created an open space between and beneath the thick canopy of bright scarlet leaves.

Yet again, Vincent felt as if he'd stepped into another dimension where reality was something of fiction. It was at that point that Vincent noticed Miles standing with his back to him, beneath the large tree on the ground that was also covered in red leaves that had fallen from their space on the branch. He was clothed in a red silk robe as if he were trying to emulate the Asian theme of his surroundings. The blood red trees and leaf covered ground created another separation from the rest of the world and looked almost too perfect to be true. He imagined this being a prime spot for photographers wishing to catch a rare glimpse of nature at its finest. If he were indeed to lose this final fight, he would definitely prefer to die in a place as naturally decadent and rich as this than in front of a hotel lobby.

He wasn't nervous even though he thought he should be. He *knew* he should be actually, but he just wasn't. It was about to be over. The long and tiring climb through the leaders of the most infamous gang probably in the country, and he was down to the last one. One way or another, his journey was teetering on the edge of coming to a blissful end. Whether he himself lost this final battle or if he would emerge victorious it was his moment at long last and he knew everything would come to a culmination.

As Miles turned around, his gaze locked on Vincent. His tone was cold, condemning and condescending as if he had some misplaced sense of self righteousness and displayed it in a manner to frighten and terrify people into obedience. Staring into his stone blue eyes, Vincent could see how easily Miles accomplished this, not a twitch in his glance or focus and overly confident. Vincent remained as confident as he possibly could, given the circumstances. He had, in all fairness, already killed four of Miles' leaders and eluded many assassination attempts but the leader, the master, the highest up, was always the most difficult to defeat as far as any story he had ever known told him thus far.

Vincent lifted one foot off the stone path and onto the bridge that bent upwards in the middle over the trickling water and landed at the red ground on the other side. A few brilliant scarlet leaves fell here and there from the majestic tree as Vincent crossed, maintaining his glare from behind his mask that was still secured to his upper face. He knew Miles knew who he was and even though the mask covered up his face, it did leave his eyes open to reveal all of his inner intents and fury.

Vincent had been so focused on finding Miles in this Japanese nirvana that he didn't realize until he was standing right in front of him that they were outside. 'Maybe this is the backyard,' he thought as he noticed the red and golden cloud streaked sky above. He darted his glance around just quick enough to see that the whole area was sunken in with a few landscape manipulations to create hilled areas leading up to the edges of four walls around them. At the point where the walls met, there were four towers from which guards in ski masks watched down over them with snipers. He had lost before he even started.

Setting his foot onto the red ground on the other side of the creek, Vincent returned his focus to Miles who hadn't shifted at all, standing ominous in red silk that matched his surroundings. His face was younger than Vincent had imagined, considering there was no picture of him in the police reports, and he sported short, light hair that seemed to reflect the red around them.

"So. You're finally here." The first words that came out of Miles mouth were shocking not because they were in any way odd or bizarre and didn't seem to logically fit the dialogue that should be exchanged between the two, but because of the calm and slightly raspy tone that carried them. Vincent said nothing in response. "I knew this day would come. I've waited for you for a long time," he continued.

"You knew I would be coming for you and that I would kill all of your leaders?" Vincent asked, mocking the absurdity of Miles' statement. If he knew who he was all along and what he would do, then why did he allow him to do it? Why didn't he continuously send someone to stop him?

"You don't believe me but it's true. I've been watching you the whole time, seeing if you'd actually manage to make your way through to me."

"Then why didn't you stop me?"

"Stop you? ... I *let* you. You didn't really think you could actually get to me and kill all of my leaders unless I wanted it to happen did you?"

"Yeah actually, I did."

"See that's where you and I differ. You need help to get where you are. You need me paving the way for you by let's say, having Andre throw an incredibly ostentatious party so you'll know exactly where he'd be. Face it; you would not be standing here talking to me right now if it weren't for me allowing it. While I on the other hand, maintain the control. I see you've noticed the guards, they're ready to shoot on my command so you better pay attention."

Vincent sat motionless for a moment before deciding to take the plunge and ask the question Miles had obviously wanted him to ask.

"So why did you let me kill all of your co-leaders?"

"Subordinates," Miles corrected assertively. "And I let you do that so that you could join me."

"*Join you?*"

"Yes join me, join us; The Daravians. I needed you - someone like you. Anyone can join really but I wanted someone with charisma and the drive to make it through the obstacles first."

"You want me to join your gang ... are you joking?" Vincent almost screamed. This was the second time he'd heard this proposition escape a leaders mouth but it still shocked him. "You killed my wife then tried to have me assassinated - three times!"

"No, Jamie went against orders and killed your wife. That was none of our doing and as for the hit men, yes those were the first of the series of hurdles I placed in front of you. You remember your old boss, don't you? Mr. Crane, I believe it is. Yes, he was the one who informed my men you were moving to Denver. I have a lot of powerful friends, Mr. Torres, but I was impressed when you managed to go 'off the grid' for a while."

It was at this point that Vincent remembered the green pocket square Patrick always wore in a strange fold out of his left breast pocket; the corporate equivalent of the green bandana. How did he not see it before? That was why they had been able to follow Vincent to Denver and not to New York; Patrick hadn't known about the latter move. He also remembered Troy mentioning the name J.P. during his discussion with the coke dealers. How could Vince have forgotten that was Patrick's nickname around the office as well as the one he'd christened his law firm with?

"That's when I decided you could be useful. Although I must confess, I didn't think you would actually do it. Do you know how long it's been since someone overcame all of the roadblocks I put in their way? Never, that's how long. I was hoping you'd make it through but in all honesty, I expected them to kill you. However, when they didn't and you made it through the hit in Denver, I made it a walk in the park for you to get here and gave the other leaders up to you on a silver platter."

With this now in mind, Vincent really had only one reasonable question to ask, "Why?"

"I've already told you why. But aside from that, they were getting overly confident. They were assuming more control than they deserved. Just like you in the beginning. That's why I put a bounty out on you. But then you proved yourself useful so I made it possible for you to dispose of them for me and this way it appears as an act of vigilantism and not my own doing. That's why you need us."

"Why do I need you?" Vincent asked, becoming more confused with the conversation as it progressed.

"To stay safe. There were a lot of people with allegiances to my former subordinates and they will want to seek revenge on you now. Not to mention all the non members that will think you are a part of the gang and must be killed or arrested. If you join us then there's no need for any of that. One word from me and all contracts out on you will be void and nobody will dare touch you."

"And if I don't join? ..." Vincent asked still starring Miles in the eye.

"Then you will become useless to me again and I will have to lose a potential valuable member whilst giving my guards up there something to do. They're just waiting for my signal."

"I've got different information. I've learned through my own connections that it was you who set everything up in order to blame me and turn the entire gang against me."

"I don't need to turn the entire gang against you, all I need to destroy you are those guys up there ... Don't be deceived by him. He has no

269

idea what he's talking about. *I* was the one who helped you, *I* was the one who let you get this far, *I* am the one who will save you from the ones who will try and harm you. *I* am the one who will decide your fate."

"Who said anything about 'him'?" Vincent asked.

"The person who told you that lie," Miles said before he stopped, looked toward the red ground and stepped forward slightly as Vincent quickly removed the small handgun from the inside of his jacket pocket and took aim. He had managed to keep it unnoticed during the party by removing it from its spot whenever somebody came close to discovering it. He raised it up to Miles who didn't even flinch. His eyes remained solid, frozen in frame, dazzlingly blue and radiant, yet still cold all at the same time. He stepped forward again slightly, apparently not the least bit afraid of the firearm being wielded in his direction before he continued.

"Look, I'm going to say this one last time. You can either join me and have all that you want, look around, there's nothing I can't give you, there's no protection I can't offer, *We* can help you ... Or I can destroy you. You chose."

At that moment Vincent bowed his head and removed the mask which he kept in his hand as he stared blankly at the ground. The last of the sun's rays caught the metal on his mask and gleamed up into the red tree above and the ground below, dotting the scene with blue and yellow lights that danced around in the air as the mask moved slightly in his hand.

Vincent lifted his head after a moment, stared Miles directly in the eye and said, "I will NOT join you!" as he pulled two fingers back on the trigger and fired, to which the only sound was the snap of the guns hammer against the bare metal. Vincent looked at Miles as a brief grin emerged on his opponents face before his body was hit from behind and red splattered into the air, then again and again and again. A momentary look of shock was etched onto his face as one shot right after the other punctured his torso, creating a permanent hole in his body as he fell to his knees then slumped over to the side. The blood flowed from his wounds into a puddle on the already red ground. A few red leaves continued to fall off the densely covered branches that encompassed the two men into their own little realm.

Vincent looked up to the four watch towers where Bale, Mathias, Parker, Sheldon and Aurora were all spread about, smiling back at him from their posts at the four corners after lifting their black ski masks. He smiled back a bit as he realized how much help friends could be, so long as you take the leap of faith and put your trust in them. He had told them he would give the signal to shoot by firing a no shot while still leaving bullets in the other compartments just in case. They had informed him that Miles usually takes people out to his garden before he has them assassinated. Especially if he holds them in high regards, such as one of his own lieutenants, so they formulated a plan in which Vincent's comrades would take out and replace the snipers at their posts. Miles always had a garden in each residence he had lived in because it provided him with a tranquil escape to nature and also produced a calming surrounding for his victims where they could relax a bit before he took them out, usually by surprise.

The irony of the situation was not lost on Vincent but as he looked down at Miles' lifeless body, the short blonde hairs on the right side of his head now catching the pool of blood, he couldn't help but feel a bit discontented. It was all over now. He had completed everything he set out to do. He had actually managed to kill all five leaders of the most notorious gang in the country. And now he felt as if he had done everything in this life that was needed of him and felt a rush of both adrenaline and depression.

What was he to do now? Miles certainly had helped him take out the other leaders, so that was no great feat. And as for Miles; well, Vincent hadn't actually even killed him himself. Looking back on the situation, he realized he should have just fired a live round at him with the knowledge that his friends would be there to back him up if something went wrong, only he hadn't. 'Hindsight is 20/20,' he figured, and this was a perfect example. Even though it wasn't a big deal it, might have made him feel better about the situation.

He now felt empty and unfulfilled, a curious outcome considering all the work he had put in. He had gotten his revenge, but now what? Vanessa was still dead and he had abandoned his career, his whole life

271

for that matter, to pursue his vengeance on these despicable people and now he had succeeded.

Head bowed in thought amongst the brilliant red hue that surrounded him on all sides, Vincent's accomplice's bolted down from their respective towers and into the garden, stopping before him under the assumption that he was paying some sort of reverence to Miles. They approached slowly after a minute and Vincent's thoughts were interrupted by their movements.

"Hey," he muttered to them, sounding much less thrilled than they had expected.

"Hey, we did it man! They're all gone," Bale said as he approached Vincent before the others.

"Yeah ... all gone," Vincent echoed dourly.

"What's the matter man? Aren't you excited at all?" Mathias piped up.

"Yeah Yeah I am, it's just ..."

"It's just what?"

"It's just that now it's all over and I have nothing else to do ..." Vincent replied, knowing he had to be truthful with them.

"What are you talking about? Now you get to live your life ... Without anyone trying to kill you! You have to be happy about that," Mathias continued as the others looked on watching Vincent's reaction.

"I gave up my life, my career, everything to get revenge on these people and now it's over and I don't know how to go back, or even what to go back *to*. That's all," Vincent said, trying to listen to their reaffirming statements and neutralize the sinking, anticlimactic feeling that overcame him.

Parker came walking down the small winding path he had been standing farther up on and sauntered over to the corpse and standing over him, he looked down and stared blankly.

"He's not so great anymore. All the illusions and facades are gone now ... He wasn't really anything without them, was he? I gotta say, I never actually thought he could be defeated. He was always this sort of elusive entity that nobody had ever witnessed much of. Now I see why. He's no different than us ..." Parkers insightful narrative struck a chord with the others as they nodded in agreement, confirming Vincent's exact thoughts about him all along.

Just then, the doors Vincent himself had been ushered into the dramatic garden from opened and out stepped a man dressed in a tuxedo with white gloves and glasses. His grey hair betrayed the illusion his mostly wrinkle free face was trying to induce. He stopped and looked at Miles as he got halfway down the path. Vincent wondered, as they all did, who this man was and if he was going to run and call the police or inform the remaining gang members, or possibly even the other servants. In unison Parker, Aurora, Bale, Mathias and Sheldon all raised their weapons, barrels pointed towards his body and he froze mid step and threw his hands up, not appearing at all frightened.

"You did it!" he exclaimed.

Chapter 21 – *The Crown*

"Did what?" Vincent asked carefully eyeing the dapper stranger.

"You killed Miles."

"Yeah ... and ... Why does that matter to you?" Vincent asked, realizing how stupid the question must have sounded, but he still needed to tread carefully in order to determine what his next move would be.

"Because I'm his chief lieutenant, Leon," the man replied replied.

"Well Leon, are you gonna go running and screaming murder and make us kill you too or are you gonna keep your mouth shut till we're gone?" Vincent asked, still eyeing him.

"Vincent, we'll just bound and gag him, we don't have to kill him. He'll go screaming if we don't confine him, but tying him up should suffice until we leave," Mathias spoke up in his deep voice, trying to talk some sense into the situation and not particularly wanting to start a massacre.

"Oh no no, I'll do quite the opposite actually, and you mustn't leave," Leon interrupted before Vincent could respond.

He was confused; quite the opposite of what? Running off and telling everyone or shutting his mouth? And why couldn't they leave? He asked as much.

"Well, because we've been expecting you. You're the new one, the leader that is."

"What? New leader for what?" Vincent asked yet again baffled at the words escaping from the mouths of these crazy people.

"The new leader of our organization ..." Leon started as Vincent's expression lost any shadow of understanding. "You are the one designated to be the new head," he finished looking confused that Vince wasn't yet aware of this fact and trying to keep his decorum.

"No I'm not ... According to whom?"

"Well ... your friends," he said cautiously, eyeing the group around Vincent hoping to catch a glimpse that indicated at least *they* understood what he was talking about.

Vincent looked over at his apparent friends hoping to also find some indication that they knew what Leon was talking about. They all wore an expression of a child who'd just been caught stealing candies they weren't supposed to have and Vincent waited for a moment in disbelief before Bale stepped forward.

"Vince, well ... we were talking and it seems there wouldn't be anyone better to do it."

"What do you mean you've been talking? You all just decided this for me?"

"Well, not just ... we've been hoping you'd do it from the beginning," Bale started again, taking an apologetic pause and starting in again before Vincent had time to become infuriated and think they had conspired against him. "Really Vincent ... there's nothing else you can do now, you said that yourself."

Vincent sat and stared at him as he tried not to shoot each and every one of them right then and there. Bale's tone switched gears from contrite to carrying an undercurrent of demand and forcefulness combined with persuasion.

"There is nobody better to do it than you and with you in the head seat you can put an end to the internal corruption. Put a stop to all the unnecessary suffering the gang causes to families like yours. You could stop it! People would respect you already because you managed to kill off every single one of the leaders. If you could change the course of their entire game being an outsider, imagine what you could do as an *insider* and their leader. Not to mention all the perks, money, women, mansions ... anything is possible, look around you. If nothing else, today proves that."

Vincent was taken aback by the absurdity of his argument. How could he stop the corruption within a system that was by nature, corrupt? It was impossible. Even if he wanted to be their new leader, it would be a useless task to take on. As he sat for a moment and his boiling blood began to cool, he realized that a few short months ago he also thought it would be impossible for him to take out every leader of this infamous gang, but he had done it. He remembered a time when he had no idea how to go about the goal he had completed minutes earlier except by simply putting one foot in front of the other and seeing where it would take him.

Perhaps it was possible to weed out the corrupt system within the gang's infrastructure and forge a new system. This seemingly impossible goal, unlike his last one, at least had other supporters who believed it could work. Maybe they were right. He began to think of all the changes he could actually make if he were to take the reins. There was still one blatantly obvious problem though.

"Just because I managed to kill all the leaders, doesn't mean I know anything about *running* a gang," Vincent pointed out.

"You've learned everything you need already," Bale answered, a supportive statement but not helping to clue Vincent in at all.

"How so? Even me managing to kill them all, Miles paved the way for that to happen and so did you guys."

"People can pave a road all the way to the end of the universe for you but only you can choose to actually take it, and you did. You could stand at the beginning of a path and get nowhere or you can actually make the decision to brave whatever may be down the road and have a chance of getting somewhere.

"And just because you take a road that's been laid out before you doesn't mean you didn't overcome anything. He may have put them in your path but you still had to travel down that path until you found them, challenge them and ultimately defeat them. He was lying to you. He offered you protection from them but what you didn't realize was that you didn't need it. He wasn't there protecting you along the way; you've had the power to do that all along."

Vincent looked up at the others who stood silent but their gazes indicated an unspoken agreement with Bale's insightful soliloquy.

"So why didn't you tell me all this before?" Vincent asked, deciding not to fight them.

"Because you wouldn't have believed us, you needed to defeat them in order to see it for yourself … And they needed to be disposed of anyway," he laughed.

Again, Vincent was momentarily at a loss for words but he realized that he still had no idea how to run a gang. And even if he did, did he really want to join and *run* the gang that was responsible for tearing his life apart. It was then that he realized that the people who had actually done this to him were now gone. As he stared at Bale, Sheldon, Aurora,

Parker and Mathias, he realized they had all had their lives ruined by these people and now that they were out of the way, maybe this really was their chance to change things.

They could now at least try to turn things around and make all the suffering and pain cease and rebuild their lives, and the organization, up in a new way. Like a new Jerusalem, they would raise up the kingdom with great power and strength, rebuilding it with a whole new philosophy, a new era that would liberate the people within from the tyranny of the previous age. Growing a little excited about this possible new venture, Vincent realized it wouldn't be easy and it may ultimately fail, but he felt like he had to try.

"Will you guys help me do it?"

They all looked exhilarated at Vincent's openness to the idea and the fact that he would continue on with them.

"You don't need any more help. I already told you that, but we'll be here with you anyway," Bale responded.

"So you're going to re-join with me?"

"Of course we are."

"Alright then, as your new leader, the first thing I'll do is tell you that you can all consider your previous records expunged, and you will all re-join the group as the new heads of your own sects. You five will replace the ones I've removed from their positions," Vincent said, taking the authoritative position rather naturally.

They sat around and discussed the details of their re-instatement until Leon spoke up about Vincent's official Inauguration.

"When do we do that?" Vince asked, looking at Leon somewhat confused, not having any idea that this was supposed to happen in the first place.

"Well ... right now sir."

"What? To who? All the leaders are dead and the members are spread over the country," Vince pointed out.

"Yes, the prior leaders may no longer be alive but all of their lieutenants, assistants and immediate subordinates are well ... here, in attendance."

"What? They are?" Mathias piped up on Vincent's behalf, indicating to him that at least they weren't in on this part of it.

"Yes sir, for the most part anyway," Leon responded.

"Did you really think that all those people were just here by chance Mathias? Miles had to have known them *somehow* ..." Aurora chimed in.

"Wait a minute," Vincent started, "you're trying to tell me that I was just in a party with a bunch of people whose bosses I'd killed? Why didn't anyone try to attack me?"

"Yes, well, with all due respect sir, who else did you think all these people would be? Miss Deloris had gathered as much," Leon asked in a submissive tone trying to not sound rude or sarcastic.

"I wasn't sure, I figured they were just other influential friends he had, and a couple of them even told me that, so I never really thought much about it at all."

"Well some of them, yes, but most of them probably just said that ... you never really know who you could be talking to at an event like this and with all the masks and outfits it's pretty much impossible to tell who's who or who could even be a potential undercover agent. We do thorough checks on all of the attendee's prior to any event but people can slip through the cracks. If anyone would know that it should be you. You really should be aware of these things if you're going to take over you know ..."

"Well, why didn't anyone try to kill me then?"

"I told you why; they probably didn't know who you were," Leon responded in a manner that alluded to his simplistic take on the situation Vincent was over-complicating in his mind.

"But *you* did ..." Vincent said, looking him in the eye and waiting for a glimmer of deceit to reveal itself beneath the glassy surface.

"Yes, Miles and I did, as did his other lieutenants, but they were given strict orders to stand down. I would imagine he kept everyone else in the dark as he usually does with these types of things."

Vincent thought about this for a second and realized that it did all make sense. What he still wasn't sure about, however, was how they were going to break the news to Miles' devoted subjects.

"So how are we going to tell everyone? Won't that start a riot?"

"Oh, I don't think so sir, they've been wanting a change for a long time. You're actually quite famous already, to the ones who've been awaiting you're arrival that is ... and you needn't worry, everyone else will come to know you and will willingly accept you very soon. Yes, some of them, most likely the ones who had it too good, will be less than thrilled at their new superiors but they won't be a problem at all," Leon continued, hinting to the fact that anyone opposed to the new way things were going to be wouldn't last very long.

Vincent looked around at his entourage and with a renewed sense of strength and meaning, acknowledged and thanked each one of them, telling them that they will always have a place with him and that together they were about to forge a new era.

"So, what do we do next?" Vincent asked, looking back to Leon once more.

"We take you inside, perhaps give you a quick tour and a change of attire," he said, darting his glance downward at Vincent's bloodied shirt and jacket for a fraction of a second. "Then we'll commence your inauguration. The sooner we make the announcement, the less here-say will be spread among your followers," he responded purposefully, clearly used to being the one sought out for advice and wisdom.

"Alright then, let's get to it," Vincent announced to no one in particular, staring past the bridge he didn't remember crossing back over, at the red stained oasis behind him then leading the way back into the estate. As they all walked behind him back up the hill towards the house, Vincent heard Aurora quietly confirming, in a tone of disbelief, that nobody else had known who all the guests were and that she simply assumed they all understood it, answering the question of why she hadn't let them in on the knowledge.

Just as they were almost back inside, a gust of wind came swooping into the garden, seemingly out of nowhere and caught the ash out of one of the Japanese stone lanterns that sat on the ground ahead and peppered it all over Vincent's body. Vincent shut his eyes and held his breath in the split second he saw it coming. Opening his eyes after it had passed, he gazed around and realized it hadn't gotten anyone else and caught glimpses of Mathias and Parker trying not to laugh.

"You think this is funny?" Vincent asked, a little annoyed, but still unable to find it completely infuriating.

"Kind of, but it's OK, Leon said you'd be changing anyway so just get inside and we'll go ahead to the party while you get changed alright?" Mathias reassured after composing himself.

"Yeah, alright," Vincent said, unable to believe his luck and wiping the soot away from his eyes and mouth before continuing through the lush greenery.

Back inside Vincent felt an overwhelming urge to have a deeper look into all that had now been blessedly bestowed upon him. He was now in complete control and had a whole new empire. Fresh and vibrant and soon to be restored to all its former glory, a revitalizing improvement on what had long since gone stale. No longer were the members of the gang interested in the old age Miles had ruthlessly reigned over, no longer would they be bound by fear of him. They were to be liberated as soon as the news of Vincent's ascendance above Miles throne broke to them.

His new Lieutenants had offered a personalized tour of the majestic estate that now belonged to him. As per law, the estate was to be handed over to Miles's 'board of directors', which was most likely really just a crime council, should anything happen to him. They, in turn, would relinquish control of the estate and empire to their new leader. But first things first; he needed a shower and a change of clothes, and then Vincent was to be given the royal tour after which his official inauguration would occur.

His ecstasy at this point was almost unbearable but his mind had not yet grasped the grandeur of his current situation and he wasn't sure that it would for some time. He had just assumed control over the gang that he had hated so much for so long. He had killed everyone on his list in this short period of time and he felt overwhelming relief now that they were all gone, even if it did all feel a little surreal.

"Right this way," Leon said, obsequiously waving his hand out over Vincent's intended path.

The black tiles felt as if they were made of air under his feet, his senses had been thrown into overdrive as if he were metaphysically connected to everyone and everything around him. Such were the emotional effects of the greatest victory he'd ever known. The revolution had come and gone and he now reigned victorious, as if striding above the stars represented by the white speckled dots in the black granite tiling. At the top of the stairs, Vincent found himself staring down the widened hallway towards the last traces of daylight emanating from the large French style window at the aft with a deep purple rug stretched out under his feet and before him, continuing on to the end.

"We'll now show you the most important of chambers first and you can continue to wherever you wish after we announce your new position as our leader," Leon continued as he started towards the unknown room Vincent was being led to.

The space behind the heavy double mahogany doors was as gorgeous and yet bizarre as he'd expected. Every room in this strange estate seemed to have a new and extravagant theme to it, this one purely dark opulence. It looked as though a savage baroness had herself once lived here before legends of her insanity began to emerge among the people and she was headed to the gallows.

The large bed was done in all black silk that shone even in the dimmed light of the black chandelier hanging above the bed. Behind the bed on the wall was a black rococo style mirror. The granite tiling continued into this room as well and slid itself under every intricate piece of black furniture in a glossy sheen. A black and white damask painting was placed all along the closest wall and looked oddly unsettling. The windows were tinted to darken the room even further and dark grey veined marble legs held up each black nightstand. On the nightstands were ivory based lamps with lampshades that were made of black chiffon draped slightly between black satin strips to create a sort of spider web effect.

Vincent walked around trying to take it all in and to comprehend that this is where he would be calling home if he so chose. He could spend an eternity wandering up and down and throughout this dreamlike mansion. That's exactly what it was; it was as if someone had taken all his dreams, both good and the eerie, and smashed them into one ludicrously large and surely ridiculously expensive piece of architecture.

The closet that he instinctively wandered into was lit by futuristic looking LED lights. A very faded bluish white colour emanated from the walls in semi-spheres that lined almost every space not taken up by dark suits. Various coloured poplins, walls of shoes, drawers and an entire wall that held a plethora of sunglasses all lit from behind along with racks of coats were the finishing touches to the normal part of the closet.

At the back of the closet, the array of masquerade masks was even more creative and impressive, enough to last a hundred of these parties without ever having to wear the same one twice. Row upon row and all sitting upon a mock-face for display, Vincent could see Miles and himself both shared an interest in masks, although Miles was obviously much more serious about the interest than Vincent was. There was an all white mask with broken pieces of mirror on the right side and chains affixed to the perimeter, strung around the eyes and finally draping off the cheek. Another one was made of black leather and had screws coming through from the other side all over the left half with tiny drops of 'blood' dripping from each screw to look as if the mask were screwed onto the wearers face from behind.

The most impressive model however, was a futuristic-terminator style robot mask that started at the nose and ran up and over half of the top of the head in a disorienting display of fake mechanisms, wires, micro chips, LED lights and outlets. One eye was completely covered with a shield of mesh wire so you could still see out through it. It too was all black and had a bit of silver detailing on a few of the wires and empty spaces lit from underneath. Other masks with glitter and feathers and various random objects attached to them in bizarre and creative ways finished off the wall that stared back at an awe struck Vincent. Behind him, Leon patiently awaited his new master's judgment.

"Does everything thus far suit your needs?" he asked formally.

"Yes, this, uh, this will be more than fine. Is this the master bedroom?" Vincent asked rather unnecessarily given the sheer size of the space but he figured he could also very easily be wrong in this fantasy induced mansion.

"It is, will you be wanting to make any arrangements or additions to it?"

"No, no, I was just curious, I haven't seen the rest of the house yet so I wasn't sure."

"Well, we had better get you changed so we can continue then," Leon said, motioning to the array of outfits Vincent could choose from.

Vincent wandered around and fingered the rich materials, running his hand up and down the jackets and perfect piles of folded dress shirts as well the racks of hung ones until he came across a section of the wardrobe that housed the more eccentric things. Here, there was a floor length black wrinkled style silk robe, an ancient roman senator looking robe in alternating black and white and a large leather trench coat with spikes around the collar

"What about this?" Vincent asked, pointing to the long black silk robe. He had at least expected a reaction from his entourage. He didn't really care if they thought he was weird anyway but he did at least expect some form of facial expression that never came. Instead, Leon simply nodded his assent, so Vincent lifted it from the closet and picked out a pair of plain black pants to go with it, choosing to leave his chest bare under the open robe. After removing his red dress shirt and plain black jacket, he washed his face and neck off in the ensuite, figuring he didn't need nor have time for a full shower considering the ash hadn't gone under his clothes.

He then reattached his monarch looking metal mask and finished it all off with some unworn black leather dress shoes with bolted silver metal plates attached to the shiny black surface.

"Alright, let's go," Vincent said with a slight smirk.

And with that, Leon started in on the rest of the *exursion grande.* They continued on towards a small, hidden stairwell behind a few turns in the hallway that led back downstairs. Leon led him to a few drawing rooms, the dining room and the greenhouse, where the thick steam pressed against the glass that contained the plush abundance of greenery surrounding a massive pool and hot tub. Setting foot back onto the black and white tile flooring in the tiny enclosure at the bottom of what appeared to be the escape staircase; Vincent looked out through the frosted glass doors to another large hallway that had not been engulfed in partygoers. This magical labyrinth was continuing to enchant him with every turn and it still hadn't really hit him that this was what he would now call home. 'To the victor go the spoils indeed,' he thought to himself.

"I hope this will be suitable," Leon said, still walking in the lead.

"Yes, it's amazing," Vincent responded without looking back at him.

"I'm pleased that you're content with your new abode," Leon said softly before continuing. "But perhaps now it's time to announce your regime."

Vincent followed him down the hallway and then down another which took them to a new room. It was undoubtedly the largest and most opulent space in the entire building, or so he thought, because each new place he entered surpassed the one before it, although this would be next to impossible to beat. It actually seemed very unnecessary and he wasn't sure what anyone did with it when they weren't throwing the most massive party he'd ever seen.

The Parisian Opera house was exactly what this room, or more like a ballroom, instantly reminded Vincent of. Up until this point, he had thought that other rooms in this place had been unnecessarily large but this was titanic. It seemed to him that there was absolutely no reason whatsoever, especially considering the plethora of other gigantic rooms designed specifically for entertaining that the house already hosted, to have something like this in a private residence.

'Only in a place as pretentious as the Hamptons would someone dare try to sell a house that had a room with what must be close to a fifty foot ceiling,' Vincent thought to himself. All ridiculousness of the frivolity aside, the room alone was breathtaking and boasted what was easily the most majestic looking staircase he'd ever seen inside a private residence before. It stood against the back wall, all curved ivory coloured marble. At the base sat large newel posts with carved stone angels sitting atop them holding elegant light fixtures above their heads. The split staircase led up to two doors flanking a balcony from the next level that overlooked the room. On the lower part of the balcony that also served as decoration for the mid-section landing, was a carved stone rendition of a unicorn between two apple trees. Its head was tilted down to watch over the room from its first class seat just below the balcony's balustrade.

A couple of women in an array of short or long flowing gowns and the requisite venetian masks walked gracefully up and down the white beauties, to and from the massive gathering of luxe-junkie beautiful weirdoes that had gathered here. Ice white chandeliers were suspended about three quarters of the way up to into the air, all situated around the vacant spot where the main chandelier should have hung. A thin, almost unnoticeable cable with a cord ran from the middle of this spot in the ceiling down to the ground where it was affixed to the decorative centrepiece of the room – 'The Fallen Chandelier'. 'That's an interesting idea,' Vincent thought to himself, wondering who on earth had planned this strange yet decadent party and what exactly all the oddities were for.

The large fallen chandelier was done in all black metal with three tiers of lights and had alternating strands of black and clear crystals draped and dangling between them. The chandelier itself was easily 7 feet tall and sat slightly off kilter to further the illusion that the alluring beauty had actually fallen from the ceiling. The cord running to the ground where it lay was obviously there so it could remain lit and the wire cable was most likely in place to hoist it back up to its proper place once the party was over. The lights however were dimmed so as not to blind the guests admiring the creative decor. The difference between this room and the others was that there were no plush sofa's on which to lounge. Everyone in the room was standing and seemed very content to do so in their champagne buzzed enthralment.

It was at this moment, for reasons still unknown to him, the sheer reality of his situation and the utter lack of limits finally hit him like a ton of bricks. He had done it. There was nothing left to do except enjoy the bliss that was now forever his. This room, along with all the others, the people, the victory all now silently assured him that he could do anything he set his mind to. Everything had been done and was now crystal clear. He could finally see what had been missing all this time, or what he thought he had been missing.

He finally realized that he had done it himself, and not just agreed because it was mentioned to him in a moment of despair as a resolution. He had saved himself from them. He hadn't physically overcome everything that would be thrown at him just yet or he may as well lay down and die, but he now understood that it was solely him that was responsible for what happens to him. Should anything challenge him, he could take it on with the knowledge that even if he should fail, he would never stop trying.

Before he started this epic journey, he had believed that everything was out of his hands and whatever happens, just happens and there's nothing you can do about it. We can't chose what happens to us, whether it be good or bad, but we can chose what to do with the time that we have and the situations that we are placed in. He believed that once they were all gone and dead, he would be safe, but what he couldn't fathom at that point was that he had the key to his destiny all along and all he need do was unlock it.

"Shall we?" Leon said motioning to the stairs where he apparently thought it would be ideal for Vincent to give his speech.

Rousing out of his reverie, Vincent nodded in agreement and looked around for a minute more with something resembling actual pride. Making his way through the chattering crowd that still had no idea their leader was dead in his own garden somewhere back in the deep recesses of this giant labyrinth, Vincent felt a newfound connection with these people. He hadn't spoken to them yet to even see if he would be able to garner their affection, but he had lost that sense of competition with them that he felt prior to his fatal discussion with Miles.

Leon started up the *escalier grand* with Vincent following behind. It seemed impossible but the staircase actually looked bigger now that he was closer to it. A few people turned to watch, possibly somehow sensing that there was news to be unveiled but most likely out of reverence for Leon, knowing that he is, was, Miles public representative when a situation called for it.

They climbed up one white marble stair at a time, Vincent's heart racing a little faster with each step. He had already done the impossible, yet facing everyone was still a daunting thought. Yes, his feelings towards them had shifted a hundred and eighty degrees in the past few minutes or so but would they feel the same towards him?

Would their train of thought shift from thinking he was another unknown guest at this party to simply accepting him as their new commander? It was a lot to take in and it certainly was big news. He hoped they would, for he knew that they were desperate for change, but would they be ready to accept it right now? Leon must have been wondering the same thing because he signalled for security to follow him up to the next level, summoning them from their posts around the room with a simple hand gesture and they obeyed.

As they made their ascent up the flight of stairs that felt like it took two years to climb and up the flight that veered off to the left from the main case, they entered into a lounge room painted in butter yellow where they immediately turned again and walked out onto the balcony that overlooked the entire ballroom. As they stood, Vincent's feet cemented to the shiny surface of the stone balcony, his heart raced even faster and he realized a second too late that someone must have made another ominous signal to allow them to begin.

The lights in the rooms behind and before them dimmed slightly as spotlights above them lit up a bit and shone down onto Vincent and Leon standing still, security closely behind, watching over the crowd. The spotlights drew everyone's eye to the five of them standing, waiting for the crowd's undivided attention which was quickly received.

"Ladies and Gentlemen, your attention please," Leon boomed in a way Vincent would never have imagined he could, considering how soft spoken and proper he sounded in a one on one conversation. Vincent spotted Bale, Mathias, Aurora, Parker and Sheldon at the bottom of the stairs looking up towards him and the group around him. He gave them a nod in salute as Leon continued after everyone had finished settling.

"It is both my sadness and great pleasure to share some most important news with you today. As you are all aware, our organization has been through a hefty share of turbulence in recent years and things were continuing their descent with little hope of recovery. You have all heard the news reports and so you will know that there has been someone out there removing our corrupt leaders from their positions within our establishment."

'Shit, this guy is good at diplomacy,' Vincent thought to himself as he listened to Leon's narration, 'I guess this is why Miles chose him to be his chief lieutenant and personal spokesman.' He darted his glance around the room searching for signs of confusion, displeasure or uneasiness but he couldn't spot any and so he turned his stare back to Leon as he continued speaking.

"It is with regret that I inform you our chief leader, Lord Deulsus, has passed away this evening. On the other hand, it is my great happiness today to announce to you all that the person who has been relentlessly working towards replacing the leaders of our various sects, is here with me now. I know you will all join me in welcoming our new leader with as much enthusiasm as he deserves."

With that, the crowd erupted into applause, betraying any thought in Vincent's mind that they would be less than thrilled to hear the news and they still had no idea who he was. They trusted that Leon would follow up his news with an answer to what they were all thinking. 'Who is he? And what's going to happen now?' … he didn't disappoint.

"Everyone, I present to you, Vincent Torres!"

As soon as the last syllables escaped his mouth and echoed through the cavernous room, the crowd erupted into applause once more as Vincent stepped forward, ahead of Leon and the bodyguards. Vincent had never been more nervous in his life even though everyone was already applauding him and he hadn't even done anything yet. A tiny bead of sweat ran down his forehead and his heart raced faster but his voice didn't falter, coming through confident and clear.

"Good evening ladies and gentlemen. It is true, what Leon has told you is now all in effect. Since the brutal murder of my wife a few months ago, I have been hunted down by your former superiors. I took it upon myself to eradicate the problem after realizing that nobody would do it for me …"

The crowd had begun to twitter and a few more people clapped spontaneously as Vincent found himself harbouring less anxiety after the initial speech. Taking notes from Leon, he continued in a diplomatic fashion.

"I managed to dissolve the problems and after a very long and tiring journey, I stand before you today. I am here to tell you that I have finished my goal of removing all leaders of this gang that had attacked me and my family, and now, as per request and heavy soul searching, I will be taking up the position as your new leader," Vincent near shouted as the audience applauded again with the ferocity of a roaring

288

lion. He found himself reprimanding his choice of words and lack of Leon's grace with public speaking, 'Heavy soul searching, where did I pull that one from?' Vincent waited for the commotion to die down before starting in once more.

"With the help of my friends who will be taking over the roles of those corrupt few I have removed, I tell you now that I will lead you into a new era of prosperity, unity and peace" Once again the applause shook the room so frighteningly that the lights over head shook and chandeliers swayed slightly.

"In the next few months, I will be working with my colleagues to produce a strategy to implement fair rights within our establishment for all of you. We will regain the abundance of wealth lost by personal greed and work to make our organization as violence free as possible within our own group. There is no need for things to continue on as they were!"

Vincent's confidence was inflating at a rate that alarmed even him upon seeing the pleased expressions on everyone's faces and he took the authoritative position on with much more ease than he had anticipated.

"Together we will unite all sects of our divided group and raise the Daravians to its former glory. We will do that by ridding ourselves of all the conventional ways that have failed us thus far and using that age old phrase that sums up the power of our ability - UNITED WE STAND!" Vincent finished his inspiring soliloquy with ecstatic enthusiasm as he threw his hands into the air and the crowd roared into applause, screams of excitement and dancing once more.

They must have instinctively known that he was finished because the lights instantly dimmed as everyone writhed beneath them and carried on. Champagne bottles popped open one after another, sending the corks flying every which way and bubbly liquid spilling into everyone's empty glasses. The music started in again and kept the rhythm of the boisterous crowd alive.

Vincent would introduce his new lieutenants in a couple days, after the party and people had gotten used to the change. Everyone had taken the news exceptionally well, proving to Vincent once again that Leon was right when he said they were indeed awaiting him.

289

Just then, an awe struck hush fell over the crowd as the large black chandelier on the ground tilted itself from it's off kilter position to stand upright then slowly lifted itself back up into the air, still fully lit. Someone had flicked the switch back on that was probably meant to raise or lower the light fixture when it needed cleaning, and the alluring beauty hoisted itself back into the air. The spectacle certainly worked to entertain the crowd. Everyone cheered while the glimmering crystals flashed their brilliance around the room like an extravagant disco ball as the hefty and dazzling chandelier rose up. Up it went, past the five other white chandeliers surrounding it and was returned to its position at the centre of the coffered ceiling as its dimmed lights lit back up to their full potential now that it wasn't at the guest's eye level.

Everyone continued to carry on as Vincent watched his friends ascend the marble staircase to join him on the balcony. Vincent had thought he'd experienced an adrenaline rush before upon finally eliminating his final target but it paled in comparison to what he felt now. A victory of unparalleled greatness, he had managed to do the impossible, at least that's what he had considered it, and had now officially gained an empire.

All the random pieces of Vincent's broken life had re-assembled into a stained glass masterpiece. From the shambles of ruin he rose to prominence where he least expected it. The truth about his journey revealed to him that life is indeed never certain and you never know where it will take you. All you can do is make the best of it and fight for what you know is right. You could end up doing wonderful things you never thought you could accomplish and all you need do is to embrace it. The reason all doors may be closed is so you can chose one at random that will be perfect for you.

As he watched out over the denizens below with the passion of fire in his eyes, he could see it all clearly now. There was nothing left to overcome, as it would seem, but even he knew that every great victory is followed by change that he would have to induct. The crowd danced and moved rhythmically to the beat, conversed and drank in newfound delight.

They had come alive in a new way that was not there before he had taken to the stage, their eyes illuminating in the dark of the room with flickers of ecstasy and hope. He thought about everything that had led to this moment and recalled the feeling of never knowing what was next. He took that leap of faith and landed safely on the other side, unscathed and untouched by all the illusions of doom Miles and the like had bestowed upon him, remembering also, that others weren't so lucky. As he sat, still gazing out over the scenery before him with his entourage at his side, he realized that the biggest question, the question of what to do when it was all over, had been answered and carried out without him even being aware of it.

Xander Sterling has been writing books since he was about seven years old. As a child, he loved the *Goosebumps* series and wrote several of his own books for the series. At age 13, he wrote a script for a fourth *Terminator* movie after seeing *Rise of the Machines*. He continues to be influenced by the pop culture and fashion worlds and had now completed his first real novel.

The idea for *Ordinary Citizen* came to him after keeping a log of several bizarre dreams he had. He started writing chapter 1 and part of chapter 10 and after showing it to a friend who said it was really good, he lost the pages he had written. A short while later he recommended writing after the storyline for the first and following six novels popped into his head one day while at work.

He wrote the first novel and began detailing the plot outlines for the remaining stories. The *Ordinary Citizen* series was born.

Like on Facebook
Follow on Twitter:
@XanderSterling1